One Good Lie

Jane Isaac is married to a serving detective and they live in rural Northamptonshire, UK with their dogs. She is the author of three critically acclaimed detective series: DCI Helen Lavery, DI Will Jackman (based in Stratford upon Avon), and DC Beth Chamberlain (a Family Liaison Officer). Her novels have been nominated as best mystery in the eFestival of Words Best of the Independent eBook awards; and selected as Thriller of the Month by E-thriller.com. Several of her books have been number 1 bestsellers in the police procedurals category and reached the top 3 on Amazon's kindle chart. *One Good Lie* is her first psychological thriller.

ONE GOOD LIE

JANE ISAAC

CANELO

First published in the United Kingdom in 2021 by

Canelo
31 Helen Road
Oxford OX2 0DF
United Kingdom

A CIP catalogue record for this book is available from the British Library.

Print ISBN 978 1 80032 401 5
Ebook ISBN 978 1 80032 402 2

Look for more great books at www.canelo.co

Printed and bound in Great Britain by Clays Ltd, Elcograf S.p.A.

In memory of Terry Lloyd, a wonderful character and sadly missed.

Also, for his dear wife, Dell. A treasured family friend.

Prologue

She wakes to darkness, a sweet earthy smell she can't place. A weight covers her eyes, pressing down. Pain. It spikes her temple as she shakes her head.

She tries to lift a hand, to free her face, and falters. Her hands are tied in front of her. Her ankles bound together.

Terror grips her. She tosses her head from side to side.

'Help!' She stretches out the word, her voice splintering as it grows louder.

Cold air penetrates her bare arms. It's soft and lumpy beneath her – not a bed as such, more like… covers strewn together on an uneven floor. The ridges and folds of a blanket dig into her back.

An engine drones in the distance. A car. No, a train. She calls out again. Louder, screaming and screeching as it passes.

Her voice is weakening now.

She wades through the fog in her brain, snags her most recent memory. At home. Checking the door locks, the windows. Double-checking them. Catching her toe on the loose carpet at the bottom of the stairs as she ascends. Hanging her robe on the back of her bedroom door, switching off her bedside light.

The images fade. Loose fragments of memory break off. She grabs at them, but they dance on the periphery, just out of reach.

The click of a lock. The air nearby displaces. Someone's entered the room.

She flinches. Every fibre of her body on hyper-alert.

'Hello.' The voice is familiar.

The realisation that follows sickens her to the pit of her stomach. And then she knows, her worst fears finally realised.

'It was you...'

Chapter 1

Nine days earlier

Sophie was sitting in her car, waiting at the traffic lights when she spotted the woman in the yellow shirt cross the road. Auburn hair, tied into a messy half-ponytail at the nape of her neck, long-limbed and svelte, she swept across the tarmac with the grace of a swan. For a moment, Sophie forgot herself. Her heart soared. She reached forward to tap the window. The woman turned. And Sophie froze, her arm suspended in mid-air.

The blast of a car horn brought Sophie to her senses. The lights had changed. She swallowed, slipped into first gear and pulled off. Glancing in her rear-view mirror just in time to see the driver in the Volkswagen behind her, tapping his temple with his forefinger.

Ignore him. Concentrate on the road. You're almost home. But she couldn't, her vision already blurring. She indicated, steered into the next side street and pulled over. She parked at the kerbside, turning off the engine. Closed her eyes, clutching the steering wheel, focusing on her breaths. Long and slow.

Almost a year had passed, yet everywhere she looked, she still saw her. In the woman on the bus reading a book, hair pinned back from her face, Calvin Klein glasses perched on the end of her nose. The glamorous mother swanning down the aisle at the supermarket. The lady in white denims, walking her dog in the park.

There was a time when auburn, or ginger as the kids at school called it, was a rarity. Now everyone wanted to look

3

like Nicole Kidman, or Gillian Anderson in *The X-Files*, and the world was awash with Titian tresses. Sophie absently stroked the curls resting on her shoulder. Few were naturally red like Aileen and her.

She'd been so proud of her mother as a child. Aileen McBride stood out at parents' evening, always smartly dressed, hair glossy and freshly groomed. Smooth, porcelain skin. She wasn't pretty, not in the traditional sense, but there was an elegance about her. People used to say she could wear a sack and make it sparkle.

Used to.

She was everywhere, and yet she was gone. *Murdered by her partner in the kitchen at the back of her shop*, the papers reported after the trial. *Strangled.* Strangled in a fit of jealous rage, the crime scene littered with his DNA. Yet Colin Halliday still pleaded not guilty, drawing out the legal process, subjecting the family to the added trauma of a trial that dredged up all the gruesome details.

Colin Halliday. A year ago, he was sitting at their dinner table, sporting a lopsided smile while they laughed at his cheesy jokes. The memory made her recoil.

Today was her mother's birthday. Aileen McBride would have been forty-eight. They should have been out shopping together now, choosing an outfit each for a family dinner tonight.

Her phone buzzed. 'Sis' flashed up on the screen. Sophie looked at it for a couple of seconds before she answered. 'Hi, Ruby.'

'Where are you, Soph? I'm at yours.'

'I just popped out to get a few bits.'

'What for? The caterers will be here in an hour.'

Sophie turned sheepishly to the array of carrier bags stacked on the back seat. They'd never had a proper funeral. When the police eventually released the body, they were all still in shock. Navigating each day as if it were their first. Concentrating on putting one foot in front of the other, too numb to make wide-sweeping arrangements. A small service ensued with close family. A burial. No wake to speak of.

'Just some crisps and drinks,' she said. 'Nothing much.'

An exasperated sigh winged down the line.

Ruby hadn't welcomed a fuss. Once the court case was over, she'd wanted to put it behind her. But their mother had lived in Market Deeton for most of her adult life. She owned a small boutique off High Street, was popular in the town. She deserved a proper send-off.

'It'll be fine, really,' Sophie said. 'I'm on my way back now. I'll see you in a few minutes.'

She cut the call and leaned back into the headrest. If she closed her eyes, she could still see Colin in court on the day he was sentenced. Two weeks ago, it was, and still so fresh in her mind, it felt like yesterday. The oak-panelled courtroom. His elevated position in the dock, the sheet of glass that separated him from the rest of the room. He stared straight ahead, his face fixed like waxwork, unblinking as the judge gave him a life sentence, recommending he serve a minimum of fifteen years.

Sophie eased forward and turned over the engine. Aileen McBride would never enjoy another birthday with her girls, never watch her grandchildren grow and flourish. They couldn't turn back the clock and save her from the pain of a violent death. But they could throw her the celebration of life she deserved: a memorial service, a proper wake, at home as she would have wanted. It was fitting to do it on her birthday, with her friends present. And it was the least she could do. Because, if it wasn't for Sophie, her mother would still be alive.

Chapter 2

Ruby stood beside the fireplace and watched the men and women sprawled over her late mother's sofas launch into another rendition of 'Danny Boy'. Pink faces swayed from side to side as they harmonised. The sun was setting outside, a swirl of oranges and yellows across a milky blue sky. All respectable guests bade their farewells hours ago, yet this lot were set in for the night.

She glanced at Sophie, sitting at the dining-room table at the end of the room, cornflower-blue eyes focused on the hands folded in her lap. Her beautiful sister. Although she didn't look beautiful today; her tousled locks hung like waxy curtains framing a translucent, empty face. Tragic loss had a habit of doing that. Of leaching every last ounce of energy, every scrap of joy.

Her gaze travelled around the room. To the open fireplace, the Moroccan rug in front covering the faux wooden floor; the photos of Sophie and Ruby at various ages on the dresser, punctuated by school pictures of Sophie's children. For nearly four years, Sophie and their mother had shared this home together. Aileen McBride died almost ten months ago, and yet Sophie had moved nothing. Every piece of furniture, every photo, every ornament still in the same place they were on the day she took her last breath. They'd agreed Sophie would stay on in the house. Hopefully, now she'd said her final goodbye, she'd make it her own.

The voices faded. Eyes shone, blooming with the possibility of what they might sing next. Ruby started collecting empty plates, clattering them together in the hope of prompting the guests to make a move. She was just leaving the room when a woman standing beside the window sang the opening line of 'Amazing Grace'.

Lewis was stepping in from the garden when she reached the kitchen, popping a mint into his mouth to quell the smell of fresh nicotine. He'd been a godsend this afternoon, working the room like a butterfly, talking to guests, keeping them all upbeat with his easy manner, his keen smile. At times like this, everyone needed a friend like Lewis.

'You okay?' he asked, discarding his cigarette stub in the bin.

The rest of the sofa crowd had joined in with the song now, a choir of voices crooning.

Ruby placed the crockery down. 'I'm not sure how much more of this I can take.'

He laid a reassuring hand on her shoulder. 'I'll take care of it.'

The second verse of 'Amazing Grace' was fading as she followed him back into the front room.

'Okay, everyone, I guess we'd better call it a day,' Lewis said, flashing his best smile. 'Let the children sleep.' He glanced up at the ceiling, to the bedrooms above, where Sophie's children were tucked up in their beds.

'That's right,' Ewan said, his Glaswegian drawl filling the room. He rose from his seat beside Sophie. 'Best get home before it's dark.'

Startled faces quickly recovered. A rumble of throat clearing followed. Shuffles as bags were gathered, arms slipped into jackets. Choruses of, 'We hope we haven't outstayed our welcome.'

'Of course not,' Ruby said, ushering them into the hallway with as much grace as she could muster. 'Thanks for coming. It would have meant so much to Mum.'

She closed the door and paused a second, shoulders softening as she relished the calm. Sophie and Ewan had moved into the kitchen and were loading the dishwasher. The sound of glasses and crockery tapping and chinking together was oddly comforting.

Lewis emerged from the front room carrying another pile of empty plates. 'Need any help clearing up?' he asked. His light brown hair had wilted and flattened to his forehead, but his black suit and white shirt remained as crisp as the glint in his eye. She envied his stamina.

'No, you're fine. We can manage. You've done enough.' She took the plates from him and gave him a grateful hug with her free arm. 'Thanks for your support.'

'No worries. Your mum was a great lady.'

'She was.'

'Have you got your car?'

'Left it at home today. Chose wine instead.'

He laughed. 'I can give you a lift.'

'Thanks. I'd prefer to walk. Be good to get some fresh air.'

'All right. Don't be a stranger.' He winked.

He was referring to the numerous calls and texts she hadn't responded to over the past months. Despite assuring him she wasn't deliberately ignoring him, that she'd struggled to keep up with everyone recently, what with the trial and the memorial service, he couldn't resist the opportunity to tease.

'I'll speak to you soon.'

Ruby balanced the plates in one hand, thanking him again as she let him out, then wandered into the kitchen. She placed the plates down beside Pru, her late mother's tabby, who was sitting on top of the microwave, washing her paws.

'You okay?' Ruby said, catching her sister's eye.

'She will be.' Ewan slotted a bowl into the dishwasher, snapped it shut and rested his hand on Sophie's shoulder. 'She's just worn out.'

Sophie placed her hand over his, lifted her head and gave him a weak smile. They were a peculiar match. Him tall and thick set with brown curly hair that tumbled into his eyes, her childlike and petite, like a china doll. Even when they were standing, he towered over her.

'I'm heading up to change,' Ewan said, pecking Sophie's forehead, slipping his hand from hers. 'I'll check on the kids.'

Ruby watched him go. He was so good with Sophie's children. In the twelve months he and Sophie had been together, they'd formed a neat bond.

She glanced around the kitchen. When the caterers arrived earlier, it had been difficult to imagine where to put all the food, let alone who'd eat it, especially with the extras Sophie had bought. Yet now the plates and servers were littered with crusts and crumbs.

They worked together to fill the dishwasher, then wash the rest of the dishes and wipe down the sides. When they were finished, Ruby opened a drawer and pulled out a clean tea towel.

'Leave them.' Sophie waved a weary hand towards the pile on the drainer. 'I'll finish up tomorrow.'

'Are you sure?'

'Of course, we're all tired.'

'Okay, I'll get off then.'

'Wait.' Sophie crossed the room, opened a cupboard, rummaged inside and pulled out a grey bag. Her late mother's favourite handbag. The gold chain handle rattled as she held it out. 'Take this.'

Ruby stepped back. 'I couldn't.'

'Please. I know you love it. It's time.'

A lump lodged itself in Ruby's throat. The faux snakeskin pressed against her fingers. She thanked her sister, took the bag and dropped her own handbag inside it.

'I'll call you a cab,' Sophie said.

'No need, I'd rather walk.' She stretched an arm around her sister's shoulder and pulled her close. 'You get some rest. I'll text you when I'm home.'

Chapter 3

Night had drawn in by the time Ruby walked down the driveway. She peeled off her jacket and blinked, suddenly aware of the heat in her face and the volume of wine she'd consumed. 'Just another glass to get through the day' had turned into several and that was before lunch. Anything to make the afternoon bearable.

At the few funeral services she'd attended in her twenty-eight years, Ruby had made excuses to wriggle out of the wake and left immediately after the service: *I have to get back to work*; *I'm looking after my sister's kids later*; *I've got the gas man coming at five*. Avoiding having to sit and smile politely while people talked through memories and wallowed in painful nostalgia.

Today, she couldn't make such excuses. And handing out vol-au-vents and quiche surrounded by photos of her dear mum – on Derrynane Beach with her girls as toddlers; outside her newly refurbished shop in the town centre; having dinner with friends – only served to remind her of how much she'd lost.

No one at the wake spoke about the murder. No one mentioned the press reports, the trial. This was a day for celebration. But it was constantly there, waving in the background like one of those Japanese cat ornaments.

It was a balmy evening, warm for September, the pavement still soaked in the heat of the day. Dreamy scents of phlox and honeysuckle swirled in the air, doing nothing to clear the fog in her head. What Ruby needed now was a cool shower, a large glass of water and her bed.

A car whizzed past when she turned the corner onto Templeton Road, catching the edge of her dress, drumming up a welcome breeze. If she continued at this pace, she'd be home in twenty minutes.

By the time she reached High Street, Ruby was feeling decidedly woozy. The small Midlands town of Market Deeton was quiet. It was almost nine on a Tuesday evening, after all, and living on the fringe of the London commuter belt, most residents had already taken to their homes to prepare for an early start in the morning. She wandered past the banks, the phone shops, the charity shops, boutiques with their windows lit, advertising their wares, and paused at the Co-op on the square. Maybe a bottle of water would dilute some of that alcohol.

A wolf whistle sounded, shrill and loud. Out of the corner of her eye, Ruby spotted a group of lads, four or five of them, on the other side of the square, cans of beer in hand. She was tempted to shout over a witty quip, berate them for their ridiculous behaviour, but decided against it. She didn't have the energy for an argument tonight.

Inside the store, a bored assistant behind the counter flicked through a magazine while twirling her hair between her thumb and forefinger. A burly man with silver hair was kneeling at the end of an aisle, filling shelves.

When Ruby left the shop, bottle of water in hand, the lads had crossed the square and gathered outside. She cracked open the bottle, took a sip of water and made to pass by.

'Well, look what we have here.' A gangly youth in a Manchester United shirt and jeans that hung loose around his backside stood in front of her, hands in his pockets. A silver ring glistened in his brow. He was only about eighteen. His mate, all crew cut, and acne-scarred cheeks, moved in beside him.

Ruby rolled her eyes and sidestepped. This was all she needed.

Baggy Jeans moved with her, blocking her path.

She lowered the bottle, screwed on the lid and met his eyeline defiantly.

'What? Don't you want to play?'

Crew Cut chuckled. 'Why don't you give me some of that water?' he said.

She glanced back at the shop, considered shouting for help. But the alcohol was dulling her instincts, bolstering her. Perhaps she should plant a fist in his gut instead.

The rest of the group circled her, filling the pavement. She slipped her hand in her jacket pocket, curled her fingers around her phone. Contemplated pushing through, though she didn't fancy her chances if they made chase. Not in these heels.

'Get out of my way,' she said, loud enough for anyone with half an ear nearby to hear.

'Or what?' Crew Cut replied.

Where was a pedestrian, a motorist, when you wanted one?

Ruby pulled out her phone and stepped closer to Crew Cut. 'I said, out of my way.' As she did so, her heel caught the edge of a paving slab. She wobbled.

A snicker travelled around the group.

She could taste their breath now; the combination of lager and nicotine made her heave. She fisted her free hand, about to lash out when...

'I think the lady wants to pass through.'

Ruby hadn't heard the assistant who'd been stacking shelves approach the door. He looked broader standing upright, arms folded across his chest, and must have been well over six foot.

'We're not stopping her.' Crew Cut shrugged and slid aside. Nudging his mates. They sniggered and moved off up the street.

'Catch you later!' Baggy Jeans called back.

The shop assistant watched them until they were smudges of colour disappearing into the night, and turned to Ruby. 'You okay, miss?'

Ruby nodded gratefully, thanked him and took off in the opposite direction to the lads. She was feeling nauseous now. The sooner she was out of town, the better.

A car cruised by. She risked a glimpse behind. Exhaled when she found the pavement empty and took another swig of water. She crossed the road beside the old grammar school and slipped down by the church. It was darker there, few of the streetlights illuminated.

Ruby glanced back again. The exchange outside the supermarket had rattled her. She should have taken Lewis up on his offer of a lift.

She was turning into Clarence Street, wondering whether to call Lewis and see if he was still up, when she heard footsteps. Someone running. Another check behind. Empty. Nothing ahead either. She sped up. Surely those lads hadn't decided to double back and follow her, after all. The steps grew louder, gaining ground. She grabbed her phone, swung around.

'Ewan!' Ruby gasped at the sight of her sister's boyfriend. He was dressed in dark jogging trousers, a fitted polo shirt. 'What are you doing? You scared the hell out of me.'

'Sorry. I saw you turn into Clarence Street, thought I'd catch you up.' He surveyed her a second. 'You okay, you seem a bit jumpy?'

She gulped. 'So would you be if someone crept up behind you in the dark.'

'I said I'm sorry.'

'What are you doing out here anyway?'

'I often come out in the evenings and jog or walk to clear my head.' He shoved his hands in his pockets. 'Sophie's out for the count,' he added, guessing her thoughts.

'And the kids?'

'Same. It's been a rough day for everyone.'

'You can say that again. Anyway, I need to get back.' She flicked her hair over her shoulder, made to move off. She didn't want to analyse the inner workings of the day. She wanted to put it behind her.

'I'll walk with you,' he said.

'There's no need.'

'Might as well, since I'm here.'

Ruby didn't argue when he fell into step beside her. She was still uneasy from the experience outside the supermarket, her nerves frayed. She turned to ask about Sophie, and twisted on her heel.

'Hey, steady!' he said, grabbing her elbow, saving her fall. The drone of an engine filled the air as a car passed. 'Good job I'm here.'

Ruby pulled her elbow back, straightened and finished the rest of the water, wiping her mouth with the back of her hand and dropping the bottle into a nearby bin.

'Are you sure Sophie's okay?' she asked. With the trial over, the reality of continuing the routine of life without their mother was kicking in now and, out of the two of them, Sophie had leaned more heavily on their mother, relying on her for child-care. Ruby had lost count of the times she'd popped by to see her mum at the shop, only to find a notice on the door saying, 'Back in thirty minutes' because she'd nipped out to do the school run. Or to find Alfie and Daisy, Sophie's children, sitting behind the counter, drawing pictures.

'She'll be fine,' Ewan said. 'She's stronger than you think. And she's got me.'

They turned the next corner and the road opened up. The sky was dotted with stars, a million tiny torchlights beaming down. It really was a beautiful evening.

'It was a nice service,' Ewan said.

'I suppose.'

'Until the vicar sang out of tune.'

Ruby remembered the startled faces and nudges that rippled around the church like a Mexican wave when they opened with the first hymn, and laughed.

'I mean what vicar is tone-deaf?' he continued. 'Surely they take singing lessons as part of their theology degree. All those services. All those hymns.'

'Mum's friends made up for it anyway.'

'Yeah, I thought they were never going to go this evening.'

'Same!'

He dug his elbow into her ribs. 'I bet they look forward to funerals. All those wakes. I can see them now, checking the obituaries online to see when the next service is. Desperately trying to find some connection to the deceased.'

Ruby chuckled again. The way his Glaswegian accent crisply enunciated the words made them sound more amusing. She felt the tension trickle out of her shoulders. They'd rarely spoken alone in the time they'd known each other, and it struck her how much quieter he was in Sophie's company. Maybe he was pumped full of wine tonight too. Either way, it made the journey more pleasant.

They crossed the road. She was only five minutes from home now. Ewan was talking about a vicar with a lisp at a friend's wedding who showered the bride and groom with spittle during their vows.

Ruby snorted with laughter.

She didn't see the cat on the wall. Didn't notice until it jumped onto the pavement in front, startling her. She staggered back, stumbled again. Her phone slipped out of her hand and crashed onto the paving.

When she knelt to retrieve it, the screen was shattered.

'Is it still working?' Ewan asked.

'I don't know.' She groaned, hauled herself up and the ground shifted. She'd drunk more of that wine than she'd intended.

'Let me take a look.' They were nearing the backs of the houses that marked Ruby's neighbouring street. Two rows of garages facing each other across a narrow channel. He moved into the gap to avoid a car parked across the pavement at the end, stepping over tufts of grass pushing through the cracks in the concrete, and switched on the phone. The splintered screen illuminated into a kaleidoscope of colour. 'I think it's just surface damage.'

'Thanks.' Ruby took the phone back and cursed the wine again. Clumsy fingers fumbling across the broken glass, checking her apps. Suddenly she became aware of how close they were standing. She could feel the heat of his body. Smell the mint on his breath. Another dizzy spell. She blew a shot of cool air up her face. Placed out a hand to steady herself and grabbed his arm. He slid his free hand around her waist. It was warm, inviting. He hooked her gaze.

Within seconds, his lips were on hers. Watery, hungry. Before she'd realised, he'd pushed her further up the cut-through. A garage door clattered as they fell into it. Fingers weaved through the back of her hair, tongue exploring her mouth. Her jacket slipped from her grasp. He tugged her hair, hard, pulling her head back. His free hand yanking up her dress. Urgent, fast movements until he found her warm flesh. His hand travelled to her thigh…

A car engine roared as it passed on the nearby road, the sound inducing a moment of clarity. *What was he doing?*

'Stop!' she yelled, pushing him away.

Ewan jerked back, releasing his grip.

He was Sophie's boyfriend for Christ's sake. She didn't even fancy him. She couldn't. Not like that.

'Sorry.' He stepped back further, held up his hands.

Ruby couldn't speak, her head swirling. She made a play of brushing down her dress, desperately trying to work through the mist in her head.

'I'm sorry,' he repeated. 'I don't know what came over me. It must have been the drink.' He tugged at his collar, twisted his head to the side.

Ruby wobbled again and pressed her hand to the door to steady herself. She could feel bile rising in her throat. Was that due to alcohol or anger? She couldn't be sure. Either way, she should go home. Sleep it off. Everything would seem better in the morning.

'I didn't mean…' His face folded, contrite. 'Look, I've never done anything like this before. I'd never do anything to hurt Sophie. You must know that.' He reached out.

She flinched, batting his arm away. Too hard. He toppled sideways, crashing against a refuse bin nearby.

'Ruby, please.' He put out a conciliatory hand.

'Get. Off. Me.' The words were shrill and louder than she'd intended.

She picked up her jacket, about to move off, when a voice called from end of the cut-through. 'Everything all right?'

They both turned to the figure, silhouetted in the street-lights.

Ruby's heart shrank to a tiny crisp. How long had he been there? She didn't recognise the voice, couldn't make out any features in the darkness, but the last thing she wanted was to be spotted in a compromising position with her sister's boyfriend, even if it was by a complete stranger.

She balled her jacket to her chest, cast one last cursory glance at Ewan and made off.

Chapter 4

There's something insidious about unfinished business. It crawls about beneath the skin like an army of restless ants.

I watch her hurry down Clarence Street, shoulders hunched, soft shoes gently teasing the paving. My unfinished business.

She's wearing a denim jacket and that skirt I like, the one that swishes around her porcelain ankles. Clasps the strap of her bag tightly, flicks her gaze to the puffball dress in the bridal shop window as she passes.

I follow behind, taking care to keep to the shadows of the shopfronts splaying across the pavement. I love this town with its mix of Georgian and contemporary architecture, its leafy avenues, tree-lined streets, posh boutiques and coffee houses. The surrounding wrap of rolling Leicestershire countryside. A haven in the midst of rural England. I can see why she came back.

That was her first mistake.

A mix in design means narrow lanes, alleys and side passages. Plenty of places to shelter, plenty of nooks in which to hide.

Her second mistake was to walk through the town centre under the cover of darkness.

She reaches the turn to Simpson's Place, turns and pauses. Dithers about entering. She knows if she continues to the top of Clarence Street, it'll take her to High Street. It's busier up there and well lit. Motorists crawl up and down the road. Cameras keep a watchful eye on pedestrians.

Go on...

She's reluctant. There are no streetlights in Simpson's Place and the cut-through, sandwiched between The Greek Deli and The Artisan

Bakery, is quiet and dark tonight. She glances back up the road. Considers continuing to the next turn, another side street but better lit. Though it'll add three minutes onto her journey. When you're in hiding, living on the edge of life, three extra minutes outside the safety of shelter, you can ill afford.

Go on…

Her shoulders drop. Another check back. She hitches the strap of her bag further up her shoulder, turns and enters.

I run my finger along the blade in my pocket and quicken my step. Once I've tied up this loose end, nothing will come between us.

Chapter 5

Sophie shifted onto her side and reached across the bed, flinching at the cold sheet, the ruffle where the covers were pulled back. She opened a bleary eye, lifted her head. The digital clock on the bedside cabinet winked as it changed time: 11:41 p.m.

'Ewan?' Her whisper disappeared into the darkness.

She sat up and rubbed her knuckles into her eyes, listening for the sound of his footfalls on the polished floor. All was quiet.

Climbing out of bed, she wrapped a robe around her shoulders and padded across the landing, wandering into the next bedroom. Daisy was fast asleep on her back, an arm hanging out of the bed. Tendrils of messy curls covered her face. She tucked the child's arm back in and brushed her hair away from her eyes.

In the other room, Alfie had pushed his covers off and was hunched in the middle, a tiny ball. She lifted him up the bed, covered him over and kissed his crown. He wriggled onto his side, opened his eyes to a tiny slit, looked at her a second and closed them again.

At the bottom of the stairs, a line of light shone beneath the closed kitchen door. She gave the door a nudge, expecting to see Ewan sitting at the breakfast bar. The room was empty, the soft under-cupboard lighting creating a gentle glow. Had he gone home? It seemed odd to leave the light on and disappear without leaving a note.

Sophie's eyes rested on her phone, charging on the side. She was signing in, about to check her messages when she noticed the amber glare of a cigarette through the window.

A whoosh of cool air raced in as she opened the back door.

Ewan jumped. He'd been leaning against the back wall, staring up at the stars.

'Thought you'd given up,' she said, nodding toward the cigarette.

'I have.' He gave a half-smile.

She reached across, grabbed the cigarette and took a long drag, relishing the rush of nicotine entering her lungs.

'Just needed a little pick-me-up.'

She ran her gaze over his jogging bottoms and shirt. 'You going somewhere?'

'I could hardly come out here in my pyjamas, could I?'

Sophie laughed. Ewan didn't wear pyjamas. She imagined the old lady over the back traipsing to the bathroom for a pee in the middle of the night, looking out of the window and getting the shock of her life at the sight of a nude man in her neighbour's garden.

She handed him the cigarette. 'I'm going to make a hot chocolate. Do you want one?'

'Fags and chocolate. You sure know how to spoil a guy.'

Sophie gave a wry smile, went back inside and busied herself with making the drinks. She was stirring the powder into the heated milk when he wandered back inside.

He blew into his palms, rubbed them together. 'It's colder than it looks out there.'

They sat in silence at the breakfast bar, hands wrapped around their mugs. 'Can't you sleep?' she asked eventually.

He shook his head, took another sip. 'We'll have been together a year on Sunday,' he said.

Sophie did her best to hide her surprise. She hadn't exactly forgotten, she knew their first anniversary must be looming, but planning the memorial service had occupied practically every waking moment, these past weeks. 'A whole year.' She smiled sleepily.

'We've not had an easy ride, have we? With everything that's happened.'

'I suppose not.' She placed the mug down in front of her and stared into it, eyes half closing.

'Can we put the investigation behind us now? Move forward? A clean slate. Just you, me and the kids.'

'Sounds like a good plan.' She raised her mug, clicked it against his in mock celebration. 'I declare our new life starts tomorrow.'

Little did she know how prophetic that statement would be.

Chapter 6

The incessant rain tapped the window like a fingernail, pulling Ruby from the depths of her slumber. A clap of thunder followed. She hauled herself forward, a pain spiking her temple at the slight movement, slid out of bed and closed the window. It was 8:05 a.m. She was running late.

Another pain, stronger this time. She threw her robe around her shoulders, pressed a palm to her forehead and padded to the medicine cabinet in the bathroom. Fishing around for the paracetamol and swallowing two tablets down with water straight from the tap.

She held onto the edge of the sink and hung her head, waiting for the pain to ease, then dried her mouth with the back of her hand and lifted her gaze to the mirror. Yesterday's wine had taken its toll. Eyes bloodshot, skin alabaster white, her dark hair limp and lifeless, she looked like she'd been in bed for days with the flu. She toyed with calling work, taking a sick day. Although, she'd noticed two appointments already booked into the diary for her this morning before she'd left on Monday. Two kitchen refurbishments to discuss with potential clients, while they scrutinised every pound sign on the quotation. And they were short-staffed as it was, with Kat, her colleague, sunning herself in Tenerife.

She dragged herself into the shower. Having taken so much time off recently with the court case and the memorial service, she ought to make the effort.

The water jets pummelled her upper back and cleared her head, making room for memories of yesterday to slither in. Of the service. The eulogy read so eloquently by her sister. The hymns. The whirlwind of faceless visitors back at the house.

Ewan in the alleyway, his mouth on hers.

Oh, God. Oh, God, no.

How could he take advantage of her when she was vulnerable? He'd been at Sophie's side throughout the trial. Finished work early to collect her children from school. Cooked dinner for the family when she arrived home late. The model boyfriend. Or so she'd thought.

Poor Sophie. She'd finally found some stability…

A late-night phone call, four years earlier, jabbed at Ruby. The tremor in her sister's voice as she told her that Greg, Sophie's now ex-partner and the children's father, had left. Right out of the blue. Ruby had driven across town in the battering rain to find Sophie in a crumpled mess at her kitchen table, sobbing her heart out. After four years, he'd arrived home from work and told her he wasn't ready for a steady relationship and kids. He'd met someone new, been offered a job in Poland and was moving out.

Later, they discovered he'd been preparing to leave for months. Stashing away money from cash-in-hand building jobs, collecting belongings together in a case already packed beneath the bed. Leaving Sophie with crushing debts and a three-year-old and a baby who couldn't understand where Daddy had gone and why they couldn't see him.

It had been a struggle afterwards. With a mortgage to pay, bills crawling out of the woodwork and only a part-time receptionist's job at the hotel in town. Sophie was torn between increasing her hours to keep the house and spending quality time with her children. Everyone rallied around to help, but eventually, with no maintenance or contact from Greg, the situation proved overwhelming.

Ruby switched off the shower and grabbed a towel. A cold shiver skittered down her spine as she recalled another late-night phone call, this time from their mother, three months later, to say Sophie was in an ambulance on her way to Leicester General. Her mother had called over late to drop off Alfie's jacket and found her slumped on the bathroom floor, surrounded by empty blister packets of paracetamol and half a bottle of whisky, the children fast asleep in their beds.

Ruby could still see her sister's ghostly face when she'd visited her in the hospital room that night. The faint summer freckles, the distance in her eyes. The medical team had pumped her stomach, yet she looked as though the very life had been pumped out of her.

By the time Greg returned a year later, saying he'd made a mistake, pleading with her to take him back, Sophie and the children were living with their mother. With Aileen assisting with childcare and the financial strain loosening, Sophie had increased her hours at work and grown stronger, more independent. And she sent Greg's sorry arse packing.

It had been four long years. Four hard years of balancing shiftwork with parenting. Four years in which Ruby tried to persuade her sister to socialise and make a new life for herself. But Sophie refused, working out childcare access with Greg, who decided to move to nearby Leicester, and choosing to spend what little spare time she did have with her kids. It was only when Alfie started school that she relaxed and started to go out with some of the mums from the PTA. And it was on one of these nights out she had met Ewan, the delivery driver who'd recently moved to the area from Glasgow in search of work. The man who showered her with flowers and took her out for candlelit dinners.

Sophie made no secret of the fact that she was crazy about Ewan, and who wouldn't be? He was handsome, thoughtful. Always there when she needed him. The children loved him, especially when he took them to the park and the cinema. He'd supported her with childcare after the death of her mother, hinted at a shared future together.

Everything was finally falling into place for Sophie.

Despite the shower, Ruby could still smell Ewan's sporty aftershave. Taste the mint on his breath. Feel his sinewy hands on her, his fingers grappling with the straps of her dress.

She cringed. How could she let this happen?

Bile shot to her throat. She dashed across to the toilet and retched, staring at the spatter of clear liquid showering the pan. Predictable really. She'd been so concerned with looking after the guests yesterday, of making the 'wake' the success her sister wanted, she'd barely eaten, herself.

Back at the sink, Ruby splashed water on her face and checked her reflection in the mirror as she patted it dry. She could only imagine the gut-wrenching heartache if Sophie found out about her exchange with Ewan. Her sister was infinitely stronger than she had been four years earlier. She'd been surprisingly resilient after their mother's death, especially considering the circumstances. But, still… sometimes, when she was tired or burdened, there was an edge of fragility to her. Ruby couldn't let her find out. She wouldn't.

Chapter 7

There was something going on at the school. Parents were gathered at the gates when Sophie arrived to drop off the children. Hunched under umbrellas to avoid the falling rain, deep in conversation. Usually, people took their kids into class and dashed off in the mornings; it was the afternoons when they gathered to chat at the gate while they waited to collect.

She picked out Louise, Daisy's best friend's mother, in the horde, talking to another mum, and parked up. Then checked the diary on her phone, wondering if she'd missed an event – an assembly, a performance, maybe even a school outing. It was empty.

A text blasted in from Greg asking if he could have an answer about his request to have the kids a day early next weekend. She ignored it.

'Is there a trip today?' she called into the back of the car.

The kids didn't answer. They were arguing over the seat belts. They were always arguing over the seat belts. The one in the middle was broken and Alfie insisted on clipping his belt into the wrong catch.

Sophie pushed the thoughts aside, pulled up her hood and exited the car. When she finally got the children out, Alfie dropped his jacket on the wet pavement and had to go back for it. Daisy trailed her book bag on the ground. It was a normal Wednesday.

Only it wasn't normal because the parents, still standing at the gates, lowered their voices and turned to watch as she waited for a gap in the traffic and ushered her kids across the road.

Sophie stared back at them through the rain. She caught Louise's eye, pulled a quizzical face. Louise jolted her head back and widened her eyes in an expression that said, *We'll speak on the way out.*

The children took time to settle in their classrooms. In the aftermath of yesterday, Alfie had forgotten his homework sheet and she needed to speak to his teacher to explain why. Daisy couldn't find her PE shoes.

Sophie left the school to find Louise beside the gate, sheltering underneath a red golfing umbrella, head down, scrolling through her phone.

'What's going on?' Sophie asked.

'Have you seen the news this morning?' Louise was short and mumsy, in jeans that became baggier by the day as she chased her Weight Watchers target, a loose navy T-shirt and sensible pumps. She pushed her dark bob out of her face and made room for Sophie to join her under her umbrella.

Sophie said she hadn't seen the news. The morning television was always on, but the kids switched it to CBeebies and she was too busy chasing her tail and making their packed lunches anyway. Plus, there was the clearing up to finish from yesterday... Her voice trailed off as Louise's expression tightened.

'A woman was killed in the town centre last night.'

'Oh my God.' Sophie pressed her hand to her throat. Ruby had walked home yesterday evening, alone. She checked her phone. She hadn't thought much of her sister forgetting to send a late-night message to confirm she'd arrived home safely; they were all weary from the day. But she hadn't messaged this morning either. Sophie's stomach knotted. 'When. Where?'

'The town centre, that's all I know. The news said a blonde woman. Poor thing, the police haven't released her name yet.'

Sophie swallowed, dry and hard. Blonde. It couldn't have been Ruby. But any relief she felt was quickly squashed by the crushing reality of what another family was waking up to this morning. And she knew only too well what that was like.

Jagged lights popped and flashed at the sides of her eyes. She stepped out from underneath the umbrella. Air, she needed air.

'Are you okay?' Louise angled her head.

'I'm fine.' Her hair was getting wet now, clumping on her shoulders. Raindrops trickled down her neck. 'I just need to get back.'

Louise reached out, touched her arm. 'Are you sure, Soph?'

'Yes. Let me know if you hear anything else.'

Back in the car, the rain was relentless, smearing the windows, blurring her view. Sophie didn't notice herself switching her wipers to maximum, pulling off down the road, pausing at the junction. Didn't register braking at the zebra crossing on High Street for a mother to push a stroller across. Didn't remember crawling down her street behind the refuse lorry as the bins were emptied, one by one. Only when the gravel of her driveway crunched beneath her wheels did she turn off her engine and realise she was home.

She closed her eyes and rested her forehead on the steering wheel, the cold plastic cooling her skin. Another murder. The maelstrom of emotions washing through another family made her pulse race. The shock. The horror. The anger. The carnival of pain. It was like someone picking at an old wound, opening it up.

The fateful day of her mother's passing slipped into her thoughts. It began as a normal Monday. Her mother was up and out of the house before they woke, just as she always was when she was preparing the shop for a winter sale, her washed coffee mug upside down on the drainer the only sign of her presence. Sophie had dropped the kids at school and worked a shift at the hotel. It was the month before Christmas and a freezing fog had hovered all day, refusing to budge. It had been a relief to come in from school, close the doors and huddle around the fire. The children were watching the television while she cooked cheese and potato pie for dinner. She was about to dish up when the doorbell rang.

Sophie could still picture the detectives on the doorstep. A man and a woman, dark suits peeping out from beneath long overcoats. Everything about them – their military stance, the way they spoke with authority, the formality – screamed of police. As soon as she set eyes on them, she knew it was serious. An accident or even a death.

The memory faded. Raindrops drummed on the car roof.

The days and weeks after her mother's death had merged as her brain had shut down and her body had moved into autopilot. Cooking dinner, keeping the house, caring for the children. Pushing the pain and anguish deep into the vaults of her brain. She'd blanked out those early months in the same way she'd blanked out the sickening details in the courtroom. Suppressed the depression, the relentless ache, the grief. Masked the anxiety brimming within. Only Ewan knew what she was going through. Ruby would have encouraged her to seek help and she refused to go down that path again. Not after last time.

A green room sprang to mind. Long olive drapes pooled at the floor either side of a sash window. The small arrangement of flowers on the coffee table, looking as fresh as those in the paintings adorning the walls. Lounging on the leather sofa, feet curled beneath her. Colin Halliday opposite, sitting forward in his chair, a pen poking between his fingers.

Ironically, it was her mother who had persuaded her to see a therapist after Greg left. 'It'll be good to talk to someone outside the family,' Aileen had said. 'You can tell them anything and you never need to see them again if you don't want to.'

And it had worked. It had taken a while, and some very painful admissions, but eventually things started to shift inside her. She joined a gym, a yoga class and opened her eyes to the world around her, all thanks to Colin.

The day she introduced Colin to her mother stuck like putty in Sophie's mind. It was almost two years after her therapy sessions had finished. She and Aileen were in the Highcross

Centre, Christmas shopping. He'd stopped, touched her arm amongst the throng of shoppers. Made her jump. For a brief moment they'd exchanged small talk. He was looking for a present for his sister and had no idea what to buy. He'd visited Aileen's shop the very next day and bought a purse. The first of many visits, it later transpired.

Tears swelled in Sophie's eyes. She'd barely been able to contain her excitement when her mother had started dating Colin. Raised by a single parent, Colin was one of the kindest men Sophie had met, the counselling father figure she'd never had. He'd coaxed her out of the dark cave, encouraged her to embrace the light. He'd healed her, made her happy. Now he would make her mother happy.

But she was wrong. He'd duped her. Listened to her bare her soul with his soft brown eyes and false empathy. The same way he'd duped her mother into thinking he was kind, thoughtful and considerate. Because he wasn't any of those things.

Raindrops clumped on the side window and trailed down the glass. Sophie wiped her face and checked the street outside, then reached over and hauled her handbag across from the passenger seat. Digging her hand in and moving aside a packet of tissues, a couple of pens, her mobile phone, she lifted out her purse. Jittery fingers opened it up and unzipped the middle pocket between the folds of change, where a small square of foil glinted at her. She unravelled it to reveal several tiny blue tablets, then sat back, placed one on her tongue and closed her eyes. No. She wasn't about to let Ruby, Louise or anyone else know she was struggling. She'd find the inner strength. Deal with this herself.

A tear broke free and slid down her face. She couldn't have known the depth of Colin's temper. How, when her mother had tried to end their relationship, his anger had exploded into a rage that culminated in her death.

But it didn't stop the niggling doubt that drip-fed into her system. A better person might have seen through him. Seen past the charm, the sweet smiles, the witty humour. Seen him for what he really was. A better person would never have introduced him to their mother.

Chapter 8

The rain was still coming down in thick needles. News-readers issued warnings about flash flooding. Cars crawled along High Street, windscreen wipers flapping back and forth. Ruby shook out her umbrella and heeled the door of Galanti Bespoke Kitchens closed. Perhaps the inclement weather would encourage some of her morning appointments to cancel. She hoped so.

'Ah. I'm glad you're here.' Mark Galanti, manager and owner of the business as he liked to remind people on a regular basis, wandered through from the staff kitchen out back, a steaming mug in hand. 'The phones have already started and there's a ton of viewings arranged.' His dark hair was slicked back, accentuating intense eyes framed with heavy brows, set into an angular face. A navy and white spotty tie hung loose over the lilac shirt stretched across his muscular chest. He marched to an arc of desks facing the door, navy trousers clinging to his thighs as he planted down his coffee on the end desk and then retreated out back.

Ruby sighed. It was only a quarter to nine, fifteen minutes before she was due to start. Start and finish times meant nothing to Mark. He was always there before everyone arrived in the mornings, watching them traipse in, and left after they'd gone at the end of the day. He even called in on his day off to finish paperwork, and that's when he actually took his day off. The housing market in Market Deeton had taken a downturn in recent months. With talk of an economic crisis, more people were choosing to stay put and renovate, which meant an increase in new kitchens. What the company really needed was another pair of hands, though that was unlikely to happen any time soon. 'The ex-wife's bleeding me dry,' was Mark's stock phrase when Ruby talked to him about the possibility of taking on someone new.

She shouldered off her jacket and hung it on a coat stand beside the archway that led into their showroom. The bottom of her trouser legs, damp from the short walk from the car park, stuck uncomfortably to her calves. She tucked her hair behind her ears and fished her phone out of her pocket. In her rush to get through the rain, she'd missed two calls from Sophie. Her chest tightened.

Sophie answered on the second ring. 'Finally!' she said. Her tone was chipped. Ruby's chest tightened another notch. Had Ewan beaten her to it and shared something? She was beginning to wish she'd spoken to Ewan first, when her sister said, 'You didn't text me when you got home last night.'

Ah. 'Sorry. I dropped my mobile and the screen shattered. Then I fell asleep on the sofa in my clothes.' Not strictly untrue. She'd woken in the early hours with a throbbing head and a mouth like sandpaper and clambered up the stairs.

'That makes a change.'

'What?'

'Nothing.'

The line crackled.

'Are you okay?' Ruby asked.

'Fine.' Sophie didn't sound fine. She sounded distinctly pissed off. 'Your phone's working now I take it?'

Ruby looked down at the splintered front. 'Yes… I just need to get the screen replaced.'

'Look, I can tell you're distracted. You obviously haven't seen the news. Are you still coming for dinner?'

'Um, sure.'

'Okay, I'll see you around six.'

The line went dead. Ruby lowered the phone. What did she mean about the news? But the thought didn't linger. Something else was battling for supremacy in her brain: Ewan.

He hadn't told Sophie about their exchange the evening before. He couldn't have done, otherwise she'd have said something. Which meant he wanted to keep it quiet too. Good.

She recalled the dark alley yesterday: his fingers weaving through her hair, grappling with her dress. She hadn't invited his advance, but she hadn't stopped it either. Not straight away. The pressing guilt was like a rod of iron across her shoulders. Perhaps they could put it down to the drink. The drink, and emotions running ridiculously high. It was a heady day yesterday.

Mark reappeared looking harried, his mobile glued to his ear, a mug of coffee in his other hand. He ended the call. Coffee sloshed about as he placed the mug on a coaster on Ruby's desk.

Ruby thanked him. 'Everything all right?' she asked.

'Not really. The contractors haven't turned up to sort out the water leak on Ise Walk. That was the customer. She's going bananas.'

Ruby rolled her eyes. It was another Wednesday.

'I'm going to have to find someone new,' Mark continued, adjusting his belt. 'We have a reputation to maintain. Can't have contractors bringing the company's good name into disrepute.'

Ruby squirmed in her seat. His habit of using stock phrases to make himself sound important grated, especially when he laboured a point. Their team meetings were full of requests to 'think outside the box' and 'get all their ducks in a row' – whatever that meant.

'Let me know if there's anything I can do.' She turned back to her computer and opened her emails.

'Isn't it awful about the news?' Mark mumbled, shuffling papers about on his desk.

'The flooding? This country never copes with sudden changes in the weather.'

'No, the murder.'

Ruby swivelled in her chair. 'What?'

Mark was twisting a pen between his thumb and forefinger, face glued to his computer screen. He tore his gaze away, looked across at Ruby. 'Haven't you heard? A woman was stabbed to death in the town centre last night.'

'Where?'

'Simpson's Place. Her body was found by the deli owner early this morning.'

A spider crawled down Ruby's back. She had walked right past the entrance to Simpson's Place last night.

Mark's mobile trilled. He moved to answer it and Ruby turned back to her emails, the attack picking away at her. So close by. Market Deeton was a small town, barely 24,000 residents, and the crime rate was low. No wonder Sophie had been agitated. Ruby googled 'Murder in Market Deeton yesterday' and clicked on a news report from the *Deeton Mercury*.

Woman's body found in Market Deeton

An investigation is under way after the body of a woman was discovered in the town centre.

Police have cordoned off the area around Simpson's Place, where the victim, believed to have been a young woman, was found by a local business owner in the early hours of this morning. The identity of the woman hasn't yet been released.

Detective Chief Inspector Chris Staples, senior investigating officer in the case, said: 'Officers were called to Simpson's Place at 5:30 this morning. The woman suffered multiple stab wounds and was pronounced dead at the scene. We are treating this as a murder investigation.'

Enquiries are ongoing to trace the suspect. Detectives are keen to speak to any witnesses who were in the town centre last night, anyone who saw someone acting suspiciously or anybody with information regarding the incident.

An icy chill. Ruby had seen numerous people out last night. The man at the end of the alleyway; the group of lads outside the supermarket; the shop assistant. Ewan. She ought to contact the police, tell them what she saw. But she needed to speak with Ewan first.

Chapter 9

Ruby drummed her fingers on the dashboard and checked the clock again. Mr and Mrs Oliver were due to meet her at their property on Mount Pleasant fifteen minutes ago. Another no-show, her third this month. Why didn't people cancel appointments when they couldn't make them? It's not like she didn't have a pile of paperwork to do back at the office.

She pushed the key in the ignition, about to make a move, when her phone rang. *Ah, here comes the apology*, she thought. *Too little, too late.*

She was mentally lambasting her clients for taking liberties when another name filled the screen. A very welcome name.

'Hello, Bridget.' Ruby smiled. Flashbacks of warm holidays in Cromer filled her mind. The sun setting over the bay, eating fish and chips on the beach, paddling in the blue-green waters. Bridget was her late mother's sister, fifteen years older than Aileen and the reason they'd moved to Leicester from Kilkenny when Aileen's marriage broke up. They'd lived with Bridget and her husband, Mick, in their younger years. Unable to have children of her own, Bridget had lavished her attention on Aileen's kids. Picking the girls up from school when their mother was working, looking after them in the holidays.

Three years ago, Mick had died and Bridget moved to Norfolk, to satisfy a lifelong dream of retiring by the sea. Ruby missed her dearly, though the miles between them didn't dilute their closeness. She wasn't sure what it was about Bridget, but she understood Ruby more than anyone else. It was as if they plucked the same strings.

'Is that our Ruby?' A rich Irish accent filled the line.

'It is. How are you?'

'I'm champion, darlin'. Good as the day God made me.'

Ruby smiled again. Her aunt suffered from fibromyalgia, a debilitating condition that marred her days. She'd broken her ankle shortly after Aileen's funeral, scuppering her plans to travel across for the trial and memorial service, but her positivity was always heart-warming. 'How's that ankle?'

'Damn annoying. How did it go yesterday?'

'The memorial service? It seemed to run smoothly. I think Mum would have been pleased. We missed you.'

'Missed you too, darlin'. And what about you, love? How are you doing? And Sophie and the kids?'

Well, apart from a tête-à-tête with my sister's boyfriend and a bunch of clients messing me around, all good. She pushed the thoughts aside, tried to sound cheery. 'We're okay, thanks. It's good to put it behind us.'

'Are you sure? You don't sound right.'

Ruby paused a split second. Bridget had a knack of being able to read her, even on the phone. 'I'm fine. Just busy. You know, at work.'

'Well, I'll leave you to it then. You know where I am if you want to chat.'

Ruby disconnected the call and squirmed in her seat. The situation with Ewan needed dealing with, and soon.

She was turning over the engine when an idea skipped into her mind. Ewan was a delivery driver for GoTo. The GoTo depot was on Ridings Street, Lodge Farm – only a mile or so down the road. Perhaps she should call by on her way back to the shop.

Buoyed up by her new idea, Ruby set off and made a right into Newton Street. Once things were sorted between her and Ewan, she could go to the police, give her account and put last night behind her.

GoTo's delivery depot was a dismal grey prefabricated building with a long frontage. Several vans sporting their swirly grey and blue logo sat beside a half-open factory door at the far end. Misgivings started to nudge Ruby as she steered into the car park. She pressed the brake. Ewan might not even be there; he spent most of his time on the road, after all. Though she didn't have his mobile number or his address and she certainly didn't want to alarm Sophie by asking her for them.

She reluctantly followed a crooked sign to visitors' parking, which turned out to be half a dozen bays close to the factory door, turned off the engine and climbed out of the car. The beeping reverse alarm of a forklift truck sounded as she crossed the threshold.

Inside was a hive of activity. Workers in navy coveralls were stacking boxes of all shapes and sizes on the grey metal shelving lining the walls of the warehouse. More racks ran down the centre. Two men near the entrance were deep in conversation while unloading a van.

Ruby caught her heel on a line of parcel twine on the floor and was bending down, freeing it up when a tall man in a hard hat rounded a line of racking. He nodded at her and pointed towards an office in the corner with a blue 'Reception' banner plastered across the top.

A bell dinged above the door as Ruby stepped into the reception area. A blue metal bench lined one wall. Scuffmarks and dents littered the paintwork. A counter ran along the end, another row of shelves behind it, filled with packages of all shapes and sizes.

Ruby stood beside the counter and shifted from foot to foot. She'd tell the receptionist she had to pass on a message from her sister (whose phone wasn't working). Ewan had worked there for some time, certainly all the time he and Sophie had been together. Presumably, they knew about his relationship. A story like that wouldn't arouse suspicion.

She was mulling this over when the door clapped back on its hinges and a man walked in. It was the man in the hard hat who'd directed her there. Not a receptionist as such.

'How can I help you?' he said. He looked harassed.

'I was wondering if I could speak to Ewan.' Ruby cringed inwardly, suddenly realising she had no idea what Ewan's surname was. She must have heard it or been told it at some stage, but, for the life of her, she couldn't recall it now.

The man narrowed his eyes. 'Ewan Wilson?'

'Yes,' she said firmly. Surely there couldn't be two Ewans working there. 'I have a message for him from my sister.' She tugged the bottom of her suit jacket and stood tall. 'It's important.'

The man's face slackened. 'I'm not sure if he's out on deliveries.'

'Could you check? Tell him it's Ruby.'

The door slammed again as he retreated.

Ruby slumped onto the bench. The cold metal seeped through her thin trouser material, making her shiver. She couldn't help thinking it would be freezing in there in winter.

Several minutes passed. It was almost a quarter to twelve. She should get back to work soon; there was only Sara, the admin assistant, at the shop with Mark and they'd be struggling to cover the phones. She was considering making a move, assuming they'd forgotten her, when the door behind the counter opened and Ewan appeared.

He closed the door behind him. 'What's up?'

Ruby approached the counter. 'We need to talk about last night.'

He viewed her warily. 'Is Sophie okay?'

'She's fine. I spoke to her this morning.'

Ewan's brows knitted. 'Then what are you doing here?'

'Like I said, we need to talk.'

'There's nothing to talk about.' He scratched the back of his neck. A coffee stain on the front of his coveralls stuck out like a cold sore. 'You and me,' he said in a low tone, 'it was a mistake. An aberration.' He met her gaze briefly, then looked back towards the factory. 'Let's forget it happened.'

'I agree.' There was something about his demeanour, his manner, that was scratchy, off. Was that due to embarrassment, shame, a hangover?

'So why are you here then?'

'Have you spoken with Sophie?'

'Not today. She was asleep when I left. Why?' He glanced again at the door. Was he worried about getting into trouble for taking time out?

'There was an attack in town last night. The police are asking for witnesses to come forward.'

'Yeah, I saw it on the news. I don't see what it has to do with us though.'

'They're appealing for witnesses.'

'I didn't see anybody acting strangely. Did you?'

Ruby ignored the question. She hadn't told him about the group of lads outside the supermarket. 'I wondered if we should speak to the police, say we were nearby.'

'Why?'

She jerked her head back. Was he being deliberately obtuse? 'Someone spotted us, Ewan! He shouted out.'

Ewan shrugged a single shoulder, nonchalant.

'Did you see the guy that saw us, or speak to him after I left?' Ruby pressed.

'No, I followed you. I wanted to make sure you got home okay. You know, with strangers hanging around.'

The fact that she hadn't seen or heard anyone following her home from the garages was disconcerting.

'Look,' Ewan said eventually. 'We weren't involved in the attack. I don't see how we could help and I don't want Sophie upset. Let's leave it there, shall we?'

Ruby glowered at Ewan. It was an impossible situation. Upset her sister or keep quiet. But she had a distinct feeling that keeping quiet wasn't going to be an option.

Chapter 10

Sophie was upstairs in Daisy's room, sorting through the washing when the doorbell chimed. Her eyes shot to her watch. It was almost time for the school run. She didn't have time for visitors right now.

She was halfway down the stairs when she recognised the outline of the single figure through the frosted glass in the front door.

'Hello, Sophie.' Bright eyes stared at her through wired spectacles, his smile carrying the warmth of friendship. Only he wasn't a friend. He was DC Hitesh Lalvani, the family liaison officer who'd supported them after their mother was killed. He was Police.

Sophie pressed her finger against the metal of the door chain and nodded a weary acknowledgement. Two weeks had passed since the trial she hoped would put an end to the exhausting whirlwind of questions, statements and police visits. What was he doing here now?

Hitesh was looking well. His hair freshly cropped and swept back from a handsome face, his beard and moustache perfectly manicured. The sweet aroma of his Kouros aftershave filled the air. 'Can I come in?' he asked.

Sophie pressed her finger harder against the metal nub. He was wearing the same navy suit he wore on the day Colin was sentenced: single-breasted jacket, tapered trousers covering long lean legs, a crisp white shirt beneath. She'd never seen him in anything but dark suits and white shirts. She pictured his wardrobe at home, a line of white shirts hanging at one end, an array of plain dark suits at the other. Not an ounce of colour in sight. 'I'm picking the kids up in a bit.'

'It won't take long.' He pushed his glasses up his nose, glanced skyward. The rain had finally abated but the clouds were thickening, promising another downfall.

A movement at the end of the driveway caught Sophie's eye. It was Christine sauntering by with her chihuahua, craning her neck to see what was going on. Christine was her next-door neighbour. A friend of the family, she'd babysat Sophie's children and shared many a coffee with Aileen over the years. She was also the town gossip.

Sophie gave Christine a wave and watched the woman move off.

Hitesh smiled again and moved forward. A subtle movement but enough for her to shift aside. He'd already decided he was coming in.

Sophie motioned for him to follow her into the kitchen and offered him a quick coffee. Hitesh liked coffee. He liked it strong and black.

He declined the drink. 'How did the memorial service go yesterday?' he asked.

She wanted to say good, though that didn't sound appropriate for a service to commemorate a death. 'It went well, I think.'

'And how are you? And Ruby?'

'We're all right, thanks.' She leant against the kitchen surface, the ridge of the wooden top digging into her lower back as she wondered what he was doing there. They'd expressed their gratitude and said their goodbyes outside the court a fortnight ago. Hitesh was an efficient detective. Supportive, yes, but not overly empathetic. After Colin was charged, he'd only called by when he had information to impart, or specific questions to ask.

He pulled out a chair, checked it was okay for him to sit and indicated for her to take the chair opposite. She did as she was told, casting a cursory glance at the clock. She really did need to leave in a few minutes.

Hitesh unfastened the button on his suit jacket and settled himself before he spoke. 'You're probably aware that a woman was killed in the town centre last night.'

Sophie froze. This wasn't how she imagined the conversation would unfold. 'I had heard.'

'The woman's identity has now been released. She was Charlotte Manning.'

Sophie's hand flew to her mouth. Photos in the press of a petite young woman with dirty blonde hair, pulled back from a heavily made-up face, sprang to mind. Charlotte Manning was one of Colin Halliday's former patients. She was also his alibi for the evening of her mother's murder. He'd admitted being at Aileen's shop on the afternoon of her murder, but maintained he couldn't possibly have killed her because he'd been with Charlotte in Leicester all evening. Despite extensive effort and a widespread public appeal, the police had been unable to trace Charlotte, who disappeared before she could be questioned.

'I wanted to come over and tell you myself before you read it in the press.'

Sophie was momentarily dumbfounded. Slowly, she removed her hand from her mouth. 'Charlotte Manning? Murdered?'

'Yes.'

'By whom?'

'That's what we mean to find out.' He nudged his glasses up his nose. 'I need to ask you if you've seen or heard anything from Charlotte?'

'No. We'd never heard of her before the investigation. I've certainly never met her. I'm pretty sure Ruby hasn't either. Why would she contact us?'

'Her name was mentioned in the news during your mum's trial. Sometimes people reach out to victims or their families afterwards.'

'I don't understand. What does this mean?'

'We're not sure yet. It may be Charlotte sought to lie low until after the court case, for some reason, and then returned to Market Deeton afterwards. It's quite possible her murder is unrelated. It's no secret she kept… shall we say, unsavoury company.'

Sophie recalled the questions about Charlotte after Colin was charged. The confusion. The suggestion he was out with another woman, a young woman unknown to the family, led to speculation of a possible affair initially and raised fresh questions about the case. She remembered scouring every press report, every news piece, to find out more about this mysterious woman.

Her mind slid to an interview with Charlotte's father, Nigel Manning, where he'd spoken frankly about his wife dying tragically of cancer when Charlotte was twelve years old. Raising his daughter alone through her rebellious teenage years. Charlotte had struggled after losing her mother and was prone to depression. She wanted her own space. They'd agreed for her to leave home at sixteen after she had found work washing dishes in the kitchen at The Crown in town and was able rent a room from a friend, and she'd seemed happier for a while.

The first time she had disappeared he'd found her crashed out in a heroin den. She'd lost her job, been thrown out of her room and lured into the underbelly of Market Deeton's drugs scene. He talked about using all his savings to send her to a private clinic, to dry out. Taking out a loan to arrange therapy with Colin Halliday. Charlotte secured a new job in a different pub and was in recovery when she fled again. It was a pitiful story of a family struggling with grief. But the press also ran other stories. Darker, sinister stories about Charlotte's life working as a call girl, renting rooms in Leicester hotels to make ends meet.

It wasn't until the trial that the barrister announced she was a former patient of Colin's he was supposedly helping out, information not released earlier due to confidentiality rules.

'What does this mean for us?' Sophie asked.

'It could be nothing at all. As I say, it may be completely unrelated. We're exploring all avenues and will keep you updated. I just wanted to let you know. Can I rely on you to tell Ruby?'

'Y-yes, of course.'

The chair scraped the floor as he stood.

'Wait.' Sophie reached out and grabbed his wrist. He stared at her and she immediately pulled her hand back, shifting awkwardly. 'You are sure Colin Halliday killed my mum, aren't you?'

'All I can say is, we're looking into everything. Where was the wake last night?'

He'd changed the subject. Again. She hated the way detectives did that. Starting with one conversation, then switching to another, avoiding having to answer her questions.

'We came back here after the church service. Around four. The last people left about seven thirty.'

'What about the family?'

'I stayed here. Ruby walked home. She left about a quarter to nine, I think. Hitesh, do you think Charlotte Manning's death is connected to my family?'

'Again, we've no reason to think that.' He fastened the button on his jacket.

Suspicion pecked at Sophie. There was *something*. She could see it in his face. 'What actually happened to her? I know the news reports say she was stabbed.'

'I can't comment on the finer details.'

'You must know.'

He met her gaze, but his lips were tight.

Sophie slumped back in her chair. Her quizzing was futile. He wouldn't answer her questions. The police played their cards close to their chest. Didn't impart information unless they had good reason to, no matter how much you probed. She'd learned that the hard way.

'Are we in danger?' she asked.

'We've no reason to believe there is any threat to the family. Try not to worry. It's probably a coincidence.'

Sophie clutched the edge of the table. It was coming back. Just when she thought there was some hope of laying it to rest, of putting it behind them, the reality of what had happened to her mother, the pain, the terror, was coming back to haunt her. 'A woman is killed on my mother's birthday, on the evening of her memorial service. Not a stranger, but the one person who could vouch for Colin, who knew where he was on the night my mother was murdered. How am I not to worry?'

Chapter 11

The children climb out of the Astra and circle the car. Around and around they run, Alfie squealing as his sister chases. He's nimble. Slipping and sliding, this way and that, in the wet. But she's quick. She turns, doubles back. Catches him by surprise. Shouts 'tag' when she reaches him.

I was like them once. The little one with the blonde curls. Curls that people stopped and admired in the street. My mother would smile. My father would grin and ruffle them with his square hand, agreeing how wonderful they were.

I watch you slide out of the driver's seat, chastise them for running in the wet and herd them into the house. You're wearing that green velvet shirt that hangs loose over your leggings. Your burnt orange mane bounces on your shoulders.

My father, Harry, used to drive me to school. Harry with his raven hair combed back from his face, his horn-rimmed glasses and his dark suits. Suits that became dusty when he sat on the bedroom floor with me at the end of the day. Finishing a jigsaw puzzle. Playing a board game. Reading me a story. And when bedtime finally came, he lay beside me. That was my favourite time of the day. We'd lie there for ages talking, just him and I. He was always interested in my day at school, always willing to help or offer advice.

When Billy Thomson punched me in the back in the gym queue, Harry said, 'When someone hits you, make sure you strike them back, hard.' I've never forgotten that.

When the Sanders twins stole my packed lunch, he went into the school and spoke to the headmaster. I don't know what he said, but the twins never came near me again.

'Sometimes people need to be taught a lesson,' he said. I've never forgotten that either.

Harry was my mentor and my best friend. Until I killed him.

You dash back out. You don't see me, peering around the edge of the bus shelter on the other side of the road. I could stand at the top of your driveway, in full view, and you'd still miss me. You're so wrapped up in your world of children, inclement weather and what to cook for dinner that you see nothing but a wet drive and a warm house.

I watch you pull your handbag out of the car and rush back inside, slamming the door behind you.

And I'm still here. Watching. Waiting.

Chapter 12

Ruby lowered herself onto the edge of the bed with a weary sigh. She pulled her shoulders back, massaged her lower spine, then wrestled a T-shirt over her head. Mark had been tied up with clients for most of the afternoon and, with Sara leaving early for a dental appointment, it was down to her to cover the phone and showroom. At least her final appointment had cancelled, giving her a chance to catch up with paperwork in between calls. It was after 5:30 p.m. when she left the office. Just enough time to dart home and change into her jeans before heading over to Sophie's for dinner.

What she really needed was two paracetamol and an early night. She couldn't cancel on Sophie though. Not tonight. This was the first murder in Market Deeton since their mother's death, and her sister had sounded shaken on the phone that morning.

A fleeting stab of conscience spiked her as she wriggled the T-shirt into place. With everything going on at work, there hadn't been time to call the police today or catch up with the news. That poor woman's family. Ruby remembered those early hours and days, only too well: sitting by the phone, waiting for a scrap of information. The overwhelming drive to find the truth. It wasn't as if she could tell them much though. After her discussion with Ewan, she'd have to say she was in the town centre last night, alone. But the people she'd seen, like the store assistant at the Co-op, would already have been routinely interviewed, wouldn't they? And the lads outside the shop walked off in the wrong direction. Unless they turned back...

The ringing of her mobile interrupted her thoughts. 'Lewis' flashed up on the screen.

'Did you hear about the murder last night?' he said without preamble. 'I've been worried about you.'

'Hi.' She grabbed her watch from the bedside table. 'It was a bit of a shock, but I'm fine, really. Thanks again for your help yesterday.'

'My pleasure. You coming to Heritage Arts tomorrow? Everyone would love to see you.'

Ruby pictured the array of keen faces at the amateur dramatics group. She'd been a member since sixth form, even travelling home for rehearsals when she was at uni to prepare for their biannual productions. It was where she'd met Lewis, a freelance events manager, when he'd joined them a couple of years earlier – to help on the publicity side. Her heart warmed. She loved the way they all mucked in behind the scenes to bring a performance together. But she hadn't been to a meeting since she'd lost her mum.

'Oh, I can't make this week, sorry. I'll be back soon.' She still couldn't face it. Not yet.

'No worries.' If he was disappointed, it didn't show in his voice. 'Anyway, I was calling to ask for your help.'

She balanced her mobile between her head and shoulder as she fastened her watch, then checked the time. She really needed to get going soon. 'What is it?'

'I'm doing a refurb on the flat. Wondered if you'd design the kitchen for me.'

Ruby remembered viewing the flat with him before he bought it a few months back – a two-bed on Cherry Tree Lodge, an exclusive modern estate on the western edge of town. The views across the River Welland and the countryside beyond were stunning. 'I can certainly help you with some ideas. I'm on my way out now. Shall I come over and take a proper look at the space?'

'That would be great. I'm going to try to take some time off next week. We could do it then. I'll get some beers in.'

'Beer and brochures. Sounds perfect,' she said with a chuckle. She grabbed a pen and notepad from her bedside table and jotted down some details. Perhaps she could talk to Mark and arrange a discount.

Ruby ended the call with a promise to call him back over the next couple of days to make the arrangements, then reached down, laced up her Converse and grabbed a cardigan from the wardrobe. She was almost at the bottom of the stairs when she caught her foot on a loose edge of carpet on the last step and stumbled. Stretching out her arms, splaying her hands. Grasping the arm of a jacket, hanging on the hooks in the hallway, to break her fall. Tom's jacket.

A flashback to just over a year earlier hit her as she straightened. The exhilaration of moving into this Victorian terrace with its tiled hallway, high ceilings and sash windows. After years of living with friends or renting flats, she'd hankered after having her own house. Something old she could lovingly restore, something with open fireplaces and natural character. And, as soon as she'd stepped over the threshold, she knew this was the perfect place.

She could still remember viewing the property with Tom. They'd been talking about buying a place together for a while. Placing the offer, biting her nails to the quick while they waited to hear. The elation when it was accepted. The urgent sex in the hallway that first night they moved in. Fighting for space amongst the boxes and bags piled up beside them.

Ruby looked back at the step, remembering them carrying in Tom's old desk, her losing her grip, dropping it down so violently it slipped and ripped the carpet. She was constantly tucking it back into place, but the gripper rod was broken and it kept breaking loose. They said they'd sort it out later. And later had never arrived.

Not for the first time, Ruby cursed the carpet – she really should get it fixed – then cursed Tom's jacket. Almost two

53

months had passed since they'd stood in that hallway, on the same tiles she stood on now, the same tiles they'd rolled around on that first night, faces numb with acceptance as she threw away their relationship in the space of a three-minute conversation. Three minutes. That's all it took to erase a relationship of two and half years.

She hadn't meant to do it that night, but creeping disillusionment had been growing for months and when he walked through the door, after yet another late drink after work, suddenly reality hit home. Where had the love gone, the intimacy? The little nudges on the sofa, the knowing smile over dinner, the footsy under the table, impromptu sex on the sofa on a Sunday afternoon. While she was dealing with the loss of her mother, shoring herself up for the trial, he was stepping back and becoming more and more distant.

They'd agreed on a break, a few weeks. He moved out and rented a room from a work colleague. Both turned a blind eye when the weeks rolled into a month and more. He called in occasionally, to collect his post or discuss a bill, and they chatted idly about their days, tiptoeing around anything remotely connected to their relationship or the future. Photos of them together still littered the walls – of them on holiday in Mexico, of a weekend in Paris when they first got together. His clothes still filled a wardrobe upstairs.

Ruby ran her hand down the back of the jacket, the soft material slipping in and out of her fingers. She'd spotted him at the back of the church yesterday, sitting there, still on the periphery of the family.

A fresh wave of guilt showered her. Tom had never gelled with Ewan. He found him awkward, standoffish. She closed her eyes. What would he make of their encounter last night?

Chapter 13

Sophie was standing beside the cooker, stirring a pan of risotto when her mobile buzzed. It was another text from Greg reminding her that she hadn't responded to his earlier message.

Sophie recalled the lights bouncing off her ex-boyfriend's balding scalp as he sat alone at the back of the church yesterday, making his presence known. Ironic really, since her mother had never forgotten how he'd treated her daughter and refused to have him in the house.

The back door opened and her sister entered. She cast the phone aside. Ruby looked tired, drawn, though she was dressed in a black T-shirt and jeans. She'd obviously found time to go home and change before she'd driven over. *Be nice to have the luxury*, thought Sophie and carried on stirring.

'I presume you know there's a car on bricks on the driveway,' Ruby said.

'It's Ewan's. An old Subaru. He bought it cheap. I've told him he can keep it here while he does it up. There's no room at the flat.'

Ruby opened her mouth to say something else when Daisy ran in.

'Auntie Ruby!' The girl hurled herself at her aunt, almost knocking her sideways.

Sophie watched her sister encase Daisy in a long bear hug.

The rice fizzed, catching the bottom of the pan. She grabbed the kettle, poured in more water.

'Where is Ewan anyway?' Ruby asked.

'He's working late tonight. He has to make up his hours from yesterday.'

'Ah.' Ruby released herself from her niece's clutches. 'What are you up to?' she asked Daisy.

'She's been drawing a picture of herself,' Sophie said, glancing at the table. She rolled her shoulders to loosen some of the tension in her neck. 'It's her homework.'

'Homework at seven? Goodness, that school's keeping you busy. Let me see.' Sophie watched Ruby move the crayons aside, stroke the blue hair on the paper and admire the child's handiwork. The rainbow of colours looked more like a children's TV character than a self-portrait.

She continued to stir the rice. A warm, hearty smell filled the kitchen. 'Can you clear the table,' she said to her daughter. 'This is almost ready.'

A chorus of groans followed.

Sophie ignored her daughter, took the pan off the heat and glanced into the hallway. Alfie was hanging off the banister by one arm like a monkey. 'Oh, Alfie, don't do that! You'll hurt yourself.' She turned to Daisy. 'Go and make your brother wash his hands, will you?' The words came out pithier than she intended.

'I'll go,' Ruby said. She left Daisy to tidy the last of the crayons into an old margarine tub, sauntered out of the room and pulled her nephew off the banisters, twirling him in the air. Daisy ran out and joined them. For several seconds Ruby swung them around, one at a time.

The sound of their laughter filling the air caught Sophie. She shouldn't have snapped at Daisy. It wasn't her fault the detective's visit was playing on her mind.

She was plating up the food when her sister re-joined her.

'I've sent them both to wash their hands,' Ruby said. She cocked her head to the side. 'You okay? You seem tense. Oh, you're not still thinking about the text, are you? I'm really sorry. I genuinely forgot.'

'A woman was murdered. I didn't know where you were.'

'I've said I'm sorry.'

'I know.' She turned to meet her gaze. 'There's something else.' She stole a glance up the hallway.

'What?'

Sophie was desperate to tell her about the visit from the police, but the sound of footfalls thundering down the stairs stopped her. 'Not now,' she said, widening her eyes as the children bustled in and wriggled into their seats at the table.

Dinner was a noisy affair. Daisy talked about a game of hopscotch she'd been playing in the school playground. Ruby regaled tales of chalking numbers on the paving outside their mother's house, and how she and Sophie played hopscotch as children. By the time they were eating their apple crumble and custard for pudding, everyone had relaxed. Even Sophie felt the tension in her shoulders lighten.

'Can we watch TV?' Daisy asked, scraping the last of the custard from her bowl.

'Okay, just for half an hour, to let your dinner go down.'

'Yay!' She slipped out of her seat and scampered into the front room, her brother behind her.

'How is Alfie doing?' Ruby asked, watching them go.

Sophie sighed. She'd followed the school's advice and attended bereavement sessions with both children. Talking about their grandmother and making up memory boxes of their time together eased Daisy, but Alfie refused to participate. A baby when his parents separated and barely a toddler when they moved here, he'd formed a close bond with Aileen and was still quiet and withdrawn at times. He refused to talk about her, even with his mother, and despite sending him to school throughout the court case, trying to shield him from the details and keep to his routine, he'd started wetting the bed again.

'He's okay,' she said quietly. 'The school are keeping an eye on him. Now all I need is for Greg to stop hounding me.'

Ruby frowned. 'What's he after?'

'More access to the children.'

'I thought he was happy being a weekend dad.'

'He's been asking for months. I put him off after Mum died, told him the kids needed their routine. He wants to play a bigger part in their lives: do the school run occasionally. I think secretly he's jealous of the time Ewan spends with them. Either that or he was too scared to ask when Mum was around; you know how she was with him.' She swiped a hand across her forehead. 'Anyway, that's not what I wanted to speak to you about.' She started gathering the plates together. 'Hitesh came over today.'

'Hitesh Lalvani?' Ruby's forehead furrowed. 'Why?'

'He asked about the memorial service.'

'Oh. That was nice of him.' Ruby picked up her bowl and wiped out the last remnants of crumble with her finger.

Sophie pushed the door closed with her toe as she moved across to the dishwasher. 'He also wanted to tell me about the woman killed last night. It was Charlotte Manning.'

'What?' The bowl slipped out of Ruby's hand and clattered against the tabletop. 'Are they sure?'

'Quite sure.'

'Where's she been?'

'Christ, Rubes. You know what Hitesh's like. If he knew the answer to that question, he wasn't about to tell me. He asked if she'd been in touch with any of us.'

Ruby's gaze widened. 'Why would she?'

Sophie met her sister's eye. 'Apparently, sometimes people close to a case reach out to the victim's family.'

'That's absurd. I mean what could she gain from us?'

'I don't know.'

'Do they know why she was killed?'

'Again, he wouldn't tell me.' She relayed Hitesh's visit, explaining how the police were working on the basis that Charlotte was lying low until after the trial. 'What I don't understand is, why she was killed last night, on Mum's birthday.' Her voice quaked. 'It's like a sign.'

'It's a coincidence. It has to be.'

'Is it?'

'Yes, of course it is. Colin killed Mum. A jury convicted him.'

Sophie wasn't so sure. She couldn't seem to crush the uncertainty growing within. 'It blurs the lines a bit though, doesn't it? Her coming back here, now.'

'Market Deeton's her hometown.'

They'd searched voraciously for details about Charlotte when her name came up in the investigation, surprised to discover she'd been raised in Market Deeton, only streets away from Aileen's shop in the town centre. Charlotte later moved to Leicester, but her father still lived in the same house. It seemed odd their paths had never crossed.

Sophie bit her lip. 'I checked her Facebook page earlier.'

'Whose?'

'Charlotte Manning's.'

'Sophie!' Ruby looked concerned. 'We've been through this. She was one of Colin's former patients.'

'I wanted to see what was written about her now. Whether she'd been on there recently.'

'And what did you find?'

Sophie's thoughts switched back to Charlotte's Facebook page, with the profile of her pouting at the camera. It was like staring at a ghost. The timeline littered with messages of condolence. She hadn't been active on there since the morning she disappeared, when she'd posted a photo of a cooked breakfast with a line beneath, *The best cure for a hangover I know*.

'I searched the comments and posts people had left, just to make sure. Couldn't find anyone we know.'

'Of course there isn't anyone. Don't you think the police would have checked?'

'Well, you never know. It doesn't necessarily mean there isn't a connection. I mean, what if the jury were wrong in Mum's case?'

Ruby's voice tightened. 'They weren't. They found Colin's spit in her hair, his blood on her clothes.'

'I don't know.'

'I do. You heard the judge speak to the jury. "Beyond reasonable doubt," he said.'

'What if someone else was involved? You know how distracted Mum was in the months before she died.'

Ruby let out a long breath. 'The verdict was unanimous.'

Sophie pinched the bridge of her nose between her thumb and forefinger and scrunched her eyes. All afternoon, she'd wrestled with the thoughts tearing around her mind. Nasty, sordid thoughts. What if Colin wasn't responsible for their mother's death? People had been wrongly convicted in the past. Though she couldn't deny, even with her attempts at shutting out the finer details, the evidence was stacked against him. He was the last person seen leaving the shop on that fateful day. Neighbouring shopkeepers reported hearing heated arguments between the two of them, on the days running up to the murder. With the shop and her family, Aileen had been struggling to give him the attention he wanted and was feeling smothered. She'd decided to put distance between them. A decision Colin hadn't welcomed.

'They found fragments of glass from his broken spectacles at the scene, for Christ's sake!' Ruby continued.

Sophie scratched the back of her neck. Something didn't feel right. 'Let's get these kids to bed,' she said, changing the subject. 'I've got a long day tomorrow. I'm doing a double shift.'

'What?'

'Agata's off sick and they need help.' She watched her sister's face fall. Ruby was worried she was doing too much, pushing herself too hard. But the hotel had been understanding since her mother had died, giving her day shifts during school hours. It couldn't go on forever. 'They've been good to me, Rubes, I can't say no.'

Ruby shrugged. 'Do you need any help with the kids?'

'No. Ewan's picking them up from after-school club and staying over.' She bit her lip and cast a doubtful look at her iPad. The murder of Charlotte Manning coupled with the visit from Hitesh still niggled her. 'Are you sure it's going to be all right?'

Ruby crossed the kitchen and wrapped her arms around her. 'This has nothing to do with us,' she said. 'Let the police do their thing.' She pulled back and wiped a fleck of dust from her sister's top. 'Hey, Kat's back from her holiday tomorrow, which means I've got the weekend off work. How about we go and visit Bridget on Sunday?'

Sophie groaned. 'Do we have to?' She didn't share Ruby's affinity with Bridget. Usually, a visit to Norfolk meant her sitting silently while they talked about crime dramas they were watching on television or compared thrillers they were reading. Bridget was kind enough and Sophie loved her as family, but her aunt could be harsh and blunt. She pooh-poohed Sophie's love of romance books – if it wasn't Jane Austen, Bridget wasn't interested – and visiting her always felt more of a duty call.

'Oh, come on. She'd love to see the kids. If it's fine, we can go to the beach. Might even get a paddle in the sea.'

Walking on the beach, listening to the gulls and inhaling the sea air, on the other hand, sounded enticing. 'Okay.'

'Great, I can't wait to tell her. She'll be so pleased.'

'Don't let's tell the kids until nearer the time. They won't sleep otherwise.'

As Ruby moved into the front room to gather the children, Sophie's mind slid back to Charlotte's murder. Coincidence. That's what both Hitesh and Ruby said. But whichever way she looked at it, Sophie couldn't get the timing out of her head. Why on that day?

Chapter 14

An hour later, Sophie pulled Daisy's bedroom door to a gentle close and popped her head around Alfie's doorway. He was snuggled up in his bed. Ruby beside him, reading *The Gruffalo* aloud. The kids had gone to bed remarkably easily that evening, helped no doubt by their auntie offering to read them bedtime stories.

'Are you still awake?' she said to her son, a smile teasing the edge of her lips.

He looked at his mother, bleary-eyed and gave her a watery grin.

'We've got to get to the end of the story,' Ruby said. 'It's only a few more pages.'

Alfie grinned again. It was good to see him so relaxed. *The Gruffalo* was his favourite book and even though he'd listened to the story hundreds of times, it was still his chosen bedtime read. Sophie said goodnight and left them to it.

She descended the stairs, edging around Pru, who was sitting serenely on the bottom step. The cat passed a beguiling look, but Sophie resisted the urge to place a hand down and stroke her head. She'd been at the receiving end of enough claws and teeth to give up trying to bond with her. Any affection Pru once welcomed had died with their mother. Ewan called her wild, but Sophie felt sorry for her. She was a feisty old lady whose beloved owner vanished one day, never to be seen again. It wasn't as if they could explain to her what had happened.

'Come on, you,' Sophie said to the cat, angling her head towards the kitchen. 'Let's get you some tea, shall we?'

Back downstairs, Sophie filled the cat's bowl, placed it down and flicked the switch on the kettle. She gathered together some empty mugs and popped a teabag in each, then moved across to the table and eyed the pile of *Homes & Gardens* on the kitchen side. Her mother used to order the magazine on an annual subscription and she hadn't the heart to cancel it, changing the payment details to her own when the renewal notice came through. A new issue landed on the doormat, month after month, encased in a shiny wrapper, and was placed on the countertop along with the others, unopened. She promised herself one day she'd go through them all, revamp the house. Ruby kept saying she needed to do something with the place, make it her own.

On top of the pile was her iPad. Her gaze lingered on its pink cover. Maybe she could take a quick peek at the news. Ruby said they should leave it, but the possible link with her mother's case and Colin left her uneasy.

She pulled the tablet over to the table and switched it on. The screen took a moment to light. Sophie glanced at the door as she keyed in 'Market Deeton news' and waited. A stream of searches came up. She changed her request to 'Market Deeton murder'. Again, numerous news reports filled the screen. She skimmed them, ignoring the old reports about her mother, focusing on the most recent. All the time listening for Ruby's footsteps. There was one article at teatime where the police had released the victim's name. Another where they'd refreshed their appeal for witnesses.

Sophie was about to check another report when a thought struck her. Leicestershire police had a Facebook page. She'd followed it last year when they were advertising calendars of police dogs to raise money for charity. She switched to Facebook and brought up the page. A post pinned to the top appealed for witnesses to the murder. Further down was a separate notice.

A witness saw an altercation between a couple beside the garages on West Way at approximately 9:15 p.m. yesterday evening. They both made off separately before he could reach them. The witness described the man as tall, with brown hair and in dark clothing. The woman had long dark hair and wore a black dress. Police are keen to trace these people. If you have any information, please contact the incident room.

Sophie reached for her bag, dug her hand in and pulled out her purse. She was unwrapping another blue tablet from the foil, when…

'What are you up to?'

Sophie jumped. She dropped the foil and her purse back into her bag. 'Just browsing…' The bag slid to the floor. She kicked it underneath her chair, moved to turn the iPad over. But she was too slow. Ruby was already there, holding it in place.

Ruby's eyes slid from the screen to Sophie. 'We agreed to leave the investigation to the police.'

'I wanted to see if they'd made any progress.' Her heart thumped in her chest now. Though looking at her sister's face, Ruby was more interested in what was on the computer than Sophie's handbag. She couldn't have been there long enough to see the tablets. Thank God. 'They're appealing for witnesses,' she said. 'Anyone who was in the town last night and might have seen something. Did you see anything?'

'No. It was quiet. What's that?' Ruby pointed at the post Sophie had been reading.

'A witness saw a couple arguing beside the garages on West Way yesterday evening. That's near you, isn't it?'

Ruby didn't answer, her eyes glued to the screen.

Sophie sniffed. 'It was probably just some teenagers having a quick shag.'

Chapter 15

Ruby drove the long way home, desperately trying to quell the nerves that were performing a jig in her stomach. The witness clearly hadn't been able to identify her or Ewan beside the garages on West Way, but there was always the chance someone else would and the appeal felt like a hand at her throat, slowly squeezing the air from her. They had to go to the police now, explain it away as some kind of silly joke. Plus, she really ought to tell them about her encounter with the lads at the supermarket.

Drinking that last cup of tea at Sophie's table had felt like an eternity. Steering her sister away from the events of yesterday evening and trying to make light conversation, while all the time Ruby's heart was in a vice, tightening by the second. She'd made her excuses and left immediately afterwards, feigning a headache. Her guilt intensifying when Sophie graciously said, 'We could all do with an early night. It's been a tough few days.' Because sleep was the furthest thing from Ruby's mind.

The murder of Charlotte Manning branded itself on her brain. It couldn't be connected to their mother's case, could it? She'd done her best to allay Sophie's fears, but the timing, on their mother's birthday, and Sophie's visit from the liaison officer, left her anxious. And the fact that she was in town herself last night did nothing to ease her frayed nerves.

It was almost 9 p.m. when Ruby turned the corner into Shetland Avenue. Cars were parked nose to tail along the kerb; she had to drive fifty yards or so up the street to find a space.

Soft lighting bled through her neighbours' closed curtains as she wandered along the pavement towards home. She was almost at the tall privet hedge encasing her front garden when she heard a noise coming from her house. A series of raps. No, clicks. She paused. It stopped. She waited a second, wondering if she'd been mistaken. No, there it was again. The juddered clicks of the handle.

Someone was trying her front door.

Ruby held her breath and turned 360 degrees. The street was empty. A part of her wondered if it was Tom, calling by to collect something. Maybe he had forgotten his key and was trying to get her attention.

She pulled her phone out of her pocket, rounded the hedge gingerly.

Ewan snatched his hand from the door. 'Oh, finally,' he said. 'I wondered where you were.' His hair was combed back off his face and slick, as if he'd recently stepped out of the shower and he was wearing another pair of dark joggers and a navy T-shirt, despite the dipping temperatures.

Ruby's gaze slid from the door to Ewan. 'What are you doing here, Ewan?'

'We need to talk.'

You can say that again. He seemed twitchy. 'I was with Sophie.'

'Ah…' He dug his hands into his pockets. 'Sorry, I didn't have much time when you came to the depot earlier.'

You didn't have any time. He was obviously here because he'd seen the recent appeal, though this wasn't a conversation she wanted to have on the doorstep. 'May I?' She pulled out her keys, pointed at the door. He was standing in front of the lock.

'Sorry.' He shuffled aside. 'Sophie mentioned you often don't hear the knocker. I was trying to get your attention.'

Ruby said nothing, taking her time to unlock the door, hovering in the hallway to remove her jacket, then indicating for him to follow her into the kitchen. The sound of his trainers squeaking against the hallway tiles went through her.

'Tea or coffee?' she said, flicking the switch on the kettle. Might as well keep this civil.

'Coffee please. White, no sugar.'

White, no sugar. Three simple words that summed up their relationship. This was a man who'd been dating her sister for a year, yet she had no idea how he took his coffee. In fact, if her memory served her correctly, he'd only been to her house a few times – to pick up Sophie or one of the kids. He'd never actually been inside. Few people had.

When the house sale was going through, she'd dreamed about the parties she and Tom would throw, the family dinners they'd organise, imagining them all sitting around the table together laughing and joking. Playing board games afterwards like they did at Christmas. This was the first house she'd owned. She couldn't wait to share it. But once they'd settled and started thinking about organising a get together, her mum died, the world turned askew and thoughts of opening her home to guests melted into the background.

She busied herself making drinks while Ewan stood quietly, scanning the kitchen: the duck-egg blue walls; the pop art pictures on the walls that Tom liked so much; the photos on the fridge of her and Tom in happier times. Ewan had never mentioned their break-up. In fact, he hadn't mentioned Tom at all since they'd separated, not even to say he was sorry for them. Odd really. He must have known.

'I take it you've heard the news about Charlotte Manning?' she said, breaking the silence.

'Yeah, Sophie told me. Bad business.'

'She's worried.'

'I know. I tried to talk her round. It's probably a coincidence.'

'That's what I said.'

Awkward silence filled the kitchen, punctuated by the coughs and splutters of the kettle.

'I suppose you've seen the appeal for the couple in West Way?' Ruby said when she could bear it no longer.

He looked up at her and nodded. 'It was dark. It could be anyone.'

'It's definitely us. The timing, the description. Everything fits.'

He lowered himself into a chair and swiped a palm down the front of his face, the calluses of his hand scraping on the thin stubble covering his chin.

'The police are appealing for people who were in the town centre last night to come forward. There are cameras. They'll be checking,' she continued.

'There weren't any cameras on the roads we walked together.'

Ruby narrowed her eyes. 'How can you be sure?'

'Because we were off the main stretch. There's no CCTV up there. The council cameras are focused on High Street.'

While his knowledge of CCTV camera placement surprised her, Ruby wasn't about to be distracted. 'We should tell the truth, Ewan.' He looked at her as if she'd gone mad. 'I don't mean… the whole truth. You know, just confirm we were there – say we were messing about, play it down.'

'Oh, you think Sophie will accept that, do you?' The barbs in his voice caught her. 'She doesn't know we were together. In fact, she doesn't even know I was out jogging.'

'You didn't tell her you went out?' When Tom and she were together, she couldn't imagine him going out at night and not mentioning it. He even shouted to let her know when he stepped outside to put the bins out.

'It didn't seem important at the time. So, now, when a description of us emerges in the press, don't you think she'd be a bit suspicious? You know how she is.'

An image of Sophie's ghostly face in the hospital four years ago skipped into Ruby's mind. Sophie had openly avoided men in her personal life after Greg. 'How could I trust anyone else?' she had said, when Ruby suggested meeting someone new. She refused to entertain discussions about a future relationship until Ewan came along. But, even now, Sophie was prone to jealousy and paranoia. And her speculation earlier about the couple using West Way for a quick shag was bound to raise suspicion, however innocent their explanation.

'We don't have to tell Sophie. We just need to tell the police.'

'There's no guarantee she won't find out.'

Ruby pushed her tongue against the side of her teeth. He was beginning to irritate her. 'If you're worried about what she might think, then what are you doing here?'

'We need to get our story straight. Make sure we're singing from the same hymn sheet.'

'Oh, don't give me that.' He sounded like bloody Mark from work.

'Look, everyone knows you were in town. You can talk to the police. I don't need to be involved.'

'What do I say to them about the appeal for the couple?' She cringed at the word 'couple'. It made the situation sound even more vulgar.

'Nothing. It could be anyone. Just say you walked home alone.'

'That's not true!'

'There was no one else around.'

'The man who spotted us near the garages. We don't know what he saw...'

Ewan huffed. 'He clearly hasn't seen much.'

'Someone else might have seen us.'

'Who? I didn't see anyone.'

The kettle clicked off. Ruby ignored it. 'I don't see why we should lie. I mean, we haven't done anything wrong.'

'I didn't see anything, did you?'

'That's not the point.'

'It's exactly the point! We can't help the police, we've got nothing to tell them, so any time they spend with us will be time wasted, away from the investigation, when they should be out there, looking for the killer. They'll have other leads. When they can't identify the couple, they'll move on to them. We're not important to the investigation, we're important to Sophie. And she's struggling right now. She puts on a brave face, but she couldn't take anything else, not least this.'

Ruby swallowed. Sophie had been tense tonight.

'I'm not saying, don't go. You be the good citizen if you want. Just leave me out of it.' Ewan's gaze flicked to the clock on the wall. 'I'll leave the drink, if you don't mind. I've got an early start tomorrow.' And with that, he pushed back the chair, stood and strode up the hallway leaving Ruby reeling.

Chapter 16

The blank screen of the television faced Ruby as she sat on the sofa, cradling a mug of tea. The same mug of tea she'd been nursing for almost half an hour. The situation with Ewan should have been straightforward. Explained away by a chance meeting, a quarrel amongst family. But nothing related to Sophie was ever straightforward. Ever since the incident four years ago, everyone was mindful of her mood. Tiptoeing around, desperately avoiding upsetting her.

Still, Ewan's unwillingness to go to the police, even to give a confidential account, irked her to the bone. Why was it such a problem?

Her mug was cold now; a dark gelatinous skin covered the top of the drink. She placed it down on the floor and massaged her temples, desperately searching for a solution, when her gaze absently went to the window. The curtains were still open. She was about to draw them when she saw a movement. The privet hedge outside was almost a foot thick. Nothing, not even passing headlights, penetrated it.

She blinked, rubbed her eyes.

Another flash, as if someone had dashed by. Adrenaline pulsed through her.

Had she locked the doors? Yes, the front door locked automatically on the Yale lock and she'd pulled the chain across after Ewan left. She'd locked the back door after she put the rubbish out that morning.

Ruby edged across the room to the window. But the front-room light was bright and she couldn't see anything in the darkness outside. Should she call the police? She'd read a report online about a resident on the estate having a prowler in their back garden last month. Another about youths stealing planted tubs and hanging baskets. But if she called the police, they'd send a patrol car. The last thing she wanted was officers in her home – she'd had enough of their visits after her mother died to last her a lifetime.

Should she phone Tom? No. She couldn't call Tom over something like this. And she didn't want to upset Sophie either. But she couldn't leave it. What if someone was out there, waiting for her to go to bed, sizing up the place to break in?

She bit her lip and switched off the light. All was quiet. The garden looked empty.

She moved into the kitchen, retrieved a large torch from the drawer and grabbed her phone. Her fingers juddered as she pressed 999, her thumb hovering over the call button. She inched towards the front door, opened it and shouted, 'Hey!', switching on the torch. The beam illuminated the front garden in a tunnel of light. It was empty. Her tubs still lined the pathway, the summer flowers waning.

'Who's there?' she called. The words were swallowed by the cool night air.

A car whizzed past on the road outside. Ruby ventured up the pathway and out onto the pavement, thumb still poised over the call button on her phone.

She stood there several seconds, checking up and down the road. Maybe her eyes were playing tricks on her. She was ridiculously tired. She walked back into the house and closed the door, but the incident left her with a lingering sense of disquiet.

Chapter 17

Peekaboo. I see you.

I peer through the window of the car on the opposite side of the road and watch you retreat into your house. Seconds later, you draw the front-room curtains.

I love it when people switch on their lights in the evenings and leave the curtains open. It's an open invitation for someone like me, a window into their world.

As a child, I'd leave school late, dawdle home. Peer inside the houses I passed and watch families sitting at the table, eating dinner together. Couples cuddled up on the sofa, watching television. Siblings playing. And I'd find myself imagining how their evenings unfolded. Maybe the kids were given ice cream for pudding. Allowed to play for half an hour to give their dinner time to settle. Perhaps someone would read them a story before bed. *An adventure story like* Peter Pan *or* Robinson Crusoe.

Harry used to read me adventure stories.

I often wonder how different my life would have been if Harry hadn't died. Whether we'd ever have met, ever have been acquainted. But it doesn't do to dwell on the past. We've been drawn together by a cruel twist of fate – you and me. And you have to play the cards that fate deals you.

Chapter 18

Ruby stood in the shower the following morning and closed her eyes, relishing the jets of water driving into her shoulders, coursing down her back. After taking to her bed early last night, willing sleep to erase the worries of the day, a fretful night had followed. Shallow dreams intersected with images of Ewan's hardened face refusing to go to the police. Watching the hazy image of them arguing in West Way, as if she was an innocent bystander. The gruesome picture of a woman on a slab. The dreams merging, morphing her memories.

Now, as she rested her forehead on the cool plastic of the shower cubicle, her thoughts turned to her mother. The drive to the morgue on that grey November morning. Sophie in the passenger seat, hands clasped together, knuckles shiny white. Remembering how she had wanted to say something, anything, to ease the tension in the car, but she couldn't form the words. Her tongue paralysed with fear.

Walking down the long corridor with Hitesh, Sophie's icy cold hand in hers. The lingering smell of bleach in the air. Her sister doubling up as they reached the door. The tears. The shrillness of her younger sister's cry still made her wince, even now. She couldn't go in. If it was their mother, Sophie didn't want to see her like that. Wrapping her arms around her, sitting her down on the plastic chair outside, telling her she'd take care of it.

Hot tears streamed down Ruby's face. Tears that mingled with the shower still beating down.

Afterwards, she was relieved she'd saved Sophie the experience because the image that stayed with her wasn't one anyone should be left with. The cream walls, the easy-wash tiled floor, the clinical smell of bleach somehow stronger in the anteroom. The long window looking into another smaller room. The clinician in blue coveralls wheeling in the trolley. Hitesh checking she was ready, before giving the clinician a nod.

A brief moment of relief, like air rushing out of a balloon, when she saw the hunched mass on the trolley. It couldn't be her mother. The body under the white sheet was too small, too thin. The stone in her chest as they lifted back the sheet. Aileen's burnt orange hair was swept away from a sallow face with sunken cheeks, pale brittle lips. They'd covered her neck and closed her eyes, but there was no doubt it was her.

Ruby slid down to the shower tray and coiled herself in a ball, shoulders quaking as she sobbed.

She wasn't sure how long she stayed there, the water streaming down, splattering her back. Eventually, the tears subsided. She switched off the shower, wrapped a towel around herself and sat on the edge of the bath.

Charlotte's murder was dredging up so many memories. In some ways, Sophie was right – it did seem like a sign. She couldn't deny, her mother wasn't herself in the months before she died. Turnover had been down in the shop all summer. She was running an early sale to boost business. At the time, they put her stress down to pressures at work and her waning relationship with Colin. Could there have been another reason?

She played out Hitesh's visit to Sophie yesterday in her mind. Sophie was wary of Hitesh. To Sophie, Hitesh, in his dark suits and polished boots, represented the investigation; the time lapse between the charge and the trial; the delay in releasing her mother's body. The anguish over her loss.

But there was another reason for her angst. Sophie felt a misguided responsibility for her mother's death because it was her that introduced Colin to their mother. Questioning his guilt appeased her conscience.

Ruby dried herself off and slipped her robe over her shoulders. She needed to speak with Hitesh herself. She needed to find out exactly what was going on.

–

'Let's go through this again,' the officer said. He met her gaze, all blue eyes and fresh faced. He'd introduced himself as TDC Foster and when Ruby asked what TDC stood for, he'd said, Temporary Detective Constable. She sighed inwardly. Fair hair, razored to number one, he looked every inch in training.

When she'd arrived at the front desk and asked for Detective Constable Hitesh Lalvani, she'd been told he was otherwise engaged. Of course he was. He'd be supporting Charlotte's father, making warm drinks, sitting on his sofa, updating him on the investigation – like he'd done for them, ten months earlier.

Now Ruby was stuck with the new boy on the block, taking her account on behalf of the homicide team.

When they were little, their mother used to say, 'Always tell the truth. You have nothing to worry about if you've done nothing wrong.' But sitting here, facing a police officer across a Formica table in a windowless room, while every sound she made, every word she uttered was being recorded, she felt a shudder rush through her. Because she wasn't being truthful. She was holding back. She was lying.

'You left your sister's house in Henderson Close at about 8:45-ish,' he said, emphasising the ish. 'Are you sure you can't be more specific?'

'No.'

'And you walked into town via Templeton Road. What time do you think you met the group of lads outside the Co-op?'

'I'm not sure exactly. You could check with the staff there. Or maybe they have' – she turned down the corners of her mouth – 'CCTV or something.'

'And your descriptions of them…'

Ruby resisted the temptation to roll her eyes. She pictured Baggy Jeans with his eyebrow ring and sneer, Crew Cut with his acne-scarred cheeks, and gave her best description. The others faded into the background. 'I'm guessing you've already interviewed the shop assistants at the Co-op,' she said, trying to make up for the holes in her memory. 'There was a guy working there on Tuesday.' Another description, this time of the burly shop assistant who came to her aid. 'He might be able to provide more detail.'

The officer ignored her comment. 'And from there you crossed the road and continued up Clarence Street...' He followed her movements, repeating the journey she'd given him earlier. His monotone voice starting to grate. '...Past Simpson's Place,' he continued, lifting his head to face her.

'Yes.'

'And you didn't see anything? Anyone hanging around?'

'As I said earlier, no. I'd have told you if I had.' She squirmed uncomfortably in her seat.

'But you'd had a lot to drink.'

'Yes.'

'What about cars?'

'Sorry?'

'Motorists. Did you see any motorists pass?'

The drone of the car engine near the garages nudged her. She blinked it away. 'Not that I remember. It was a quiet night.' She was beginning to feel more like a suspect than a witness.

'So it seems.' He looked down at his notes again.

'Is this going to take much longer?' Ruby asked. She was starting to feel claustrophobic. 'Only I really need to get back to work.'

'Almost done. I see you walked along West Way.'

Ruby suppressed another shudder. 'Yes.'

'And what time would that be?'

'I can't be sure exactly. I didn't check.'

'You must have some idea.'

She blew out a slow breath, as calmly as she could. 'Around ten past nine.' An imperceptible shrug. 'Possibly later.'

'And you didn't see anything there?'

'No.'

'Are you sure?'

'Yes, I'm completely sure.'

Chapter 19

A cocktail of guilt, frustration and disappointment needled Ruby as she left the police station. The lie she'd told TDC Foster lodged itself like a fish bone in the back of her throat. Plus, when she'd asked about Charlotte Manning's murder, the officer had met her gaze – his face tightening, betraying the fact that he knew exactly who she was, who her mother had been – and said he wasn't able to give her any details. Not the most productive hour she'd spent.

She checked her phone, relieved to find no new messages, and texted Mark to say she was on her way to work.

The weather was brightening, a shard of sunlight breaking through the clouds, helped along by a bustling wind. Ruby wandered down High Street to the sound of freshly fallen leaves crunching beneath her feet. Autumn had definitely arrived.

Her phone vibrated in her pocket. She moved to the side of the pavement. By the time she retrieved it, the caller had rung off. Through the splintered screen, she was surprised to find it had been Tom calling. It couldn't have been important; he didn't leave a voicemail. She was about to slip her phone back into her pocket when it buzzed with a text. Tom again.

Are you free to meet on Sat?

This was her only Saturday off this month. Not that she had anything particular planned. She'd promised Sophie she'd go through some of their mum's clothes, but that wasn't until the afternoon.

Sure. She pressed send and slipped it into her bag. She was back at her car now. She had just placed her keys in the ignition when she received another text.

> OK, let's meet in Martini's Bistro on Carvel Street at one. I'll book us a table.

Ruby frowned. She crossed paths with Tom every couple of weeks, usually when he came by the house to collect his post. They'd never arranged to meet though, not since he'd left. Was this the discussion she'd been avoiding? Were they about to address the future of their relationship, once and for all? They couldn't go on as they were. He was still contributing to the bills and it wasn't fair to him to be living in a mate's spare room when he had a perfectly good home himself.

She punched back, *OK.*

No sooner had the message sent than another came through.

> Great, see you then.

She chucked the phone on the seat beside her and turned over the engine. That was one lunch she wasn't looking forward to.

–

The morning sun bounced off a car windscreen, temporarily blinding Sophie as she walked along Ablett Street on her way into work. Past the charity shops and boutiques, the chemist and the nail bar. She was about to turn the corner, when she paused and glanced further down the road that led into town. The road that contained her late mother's shop.

Since the murder, she hadn't allowed herself to venture down there. It was almost as if she was holding onto a precious memory, savouring it, and if she wandered past and viewed the frontage, witnessed the traffic, the shoppers browsing, life rolling forward, it would burst and be lost forever.

But, today, she felt a magnetic force, pulling her towards it. This was her direct route to the hotel, to work. For months she'd taken the long way around, down Hilton Street and into the top of High Street. She continued up the road two more blocks and stopped, turning on her heel to survey the phone shop set into the white-washed building opposite. Flanked by Deeton Books on one side and Thompson's Bakery on the other, it barely resembled the shopfront that had been part of her life since she was a teenager. The woodwork had been painted navy by the new tenants, although if she looked carefully, she could still see smudges of yellow at the edge of the windows. The sign above the door had changed, but in her mind she could still see the gold 'Hattie's' in swirly letters.

She hovered beside the kerb, taking in the window display, featuring the latest phones hanging from wires, the racks of phones and accessories lining the walls inside. The soft seating at the back beside the counter. Mentally turning back the clock to the clothing and accessories draped artistically in the window. More clothing strategically arranged on chrome racks inside.

The door to the bookshop next door snapped open and Becky, the owner, emerged.

Sophie dipped her head, pretending to look away, hoping she hadn't seen her. Becky Tyler was a forceful woman in her early thirties, one of those gushy people Sophie tended to avoid.

It was too late. Becky was already bustling across the road, her bohemian dress flapping around the ankles of her lean frame.

'Hi, Sophie,' Becky said. 'How are you doing?'

Sophie said she was okay, and that Becky was looking well, even though with her cropped white-blonde hair pinned off her face she appeared tired and drawn. Barely two weeks ago, Becky had been sitting in a courtroom in her best suit, eloquently regaling how she'd returned to her shop to collect her purse after hours on that fateful evening ten months ago and noticed the rear fire door of Aileen's store ajar. Pushing it open, wandering inside, only to find her crumpled body on the floor. Sophie shivered. It couldn't have been easy, picking up the pieces, coming back to the same shop, day after day, after finding your neighbour like that.

Becky was chattering away, congratulating Sophie on her speech at the service yesterday when a man emerged from the bookshop.

It was Lewis, helping out. He often helped Becky out when he wasn't busy.

'Becky. A customer's asking about the possibility of ordering one of P. G. Wodehouse's collections,' he called across the road.

Becky rolled her eyes. 'Excuse me,' she said to Sophie. 'It's good to see you.'

She watched her cross the road, only to be replaced by Lewis.

'How are you doing?' Lewis said.

Sophie gave a backwards nod and sighed inwardly. Market Deeton was a small town, but still large enough to fade into the background or go unnoticed – one of the things she'd liked most about living there until the death of her mother and the subsequent trial thrust her into the limelight. It was easier for Ruby. With her dark hair and nondescript features she looked like any other twenty-something on the High Street. Sophie was the image of her mother and her flaming red hair was like a beacon to concerned locals, who buzzed around her like flies.

Though Lewis wasn't exactly a stranger. He was Ruby's friend and he'd been to their house for dinner several times when Aileen was alive. One of the sorry locals her mother took pity on because he didn't have family nearby. Becky was another. She'd opened the shop after her husband of twelve months had been killed in a tragic car accident in her late twenties. There'd been plenty of them over the years, clogging their house on a Sunday when the shop was closed.

Sophie forced herself to be polite. 'Okay, thanks,' she said. 'I'm on my way to work.' She wanted to move on, but he was standing right in front of her, blocking her path. He followed her eyeline to the phone shop.

'Must be difficult seeing it now,' he said, guessing her thoughts.

Sophie chewed the side of her mouth. The shop had remained vacant for ages after the police released the crime scene. Only last month did she hear that a large phone company had signed the lease.

'They've done a good job, I think,' he continued. 'You know, to make it look different. Your mum would be pleased.'

Sophie's legs weakened. She liked Lewis. She knew he was only trying to be helpful, but she wasn't in the mood to chit-chat about her late mother's shop. Not here. Not now. 'I've got to go. I'll be late for work.' She shuffled past him and continued down the road.

Chapter 20

Kat forked a final mouthful of rice into her mouth and placed her plate on the floor. 'I do love a good curry,' she said, licking her lips. 'Didn't have one of those in Tenerife.'

Ruby chuckled and filled up their glasses. She'd missed Kat this past week. Their little chats over coffee. Talking about what they'd been up to at the weekend. Moans about the daily grind. It was easy to forget Kat had been Sophie's friend from school. These days, Ruby saw far more of Kat than Sophie and, in the three years they'd worked together at Galanti's, they'd grown close. It was good to have her back.

There had been little time to talk at work today with half the town, or so it seemed, trotting in, making enquiries about a new kitchen. It was lovely to finally kick back at home now, have a glass of wine and a catch-up.

Kat swirled the wine in her glass, watching it drift around. She looked like an advertisement for Expedia, with her bronzed skin and ponytail of white-blonde hair. 'How are things with Tom?' she asked.

Darkness was drawing in outside. Ruby switched on the lamp in the corner and lit some candles. The light created a soft hue in the room as she told her friend about Tom's lunch arrangement.

'What do you think he wants?'

Easing herself back onto the other end of the sofa, Ruby kicked off her shoes and tucked her feet beneath her. 'No idea. Maybe he wants to sort all this out.' She waved her hand at the room, gave a wistful smile. She loved this house with its

84

chipped doors, its rattling window frames, the old Victorian tiled fireplaces in every room. She had so many plans for it, the idea of leaving made her ache inside.

'You think he wants to sell?'

'Why wouldn't he? It's been a couple of months. Perhaps he wants me to end the relationship properly, so he can look for somewhere more permanent.'

'Or he wants to reconcile.'

'He hasn't made any noises to say so.'

'What about you? What do you want?'

Ruby rested back into the sofa. She could still see Tom's square jaw, his sparkly brown eyes beneath his cycling helmet on the day they first met. It was the middle of summer. She'd taken a week off work to catch up with chores and decided to dust off her old bike and take a ride, maybe start a new fitness regime. She was less than a mile outside Market Deeton, admiring the rolling Leicestershire countryside, when she caught a puncture.

She remembered standing at the side of the road, staring hopelessly at the round pieces of rubber and glue in the puncture repair kit. Toying with whether to wheel the bike back home or try to locate the source of the puncture, when Tom pulled up on his mountain bike and offered to help. It was a nasty tear, scuppering her plans for an afternoon ride. He'd patched it up and followed her back to make sure she got home safely.

A coffee, to say thank you, turned into hours sitting on the patio in the sunshine, chatting. He was witty, easy-going, and there was a boyish enthusiasm to him as infectious as his laugh. Not bad-looking either, a touch of Brad Pitt about him, though Tom was taller, sleeker.

'Honestly, I don't know,' she said. 'If he was the old Tom, the guy I met two and a half years ago, I'd love to get back together. He's just been so weird recently. Going out drinking with his mates, while I was sitting here trying to organise a funeral for my mother. I'm not sure I know him any more.'

'This whole year's been difficult for all of you.'

'I know. But do I really want to spend my life with someone who bails out as soon as we hit a problem?'

Kat raised a manicured brow. 'You lost your mum in the worst possible circumstances. I'd say that's more than a problem.'

'He wasn't there when I needed him.'

'Perhaps he couldn't cope.'

'Neither could I. Anyway' – she lifted a cushion with her free hand and chucked it at her friend – 'you're supposed to be on my side.'

Kat held out her wine glass and dodged the cushion, laughing. 'I'm just playing devil's advocate. I will say this though: Don't make any rash decisions. Tom's a good man. You've all been through a lot.' She took another sip of wine, a teasing smile tugging at her lip. 'I think a certain Mr Galanti would be pleased to hear you were free though.'

'Don't start!' Ruby tossed another cushion, narrowly missing Kat's head.

'Oh, come on. You know you're his favourite.'

'So you keep telling me.' Ruby cringed at the idea. She could never fancy Mark Galanti with his greased hair and slick comments.

'I can't believe you don't see it. The way he leans over your desk, calls you his *senior designer*.' She pulled a cheesy face.

'That's my job title. He's mentoring me.'

'Hmm. If you say so.'

A memory swooped in. Wandering into the kitchen at her mother's, announcing she'd been offered her job. She'd been so thrilled, so elated. Yet her mother's congratulations had been tainted by the name and she had simply said, 'Oh, for the love of God, not Mark Galanti. You'd better watch yourself there, girl.'

But Aileen wouldn't expand, wouldn't be pressed, and when his name came up in conversation, she shuddered disapprovingly. Ruby knew they'd fallen out when they were on the local business association together, a couple of years earlier. She'd tried to probe Mark, but he dodged her questions, refusing to acknowledge there was an issue, even though he avoided Aileen like the plague. It was an odd situation. One of those unresolved issues. A stone in her shoe. Though, she had to admit, Mark was an intensely private man. Someone it was difficult to warm to, however much Kat said he favoured her.

She finished her wine and topped up their glasses.

'How are you anyway?' Kat said. 'I mean really?'

'I was doing okay, you know, set on putting it all behind me. Ready to start a new chapter and all that. Then… You heard about the murder?'

'I did! My mum texted me when we got back last night. It was late, otherwise I'd have messaged you. Charlotte Manning, after all this time. Have the police told you anything?'

'Not really. I need to speak with Hitesh, our liaison officer. I'm waiting for him to contact me.'

'How's Sophie doing?'

She was reminded of Sophie's jumpiness last night, the anxiety in her face. 'Difficult to say. She seems to be coping, but you can never be sure with Sophie.' Kat's face contorted when Ruby told her about Sophie's visit from Hitesh yesterday. 'I think it really knocked her for six.'

'I can't say I'm surprised.' She reached across, placed her hand on Ruby's forearm. 'Try not to worry.'

'There's something else,' Ruby said, her eyes fixed on the shadows of the flickering candle flame. She was wrestling with keeping the exchange with Ewan to herself, the pressure to share the burden, to ease the load, eating away at her.

Kat pulled her hand away and took another sip of her wine. 'What?'

'I…' She drew a deep breath, cheeks billowing as she blew it out. It was a struggle to find the right words. 'I think I need to start from the beginning.'

Ruby took her time to tell Kat about her walk home from the wake on Tuesday evening. When she relayed the incident in West Way, Kat gasped.

'Bloody hell, Rubes, you don't do things in half measures.'

Ruby felt heat in her cheeks. She took another sip of wine. 'Nothing happened as such. I stopped it. I just feel so guilty.'

'Why? From what you're telling me, he took advantage of you when you were drunk.'

'I don't know. We both drank too much. But I should have stopped it sooner.' Ruby told her about the witness spotting them.

'That description was of you? I saw it on the news!'

Ruby gave a sombre nod.

'Do the police know?'

'It's complicated.'

Kat sat forward, placed down her glass and frowned. 'What do you mean, complicated?'

'Ewan wants to forget it, put it behind us.'

'Okay.' She dragged out the word, her face creasing in confusion. 'Why do I get the feeling you're not telling me everything?'

'Ewan won't go to the police. Sophie doesn't know he was out. He doesn't want her to find out about our… Anyway, when I gave my account today, I… I didn't mention it was us in West Way.'

'Whoa!' Kat held up a flat hand. 'Wait a minute. Are you saying Sophie doesn't know he was out, let alone with you?'

'Yes. You know how jealous she gets, after what she went through with Greg.'

'It's one thing her not knowing he was with you, especially after… Well, you know. But why shouldn't she know he was out? I mean, what was he doing in town anyway?'

'Apparently, he goes out a lot in the evenings. Jogs, walks. He says it clears his head.'

'Does he now? And does he always keep it from Sophie?'

'What are you saying?'

Kat looked down at her glass and exhaled a long breath. When she looked up, she levelled Ruby's gaze. 'Don't you think Ewan's a bit weird? I mean, generally.'

Ruby was taken aback. She'd never really thought about him much. Sophie seemed happy and that was all that mattered really. 'He's really supportive of Soph. I don't know how she would have managed without him this year.'

'I don't mean that!'

Ruby frowned. 'He is a bit quiet, I suppose. Doesn't talk much.'

'Doesn't talk much? He barely speaks to anyone, as far as I can see. Even the cat avoids him.'

Clearly, Tom wasn't the only one who thought him aloof. 'Pru avoids everyone,' Ruby said, taking another mouthful of wine.

Kat grabbed her glass, lifted it to her lips, then promptly lowered it again. 'Hey, what if he was involved in the attack and you were covering for him?'

Ruby spat her wine back into her glass. 'Don't be daft! I can't see Ewan attacking Charlotte Manning. Why would he?'

'All right. How do you know he hasn't snuck out and tried it on with other women before?'

Ruby stared at her friend. It was true, she knew very little of his life outside the family. Was he prone to straying? Surely not… She thought about his Subaru parked on Sophie's drive, the promises he'd made. Everything about their relationship screamed of permanence.

'What do you know about his other relationships?' Kat asked.

'Not much.' Ruby was starting to feel uncomfortable now.

'What about friends here?'

'I don't know. He spends most of his time with Sophie as far as I can see, helps out with childcare. What are you getting at, Kat?'

'I just wonder if he's as genuine as he appears. You don't want him setting Sophie up for a fall. You've all been through enough.'

Chapter 21

The following morning, Ruby sat at the kitchen table nursing a fresh mug of coffee. It was almost 6:30 a.m. A semicircle of amber sun lit up the sky outside, glowing through the uncurtained window. A newsreader on the television babbled away about an upcoming by-election. She took a swig of coffee and held her head back, swilling it around her mouth before swallowing it. Her eyes were dry and scratchy; a dull ache pulsed above her left brow.

All night, Kat's comments about Ewan had swirled around her stomach like dirty dishwater. At the time, she hadn't thought much about Ewan being out on the night of the memorial service, accepting his explanation he was jogging to clear his head. He was ultra-fit, always badgering Sophie to go to the gym more often. Plus, she'd polished off the best part of two bottles of wine and with everything that went on afterwards – their exchange, the murder – she'd wrapped herself up in a tangled ball of guilt. Now Kat was starting to unravel the tangles, it did sound dubious. There was nothing wrong with him going for a run, getting some fresh air, if that's what he normally did. What was odd was he didn't want Sophie to know and he'd gone to great lengths, including evading the police, to cover it up. Was he protecting Sophie? Or had he targeted Ruby?

He'd fallen into their lives a year or so earlier when Sophie, on one of her fortnightly evenings out with some of the mums from the PTA, met him in a bar in town. Ruby could still remember Sophie telling her about Ewan the next day. He'd offered to buy her a drink and plagued her for her number.

She'd refused to give it to him. She liked him though, it was obvious from the way her eyes shone and her lips danced as she told the story. Two weeks later, she'd seen him out in a different pub and he'd rescued her from a drunken lout at the bar. Again, he'd tried to talk her into going out with him. Again, she'd turned him down. Sophie liked to play hard to get and was often brusque and sarcastic with people she didn't know.

A few days later, Ewan had delivered a parcel to her home and finally coaxed her out for coffee. And on that first date she'd shared her concerns about a relationship, her experiences with Greg, even her attempt on her life. 'He's so easy to talk to,' she had said to Ruby afterwards. 'He just seems to understand me.'

Another date ensued and within a couple of weeks they were seeing each other every night and she was introducing him to her family. Sophie had always been the same. Ever since school, as soon as she met a guy, as soon as she let them in, it was full on. Ewan was no exception and the fact that he made a real effort to spend time with the children, build a bond with them from the beginning, only cemented his position further.

When their mother died, a couple of months later, he took time off work, stayed over with Sophie, babysat the children. He might be the quiet, reserved type, but even Ruby had to concede, he was good for her sister.

What troubled Ruby now was that she knew so little about his life away from Sophie. He told Sophie he'd come down from Glasgow after his parents passed away, in search of work. He'd been with GoTo about eighteen months. He had mentioned a sister in Glasgow a couple of times. He'd talked about taking Sophie up to visit her, but it hadn't happened yet and she couldn't recall him talking about friends or relatives nearby.

Ruby grabbed her phone and opened Twitter. People shared personal details of their life on social media – information about family, places they visited, restaurants they'd been to. She typed in Ewan Wilson and a list came up, though none of the avatars matched. She switched to Facebook and tried again. An Ewan

Wilson in Worcester flashed up with the profile picture of a German Shepherd dog. Another at University College London. The next profile photo was a motorcycle, the timeline full of skylines and engine parts. She went back to the search and tried another. The privacy level was set high; she couldn't view the details.

She switched to Sophie's page and scrolled through various posts about the children, a photo of the beach in Cromer, the view from Bridget's house. Sophie rarely posted, but the more Ruby looked, the more peculiar it seemed. There was no mention of Ewan. No photographs of them out at dinner or visiting the park with the kids.

Was it possible for Ewan to have no presence on social media? Unlikely for a man in his early thirties. Perhaps he preferred Snapchat or Instagram. Maybe he used a pseudonym. But the absence of information about him on Sophie's page was strange. Ruby was mulling this over when her mobile rang in her hand. It was Sophie.

Ruby jumped. The phone slipped. She grappled with it in mid-air, catching it just before it hit the side. The last thing she needed was another a cracked screen. It had taken almost an hour to sort it out yesterday evening, especially since she couldn't face her mother's old store, which meant she'd had to walk to the phone shop at the other end of town.

Her eyes flicked to the kitchen clock as she answered. It was only 6:45 a.m.

'Hey.' Sophie sounded stressed. 'You're awake, thank goodness.'

'Is everything okay?'

'Yes. Can you take the kids to school for me this morning?'

'I thought Ewan was there with you.'

'He was. He left half an hour ago. And now work has phoned. The early relief receptionist has called in sick. They've asked if I can help again. If you could come over, drop off the kids at school before you go to work, I can pick them up later.'

'Okay. I'll be there as soon as I can.'

–

Daisy was sitting at the table in her pyjamas, eating her cereal when Ruby walked through Sophie's back door.

'Morning, darling,' Ruby said.

Daisy looked up wearily, clearly still half asleep. There was none of the bounce she'd seen in her a couple of nights earlier. Pru was sitting on the kitchen surface, peering down at her empty food bowl.

'Where's Mummy?' Ruby asked, taking a box of food out of the cupboard and filling the cat's bowl. Pru instantly jumped down to join her and graciously rubbed herself along Ruby's ankle.

'She's upstairs with Alfie. He can't find his school shirt.'

Ruby climbed the stairs and popped her head around the doorway of Alfie's room to find Sophie in her smart suit on her knees, reaching beneath the bed. A bewildered Alfie sitting on the floor beside his mother in his Batman pyjamas. He'd had a growth spurt since she'd bought them for him last Christmas and inches of bony wrist poked out the cuffs.

'Want me to take over?' she said.

Sophie didn't answer. 'There it is!' She pulled out a red polo shirt and handed it to her son. 'Now go and eat your breakfast.'

Ruby ruffled his hair affectionately as he wandered out of the room, polo shirt in his hand.

'Thanks for coming over,' Sophie said, scrabbling to her feet, furiously brushing flecks of dust from her jacket.

'That's all right. Everything okay?'

'Yes. Ewan had to leave early for work.'

Ruby followed her sister downstairs and waited in the kitchen while she hugged her children.

'Don't forget Daisy's reading book. She needs a new one,' she said on her way to the front door.

'We'll be fine,' Ruby said. 'I have done this before.' She was helping her sister on with her coat when she noticed something on her neck.

'What's that?'

Sophie pulled up her collar. 'It's nothing.'

At first, she thought the mark, poking above her collar, was a rash, but, on closer inspection, there was a blueish cloud circling it. A series of red dots. A love bite? 'It looks sore.'

'It's not.' Sophie shrugged her sister off. As she did so, her cuff slid up to expose a red line, no, a welt, on her wrist.

Ruby grabbed it. 'Sophie, what happened?'

'I said, it's nothing.' She pulled her hand away.

'It doesn't look like nothing. How did you do that?'

'You don't want to know.'

'Oh, I do.' She moved in between Sophie and the door. 'I mean, if you're struggling, you need to talk to me.'

'I'm not!' Her cheeks pinkened. 'I shut it in the bedside drawer. God, Ruby. I don't need the Spanish Inquisition every time I catch myself.'

'That's more than a catch.'

'It's fine.' There was a tightness in her tone that said it wasn't fine. 'It's nothing.'

Ruby grabbed her arm as she turned to go. 'Soph,' she said, gently, 'are you sure you're okay? Really?'

'Yes! You're making a fuss for no reason.' She pushed her hand away. 'Make sure the kids take their jackets. It's supposed to rain again later.'

And with that she yanked open the door and stomped up the drive, leaving Ruby standing there, aghast. What the hell was going on?

Chapter 22

Ruby was fiddling with a pile of paper clips looped together on her desk. Absently winding them in and out of her fingers. She'd been writing the same email to a client for the last ten minutes and couldn't focus, the mark on Sophie's neck and the welt on her wrist playing on her mind. There was something her sister wasn't telling her. She hadn't explained the mark on her neck, and it was unlikely she'd get a welt on her wrist like that from shutting it in a drawer – it was raw, more like a burn. Ruby had gone through the motions of getting the children dressed, taking them to school, then crawled through the traffic to get to work, yet she couldn't shut the exchange out of her mind.

She wanted to call Sophie, to check on her again, but her sister was at work and wouldn't welcome the intrusion. With Sophie, she needed to tread a fine line. Ask enough questions to show care, not so many that they morphed into concern. Too much interest or any mention of her past problems and Sophie shut down.

Could the mark on her neck be a love bite? If so, Ewan had been overeager. It must have hurt. She was reminded of Ewan's hands on her, the way he'd tugged at her hair, hard. Kat's comment about him being weird pressed on her. Was Ewan responsible for Sophie's bruises? It might explain why she was so agitated. Something wasn't right. Ruby could feel it in the depths of her stomach and suddenly the urge to find out more about him and his background was crucial.

The older sister in Glasgow sprang to mind. Shauna, Rhona… no, Isla, that was it. She remembered him mentioning she wasn't married. Isla Wilson then. Mark was at his desk, sifting through paperwork. Kat was out with a client. Sara's head was buried in a pile of brochures. Ruby slid her phone across the desk and brought up Facebook. Internet usage at Galanti's was monitored. Mark was quite explicit – he couldn't afford for it to be used for personal reasons. Him and his bloody budgets. She'd have to use her mobile, be discreet.

She switched to Facebook search and typed in Isla Wilson. Three entries came up. The first lived in Canada. The second in New Zealand. She was reminded of her earlier search for Ewan. Perhaps they were a family that didn't use social media. The last avatar was a sunflower with a location of Hamilton beside it. Was Hamilton near Glasgow? More in hope than expectation, Ruby switched to Google and typed in Hamilton, Glasgow. Her heart skipped a beat. Hamilton was twelve miles south-east of Glasgow. Could this be her?

She clicked on the sunflower. The timeline showed a picture of someone's back garden. A rose. A happy new year sign. Clearly Isla didn't post often.

Ruby looked up, out into the street beyond. A car whizzed past. A woman pushed a pram. A man stood in the doorway of the newsagent's opposite, vaping. She snuck a glance behind. Mark and Sara were still engrossed in their work.

A voice from deep inside whispered, *Message her. What have you got to lose?* True. The best she could hope for was to find out more about Ewan, to allay her fears. The worst, that she wasn't the right Isla Wilson, or maybe she was, and she alerted Ewan or even Sophie. Ruby could deal with that later. Perhaps she could explain it away as trying to unite the families after everything they'd been through.

She typed out a quick message, introducing herself as Ewan's girlfriend's sister and saying she was interested in getting to know the family better. Re-read it twice. Dithered about adding something more, about his character, then changed her mind and pressed send. No point in overcomplicating it.

From what she could see, Isla didn't have any privacy levels set, which meant Facebook would notify her she'd received a private message from someone outside her friendship list. Now all Ruby could do was wait.

The sound of the door flapping open caught Ruby's eye. It was Hitesh. He was wearing another of his flashy tailored suits.

'Morning, officer!' Mark called from behind her. 'Didn't know you were after a new kitchen.'

Hitesh forced a smile. 'I'm here to see Ruby.'

Ruby could feel Mark's eyes on her as Hitesh approached.

'How are you, Ruby?' he said.

'Fine. Why?'

'I was told you were in the station yesterday asking for me.'

'Yes.' She glanced furtively at Mark. 'Any chance I could take ten minutes?' she said. 'It's personal.'

Mark looked from her to the detective. He'd tolerated the detective's occasional presence while her mother's case was awaiting trial though it was obvious from the expression on his face, he wasn't expecting the visits to continue now the case was closed. He narrowed his eyes. 'What kind of personal?'

'To do with my mum.'

'I need to update Ruby on a few things,' Hitesh said brightly. 'Shouldn't take long.'

'Okay. You'll need to make the time up,' he said to Ruby.

So much for favouritism, Ruby thought.

'Thanks. We'll pop into the café next door so we don't disturb you,' Hitesh said.

A feeling of déjà vu washed over Ruby as they traipsed into Croft's Coffee House. They'd been in there many a time after the charge, as he updated her on the investigation and preparations for the trial. This was the first time they'd been in there since the conviction though and something about his visit to Sophie the other day unnerved her.

She followed him to their usual table in the quiet corner at the back of the café, away from the glare of shoppers passing by.

A waitress approached, wisps of brown hair falling out of a high ponytail. A long grey apron tied around her waist puckered her black T-shirt. She held her order book up, poised, as soon as they sat.

'Latte?' he checked with Ruby.

She nodded, cringing at his familiarity with her coffee choice.

He ordered himself his usual black coffee, undid the button of his suit jacket and sat.

The waitress scurried back to the counter.

'So, what did you want to see me about?' he asked.

'Sophie was worried about your visit. We both were.'

'There's nothing to be concerned about. I just wanted to deliver the news before you guys heard it elsewhere.' He rested back in his chair. 'The press might come knocking, now Charlotte's name is out there. I'd ask you not to speak with them. We are treating this as a separate case.'

'You asked if we'd seen Charlotte. You must have had a reason for asking.'

The beep of a mobile phone interrupted them. Hitesh reached into his inside pocket, pulled out his phone and swiped the screen. 'Sorry, I need to respond to this.'

Ruby wondered if it was an update on the murder. She strained her eyes to see, but the screen was turned at an angle and she couldn't quite read the message.

The waitress returned with their drinks as he finished.

He waited for her to place them down and retreat before he spoke. 'She was linked to your mother's investigation. It's quite normal for us to ask questions.'

'Have you found out anything else? Who killed her, or why?'

'I'm sure you've read our press updates.'

She had, but all they contained were the basic facts about the case and the usual appeal for witnesses. None of the intricate details. And it was the intricate details she needed. 'Do you know why she came back?' Ruby asked. 'Or how long she's been here?'

'We're still trying to establish her movements and how long she's been back in Market Deeton. It's difficult, her old friends aren't talking – either they know something and are keeping it to themselves or they haven't seen her. She tended to live beneath the radar.'

'You must know something!'

He eased back into his chair. 'Come on, Ruby. You know better than that. The investigation's ongoing, that's all I can tell you.'

'What about Colin's conviction?'

'Colin Halliday had a strong motive to kill your mum. The evidence against him was tight. There's nothing to suggest the conviction is unsafe.'

'Why do you think she came back now?' Ruby pressed. 'After the trial.'

'We don't know when she returned. All we know is that the details of the trial were well reported in the news. But we shouldn't jump to conclusions. As I said to Sophie, Charlotte's murder is probably completely unrelated to your mother.'

Ruby got the distinct impression there was something he wasn't telling her. She was tempted to tell him about what she'd seen at home the other night – the movement in her front garden – but stopped herself at the last minute. She hadn't seen them clearly enough to determine whether they were male or female, let alone to pick out an identifying factor and, in the cold light of day, the whole event sounded silly and more like her mind playing tricks on her.

Hitesh took a sip of his coffee. 'There's nothing to worry about. The visit to Sophie was routine. Be assured, I'll update you again if I need to.'

But Ruby stared into her coffee, unconvinced. If there was nothing to worry about, why did she feel so uneasy?

Chapter 23

Ruby opened her eyes on Saturday morning and, for the first time in days, felt refreshed after a deep slumber. It was just after ten. She sank back into the pillows, relishing the beginning of her weekend off. She wasn't meeting Tom for another few hours. Plenty of time to relax. She grabbed her phone off the bedside table. No new messages. Sophie hadn't been in touch since yesterday morning – not even to thank her for taking the children to school. Was she still smarting over Ruby's remarks about the bruises on her wrist and neck? Had she struck a nerve?

She slid out of bed, opened the curtains, looked out at the pebble grey sky, then switched on the radio and snuggled back under the duvet. A Coldplay song was playing. She recognised the beat but couldn't place the title and as she listened to the tune her mind drifted back to Sophie. Maybe she was over-reacting. Sophie was a big girl, and inordinately stronger than she had been four years ago. She remembered her reading the eulogy at the funeral. Crisp, clear words, her face stoical. While Ruby had dealt with the wider issues – the police, the court case – Sophie had surprised everyone by showing immense strength after her mother's death. She'd cooked and cleaned and maintained a routine for all of them, and she was doing a great job raising Daisy and Alfie. She couldn't imagine her tolerating an abusive relationship. And there was also the question of time. Sophie and Ewan had been together a year. Surely, if he had violent tendencies there would have been other signs before now?

The song ended. A newsreader rambled on about changes in the council refuse collection policies and then speculated about road closures with more rain expected. Ruby was only half listening now. She thought of Tom and what he might want later. They'd visited Martini's Bistro several times while they'd been together, most recently for his birthday earlier in the year. She'd had crab, him lobster. Tom had been in a mischievous mood that night, pinching her food, flicking water at her from the finger bowl. She doubted there would be any of that joviality today.

A gravelly voice filled the room. '*This was a brutal attack. We are treating it as an isolated incident and interviewing everyone who came into contact with the victim. If anyone has any information…*'

A senior police officer was talking about Charlotte Manning's murder.

A text pinged on her mobile, interrupting the news report. Ruby sat up and retrieved her mobile from the bedside cabinet. It was Sophie.

> Bit busy today – need to get Alfie new school shoes. He's gone right through the toe on one foot! Can we sort Mum's clothes another time? Let me know how you get on with Tom x

Ruby stared at the message. Her sister sounded upbeat, the exchange over her bruises long forgotten. But she would still like to see her today, to check on her properly. To make sure all was well. She typed a text back to say she'd call by later when they were home.

The door knocker sounded downstairs. She groaned, placed her mobile down and climbed out of bed, dragging her bathrobe off the door and stretching it around her shoulders. So much for a lie-in.

Downstairs, Ruby left the chain fixed and opened the door to a narrow slit. A man in a dark overcoat stood on the doorstep, a satchel over his shoulder.

'Sorry to bother you,' he said. 'I'm James Newton from *Deeton Mail*. I wondered—'

He was just holding up a card when Ruby slammed the door. Goodness, they didn't waste their time. She thought about the days after her mother's murder, later during the trial. The press camped outside their homes, waving microphones in their faces as they came and went.

She needed to warn Sophie.

She was at the bottom of the stairs, typing out a quick text to her sister when the letterbox snapped open. A pair of eyes were fringed with a row of fingers.

'I just want to talk to you about Charlotte Manning,' he said. 'Get your account of how the family feel about her murder. Do you still think Colin Halliday's conviction is safe? This is your chance—'

'I'm not interested,' Ruby said.

She marched up the stairs, finished her text to Sophie and got back into bed.

A car engine ignited outside. The journalist, hopefully.

She was snuggling back under the covers when her phone buzzed again, sliding down the pillow beside her. A sunflower avatar graced the screen. Ewan's sister – responding to her message from yesterday. The message was brief: *I don't know who you are. My brother and I are estranged. Please do not message me again.*

Ruby shot forward. *Estranged!* Ewan hadn't given them the impression they were estranged when he'd talked about visiting her in Glasgow during the summer. Perhaps she hadn't got the right Isla Wilson. Although there couldn't be many Isla Wilsons with a brother called Ewan who came from the Glasgow area. Or maybe they'd argued since, and Sophie hadn't mentioned it.

She read the message again. Estranged was such a big word. It suggested hostility, a separation over a long period, not a recent change. Why would he lie?

Chapter 24

Martini's Bistro was heaving, every table occupied. It was one of those casual affairs, with rickety, round, 'shabby chic' tables and chairs that resembled garden furniture. A warm, meaty smell pervaded the air inside.

Ruby followed a harried floor manager to a table in the far corner. She'd opted to wear navy jeans and a long white linen shirt with a denim jacket over her shoulders. Tied her hair into a loose ponytail. It didn't seem right to get glammed up. They were on a break, after all.

Tom was already at the table. He stood as she approached, towering over her, and gave a gentle smile. His chestnut hair was shorter than when she'd last seen him and spiked at the front. She could see the outline of his pectoral muscles through the checked shirt that hung loose over dark jeans. Same old Tom – looking handsome in his usual laid-back way.

Ruby ordered a lemon and lime and they sat. She was reminded of their first date. The flutter in her stomach, the race of her pulse. The excitement of what the evening would bring. Today, she didn't feel any of those things. Today, if anything, she felt a touch of nerves.

'On the hard stuff, I see,' Ruby said, nodding towards his coffee.

'Late night.'

'Oh?'

'Yeah. I'm putting in a lot of hours at work. We've got a big project on.' Tom was a draughtsman for a manufacturing plant in Leicester, a job that required an early start and laboriously long hours staring at a computer screen intersected with site visits and client meetings. He rarely talked about his work, apart from to moan about the occasional disgruntled customer, or celebrate the end of a project, and she was never sure if he genuinely liked it or whether it was a job he'd fallen into and it had become too comfortable to leave. He certainly had a lot of friends there. 'How are things at Galanti's?'

'Okay. Busy, you know.' Ruby lowered her eyes to the sheet of card on the table. 'Ooh, new menu,' she said, skimming through. She'd skipped breakfast and the idea of calamari and triple-cooked chips sounded heavenly. 'This looks lovely. Are we doing starters?'

'I thought we'd go straight to mains.'

She shifted in her chair. *Straight to mains.* 'Sure.' It's not like this was a date.

'You should try the king prawns,' he said. 'They're to die for.'

She eyed him a second. 'You've already tried the new menu?' As soon as the words dripped from her mouth, she wished she could take them back. He could have been there a million times over the last couple of months. They weren't together, it wasn't any of her business.

'I've brought a few customers in,' he said, then winked. 'Only the important ones.'

'Lucky you.' She glanced around the restaurant at the families, the couples, the friends, all lunching and felt herself slowly starting to relax. Months had passed since she'd been out socially; she was beginning to forget what it was like.

A different waitress arrived with her drink, a tall blonde who introduced herself as 'Carrie, your waitress for the day' and flicked a page on her pad dramatically. Ruby wondered how many times she delivered that line during a shift and ordered the calamari with the promise of trying Tom's prawns when they arrived. The floor manager was turning people away at the door now.

'So, what did you want to see me about? Your text sounded formal.'

Tom dropped his napkin into his lap. 'How are you doing? I heard about Charlotte Manning.'

Ah, so it was a welfare call. The fact he still cared enough to do so was touching. 'I'm okay, thanks. It was a bit of shock, but the police seem convinced it's not connected to Mum's case.' She took a sip of her drink. 'Thanks for coming to the service on Tuesday.'

'I wouldn't have missed it. Your mum was a great woman.'

'She was.'

'I'm sorry I didn't come back to the house.' Wrinkles rippled down his nose as he scrunched his face.

'Oh, no worries. I'd have missed that part out too if I could.'

He snorted. 'Did it all go off all right? I was thinking of you.'

'I think so.' She talked about the Irish songs, the numerous renditions of 'Danny Boy'. By the time the waitress arrived with their plates of food, he was laughing.

'What about Sophie?' he asked as he picked up his cutlery.

Sophie's bruises flashed into her mind. Dark blue and spotty. She pushed them away. 'Okay, I think.' She paused as she burnt her tongue on a chip. 'She seems to have adjusted well under the circumstances.'

'Yeah. Well, she has Ewan. Hopefully, he'll help to take her mind off things.'

Ruby recalled how the two men had never really hit it off. When they first met, a dinner out at a posh Italian in town with all the family together, they'd barely spoken. Strange really. Tom usually got along with everyone. She was tempted to share Ewan's sister's message when something made her hold back. 'You've never liked Ewan, have you?' she said.

'I wouldn't say that. We're just different.' He pressed his napkin to the corner of his mouth.

'You're being polite.'

He shrugged.

'What is it you don't like about him?'

Tom forked another prawn and put it into his mouth. It was a while before he answered. 'I don't know. He's just quiet. I didn't see him as a partner for Sophie.'

'Why?'

'I can't put my finger on it exactly.' He lifted his napkin again, wiped his mouth. 'I had a drink with Lewis last night,' he said, changing the subject.

Ruby met his gaze. She'd introduced Tom to Lewis shortly after they'd met and the two men had hit it off instantly, identifying a shared interest in indie rock music. She recalled a late-night drunken conversation with them extolling the virtues of Leicestershire bands and both cheering when they realised they'd attended the same Kasabian concert a year earlier. There was no reason why they shouldn't continue their friendship – they got along famously, after all. But their meeting made her uncomfortable. Last year, it was the three of them going out, drinking, chatting, and she couldn't help feeling excluded.

'That's nice,' she said, fighting to keep her voice even.

'He's worried about you.'

'I'm fine.'

'He says you've been distant. Not returning his calls. And you haven't been to Heritage Arts for ages.'

Shit. Shit. Shit. She hadn't got back to Lewis about his kitchen. She made a mental note to ring him later. And she'd explained to him about the other messages, hadn't she? 'I saw him on Tuesday. He came back to the house.'

'He meant generally.'

'Everything all right with the food?' It was the attentive Carrie.

They both nodded and made the right noises and Carrie moved off. The moment passed, but Ruby couldn't suppress the bubble of guilt inside. She hoped Lewis wasn't feeling neglected; he'd been good to her, good to her family.

'Are you in later?' Tom said, pulling her back to the present. 'Jake, from work, is doing the Brockleton Park run with his kids on Sunday morning. Thought I'd tag along. Could do with picking up my running shoes.'

'Um... sure. You've got your keys if I'm not about.'

'I think I left them at work.'

She rolled her eyes. 'Okay, text me before you come. I'm popping to Sophie's in a bit.'

Ruby was interrupted by a nudge in her back. It was the couple at the table behind. He was putting his jacket on. She leaning over the child's car seat indulgently. The man apologised for knocking her. Ruby shook it off and looked down at the sleeping baby, barely a few months old. The child turned its head, oblivious to her interest, as its mother covered him with a blanket. She'd imagined Tom and she would have children one day. Possibly two or three. She turned back to Tom and noticed he was watching them too.

'How did we get here?' she asked.

Tom stared back at her, his cheeks hollowing. 'What?'

'We're like strangers.'

'You asked for the break.'

It wasn't about the break or that one conversation they'd had in the hall. 'How did we become so distant?' They used to talk about everything. Or so she thought. 'How did we stop talking?'

'I didn't. I tried to talk. You wouldn't let me in.'

'Are you seriously saying the break-up was my fault?'

'I didn't know how to help you, Rubes. You were so sad, so grief-stricken. It was torture.'

'I can't believe you're blaming me!' Her jaw dropped down, incredulous. 'I'm not the one who avoided coming home. Stopping out until all hours. We went days without seeing each other. And all after...' Her eyes grew warm. 'How dare you?'

He looked down at his food. 'This isn't all about what happened to your mother.'

'This is exactly about what happened to my mother.'

When he met her gaze, his eyes were watery. 'I don't know what it is with you. It's as if you put up an internal barrier, a wall I can't get through.'

Ruby could barely believe her ears. The fact of the matter was, he was never at home to try. Always going to the gym, or off to drinks with friends after work. It was as if he couldn't bear to spend time with her.

'Don't take this the wrong way,' he continued. 'I think you need help. I think everything that's happened with your mum—'

'Oh, this is my mum's fault, is it?'

'No, Ruby.' He sighed. 'You close down, refuse to talk. You're doing it now.'

'I've done plenty of talking. To the police, the lawyers—'

'About the case, yes. Not about *you*.'

'I'm not listening to this.' Her chair scraped the floor as she slid it back. She pulled the napkin from her lap, threw it across her half-eaten plate of food and stood, the pressing desire to get out of there overwhelming.

'Ruby, please…'

'No. No way. You're not putting this on me. And you're certainly not putting this on my mother.' And with that she stalked out.

Chapter 25

Sophie was in the front room, curled up on the sofa beside Ewan when Ruby sauntered in later. She was flicking through a magazine, while he watched a football match on television.

'Hey,' Ruby said. She perched herself on the arm of the chair.

Ewan gave an impassive nod and turned back to the television. This was the first time she'd seen him since his visit to her house and he couldn't have been more detached.

'Hello,' Sophie said. Her curls bounced on her shoulders as she looked up. She was wearing a collared shirt, the cuffs pulled down over her hands, and a pair of fitted jeans – no chance of checking up on those bruises then – and her face, devoid of make-up, was achingly beautiful. An English rose. 'How was your lunch?' she said, sounding unusually chirpy.

Ruby widened her eyes and shook her head in a 'not now' way. She was still seething at Tom's comments over lunch. How could he blame her for the cracks in their relationship when he hadn't been there for her? 'Where are the kids?' she asked. The house was inordinately quiet.

'Playing on Ewan's Xbox upstairs.' Sophie closed the magazine.

'I take it you haven't had any visitors from the papers?'

'No. Thanks for your text. Looks like we've been the lucky ones. Shame really, 'cos Ewan's ready for them. Aren't you, darling?' He smiled as she nudged his shoulder but kept his eyes on the screen. 'He'll give them short shrift.'

Sophie hauled herself up and indicated for Ruby to follow her into the kitchen.

'Did you meet with Tom?' she asked in a low voice, closing the door behind them.

'Don't ask.'

'Oh.' She sounded despondent. 'I rather hoped you were going to say you'd talked things through.'

Ruby leaned against the side, crossing one ankle over another, and told Sophie about her lunch. A wave of sadness washed through her as she finished up. 'He made me sound cold, detached.'

Sophie pulled a face. 'Sorry.'

Ewan roared 'goal' from the front room and clapped his hands loudly.

'Somebody's happy,' Ruby said mournfully. 'Everything all right with you?'

'Think so.'

'Doesn't sound like it.'

'I need to ask you something. It's a bit awkward.' She scrunched her face.

'Right.' Ruby stretched out the word.

'Do you mind if we don't come along to Bridget's tomorrow?'

Ruby sighed inwardly. Bridget had sounded so excited when she'd phoned to announce their visit. 'What, all of you, or just you?'

'All of us. It's our anniversary. Well… a year since we met and Ewan wants to mark it by taking us to the new farm down the road. The children can pet the animals there. The weather is supposed to be fine tomorrow and you know how much Alfie likes goats. Greg's got the kids next weekend; it'll be a while before we get the opportunity again.'

'Ewan's taking you?' *Is this his way of making up for something?*

'Yes. It's been a shit week. What with the service, and… well, you know?' She hesitated a second. 'He's been feeling pretty low. He thinks a family day will cheer us all up.'

A family day. Did Sophie know he was estranged from his real family, or his sister at least? If she did, she'd certainly never mentioned it. Ruby itched to tell her, to discuss it, but it wasn't a subject to be raised now, not with him sitting in the front room.

'What's he got to feel low about?' she asked.

'It's been hard with Charlotte Manning's murder... It brings everything back. It's probably my fault, I can't stop thinking about it. I hope they catch the killer soon.' Tramlines travelled across her forehead. 'You don't mind if we don't come, do you, Rubes? I think a day at the farm would take our minds off things. You're welcome to join us.'

'Thank you. I'll think I'll go ahead and see Bridget on my own.' Even if Bridget hadn't been geared up to see them, the idea of spending the day playing happy families with Ewan didn't sound particularly palatable.

'I hope she's not too disappointed we aren't coming.' Sophie turned to the sink and started rinsing a mug.

'I'm sure she'll understand.'

The door flapped open and Ewan entered, grinning from ear to ear. He didn't look low to Ruby. In fact, if anything, he looked ecstatic. '3-1,' he said. He ignored Ruby, instead wrapping his arms around Sophie. Nuzzling her neck.

'Nice one!' she said.

If he was making a point, he was going overboard.

Ruby's phone erupted. It was Tom. She swiped to decline the call and slipped the phone into her pocket. She wasn't ready for another conversation with him at the moment. 'I'll go and see the kids,' she said.

Sophie didn't reply, instead turning and embracing Ewan. The faint sound of whispers filled the hall as Ruby climbed the stairs.

The kids were in Daisy's room, eyes fixed on the screen in front of them, little fingers busily working the handsets they were holding. Ruby could have worn a moustache and they wouldn't have noticed her.

She could hear Sophie and Ewan still talking in low voices as she traipsed back down the stairs. There was an urgency to their tones, a tightness. They stopped as she walked into the kitchen. Ewan averted his gaze. If he was affected by what had gone on between them, it certainly didn't show. Yet again, it was she who felt uncomfortable. 'I'm going to head off,' she said.

'Okay,' Sophie replied, opening the back door for her. 'You have a good day tomorrow. Give Bridget our love.'

As Ruby wandered up the driveway to her car, Ewan's family situation niggled her. Why exactly was he estranged from his sister? And why was there no record of him online, no social media footprint? It was almost as though he was avoiding someone, or that he had something to hide. And why would Charlotte Manning's murder upset him so much? Did he know her better than he was letting on? Nobody, apart from her, knew he was out that evening in Market Deeton. Did Ewan have a history of affairs, or worse, a violent background? As much as she couldn't believe he'd have anything to do with the murder, she needed to find out more. She needed to ensure Sophie was safe.

Back at the car, she pulled her phone out of her bag. Tom had followed up his call with a text – *Call me when you are free.* She ignored the message – it was probably something to do with the running shoes he wanted anyway – and switched to Facebook Messenger, typing out another quick message.

> I'm sorry to bother you again. Ewan is dating my sister and I have some important questions I need to ask. If you could spare a few minutes of your time, I would appreciate a quick chat. Please call me as soon as you are able. Thank you.

She re-read the message, added 'in confidence' after the 'chat' and typed her mobile number at the end. Then clicked send.

Either their situation was due to a family argument, a private squabble of little substance in the wider world, or there was something more sinister afoot. And Ruby desperately hoped it was the former.

Chapter 26

Sophie stood at her bedroom window and watched Ruby drive off. She wasn't herself, the unresolved issues over her relationship with Tom obviously bothering her.

Her phone tinkled in her pocket. Another text from Greg. *Any news on next weekend?* This access issue wasn't going away. She needed to make some decisions, talk it over with the kids.

A hand pressed on her shoulder. Sophie jumped and turned to find Ewan beside her. 'I didn't hear you come upstairs,' she said.

'You disappeared suddenly. Everything okay?'

She tucked her phone in her pocket. 'I came up to check on the children.' She gave a rueful smile. 'Do you think Ruby's all right? I'm worried there's more to this break with Tom than we realise. I'm wondering if I should go to Bridget's with her.'

'She'll be okay, she's a big girl. Come on, we need this day out tomorrow, it's our anniversary. The beginning of the rest of our lives, remember?' He was standing awkwardly, hands tucked behind his back.

'What are you doing?'

'Which hand?'

'Ewan!'

'Come on.'

She tapped his left arm.

'I got you something.' He pulled out a dress scarf in soft pastel shades of pink, yellow and milky blue.

'Oh my goodness, Ewan! It's beautiful. It'll look perfect with my denim shirt.' The silk slipped in and out of her fingers. 'But you can't afford—'

He pressed a finger to her lips to silence her. 'What we have is special. You know that, don't you?' He slid his hand to her waist and drew him to her.

The kiss was watery and light, his nose brushing hers as he pulled back. Sophie's heart melted.

'Allow me,' he said, taking the scarf and wrapping it around her neck.

She moved across to the mirror. He watched her reflection over her shoulder as she stroked the soft threads. 'I love it. Thank you.'

He took the ends of the scarf and gently twisted her to face him. Winding it around her neck again. It was taut to her skin now. Another tug.

Sophie lifted her hand to her throat. 'What are you doing?'

He didn't answer. Pulled again, his gaze glued to hers.

'Ewan, don't.'

She felt her windpipe constricting as he tightened again. Gasped for air.

His face relaxed. He released his grip. 'It's only a bit of fun,' he said, smiling.

'Mum!' Alfie rushed along the landing. 'Daisy's got my handset. She won't give it back.'

Sophie loosened the scarf and coughed, rubbing her throat.

'Has she now?' Ewan said, ignoring Sophie. He bent down and scooped the little boy into his arms. 'Well, we'd better go and sort it out then, hadn't we?'

Sophie watched him walk across the landing with her son balanced on his hip and move into Daisy's room, and rubbed her throat again. She pulled the scarf from her neck and looked in the mirror to find two pink lines where it had been.

Chapter 27

It was almost four when Ruby pulled into Shetland Avenue.

A couple emerged from the house opposite as she climbed out of her car. The man dressed in a dark suit, a blue open-collared shirt. The woman in a strappy red dress that flowed to her ankles. They gave one of those awkward acquaintance-type waves. Ruby waved back and watched them move off down the road hand in hand. They seemed happy, relaxed. Blooming with the optimism of a long evening in front of them. She wondered where they were off to. A wedding reception, a party, a dinner? There was a time when she and Tom would dress up and walk into town on a Saturday night. It was the only night he'd go into town; he preferred local pubs during the week. But on a Saturday, he'd groom his hair and beard, the sweet smell of his aftershave wafting through the house, and it would feel new and special, like their first date all over again. The memories induced a pang of sadness.

She rounded the privet hedge surrounding her front garden, approached the front door, and stopped, her eyes resting on the handle. It was sitting bolt upright. Instinctively, she turned back and checked over her shoulder. The road outside was empty. She looked back at the handle. The lock worked fine, but occasionally the handle didn't drop down properly. Ruby always lifted it down and left it horizontal because she didn't want people to realise it was broken and try to force the door. Clearly someone had been there.

She was reminded of Ewan trying the handle. Had he been back? He hadn't mentioned it when she saw him earlier.

Perhaps it was Tom, dropping by to collect his running shoes. That would explain his call. Maybe he'd found his key. Her stomach dropped. She desperately hoped he wasn't still there. She certainly wasn't ready to continue their lunchtime discussion. Not yet.

She tried the handle, relieved to find the door still locked, used her key and moved inside. The air in the hallway felt displaced, as if someone had recently been inside. Her gaze immediately went to the dish on the hallway table. Her spare keys sat there alone.

She called out Tom's name, her voice echoing around the walls, and wandered into the front room. The cushions were still arranged across the back of the sofa, the remote control beside the television where she'd left it that morning. In the kitchen, her used coffee mug sat in the sink. Nothing had been moved. It must have been Tom. A fleeting visit to collect his running shoes or something else he needed.

A shiver ran through her. The temperatures had plummeted over the last few days. She climbed the stairs, opened the door of the airing cupboard and flicked the central heating switch on. She was just pushing the cupboard door to a close when her eyes dropped. Sitting on the floor were Tom's running shoes. She remembered now. He'd done a park run on a wet day back in May. The rain had been relentless; he was soaked to the skin when he finished. He must have left his running shoes in there to dry off. Though that didn't answer the question of why the door handle was raised.

Ruby crossed to her bedroom. The bed was made with the throw laid across the bottom as she'd left it that morning. Her bathrobe hung on the back of the door. She opened her bedside drawer – her passport and chequebook were still there. Her jewellery box on the window ledge still contained her mother's gold St Christopher necklace. She must have been mistaken. Perhaps the postman had caught the handle. She shook it out of her mind. She needed to get a grip. Charlotte's murder and the incident with Ewan were making her jumpy.

In any event, Tom wanted those shoes for a park run tomorrow, which meant he'd be calling by for them soon. The prospect of him turning up, wandering in while she was sitting in front of the television or taking a bath put her on edge. She wasn't ready to talk, she realised that now, and she wouldn't relax if she thought he was going to come in at any moment, not after the way things were left at lunchtime.

Ruby picked up the shoes, descended the stairs, popped them in a carrier bag and grabbed her keys. She might as well save him the trouble of coming over and drop them at his. She could make it short and sweet, say she was on her way out somewhere. At least it would keep him out of her hair for a while.

Chapter 28

The Saturday afternoon traffic was thick with shoppers. It took almost fifteen minutes to drive across town and by the time Ruby arrived in Tom's road, her patience was wearing thin. What she needed was a warm bath and an early night before the journey to Norfolk in the morning.

Tom was living with a friend at 43 Cumbernauld Street, on the eastern edge of the town centre. It was a pleasant location: three-storey terrace houses faced each other across a tree-lined road, all with small front gardens edged with drystone walls. Ruby wasn't sure how far down the street the house was, and she inched along, squinting to check the numbers and then parked up in a space diagonally opposite on the other side of the road. She was climbing out of her car when the door of number 43 opened.

Ruby wasn't sure why she felt the need to hide. It was almost instinctive to duck down behind a nearby Volvo, directly opposite. Peering through the car window, she watched Tom at the door. He'd changed into a loose T-shirt and jogging bottoms, his hands bulging the pockets. He was deep in conversation with someone, she was pretty sure they were male, but they were standing with their back to her and she couldn't see who it was.

Seconds flitted past. Ruby was beginning to feel self-conscious. Had it come to this? Spying on her former boyfriend. Though, she'd been there a while now; she could hardly suddenly appear. Finally, the man stepped back. He was hunching his shoulders, nodding. He turned. There was something familiar about him.

Ruby peered closer. Yes, it definitely was him – the police officer who'd taken her account at the station. What was he doing with Tom?

They shook hands and the officer walked down the short pathway. He was coming towards her.

Ruby bowed her head and placed her hand in the carrier bag she was holding, pretending she was checking for something. She pushed the running shoes about. The officer didn't look in her direction. He climbed into his car opposite, turned over the engine and drove off. Tom had gone back into the house now and closed the door.

Ruby dithered for several seconds. Maybe she could hang the bag on the door handle and make off quickly. She wasn't in the mood for conversation, although she was dying to know why the police at been at Tom's door.

As it turned out, she didn't have to make the decision. She was bustling across the road when the door opened again and Tom stepped out. He walked down the pathway to meet her.

'Hey,' he said.

Her eyes dropped to his feet. He wasn't wearing any shoes. Good job the rain had held off. 'Hi.' She felt distinctly uncomfortable.

'I saw you out of the front window.'

'I brought your running shoes over.' She held out the bag.

'Thanks.' He took the bag without looking inside. 'That's really kind.'

'Okay, well I'd better go,' Ruby said, pointing towards her car. 'I'm on my way out.'

'I'm sorry about earlier,' he said, ignoring her statement. 'It came out all wrong.'

The sight of his face softening, brown eyes gazing down at her, dissolved her former anger. 'I'm sorry I missed your call.'

'We really should talk.' An uncomfortable steeliness crept into his voice. 'You could come in now…'

'I'm afraid I can't.' She pulled back her sleeve, made a play of glancing at her watch. Though she didn't move. The need to know what the policeman was doing there poking her like a cattle prod.

'Of course.' His face fell. 'Tomorrow then?'

'I'm going to see Bridget. Next week would be better, I've got a busy few days coming up,' she said. 'Let me know when you're free.'

'All right. Give Bridget my love.'

'What was the officer doing here?' she asked, changing the subject.

'What?'

'The police officer.' She pointed at the house. 'I saw him leave.'

'Oh. I was in town on Tuesday evening, when... well, you know. I saw some lads hanging around in High Street, wanted to let the police know. They insisted on coming out when I called them. Probably wanted to check where I was living, make sure I was who I said I was. This isn't my address on the voters' register.' He avoided her eyeline. 'Saw your boss out too. Looked like he was on a date.' He pulled a face.

'Mark?'

He nodded.

Odd that Mark hadn't mentioned being out on Tuesday evening, especially as there'd been so much talk about the murder over the last few days. But it was Tom that really bothered her. Out in town, during the week. It didn't sound like him. Granted, he'd been going out more this year, but he still spoke about avoiding the town pubs midweek. She waited for Tom to expand, to say he was with a friend, or it was a work commitment. But he buried his eyes in the pavement. Unless of course he was seeing someone new...

'Okay, well I'd better get off,' she said.

'Right.'

She turned towards her car and shouted back over her shoulder. 'Enjoy your run.'

He was still standing on the pavement in his socks when she pulled away down the street, confusion tumbling through her insides. She needed to put distance between them. Distance to sort out what she wanted, distance to stifle the permanent drum beat in her head. He hadn't mentioned he was in town on the night of the murder when they met earlier. Occasionally, he met with clients but usually during the day. And his tone was off. Why was he so uneasy?

Perhaps he had met someone. Ruby and he had been close. He wouldn't want to hurt her feelings by slipping it into conversation, he'd want to tell her properly, face to face, to cushion the blow. It was the only explanation she could think of. Was that why he'd asked her for lunch – to finish it and make room for someone new? Though she'd left abruptly and he'd missed the opportunity.

Ruby's chest knotted as she turned the corner at the bottom of the street. He'd had ample opportunity to meet someone else during their break. He could have slept with half of Market Deeton for all she knew.

The knot tightened as memories from the past couple of years swooped in. Tom in the kitchen, cooking bacon for breakfast, wearing nothing but an apron and a postcoital glow. Long walks over the fields, picnics in the summer. Unlike other men she'd dated, Tom didn't care whether she wore make-up, or if her hair was groomed. He was easy, natural. Said she was beautiful either way. Didn't complain when she picked the skin around her nails when she was nervous. Suddenly she realised that, deep inside, a part of her had held onto a tiny thread of hope that, after the trial, they might be able to patch things up and go back to the way they were. Though any prospect of a reconciliation seemed unlikely now. Because Tom had already moved on.

Chapter 29

I watch you drive off down the road. It amuses me how much alike we've become. Both creeping around, avoiding confrontation, while keeping a watchful gaze on unknowing others.

The truth is, it's surprisingly easy to watch people, learn intimate details about them when they don't feel vulnerable. Most people drift through life, concentrating on the task at hand. They take the kids to school, drive to work, get the car to the garage on time for its service, and block out what's around them. Murderers, rapists and paedophiles are released from prison and walk among us, yet most of us are so wrapped up in our own lives, we don't even realise they're there.

I see everything.

And we are all creatures of habit. Even you. You start work at nine, but always arrive fifteen minutes early. You pop out to the café next door for a takeaway coffee mid-morning. The barista asks you if you'd like anything else, a cake or a biscuit, but you pat your waistline and say you're watching your weight. He knows what you are going to say, but every day he continues to ask. It's one of those routine conversations that makes you both chuckle. In the evenings, you sit in front of the television. I can tell if it's a favourite programme because you twiddle your hair around and around your middle finger, rapt. And you leave your curtains open.

You think you are safe, hiding behind that tall hedge. You think it protects you from prying eyes. You're wrong.

Chapter 30

A gull screeched overhead as Ruby locked her car outside the red-brick bungalow. The gravelled front garden was neatly edged with a split-flint stone wall. A hanging basket filled with white geraniums beside the front door swayed from side to side in the soft breeze. It was a clear day, if a little chilly, and the smell of fresh bread wafting towards her as she walked up the pathway made her stomach growl.

The door opened before she reached it and a grey-haired woman in navy slacks and a linen shirt appeared, smiling from ear to ear. Bridget looked smaller than when she'd last seen her, as if she'd shrunk in the last month.

'Hello, my darlin'!' Her aunt flung her arms around Ruby. The embrace was so tight she could feel the woman's shoulder bones jutting out.

Ruby pulled back. 'You've lost weight.'

'Ah, it's just old age, so it is,' Bridget said dismissively.

'You're not old. Not yet.'

Bridget ignored her and peered past her into the road. 'Didn't change their minds then?'

The disappointment in Bridget's voice when she'd phoned yesterday to tell her Sophie and the others weren't able to come still tugged at Ruby. 'No, sorry. Some confusion over a school thing.' The lie slithered around Ruby's mouth like an annoying hair.

'Well, at least you're here, love,' she said, rubbing her back and ushering her inside. 'I've made some banana bread. Your favourite.'

The aroma of fresh baking was stronger in the hallway. She followed Bridget into a room at the back of the house. The kitchen table was set neatly with a red tablecloth and grey mats, and cutlery for five. A bottle of lemonade, bought especially for the children no doubt, sat in the middle. Ever hopeful.

Ruby stared out of the back window. Following the view across the small lawn of grass, over the short fence edging the garden and through the field behind to the edge of the cliff, where an expanse of green–blue sea reached out to the horizon. Gulls swooped overhead. She'd missed this. It was the location and the vista that had sold the house to Bridget and it was easy to see why. When the wind blew south, they could hear the waves lapping up the beach below, taste the salty sea air.

'Sit down,' Bridget said, flicking the switch on the kettle. 'I'll make us a cuppa and you can tell me all about your week. I want to hear everything.'

Ruby managed a thin smile. Bridget had always been one of those capable women who bustled around at a hundred miles an hour and even now, limping around the kitchen, her days dogged by fatigue, a by-product of the fibromyalgia that crushed her energy levels, she still struggled to stay still. She watched her as she pulled mugs out of the cupboard and filled a teapot to the brim. There was no point in offering help. Bridget loved entertaining and was affronted if people tried to take over. 'I'm not on my deathbed yet,' she'd say. 'Now leave me be.'

'I thought we'd go for a walk later,' Ruby said. 'I could take you along the pier in your wheelchair.'

Her aunt passed a derisory glance at the wheelchair folded beside the back door, then looked out of the window. 'Maybe. If it stays fine.' She placed the teapot and cups and saucers out on the table, then cut two generous wedges of banana bread and laid them on plates between them. 'Dinner won't be ready for a couple of hours, so this'll keep us going. I've got lamb stew in the slow cooker,' she said with a wink.

Ruby's mouth watered. She hadn't eaten a home-cooked meal since the risotto at Sophie's. There never seemed much point when it was just her.

'Now what have you got to tell me?' Bridget probed.

There was no avoiding telling her about Charlotte Manning's murder, although Ruby deliberately played down the visits from the liaison officer. 'The police are treating it as a separate incident,' she said.

'And she turns up on the night of your mother's birthday?' Bridget sniffed dismissively. 'A likely story. Sounds like there's more to that than meets the eye. What does Sophie think?'

Ruby pictured the worry lines on her sister's face. 'She hasn't said much really. We're leaving it to the police.'

They sipped their drinks and mulled over the gossip from home. Ruby talked about Daisy's self-portrait homework and Alfie being invited to join the football team, and skimmed over her lunch with Tom. Bridget told her about a trip she'd taken earlier in the week to King's Lynn and then decided it was too windy and cold for them to go outside today, and why didn't they stay inside in the warm? It's not as if they didn't have plenty enough to talk about.

Before Ruby knew it, a couple of hours had passed, and she was tucking into a richly seasoned lamb stew with mashed potato so soft it melted on her tongue.

'It is a shame Sophie and the kids couldn't come,' Bridget said. 'I got some of those cakes in they like for pudding.' She pointed to a pink box on the side.

'Macaroons.'

'That's it. Beryl went all the way to Norwich to get them for me. Would you like one?'

Ruby finished her last mouthful, sat back in her chair and loosened her belt. 'No, thank you. I'm stuffed.'

'Well, you'll have to take them back with you.' Bridget sat forward, narrowing her eyes. 'Are you sure everything's okay with Sophie? I haven't heard much from her.'

Ruby was tempted to share her concerns about her sister, but Bridget's condition had deteriorated after their mother's death. The loss of her sister had hit her hard, especially in such shocking circumstances and, acutely aware that stress was a factor in triggering a fresh flare-up of pain and fatigue, Ruby felt the need to shield her aunt from more anxiety. 'It's just been one of those weeks, you know.'

'Hmm. Always been a worrier, our Sophie,' Bridget said, gathering up the plates. 'She gets that from your mother.'

Ruby gave a wistful smile. Sophie was very similar to her mum, both in looks and personality. Many a time she'd wandered into Aileen's house of an evening to find them sitting on the sofa together, watching the soaps, or some soppy period drama. With her love of thrillers and mysteries, she couldn't have been more different if she'd tried.

'I found a box of old photos when I was clearing out last week. Saved them for the children. Daisy was the image of your mother at that age. Do you want to see them?'

Ruby winced. They'd spent months going through old photos after their mother died and all it did was leave her hollow, reminding her of the depth of her loss. Though Bridget's face was so keen, so hopeful, she didn't have it in her to refuse. 'Why not?'

'Great.' Bridget made a play of clearing the table, then disappeared into the front room. When she came back, she was carrying an old shoebox. The lid torn and tattered at the corners, the sides bulging. She snapped off the elastic band holding the lid in place and pictures toppled over onto the table. 'Now, where are they?' Bridget said. More photos slipped out as she sifted through, clearly enjoying herself. With the fifteen-year age gap, Bridget had always seemed more like a mother than a sister to Aileen.

Ruby picked up a picture of an austere woman in a long floral dress. Grey hair was pulled back from an angular face and tied into a bun at the nape of her neck. She couldn't remember a time when she'd seen her grandmother's hair loose; it was always tied up in the same tight bun. 'Was I like my grandmother?' she asked.

'My mother?' Bridget said, peering across at the photo. 'No, nothing like.'

Ruby sighed. They'd moved to Leicestershire before she started school and only saw their extended family during a couple of visits back to Kilkenny while she was growing up. 'It's too expensive,' her mother would say when the conversation came up. 'They know where we are, they can always come here.' But they never did and contact was mostly limited to birthday and Christmas cards, with the odd phone call thrown in, and that was a rarity. Aileen didn't like to talk about her family in Ireland. It wasn't until her late teens, when her grandmother died and Aileen went across for the funeral, that Ruby learnt from Bridget that her grandparents hadn't approved of her mother's decision to divorce their father and move to England.

Ruby pulled out another photo of a boy in a peaked hat. 'What about my uncle?' The five-minute phone call to inform him of Aileen's death last year was the longest conversation Ruby had ever had with her mother's brother. He'd listened, offered his condolences, though sent no card and made no effort to come across for the funeral or the memorial, despite being invited.

'Derren? No, you are nothing like him. You can trust me on that one, my girl. Nor the folk on your grandfather's side... Ah, here we are.' She held up a couple of photos of Aileen as a young girl and cooed over them. The resemblance to Daisy was stark.

Ruby smiled and eased back into her chair. With the question marks zooming in and out of her head about Charlotte Manning and Colin Halliday's conviction, she felt the need to understand her mother better. Could someone else be responsible for her death? A member of the family possibly. Perhaps there was something about them she didn't know. 'What were Mum and Derren like, growing up?' she asked.

'Ah, well... They both came along late, Derren was twelve years after me. Olive, your grandmother, didn't think she could have any more kids and had thrown herself into the church. She was in her late thirties when Derren arrived.' Bridget's eyes glazed. 'He was the pride of her life, mind you. Honestly, she'd have dressed that baby in gold if she could have. He could do no wrong. For Aileen, it was a different matter. She arrived three years later, a shock right from the beginning.'

Ruby recalled her hot-headed mother and smiled. 'How do you mean?'

'My mother was the pious one, a proper Catholic woman. She was tough on me, but when Aileen came along, she expected more of her. Oh, that girl!' She smiled wistfully. 'She was full of spirit from the day she was born, and I loved her for it. Sadly, my mother didn't feel the same. She was stricter with her. Partly because she was an older mum, trying to show she knew what she was doing, and partly because she wanted to bend her into shape. It was never going to happen though.'

'Mum did have a strong will.'

'You can say that again.' Bridget rolled her eyes. 'Olive tolerated her when she was young. Couldn't abide her in her teens, especially when her head was turned by boys. That's why your mum married your dad, and so young. Any hint of romance and my mother had her whisked straight down the aisle.'

Ruby watched Bridget gather up the photos and shove them back into the box, her mind turning to her father. Mick, Bridget's husband, had been a father figure to her and Sophie growing up, but Ruby had often wondered what her real dad was like. There were no photos of him at home. 'Did they like my dad?' she asked.

'No. Not at all, as I recall. He was from one of the villages and much older than your mother. A waster, right from the beginning. His wages frittered away on drink. Liked a flutter on the horses too. I could see where it was going, tried to talk them out of it, but upholding their reputation as a good

Catholic family was more important to my mother than my sister's happiness. When Aileen refused to give him up, as far as they were concerned their only recourse was marriage. I think that's why Aileen never pushed you girls into marriage. She wanted you to be happy, first and foremost.'

'Must have been difficult.'

'I'd say so. I was lucky. I managed to get away when Mick got the job over here. Your mam wasn't that fortunate. Help me with the band, will you?' She placed on the lid and lifted the box. Ruby stretched the elastic wide between her hands.

'What did my dad look like?' she asked.

'Tall, dark. A bit like you. Though, mark my words, that's all you get from him, darlin'.'

'I searched for him online after Mum died,' Ruby said sheepishly. 'Even thought about employing one of those agencies, you know, that finds people.'

'Really?' Bridget lifted a brow. 'Aw, he moved away after the divorce. I don't even know if he's still alive.'

She started to slide the box into the band. The ruffled edges of the lid caught. She rocked the box back and forth, but bits of broken cardboard kept catching. The band was digging into Ruby's skin now. Bridget gave the box a final hard shove, and suddenly the bottom broke open. Piles of pictures splashed onto the table, dropping off the edge and cascading to the floor.

'Oh, for the love of God!' Bridget said.

She bustled across to a kitchen drawer, pulled out a carrier bag and started scooping photos into it. Ruby was kneeling on the floor, gathering up others, when something caught her eye. She pushed a couple of pictures aside. It was a red plastic bracelet – one of those secured on wrists during a hospital stay – and tiny. It must have belonged to a small child. She picked it up and peered closely. It was scrawled with a name and date of birth, but the writing was too smudged and faded to decipher. She could just about make out the number 85 at the end.

Bridget glanced across, and started. 'How did that get in there?'

'Whose was it?' Ruby asked.

She whisked it away. 'Oh, no one special.'

Ruby watched her toss it into the bag, but the wristband bothered her. If it belonged to no one special, why keep it?

Chapter 31

Bridget's comments about her extended family skipped in and out of Ruby's mind on the drive home. It was true, her father hadn't bothered with her all this time. The news of her mother's murder would have spread like wildfire in the close-knit communities of Kilkenny. He could have easily reached out if he wanted to.

Aileen's relationship with her family might have been acrimonious, but so many years had passed and, even if Colin had been wrongly convicted, as much as she tried, Ruby couldn't think of a viable motive for any of the extended family to be involved in her murder.

Bridget had been unusually quiet after she put the bag of photos away. When Ruby quizzed her again about the hospital band, she'd ignored the question, said she was tired. It was so unlike her and the fact that she'd kept it all these years niggled Ruby. She remembered her mother telling her Bridget couldn't have children. Unless... Bridget fell pregnant and gave birth to a stillborn. That would explain the secrecy and possibly Bridget's need to hold onto the wristband. Perhaps it was too painful to talk about. Ruby's heart wrenched. Poor Bridget. She made a mental note to call her tomorrow, check she was okay.

Ruby shifted in her seat. Usually, she enjoyed the journey, but today the empty road seemed to go on forever. By the time she joined the A47, the weight of fatigue was pressing down hard, and she was struggling to keep her eyes open. She'd eaten far too much of Bridget's home cooking.

She switched up the air conditioning and turned on the radio. A newsreader was talking about ongoing troubles in Syria. Sophie and the kids would be at the farm now. It was a clear day, if a little windy. The children would love it. She should make more of an effort with Sophie. There were only the two of them left in Market Deeton now, they needed to look out for one another.

The sign for the services couldn't have been more welcome, especially when she spotted the peaked roof of Starbucks. It would be good to take a short break from the wheel and have a coffee. She could refuel too.

While Ruby filled up her car, a coachful of travellers arrived. When she'd finished, the queue for the counter at Starbucks ran to the door and the café tables inside were all taken. Ruby joined the end of the line, her gaze falling on a couple sitting at a table beside the window, eyes glued to each other, as if they were the only people in the room. She watched as he reached across and entwined his fingers in hers. He must have said something amusing because she chuckled and snatched her hand back, coyly. It was a tender moment and once again she was reminded of her and Tom, in their early days. When they were immersed in each other, when she couldn't wait to see him, when her stomach fluttered with excitement at the prospect. She thought of Tom, standing in his socks outside his temporary home yesterday, and her heart ached afresh at the distance that now stretched between them.

The queue inched forward. Ruby pulled out her phone. She'd switched it to silent when she arrived in Norfolk – Bridget couldn't abide people using their mobiles in company. She turned the ringtone back on and numerous Facebook notifications flicked up: friends' news, book clubs she was a member of. She was idly scrolling through the posts when the phone pinged and the sunflower graced the screen. Ewan's sister.

A short guttural cough behind. Ruby checked over her shoulder to find an elderly man frowning. He lifted a hand, muttered something about the queue moving. She apologised, shuffled forward again and opened the message.

> I really don't think I can help you. Sorry.

Short, curt. Disappointment gripped her. Why was she so reluctant to talk?

'Can I help you?'

Ruby looked up. Without realising, she'd edged forward again and was now at the counter. She lowered her phone. 'A latte please.'

'To drink in or take away?'

'In, please.' She went through the motions of giving her name, pulling out her card and paying. The screen on her phone, still in her hand, went blank. 'Sorry, could I have that to take away please?' she said, changing her mind. The fresh air would do her good, give her space to think after being cooped up in the car for so long.

The assistant gave her a hard stare, then changed the mug to a paper cup, wrote her name on the side and indicated for her to wait at the end of the counter.

The tables outside the café were empty, not surprising as the late September air was beginning to feel distinctly cool. Ruby zipped her jacket up to her chin and sat at the table furthest from the door. She took a sip of her drink and re-read the message. There was nothing much to grab onto, but Ruby found herself coming back to that earlier message – estranged. People often dropped off with phone calls, messages and emails, especially when they moved away, some even lost contact, but the word estranged suggested an argument or a disagreement. What had happened between them?

A crow cawed overhead. A man emerged from the services and hovered nearby with a vape, the menthol smell of the vapour cloying her nostrils. She idly switched to the internet and typed in Market Deeton news to see if there was an update on the murder.

Numerous searches came up. Ruby scrolled through a new planning application for a town centre factory conversion, residents complaining about dog owners not picking up after their pets. She was about to give up when she clicked on the next page and found an entry from *Deeton Mail – New Witness Sighting in Murder Investigation*. Her gaze dropped to a photo beneath the title. And she froze. The image, black and white and slightly blurred, was of the rear of a man and woman walking along. Ewan and her.

Do you know these people?

A driver captured this image on his dashcam of a man and woman walking through Market Deeton town centre on Tuesday evening. They are thought to be the same couple spotted later in West Way. Police are keen to trace them. If you have any information about their whereabouts, please contact the incident room.

Ruby's stomach twisted. She examined every inch of the dashcam photo. It had captured them walking down Clarence Street. She knew that because she recognised a clock hanging from above a café entrance in the top corner. The lens caught their outline in the car's headlights, leaving a soft glow around them. She couldn't remember a car passing. Not surprising really, she had been pretty tipsy. Her head was tilted towards Ewan, as if they were in deep conversation. And… What was that? The pixels blurred even more as she enlarged the image.

His hand was touching her elbow. He must have been helping her, steadying her. She had been wobbly on her feet. Although the image was hazy and, to an unknowing eye, it looked as though they were linking arms. But – she suddenly realised she was holding her breath and blew it out – she couldn't see anything particular, anything to specifically identify them. Thank goodness.

A car crawled by. She watched it go, only half-concentrating. The question mark, the appeals for this 'couple' troubled her. Did the police really believe they might have some information? Or, worse still, did they think they might be involved in Charlotte's murder? The thought that they might be directing their resources towards searching for them when they should be searching for the killer made her reel. Once again, she cursed herself for lying to the police, then cursed Ewan for asking her to do so. It would have been so much easier to tell the truth from the beginning. They weren't doing anything wrong. Well... not in the eyes of the law anyway.

She looked down at the image and something at her hip caught her eye. She enlarged the photo again, stretching it out on the screen. And that's when she saw it – her mother's faux snakeskin handbag. The gold clasp and matching chain strap were barely recognisable, but it was definitely the same bag. The bag Sophie had given her when she'd left on Tuesday evening. One of a kind, a sample.

If Sophie saw this image, if she examined it closely and noticed the bag, she'd know it was her sister. Would she recognise Ewan too?

Shit. Shit. Shit. Ruby couldn't deny that however innocent the situation may have been, it looked compromising on camera. This wasn't going to be an easy one to explain. She needed to come clean to the police, stop the search for this 'mysterious couple'. But first she needed to speak with Sophie.

Chapter 32

Ruby arrived at Sophie's to find Ewan's silver Golf parked on the drive. She hesitated, her stomach twisting afresh. This conversation needed a delicate touch. It would be much easier if she was alone with Sophie. She might as well go home first. Take a shower. Have a coffee. Calm the nerves buzzing like a beehive in her chest. Call round later when Ewan had left and the children were in bed. Ewan's shift started early on a Monday; they often caught up on a Sunday evening after he'd gone home.

Ten minutes later, she was in Shetland Avenue, reversing her Fiesta into a tight gap between a BMW and a Toyota, yards from home, when a flash of colour in the wing mirror caught her eye. Ruby checked over her shoulder. A man was wheeling a bike towards her in a red hoody and denims, a lit cigarette poking out of his mouth. Lewis.

She gave him a wave, to let him know she'd seen him, shunted back and forth to straighten, then cut the engine. He'd pulled back his hood and was beside the car when she climbed out.

'Hey,' she said. 'What are you doing up this end of town?'

'Visiting a mate around the corner,' he said, taking the cigarette from his mouth and flicking the end. A spray of ash showered the pavement. 'I'm going for a beer now. You're welcome to join me.'

'I can't, sorry. I have to head out again in a bit.' Tom's comment about her not returning Lewis's calls nudged her. She scrunched her nose. 'Another time?'

'Course. You okay? You look like you've seen a ghost.'

'Oh.' She shook her head, trying to loosen the anxiety within. The dashcam image was gnawing away at her. 'It's nothing.'

'Are you sure?'

'Yes.' She remembered she still hadn't called him to make the appointment for his kitchen refurbishment and apologised. 'Are you sure you don't want to come inside for a coffee?' she said, forcing a smile. 'I have a few minutes. We could fire up my laptop, have a look at some ideas now, if you like? Might even have a beer in the fridge.' Not a suggestion Mark would approve of. She could hear him now, punching out his mantra, 'People choose Galanti's because we're high end. They expect to be treated like royalty.'

Lewis took a final drag, stubbed out his cigarette on a nearby wall and placed the end in his pocket. 'I've decided to take next week off work to concentrate on flat stuff,' he said. 'There's so much to do. I'm staying with a friend while they finish the rewire. The dust is driving me nuts.'

'I can imagine.'

He checked his watch and Ruby looked across at her house, the front door hiding behind the privet hedge. Going home, walking through her front door, was starting to make her jittery, especially after yesterday; she was convinced someone had been in there. Could Tom be playing games, making her feel uncomfortable so that when he officially ended their relationship, she'd be eager to sell? He knew how much she loved the place.

'I was hoping to meet Kev in The Prince,' Lewis said. 'But… I guess he can wait a bit longer. Might as well make a start since I'm here.'

Ruby's shoulders slackened as they crossed the road. Him wheeling his quirky bike with the little wheels. 'Never seen one of those before.'

'It's a Brompton, a city bike. I dust it off occasionally.'

Ruby breathed a sigh of relief when she saw the door handle sitting horizontal. At least no one had tried it today.

Lewis hovered beside her, twisting the handlebars, folding his bike down into a neat square.

'That's impressive,' she said, letting them both inside.

He placed the bike down and waited for her to shed her jacket. This was the first time Lewis had been to the house since Tom had moved out and it suddenly felt strange, awkward. The three of them had enjoyed so many evenings together before her mum died. Lewis was good company, always full of jokes to keep them amused. Easy on the eye too. Tall, sporty. In other circumstances, and if she hadn't met Tom, she might have viewed him differently...

'Can I get you a beer?' she asked.

'No, I'll have a coffee.'

'Still white, no sugar?'

'Oh, you remember,' he said, teasing.

She told him to go and make himself comfortable in the front room, then moved into the kitchen. Logging into her laptop while the kettle boiled, wracking her brains to remember the layout of Lewis's kitchen and searching her database for designs that might suit.

Back in the sitting room, Ruby talked through ideas while they sipped their drinks and showed him photographs of finished projects. He was pretty happy to give her free rein with the space. It sounded like a relatively easy project to put together and they made an appointment for her to visit him on Tuesday and measure up.

'How are things with you and Tom?' Lewis asked, easing back into the sofa when they'd finished.

'Oh, you know. No change.'

He pulled a face. 'That's a shame. I always thought you were good together.'

They fell into nostalgic chatter about nights out and silly drinking games they'd roped each other into as they finished their drinks. Time passed easily and Ruby felt the tension loosen in her shoulders. A bird cheeped in the hedging outside.

Lewis turned to place his empty mug on the coffee table beside him and caught his cuff on the edge of a photo. It rattled as it landed on the hardwood flooring. 'Oh, sorry,' he said, lifting the silver frame from the floor. It was a picture of Daisy sitting on Santa's lap with Aileen beaming beside her. She could have only been about three. A hairline crack ran through the corner of the frame. Lewis looked horrified. 'I'm so sorry, I'll replace it.'

'Please, don't worry.' Ruby took it from him, swiped her finger along the tiny crack as if it was nothing and placed it back with the other photos. Photos of Sophie and her growing up, pictures of them on shopping trips with their mum, sitting around the dinner table at Christmas.

'Your mum cooked the best Sunday dinner I've ever had,' Lewis said, studying the other pictures. 'Never tasted roast potatoes like hers.'

'Goose fat and rosemary,' Ruby said. 'She covered them in it before they went in the oven. Called it her own secret recipe, although I don't think it was much of a secret.' She could see her mother lifting out the oven tray, hands enclosed in charred gloves, face pink from the heat of the stove. Aileen loved to cook Sunday dinner, inviting friends and family over to sit and eat together. 'A full table is a happy table,' she used to say. Her mother's infamous Sunday gatherings were one of the things Ruby missed most. She felt her eyes fill.

Lewis sat forward. 'Oh, I didn't mean to upset you.'

'It's okay. It's quite refreshing to hear someone speak about Mum. Most people don't know what to say, so they don't say anything.'

'That's tough.'

Ruby shrugged. The situation with Sophie, Ewan and her, the bruises and the messages she'd exchanged with Isla clawed back into her mind. If ever she needed her mother's counsel, it was now. She closed her eyes, rubbed her forehead.

'Are you okay?' Lewis asked.

She waved away his comforting hand. 'I'm fine.'

'Can I do anything?'

'That's kind of you, but no. It's been a difficult week.'

'Yeah, I guess. The news about Charlotte must have been a shock.'

'It's not just that.' To Ruby's dismay, her throat tightened. A tear traced her cheek. She swiped it away. 'Everything is such a mess.'

'Why?'

'Stuff. You know, life. I'm about to quarrel with my sister.'

'I find that hard to believe. You always seem so close.'

'We are usually.' Her words dissolved.

'Look, you know I'm here if you ever want to talk. Crap at advice, but happy to listen.'

She smiled at his attempt at a joke. Her heart pushed her to tell him, to spew it all out, though her head said otherwise. She'd already betrayed Sophie in the worst possible manner. Sharing her concerns further before she faced her sister wasn't going to help the situation, especially if any of the details got back to Sophie.

'Thanks. I'd better go and see Sophie, get this out of the way,' she said, gathering up the mugs.

'I can come with you, if you want? Moral support and all that.'

'Thanks, but no. It's a family matter. I need to go alone.'

Chapter 33

A line of cars stretched in front like little boxes as far as the eye could see. Ruby pressed her head into the headrest. It was almost 7:30 p.m. Sophie would have put the kids to bed by now and be settling down for the evening.

It was critical she reach Sophie before she looked at the news appeal herself. This wasn't a conversation she could have over the phone. She needed to be there with her sister. Watch the comprehension unfold on her face. Make sure she understood what really happened in West Way. She only hoped she hadn't already seen it and made the connection. That after a long day out, she would have been far too busy sorting out the children, making their tea, getting them ready for the week ahead.

The cars started moving. She inched forward and pressed the brake again. High Street was more congested than she would have expected for a Sunday evening and sitting idly in the traffic, her nerves were starting to perform somersaults. What if Sophie didn't believe her about Ewan? Or what if she didn't think this was a one-off, a mistake?

She grabbed her phone and checked the local traffic news. There was an accident on the High Street intersection: a lorry had shed its load. The road had been closed and motorists were being diverted. No wonder they were practically at a standstill. Leapers End was a few metres or so ahead. If she reached it, she could turn off, take the back route. She waited for the traffic to move. The Peugeot in front edged forward, leaving just enough gap for her to swing off the main drag into Leapers End and then queue for Templeton Road.

7:38 p.m. Itches travelled up and down her back. She could imagine Sophie, trotting down the stairs, ironing the school uniforms, making packed lunches for the morning. Moving into the front room, switching on the television.

Ruby yanked down her wheel, making a sudden manoeuvre to steer to the side of the road and climbed out, ignoring the motorist behind yelling expletives out of his open window. She might as well walk from here. It would only take ten minutes or so.

The traffic along Templeton Road coming into town was no better. Thank goodness she'd abandoned her car. She picked up her pace, continued up the hill. 7:44 p.m.

As soon as she glimpsed Sophie's drive, the hairs on the tops of her arms pricked. Ewan's Golf was still there. She really wanted to speak with Sophie alone, to level with her. Maybe even tell her about the message from Ewan's sister. It was going to be doubly difficult now. But she couldn't leave it any longer.

She slipped down the side of Ewan's car, past the Subaru at the bottom, still on bricks, and around to the rear of the house. Only to find the back door locked. Odd. It was never locked when Sophie was home, not until she went to bed in the evening. They all used the back door for access – her mum used to say the front door was for guests and deliveries.

Ruby backtracked to the front and studied the upstairs window above the door. The curtains were drawn at Daisy's room. The children were in bed. Not wishing to disturb them, she bypassed the doorbell, knocked the door gently and waited. Seconds flitted by. Eventually it was answered by Ewan. He peered quizzically at her.

'Everything all right?' Ruby said.

He let her in, unspeaking.

A step creaked. Ruby looked up to see Sophie coming down the stairs. Her hair was tied into a knot on top of her head, her face blotchy. She was wearing her yoga bottoms and a long pink sweatshirt.

'The back door's locked,' Ruby said.

Sophie was at the bottom of the stairs now, standing beside Ewan. They both seemed dazed.

'Soph?' Had they had a row? Maybe now wasn't a good time. But was there ever a good time to tell your sister her boyfriend wasn't the man she thought he was? 'The back door's locked,' she repeated as if no one had heard her the first time.

'I know.' Sophie's voice was tight.

'Can I come in?' Ruby said. She flicked her gaze upstairs and gestured towards the kitchen. She really didn't want to wake the children.

Sophie said nothing, but stepped aside, allowing Ruby to walk in and they made their way down the hallway. As soon as they were in the kitchen, Sophie pushed the door to.

Ewan leaned up against the surface, dug his hands in his pockets and stared at the floor. They'd had a row. They'd had a row and she'd disturbed them. Her timing couldn't have been worse.

'I'll come back,' Ruby said, angling her head to meet Sophie's gaze. 'I can see you're busy.'

'I think you've got something to tell me, haven't you?' Sophie folded her arms across her chest.

She knows.

'You can say what you need to in front of Ewan,' she said. She moved to stand beside him.

'It's tricky. I—'

'What, cat got your tongue?'

Sophie's icy tone cut through her. *She definitely knows.*

Ruby glanced from one to the other. 'Why don't we all sit down.'

'I'm happy to stand.'

'What I've got to say is sensitive.'

'Got anything to do with a dashcam image, by any chance? Or a "couple" spotted in West Way?' Her emphasis on the word couple made Ruby flinch.

She did know. And from the pained look on her face Ewan hadn't done a particularly good job of talking her through it.

'Sophie, I can explain.' She turned to Ewan for support, but he seemed more interested in a fleck of dust on the floor beside his feet. 'It was a misunderstanding, a silly moment. Ewan, tell her…'

'I don't think that's entirely true, is it?' Sophie said. She uncrossed her arms and straightened, a muscle flexing in her cheek. 'You see, Ewan's already told me everything.'

'Then you'll know I'm telling the truth.'

'So you weren't the couple having the altercation at West Way, or walking arm in arm up Clarence Street?'

'I didn't say that. But it's not what it seems.'

'Isn't it? Then why don't you explain it to me, eh? Explain to me how you tried to seduce my boyfriend on the night of our dead mother's birthday.'

What? Was that what he'd said? That *she* had tried to seduce him?

Hot shame filled her cheeks. 'No! That's not true.' She cringed at the indignation, the desperation in her voice.

'That's exactly true.' Sophie's face contorted. 'No wonder your lunch with Tom didn't go well. You'd already set your sights on someone new.'

How dare he? 'Sophie, no. You've got it all wrong.' She pointed at Ewan, listening to the decibels in her voice rise. 'He's not who you think he is.'

'Oh, you know my boyfriend better than I do now, do you? Think sticking your tongue down his throat makes you qualified.'

'Sophie.' Ewan's voice was barely a whisper.

'No, she needs to hear this. Ewan's already told me why he didn't say anything the other day, because he didn't want to upset me, because he didn't want to do anything to jeopardise *our* relationship.' A stream of spit blew out of her mouth as she pointed from herself to Ruby and back again. 'Thought we'd had enough misery in the family. He was looking out for me. We trust each other, you see. We're not like you.'

'If you trust each other so much, why did he wait until a dashcam image appeared in the news before he told you?' Ruby regretted the words as soon as they left her mouth. This was not doing her argument any good.

Sophie stiffened. Her face was taut with anger. And something else. Something else Ruby couldn't put her finger on. *Fear?*

'Because he was protecting me! We'd just said our final goodbyes to our mother. And with Charlotte Manning's murder in the news, this was the last thing I needed.'

'You don't understand. There's a lot more—'

'Oh, but you see I do,' Sophie cut in. 'Ewan told me first thing this morning. We haven't been to the farm. We've had all day to sort this out. Hours to talk about it. Plenty of time for him to go down to the station and give a correct account to the police. Unlike yours.'

'What?' Ruby was incredulous. How could he do this to her?

'Yes, he's been down there this afternoon, straightened everything out. You should be thanking him for getting you off the hook.'

Ruby opened her mouth and closed it again, clamping her teeth together, gagged by frustration. This was the moment she was supposed to fight for herself, to prove to her sister her sleazy boyfriend was lying, but she was so rankled now, she was fearful she'd say something she'd regret. Worried about upsetting her sister further, pushing her over the edge. Plus, the children were sleeping upstairs.

Sophie tossed her head from side to side. 'How could you?'

Exasperation needled her. She couldn't let him get away with this. 'It's not what you think. If you just listen, if you let me explain…'

'Explain what? That you're a tart who couldn't keep your hands off your sister's boyfriend? I hear it's not the first time you've flirted with him either.' Her nostrils flared. 'Poor little Ruby. Everyone thinks you're so capable, so organised, so kind. When really you're just a conniving little bitch!'

What the hell had he said? Ruby shot Ewan a hard look. But he wouldn't meet her gaze, his face puce. 'You've got it all wrong,' she said. 'He's filled your head with a pack of lies.'

'I don't think so.' Sophie glanced askance at Ewan and then back to her sister. 'Tom was right, you are a cold fish. Too high and mighty to talk about your own problems, instead you stick your nose into everyone else's. Then you push people away. Well, this time I'm pushing you away.' She took a step forward. 'I don't want to see you. I don't want to hear from you.' She flung open the door to the hallway. 'Now, get out!'

Chapter 34

Sophie gripped the work surface with both hands as Ewan shut the front door on Ruby.

'You okay?' he said, re-joining her.

'Could you check on the kids? I want to make sure they didn't hear any of that.'

She pushed the kitchen door closed after him and sank into a chair. She needed to iron Alfie's PE kit for tomorrow. Check Daisy's homework was in her bag. All the usual chores that plagued her Sunday evenings. But the domesticity of life tumbled away, loose stones rolling down a mountain, as her world shifted afresh.

All day. All day she'd had to come to terms with what had happened between Ewan and Ruby. A day consumed by visits to the police station, taking the kids to McDonald's to make up for missing their precious family day out. Talks, discussions, explanations. Yet only now, when the children were in bed and the house had quietened, did the reality of the situation dawn. Her sister, the person closest to her in the whole world, had betrayed her.

I can explain. Ruby's words rang out in her head. Explain what? Ruby might have devoured the best part of two bottles of wine that day, but she was by no means paralytic. She knew exactly what she was doing and she also knew there was no excuse to justify her actions.

Good old Ruby. Who looked after people, who could always be relied upon to do the right thing. Only this time she hadn't.

She'd looked lost this evening, a fish out of water, fumbling to find the words to talk her way out of things.

Sophie glanced at the clock. The same clock that had been there this morning when they were preparing for their day out. The kids were so excited about going to the farm. Alfie was up at the crack of dawn, climbing into her bed, wriggling around until she agreed to google animals with him on her phone. Ewan went downstairs to cook pancakes with maple syrup, a special treat, before they left. The sun was shining when she opened the curtains, the sky pale blue and clear of clouds. It had all the makings of the perfect family day…

She'd thought Ewan was joking when the kids and she traipsed downstairs for breakfast and he'd taken her into the front room to speak to her, alone. Thought it trivial, like a chocolate treat he wanted to sneak into their lunchbox, a surprise for the kids later. Ewan was good at surprises. But his face was grave, and when he asked her to sit, she experienced a touch of déjà vu. She'd been asked to sit on a sofa four years ago when Greg announced he was leaving. She recalled pressing her hand to her chest, lowering herself onto the seat, desperately wondering what could have happened. Though she couldn't have guessed, not in a million years. Ruby was her older sister. The one person she looked up to and trusted implicitly.

The confusion as he showed her the fresh appeal and the dashcam image on his phone. It wasn't until he enlarged it that she noticed her mother's bag, the one she'd given to Ruby on Tuesday evening. Still, she didn't understand. Who was Ruby with? Then he'd flicked back to the description of the couple at the garages and suddenly she saw the resemblance. It wasn't obvious at first, but when he put the description and the image together, side by side, it was as clear as glass. Ewan and Ruby together. In West Way of all places!

The explanation of him out jogging jarred her. Him out on the night of her mother's wake, when she believed he was lying in bed beside her. That's why he was dressed when she found him in the back garden. But… it was a day of twisted emotions. Of celebrating a life and also saying their final goodbyes. They'd all been cocooned by grief for so long, a part of her could understand him wanting to feel the air in his lungs, to flush out the cobwebs. A chance meeting with her sister walking home through the town centre didn't sound unreasonable either.

So why keep it secret?

Then his face had twisted and he'd started saying things like, 'please don't judge me', 'it wasn't my fault' and 'I was only trying to protect you' and her heart had plummeted to the floor. It sounded serious. And it was serious. Ruby had made a pass at her man when he'd kindly offered to walk her home. Pushing him against the garages, sticking her tongue in his mouth, becoming angry with him when he rejected her.

How dare she? Sophie pictured Ruby sitting at the table eating dinner with them the next day. She'd showed her the appeal for the couple in West Way that evening too, and all the time Ruby knew it was her and Ewan, yet she never said.

When Ewan went on to say Ruby had been flirting with him for a while, making suggestive comments, she'd been gobsmacked. How could Ruby do this to her? Her sister. Her one constant.

The door swung back and Ewan entered. 'They're both out for the count,' he said. He moved to her side. 'I'm so sorry. You can see why I didn't tell you now. The last thing I wanted was to come between you and your sister.' He pulled a chair close to hers, sat and wrapped his arms around her.

Sophie wanted to weep. She wanted to howl hard tears, feel the relief of them as she cried it all out until she was empty, spent. But her insides were so tightly wound the tears wouldn't come.

'Why don't I stay over tonight?' he said, rubbing her back, touching his forehead to hers. 'We can put our coats on, sit on the patio, have a glass of wine under the stars. Take your mind off things.'

It was a tempting offer. Anything to numb the gloom simmering within. Her head hurt and her throat was raw. She'd lost her mother and now it felt like she'd lost her sister too.

She pulled away, sniffed. About to answer, when a nasty thought elbowed her. The same nasty thought that had been bothering her all day. Why, oh why, hadn't he told her he'd been out on Tuesday? Yes, she knew he liked to jog of an evening, but he usually announced it before he left. That night, they'd waited for everyone to leave and gone up to bed together. The very notion he'd dressed and slipped out when he was supposed to be lying beside her, and then returned without saying anything, was staggering. Had he done this before?

Again, Ruby's stricken face nudged her. Was she shocked because all had been revealed, or was she wondering exactly how much Sophie knew?

She would have known if there was anything more to it, if something had been going on between them for longer, wouldn't she? There would have been signs. He'd smell different. Of the sweet fabric conditioner Ruby insisted on using, or the bohemian-scented sticks she burnt at home.

Though she hadn't noticed with Greg.

But things were different now, weren't they? She was different. With Greg, the children had been young. Alfie suffered with separation anxiety and wouldn't leave her side, even sleeping in their bed. They were rarely alone and when they were, they were worn out. She was more independent now. She made time for Ewan; she'd made sure of that from the start. He was less detached too, more intense. Telling her he loved her at every opportunity, saying they were special. It wasn't possible to feign those feelings, was it?

She looked across at Ewan. 'I think I need some time on my own.'

'Don't do this, Soph.'

'I'm not doing anything. I'm tired. I need some time. You go home, you're on an early shift. We'll talk tomorrow.'

Chapter 35

Ruby marched up Sophie's driveway, thoughts whizzing around her head like a racing car on a Formula One track. *Did that really just happen?*

When she reached the pavement, she turned back and checked over her shoulder, just in time to catch Ewan's pointy face at Daisy's window. He disappeared around the edge of the curtain as soon as he met her gaze.

What on earth was going on? She'd prepared herself for telling Sophie about their chance meeting in town the other night. Walking back together. Playing down the scene beside the garages as some kind of silly quarrel or a bit of banter, smoothing things over – they hadn't said anything at the time because it was an important day and they didn't want to upset her. The main issue was to admit it was them in the photo and to convince Sophie it was an innocent encounter. Why would Ewan tell her about their kiss? What good would that do? And how dare he say that she'd come on to him, and that this wasn't the first time she'd flirted with him? What the hell was he playing at?

She was tempted to go back, confront him. But the children were upstairs and with Sophie there…

Ruby turned into Templeton Road. She needed space. To think. To work out exactly what had happened back there. Why, oh why, hadn't she brought the car nearer to Sophie's?

Cars were still piled back, lining the kerb on the way into town. Bored drivers lowered their windows, leaning out elbows. Others were searching their phones. Some had even left their cars and stood chatting on the pavement together. The earlier collision was still blocking the road into town and nothing was moving any time soon, apart from those squeezing out to do a U-turn.

Brockleton Park was on her left, edged by a long line of ancient oaks. Halfway down was a children's play area, enclosed by yellow picket fencing to keep out dogs. Her eyes fell on the empty area. It would be good to take a moment, to order her thoughts.

Ruby stepped out into the road. And jumped back as a motorcyclist missed her by millimetres. She'd zoned out, hadn't looked, hadn't considered the traffic coming out of town. Clearly that side of the road wasn't so affected by the blockage. She took a couple more steps back and waited for a clear gap, then crossed.

The play area was quiet, the roundabout squeaking gently as it turned in the soft breeze. She entered at the little gate, wandered past the climbing frame and the slide. The swing chains juddered as she sat on the plastic seat and rested her feet on the ground.

They'd agreed to keep things secret. Now Ewan had turned everything upside down, told the whole story, embellishing it and placing the blame firmly on her. Why?

She was reminded of Sophie's bruises. How many more were there, lingering beneath her clothing? Perhaps Sophie had told him she'd noticed them and been asking questions. If they were down to him, if he was of a controlling nature, if he did have violent tendencies, it would make sense to want Ruby out of the way.

The notion began to fester in her mind. Was her sister in danger?

Violent tendencies… She couldn't help but think of Charlotte Manning's lacerated body, left for dead in a dark alley. Ewan had gone to great lengths to cover up being out on the evening of her murder. Though he'd been to the police now.

If they placed him in the vicinity, they'd look at him further, wouldn't they? Ewan claimed he didn't know Charlotte. Unless of course he'd lied.

The urge to find out more about this man pressed on her. She needed to delve into his life in Glasgow, find out why he was estranged from his family and whether he'd been acquainted with Charlotte Manning.

She grabbed her phone, pulled up Facebook Messenger. Isla Wilson's note sat at the top. Whatever happened now, Ruby needed to find some way of persuading the woman to talk. Because if her gut feeling was right, Isla knew something. Something that she could use as ammunition to fight for her sister.

Ruby typed out a quick message: *Thanks for coming back to me. I'm sorry, I had no idea you were estranged. I still need to speak with you, it's an emergency. Would you be available to talk to me tomorrow? Please. I'd be so grateful if you'd help out.* She read it through, backtracked and added, *Everything you say will be treated in the strictest confidence.* Then pressed send.

Chapter 36

The gate to the play area squealed on its hinges as it opened. 'Ruby, is that you?'

Ruby's hand flew to her stomach. She'd been so consumed with her phone, she hadn't seen anyone approach.

'Lewis! What are you doing here?' He was still wearing the same red hoody and denims from earlier, but his hair was wet, as if he'd just stepped out of the shower.

'Sorry, I didn't mean to startle you. I'm staying here' – he pointed at a grey pebbledash building overlooking the park – 'with a mate.'

Ruby looked up at the block of flats, vaguely recalling him telling her something about moving out of his flat because of refurbishment. It all seemed like a long time ago now, as if days had passed, not hours. 'Stephenson House?'

'Yes. On the second floor. I spotted someone sitting alone in the children's play area. You okay?'

Is that what she looked like? A forlorn figure hunched on the swing. In need of assistance. How many other people were watching her sitting there?

'Yes,' she said automatically. Although she wasn't fine. Nothing was fine. Her world was crumbling around her and she had no idea how to fix it.

He hovered awkwardly. 'I can go if you want, now I know it's only you?'

'No, please.' She motioned to the swing beside her. Lewis oozed a calm stillness. Just the sort of influence she needed right now. 'Stay.'

The chains jangled as he shuffled onto the seat. 'How did your talk with Sophie go?' he asked.

Ruby pictured her sister's twisted face and felt a fresh stab of pain. Then, to her horror, she found her eyes filling. All the suppressed rage, the pent-up frustration at the situation she found herself in, turning to tears which now streamed down her face. She bowed her head, choking on the sobs that followed.

Lewis leapt off his swing and crouched in front of her. 'Hey! I'm sure it can't be that bad.'

But it was bad. It was very bad. They hadn't argued, not properly, since their teenage years and this wasn't some tiff over who was in charge of the remote control for the television, or a quarrel over borrowed and trashed clothes. This was raw and deep and she couldn't see a pathway out of the darkness.

She cried and cried. Weeping until her face ached and her nose stung.

Eventually the sobs subsided. She wiped her face with the sleeve of her jacket, dragging it across her the skin. 'I'm sorry.' Her voice was barely a whimper.

'No need to apologise.' Lewis was still crouched in front of her, looking up at her, eyes like pools. He leaned sideways, reached into his pocket and passed her a tissue. 'It's clean, just a bit crumpled.'

She thanked him, wiped her face again and stared out into the half-light. An owl called to its mate. Another hooted back. An engine revved on the road nearby. Lights switched on in Stephenson House. Curtains were drawn, the residents of Market Deeton settling down for the evening.

Lewis moved back to the swing beside her.

'So, have you rescued many dejected souls on swings since you've been staying here?' she said.

'Strangely, no.' He scanned the children's play area. 'I doubt their mothers would appreciate it.'

She couldn't help but laugh.

'Seriously, I can't ignore someone in trouble,' he said. 'I've been through hard times myself.'

It was unusual to hear him sombre, serious. He was normally so chirpy, one of those easy-going, convivial people who lit up a room when he walked in. 'Sorry, I didn't realise.'

'Why would you? It was back when I lived in London.'

Another part of his life they rarely talked about. He'd taken her and Tom down to London last summer to a swanky restaurant and bowled Tom over by introducing him to some premier league footballer she couldn't remember the name of. She recalled him saying he'd moved out of London for work – he was often going back to visit friends and family. But she'd never really given much thought to his life before he moved here. 'You don't need to tell me about it if you don't want to,' she said.

'I don't have a problem with it.' He inhaled deeply. 'A few years ago, I had a good job in events management, my own car, shared a flat with my girlfriend, Tonya – many of the things we're supposed to aspire to. Then the company went into administration. I wasn't bothered at the time. Was pretty sure I'd land another job easily. But the market had taken a downturn. None of the big companies were recruiting.' He sniffed. 'I wasn't exactly good at being unemployed. Within weeks, I lost the car – couldn't keep up the payments. Tonya and I split up a few months later and I left the flat. I stayed with friends for a while, moving around – sofa surfing. But you can't exist on people's goodwill forever.'

He leant back on the swing, swayed it back and forth gently.

'It was a friend of mine, Al, who pulled me out of it. He came up to the Midlands and was organising corporate events: training courses, team building – said there was work in the area. I stayed with Al in Birmingham for a bit, but there wasn't really enough to keep us both going, so I saved up, moved across to Leicestershire and went freelance.'

'That was brave.'

'Or stupid.' He snorted. 'I stayed in the centre of Leicester at first. Came out to Market Deeton one day to run an event at The Jubilee Hall and fell in love with the place. It's so quiet and friendly. So different to city life.'

'I always thought it was Becky that brought you here. You two seem close.' A teasing smile tugged at Ruby's lips as she pictured the tall, formidable Becky, her mother's shop neighbour.

Lewis chuckled. 'Becky's all right, you know. You should give her a chance.'

Ruby didn't answer. It always surprised her to see them out drinking together. Lewis, warm and friendly. Becky with her outwardly frothy personality and the smile that didn't always reach her eyes.

'When I first came here, I knew no one. I rented a flat in Bordwell Road, off High Street. I was working from home, trying to expand my freelance business and struggling to establish contacts. Everybody here works on recommendation. I used to walk along Ablett Street to get an espresso in the mornings. It was summertime and Becky would often be sitting outside her shop, watching the world go by, chatting to passing locals. She knew everyone. One morning, I bought her a coffee and we got talking. The kindness of that woman.' He shook his head. 'She recognised me as an outsider, made a point of introducing me to the right people. That's why I like to help her out, when I can, in the shop.'

'You're certainly there a lot. Sophie used to think you were a couple.'

He chortled. 'I don't think I'd be her type, even if she was mine!'

Ruby stayed quiet. She couldn't see them together either. It amazed her how her mother had managed to work alongside Becky for so long. They'd certainly had their fair share of clashes over the years. She could still remember the stand-off over parking for deliveries last summer – they hadn't spoken for a week. But that was Aileen and her fiery temperament. It was soon forgotten. And Ruby couldn't deny that Becky was incredibly adept at networking.

'Becky's always busy, out and about,' he said. 'She's on every committee, every business association you can think of. She helps me and occasionally I cover for her. Plus, the shop keeps my hand in with the locals. They get to know me. If someone's planning a wedding or a celebration, they'll often come to the shop and Becky gives them my details. It was her that extolled the virtues of Heritage Arts – said it was a quality set-up and would be a good place to build up local contacts.'

Ruby remembered Lewis wandering into their Heritage Arts meeting almost two years earlier, with his sleek suit and manicured hair, offering his services to promote their next play. She'd seen him with Becky, passed the occasional greeting, but it was the first time they'd really spoken, and she'd been blown away by his drive and enthusiasm. Some of the older members were sceptical. They were a small amateur group, less than forty members. What promotion did they need apart from a few flyers to advertise their next performance? Only friends and family tended to come along anyway. When he said there was no charge, he was looking to give something back to the community, they could hardly refuse. It paid off because he knew the right printing companies, sought out the best places to advertise. At their performance of *Romeo and Juliet* that summer, he doubled their audience, and their Christmas performance attracted families from the city.

'You're very generous with them.'

'Not really. The drama group turned things around for me. People started to contact me to organise comedy gigs, music festivals. Most of my business comes from this little town now and that's all down to Becky. I owe that woman a lot.'

Ruby swayed back and forth on her swing. 'I had no idea.'

'Everyone's got a story,' he said.

A stream of car engines started. It sounded like the road nearby was clearing.

'It's not worth it, you know,' he said eventually. 'The argument with your sister. Family's important. You're lucky to have her nearby.'

She thought of the hard faces at Sophie's earlier, the harsh words. 'What do you think of Ewan?' she asked.

Lewis gave an imperceptible shrug. 'Seems all right. Keeps himself to himself. Sophie's happy with him.' Another vague answer, practically mirroring Tom's yesterday.

Ruby wasn't sure whether it was Lewis's generous nature or the story he'd shared, but, to her surprise, she opened her mouth and told him all about the argument. He didn't flinch when she ran through her brief exchange with Ewan in West Way. Listened quietly while she talked about their agreement to keep it secret, her lying to the police, the description in the news, the photo today that incriminated them both. The allegations he'd made against her. She kept her misgivings about the possibility of Ewan being involved in Charlotte's murder to herself. It was only conjecture at this stage and Sophie wouldn't thank her for spreading rumours. No sense in doing more damage to their ailing relationship.

'Why do you think he blamed it on you?' Lewis asked.

'I don't know.' She went on to tell him about the nasty love bite, the bruises on Sophie and how she'd reached out to Ewan's sister in an effort to protect her own sister.

'Blimey!' he said. 'He sounds like a real shit.'

Engines thrummed as the cars pulled away nearby.

'Why don't you go back and see Sophie?' Lewis said. 'I'll come with you, if you like?'

It was a tempting proposition. It was less than a ten-minute walk back to Sophie's and Ewan might have left by now. They could reason it out together. Although, what could she tell her? She could only correct what Ewan had said and shift the blame onto him. Problem was, he'd got in first and already planted the seed, allowing it to well and truly germinate. No. If she was going to speak with Sophie, she needed something else to convince her. Perhaps she could trace the witness who saw them at the garages. If they'd been there a while, they might have seen exactly what happened. Or maybe Ewan's sister would come up with something.

'Thanks, but I think I'll go home. Let her cool down.'

'He can't be allowed to get away with this.'

'He won't. But I don't know his address. It's not like I can go over there, wait for him to arrive home and give him a piece of my mind.' She hauled herself out of the swing. 'I need to think this through.'

'I'll walk you back.'

'No need. My car's around the corner.'

'Then I'll walk you back to your car.'

The gate hinges squeaked again as they left the park behind them. Night had drawn in, a million stars peeping out from the blanket of darkness above.

The road was clear when they reached Ruby's Fiesta. 'Thanks,' she said to Lewis.

'For what?'

'Listening.'

'Any time.' His face brightened. 'I'm happy to talk to Sophie myself, if you think that'd help? I know she struggles.'

Ruby was opening her driver's door when something in his last sentence jarred her. She turned back. 'I'm sorry?'

'What?'

'You said, "I know she struggles".'

'After everything she's been through, it's not surprising—'

'What did you mean, Lewis?'

'Oh, just…' He shrugged, hanging his head awkwardly. 'I'm glad she's off the V, that's all. It's a trying time for anyone without—'

Ruby cut in again. 'I'm not with you.'

'Valium.' He looked at her and his eyes widened. 'Oh, God, you did know, didn't you?'

Ruby's heart thumped her chest. Sophie taking Valium? Since when? 'The point is, how did you know?'

'It was common knowledge in The Crown. Aileen's youngest daughter buying V from Tony G. Nobody begrudged her, she's been through hell this past year.'

Common knowledge. The words scraped through her.

'But she's off it now?'

'Tony G was banged up last month for ABH. The Crown cleaned up and kicked out his cronies. She's not getting it from there any more, that's for sure.' He closed his eyes a second and when he opened them, his face was full of regret. 'I am sorry, Rubes, I genuinely thought you knew.'

Ruby swallowed, dry and hard. How come she was the last to know? What other secrets were people keeping from her?

Chapter 37

Ruby flattened her foot on the accelerator as she drove down the road. The box of macaroons, the kind present to Sophie's family from Bridget she'd forgotten to take in, crashed into the back of the passenger seat. Not that it made any difference now.

The idea of Sophie taking Valium wouldn't have bothered her if it had been prescribed. If she needed it, she needed it. Whatever it takes. Ruby had taken sleeping pills herself this past year. But bought off the street... Was it pure? Was she taking the right dosage? Was it even something she should be taking considering her history? She felt a burning desire to go back and speak with her. Paused at the next junction, toying with the idea. But she had no proof, and what more could she say?

How could she not have known? Granted, The Crown wasn't a regular haunt for her. She tended to drink in The Prince. With its polished floors and spacious layout of high and low tables, it had more of a light and airy feel. But Market Deeton was small. It wasn't easy to keep secrets, especially from the crowds in town.

A car approached from behind. She indicated left and turned towards home, slowing at a roundabout. She was waiting for a gap in the traffic when she noticed a man at the corner, a mobile phone pressed to his ear. He was tucked back, away from the streetlights, in the shadow of a nearby bank of shops. Flailing his free arm around animatedly, clearly unhappy about something. He was wearing denims and a long dark jacket with the collar flipped up. She caught the edge of his profile and squinted. It couldn't be? She narrowed her eyes to tiny holes. He turned, only a few inches, but enough to see a lock of light brown hair, falling onto his face.

Ewan.

He started pacing back and forth, distracted by the conversation.

A car horn blasted. Ruby jumped. She was holding up the traffic. She placed her hand up to the driver behind in brief apology and glanced back at Ewan. He was engrossed in his conversation, oblivious to her presence. Ruby sped over the roundabout and checked again in her wing mirror. Watching with half an eye as she continued down the road.

She recalled the tightness in his face earlier. His eyes sliding away from her gaze. He couldn't wait for Sophie to usher her out of the house. What was he up to?

Frustration twisted her insides. She hadn't been able to speak to her sister properly, to reassure her, to tell her exactly what happened because he'd got in first and filled her head with a deluge of untruths. Anger grew inside her, burning into a fireball of tension. She'd learned to bite her tongue and suppress her emotions in front of Sophie, fearful of pushing her too far, and Ewan had played on this vulnerability.

Ruby ground her teeth, and took a sharp right into the next side street. Well, he couldn't hide behind her fragility here. Even if she hadn't already been concerned about his relationship with her sister, even if she didn't harbour some suspicions about a potentially controlling and abusive nature, there was one thing Ruby couldn't abide and that was deception. He might be able to twist things to manipulate Sophie, but there was no way he was going to get away with it with her.

She crawled down a terraced street. Cars were parked nose to tail along the kerb. The rage intensified as she desperately searched for a space. *Come on!* Ewan looked as though he was waiting for someone. Perhaps they hadn't turned up and that's why he was so agitated on the phone. She had no idea how long she'd got before he made off.

Finally, she found a space, a third of the way down on the other side of the road. She parked hastily, leaving the car at an angle – desperately hoping there wouldn't be any attentive traffic wardens working late – and slammed the door, already several paces away when she clicked the locking mechanism on her key fob.

The junction was fifty yards or so up the road. She broke into a jog. Had to wait for a van to pass before she could cross. Headlights flickered across the windscreens on the main road. Night had really drawn in now. She could see the roundabout in the distance. From this angle, only the edge of the corner was visible. It was empty. But Ewan had been tucked back, hadn't he? Lingering in the shadows of the shopfronts.

She sped up, breaking into a run. At the roundabout, the area opened up. She weaved through the traffic. The bank of shopfronts – a café, a newsagent, a hairdresser's and a charity shop – were in darkness. And there was no sign of Ewan.

Ruby ran across the road and stood where he'd been standing, hands on hips, desperately searching every which way. Nothing. Disappointment sliced through her. Surely he hadn't gone. She'd only been a few minutes. She was working this through when she wheeled round and caught a figure in her peripheral vision. He moved into a side entrance, a narrow aperture between the charity shop and the hairdresser's next door.

The opening was barely two metres wide, and dark. Ruby tensed, her instincts screaming caution. But tonight, a wild fury clouded her judgement, all thoughts consumed with confronting Ewan.

The smell of urine, strong and sweet, hung in the air as she stepped inside the opening. Her phone torch lit up the area in a weak channel of light. The passage led to the rear of the shops. It was cold and damp. Moss and lichen grew in the gaps between the bare bricks. An overflowing guttering dispersed rhythmic drips. A pair of industrial waste bins sat halfway down. She couldn't see anyone.

'Ewan?' Ruby's voice faded into the darkness. She walked slowly towards the bins, angling the light, trying to see past them.

'You want sommat?'

The chipped voice made her jump back.

A tall skinny man stepped out from behind the bins. He was wearing denims and a black jacket, similar to the one Ewan wore, with the collar pulled up, though from here she could see his brown hair was cropped to number two all over. A scar ran the length of his cheek.

'I'm looking for someone,' Ruby said. 'He came down here.' She tried to peer around him.

He stepped out further, blocking her view. 'Oh, yeah?' He raised a brow.

Again, she tried to look round him.

'Ain't no one else down here,' he said. 'Apart from you and me.' His eyes bore into her. Dark, menacing. She suppressed a shudder. 'Unless you're after Mandy or Charlie. Might be able to help you out there.' He tittered at his attempt at a joke.

Oh, shit. She'd followed a figure she'd mistaken for Ewan and ended up in a drug dealer's lair. That was all she needed.

'Why don't you tell me what you're really after?' he said.

'I'm looking for Ewan,' she said, fighting to keep the nerves at bay.

He moved in close. 'Ain't no Ewan here.'

'I saw him.' She checked behind. There was no one there. When she turned back, he'd moved forward again. So close she could smell his breath, thick and oniony.

'I said, ain't no Ewan here.' His face hardened. 'You must have been mistaken.'

Ruby heard blood rushing through her ears. Right now, everything felt like one big mistake.

Later, Ruby descended the stairs and tried the front door handle again. Having checked every room in the house on her return, she moved into the kitchen, double-checked the back door and slid into a seat, running her hands through her hair, cursing her paranoia. She was convinced she'd seen Ewan going down that side passage. Was it possible she was mistaken? Or was someone covering for him?

An image of the dealer standing there, watching her, feet rooted to the spot as she'd retreated pulsed through her. It wasn't until she reached the shopfronts that she turned back, relieved to find the path behind her empty and broke into a run. A run she didn't break until she got back to her car.

Her anger at Ewan intensified. She'd placed herself in a potentially dangerous situation in her quest to speak with him and yet again he'd thwarted her. It was as if he was working her like a puppet, all the moves in his favour. Well, if she couldn't confront him, face to face, she needed to find another way. She needed to get evidence, to make her sister see sense, to prove to her what he was really like. Because she was in no doubt now that something was seriously awry.

Lewis's words rattled around her brain. Sophie taking Valium from a street supplier...

She'd read something about a Tony Garratt being arrested outside The Crown last month for drugs offences. The police were clamping down on drugs-related violence in the area. Operation Hawthorn they called it. But someone was bound to have filled Garratt's shoes. Someone like the guy tonight.

Ruby's mind was awash.

Sophie hadn't gone to a doctor and requested a prescription because she was sceptical about going to the surgery, worried about them pressuring her into counselling after what had happened with Colin. Despite Ruby expressing concern, she'd adamantly refused to see a therapist after their mother died.

Lewis also said it was common knowledge in The Crown. Common knowledge! How could Sophie be so stupid? Greg was already angling for more access to the children. He didn't live in Market Deeton, didn't socialise there, but there was always the chance he could find out. The last thing Sophie needed was for him to use it as ammunition to question her parenting skills.

Ruby picked and pulled at her memories of the last twelve months, searching for instances where her sister might have taken something, or displayed unusual behaviour. There was nothing. She had been remarkably calm recently. Was still driving, had gone back to work, was ferrying the kids to school and back, taking care of them. She'd even insisted on reading the eulogy at their mother's memorial service, a task that would normally fall to Ruby. Was this down to the influence of the drug?

The buzz of her phone made her jump. A text from Lewis.

> Can't tell you how sorry I am. Thought you knew about Soph. Let me know if I can help. Feel bloody awful.

She pushed her phone aside, switched to her iPad and googled Valium. Part of the benzodiazepine family, more commonly known as diazepam, prescribed to address myriad issues, including anxiety. Perhaps the Valium was keeping her calm, helping her to deal with the grief. *Highly addictive*. She didn't like the sound of that. Sophie was vulnerable.

Did Ewan know? Was he helping her now Tony Garratt was out of the picture? She recalled a flatmate at uni who bought ecstasy and ketamine from the same supplier. Ewan had been standing close to where the dealer was operating tonight. Did he supply Valium too?

Ruby checked Facebook. Ewan's sister still hadn't opened her private message. She desperately hoped she would and soon, because right now she was pinning all her hopes on her.

Chapter 38

The front doors were locked when Ruby arrived at work the following morning. She knocked the door, rattled the lock, placed a hand up to shield her eyes and peered through the glass. It was 8:30 a.m. Mark wasn't scheduled for a day off. She tapped the glass again. Perhaps he was in the back office. She fished about in her bag for her keys. It took her a while to locate them – they'd slipped to the bottom, amongst her purse, a packet of tissues, her hairbrush. Finally, she found them and let herself in.

The shop was quiet and still inside, and freezing cold. No whirr of computer fans, no sound of the kettle bubbling away in the background. She slipped off her jacket, called out and switched on the temporary heater near her desk. They'd need to switch the central heating on soon if this cool spell persisted.

Ruby hung up her jacket, fired up her laptop, then crossed into the kitchen and filled the kettle. Her head was fuzzy after a fretful night's sleep: concerns about Sophie and Ewan skipping in and out of her mind, the question mark over the drug dealer in the alley. Her broken slumber hindered further by her mobile ringing at 2 a.m., the line cutting when she answered. A withheld number. Could it be Isla? Ruby had put her mobile number at the bottom of her last message, in case she preferred to talk, but why would she call at that time of night? The woman had read her Facebook message though, and left it unanswered. What did that mean?

The kettle was popping behind her, rising to a boil when her mobile rang. It was Lewis.

'Hey. How are you this morning?'

She remembered him saying something about taking the week off work. 'I'm okay.' She told him about spotting Ewan yesterday evening.

'What do you think he was up to?'

'No idea. He usually goes home on a Sunday to prepare for his early Monday shift. Well, that's what he tells Sophie.'

Lewis was quiet a second. 'Look, do you want to meet for a coffee tonight? I'm worried about Sophie. I feel awful about the drugs thing – I really thought you knew. Maybe we can come up with a way to help her together.'

'Sounds good. You didn't call me in the night by any chance, did you? From a landline, or a different phone?'

'No, why?'

'Some idiot rang me in the early hours. Called off when I answered. Number withheld.'

'That's odd.'

'Probably a misdial,' she said with more bravado than she felt. She'd brushed it off last night, fallen back asleep, but in the cold light of day it was starting to bother her. Someone, somewhere was trying to making her uneasy.

A voice called, 'Morning!' from out front.

'Listen, I have to go,' she said to Lewis. 'I'll meet you in The Prince at eight.'

Ruby wandered out to meet Kat. 'Morning. I'm making a cuppa. Have you heard from Mark? He wasn't here when I arrived.'

'No.' Kat glanced at the clock. Ten to nine. 'Let's hope he's overslept and rushes in late. I can only imagine the mileage we'll get out of that.' She gave an acerbic chuckle and wrestled off her jacket.

By the time Ruby had returned with drinks, Kat had logged into her computer and was staring at the screen.

'Thanks,' she said as Ruby placed a coffee mug on her desk.

'How was your weekend?' Ruby asked.

'Oh, the usual boring stuff. We're supposed to be redecorating the bedroom. Graham's gone all mardy on me, says we can't afford a decorator after the holiday and we'll have to do it ourselves. Tight git.'

Ruby snorted. Graham was Kat's boyfriend of three years, a young solicitor who worked in Leicester. They'd moved in together six months earlier and now they always seemed to be arguing. She often wondered why they'd bothered.

'Anyway,' Kat said. 'More to the point, how was yours? I nearly called you yesterday.'

'Oh, you don't want to know,' Ruby said, sliding into her seat and scrolling through her emails.

'Oh, I do.' Kat picked up her coffee and rolled her chair across. Her pink lipstick accentuated the blue in her eyes as she widened them. 'How did your lunch with Tom go?'

Ruby sipped her tea and filled Kat in on Saturday's lunch. When she got to the part about her walking out of the restaurant, Kat tutted.

'So now you have no idea why he asked to meet.'

'I don't know what to think. I mean, he puts the blame on me for why things fell flat, then says we need to talk...' Her words melted into the air as she was reminded of the phone call in the middle of the night. Surely, he wouldn't play those sorts of games?

Kat blew across the top of her coffee. 'What about Sunday?' she asked. 'Was it nice to see Bridget?'

Ruby skimmed over her visit to Norfolk, mentally reminding herself to call Bridget and check on her when she had a moment, then mentioned the fresh police appeal and the dashcam footage. When she talked about her argument with Sophie, Kat's eyes were agog.

'Oh my! Ewan, how dare he?'

'I know.' Ruby rubbed the back of her neck. How she wished she hadn't listened to Ewan. Hadn't lied to the police. She'd done it with the best intentions, to protect Sophie. And now it had backfired in her face. 'He's got me cornered. My word against his. I'm tempted to go to his work, have it out with him.'

'You should, the bastard.'

'Hmm. I'm not so sure. If it gets back to Sophie, it'll do more harm than good.' She did need to do something though. All night, thoughts of Ewan being out on the night of Charlotte's murder had wormed their way in and out of her mind. Could he really be involved in some way? And what did that mean for Sophie? 'There's more,' Ruby said. 'I noticed bruises on Sophie last week. When I asked her about them, she got all churlish.'

'What kind of bruises?'

'On her neck and wrist.'

'You don't think he's knocking her about?'

'I don't know what to think. Mentally, she seems in a better place…' Ruby passed on Lewis's comments. 'Did you know she was taking Valium?'

Kat gasped. 'Of course not, no.'

Not everyone knew then. 'What about Graham? Lewis gave me the impression everyone in The Crown knew. Isn't that where Graham drinks?'

'He's never mentioned it. I'll ask. Hey, do you think I should ring Sophie? Arrange a catch-up and sound her out.'

'It's got to be worth a try. Thanks. I'm trying to work out how I can get her back on side. Even considered contacting Hitesh, our liaison officer, about the witness who saw us at the garages, but I doubt he'll give me the details.' She relayed her fleeting contact with Ewan's sister.

'You need to go to the police,' Kat said.

'And tell them what? My sister *might* be being knocked around by her lying arse boyfriend.'

'Well, you need to at least put the record straight and tell them it's you in their appeal. Your original account will conflict with Ewan's. Imagine if they think you've lied because you're involved. People get put away for giving false accounts and perverting the course of justice.'

'I intend to. I think you have to deliberately lie to protect someone to be charged with perverting the course of justice.' Though the notion made her uncomfortable. 'I can't see that applying to me. Do you really think I'm going to be in trouble?'

'I doubt it. Not if you put the record straight, and soon. I can ask Graham, if you're worried?'

The office phone rang. Kat rested a reassuring hand on Ruby's shoulder and moved across to her desk. The mellifluous sound of her voice filled the room as she picked up the receiver and introduced herself.

Ruby turned back to her laptop and brought up the weekly diary, but pictures of the weekend's events kept flashing up in her mind. Sophie's taut face, the anger in her eyes. She recoiled afresh. It was difficult to see how they would ever resolve this.

She was aware of Kat ending her call.

'Do you think I'm difficult?' she asked.

Kat was making notes on a pad beside the phone. 'I'm not sure what you mean.'

Her attempt at sarcasm was wasted. 'It's something Sophie said yesterday. She called me a cold fish.'

'She was angry. She didn't know what she was saying.'

'Tom made a similar remark when he alluded to the break-up being my fault. He said I clam up, don't talk about my feelings.'

Kat clicked a couple of buttons on her keyboard before she looked up. 'Are you asking for my opinion?'

Ruby didn't like the sound of this. 'Go on.'

Kat swivelled in her seat to face her. 'I've known you a long time. What you went through, losing your mum in that way, was horrific. No one should ever—'

'Just cut to the chase.'

Kat wetted her lips and rubbed them together. 'Okay, I'm sure you'd be the first to admit you weren't yourself after your mum died.'

'Not you as well.'

She held up a flat hand. 'You had every right to be out of sorts. It was horrendous. But you have been quite withdrawn. You've dealt with everybody else's problems. Sorted out the police, your sister, helped with the children. When it comes to you...' Her words trailed off. 'We've all been worried about you.'

'You didn't say.'

'People don't, do they? Because they expect it to pass. But you have been quite reclusive. I mean, when was the last time you went to your drama group? You must have missed at least two performances now, it's so unlike you. Sooner or later, you do need to start thinking about getting back into things.' Her tone softened. 'Is it possible... Hear me out here, this is a long shot. Is it possible, Tom thought you were pushing him away?'

Ruby was flabbergasted. She stared out of the window, at the cars trundling past.

'It's understandable really,' Kat continued with her usual bluntness. 'Everyone relies on you, especially Sophie. Talks to you about their issues. Leans on you. Listens to your advice. *Ask Ruby, she'll know what to do.* You're so level-headed with other people's problems that when it's your turn, when something goes wrong in your world, there's nothing left. I'm sure you believed you were doing the right thing.'

An ache spread through Ruby's chest. 'I did talk about things.'

'Things, yes. Feelings, no. Oh, you'll chat about surface stuff. But never about what's going on inside your head.'

'My mother had been murdered.'

Kat looked affronted. 'You did ask.'

Immediately Ruby was sorry. Kat's frankness was a rare quality in friendship and something she'd always cherished. 'I didn't mean to snap. It's just an easy cop-out to say our relationship breakdown was my fault.'

'You're right. It's rarely one person's fault anyway.'

Ruby turned back to her desk and opened her diary, but she couldn't shake off Kat's comments. Was she really that difficult?

Chapter 39

They were halfway through the morning by the time Galanti's door flapped open and Mark marched in, closely followed by Sara. Both laden with boxes and bags. They'd been to the cash and carry.

'Did you get my text?' Mark asked them.

Kat lifted a brow at Ruby. 'No,' she said. 'Don't worry. Everything's in hand here, as usual.'

Ruby sighed and hauled herself up, grateful for the break. She'd barely been able to concentrate since her conversation with Kat earlier. Had she really pushed people away? She'd practically lived with Sophie the first months after the murder. Dealing with the police, the paperwork. Cuddling up with the children when they had nightmares. It wasn't intentional, not a conscious act, more that she didn't know how to deal with the ongoing pain, the anguish, the grief, so it was easier to push it aside. Had that made her impossible to live with, impossible to be around? Recently, she'd been so absorbed with the upcoming trial that between work and family, life had become utterly exhausting.

She relieved Sara of the large bag she was carrying and the young woman scurried back out to the car. Mark only went to the cash and carry once a month to buy basics like coffee, tea, kitchen consumables, and he always seemed to pick up half the store.

She carried the bag of toilet rolls into the washroom out back and was reminded of Tom's comment about seeing Mark on the night of the murder. It struck her as odd that he hadn't mentioned being out. She wandered into the kitchen to find him reading a message on his phone.

'How was your weekend?' she asked casually, leaning against the work surface.

He shrugged a single shoulder. 'It was okay. We finished the project on Lipton Lane. I'll be glad to see the back of that one. A few new enquiries – a commercial one for you to get your teeth into. We could work on it together. What about you? Enjoy your weekend off?'

Ruby wanted to say not at all, but a little voice inside stopped her. Perhaps it wasn't a good idea to share too much with him, especially after Kat's comments about him being soft on her the other day. 'It was all right,' she said. 'I saw Tom, he sends his best regards.'

Mark didn't answer, his fingers sliding across his phone screen, responding to a text.

'He said he saw you last week in town,' she continued.

He didn't look up. 'What? When?'

'Tuesday. The night of the murder. You didn't mention it.'

'Must have been working late.'

They were interrupted by Ruby's mobile trilling, an unknown number.

'You should get that,' Mark said. 'Might be our order of the year.'

She watched him wander back into the showroom. Strange. Tom was convinced he'd seen him out with a woman. Mark rarely went on dates. In fact, in the three years she'd worked there, she couldn't recall him seeing anyone. Surely, he'd remember.

Her mobile was still singing in her hand. She snapped to answer. 'Hello?'

'Ruby?'

The hairs on the back of Ruby's neck upended. She *knew* that voice.

'Ruby, it's Colin.'

'I know who it is!' she hissed, spots of spit flying out of her mouth.

'I wasn't sure I'd remember your number.'

Suddenly Ruby felt excruciatingly cold. As if his words were turning her to ice, inch by inch. Ten months. It was over ten months since they'd shared a conversation and so much had happened since then. She recalled his unflinching face in court as the jury read out their guilty verdict. Fixed straight ahead. He wouldn't meet her gaze, not once.

'How are you, and Sophie?'

She gritted her teeth. She wanted to say he didn't have the right to ask that question. He'd given up that right when he killed her mother. But her tongue filled her mouth, and she couldn't form the words.

'I wanted to call…' He hesitated. 'Only I heard about Charlotte. It's so awful. I wanted to check you were both okay.'

Okay? The question was incomprehensible. Their mother had been murdered. They'd never be okay. The sheer gall of the man kick-started her voice into action. 'How dare you?'

'Ruby, please. I wanted to caution you to take care. Whoever killed Charlotte, whoever killed your mother… They're still out there.'

'They're not connected.'

'I don't believe that's true. I didn't kill your mother. You must know that now.'

Ruby's head was spinning. She didn't know what to believe. And she couldn't take this. Couldn't listen to another word. 'Don't call me again!'

She cut the call and leaned up against the wall, the cold plaster seeping through her thin shirt. Endless questions ricocheted around her mind. Was he digging for information? Was he trying to take advantage of a toxic situation to profess his innocence? Did he really think they were in danger? But one question overrode all others, reigning supreme. Charlotte was killed almost a week ago. Why call her now?

Chapter 40

Sophie was lifting her shopping out of the car when she noticed the van pull up at the end of the driveway. She sighed, shoulders slumping as she replaced the bags and watched her ex-partner walk down to meet her. It was her day off work. She had a dental appointment in an hour.

'How are you doing?' Greg asked. He was wearing his dusty builder jeans and he'd had his hair cut since she'd last seen him. Short and neat. It suited him.

'Fine.' Sophie glanced at the bags filling her boot and then back at Greg. He lived on the other side of Leicester city, a good twenty miles from Market Deeton. This wasn't an *I was in the area* visit, not that he ever called by without arrangement. He'd made the journey specifically.

'You haven't replied to my messages,' he said.

He was banging on about his request to take the kids early at the weekend again. 'I sent you one yesterday.'

'To say you were thinking about it.'

'The kids love seeing you, Greg, you know that. I just want to make sure they're ready to change their routine.'

His gaze slid to the Subaru, the bricks beneath the axles. 'Is he living here now?'

She was tempted to ask him who he was talking about, but there was no sense in antagonizing him further. 'Ewan stays occasionally. He's leaving his car here while he does it up.'

'You need to be careful. He's getting his feet under the table.'

'It's none of your business.'

He crossed his arms. He seemed shorter, stockier than usual, today. 'It's completely my business. My kids live here.'

'Ewan's great with the kids.'

He huffed and looked away. 'He's not what you think.'

Sophie pressed her teeth together. An argument wouldn't do the kids any good; an argument was what she'd been trying to avoid. But his jealous behaviour was really starting to grate. She took a step closer. 'That's rich coming from the man who walked out on us all.'

'Don't start, Soph. We've talked about this. You know I made a mistake. I'd do anything to turn the clock back.'

'Then let's get down to the real reason you want to spend more time with the kids, shall we? Because you're jealous of Ewan. You weren't bothered before he came on the scene.'

'That's not true.'

'Isn't it? Come on, tell me. What's so wrong with Ewan? What is it I don't know about him?'

He stared at her, his gaze long and steadfast, as if he was harbouring a secret.

She angled her head. 'Well? What is it, Greg?'

'What's going on?'

Neither of them had noticed the Golf pull up and park on the road.

Ewan walked down the driveway, looking from one to another. 'Sophie?'

She tore herself away from Greg. 'We were discussing the kids.'

'I was just leaving,' Greg said. He turned to Sophie. 'I want your decision by tomorrow.'

She watched him stride up the driveway, trying to work out whether he'd been on the brink of saying something, or whether this was yet another ploy to get her to question her relationship choice, and decided it was the latter. If he had something on Ewan, he'd have damn well made sure he'd told her by now.

'What are you doing here?' she said to Ewan. He was dressed in track bottoms and a sweat top. No work uniform.

'Nice welcome. Can I come in?'

He was acting weirdly. Sulking because she'd sent him home last night. Sophie lifted a couple of bags out of the boot. She really had no time for this. 'Grab a bag. I need to get these unpacked, I've got a check-up at the dentist.'

She carried the bags into the house.

'Shouldn't you be at work?' she said, dumping the shopping on the kitchen table.

'I've taken the rest of the day off. I needed to see you.'

Sophie busied herself with putting the shopping away.

'I'm going out of my mind, Soph. I haven't slept, I can't eat. Please tell me everything's going to be okay.' He caught her arm, stopped her in her tracks. 'I can't lose you, Soph. I won't.'

Sophie shrugged him off, placed the cereal packet she was holding on the side and rubbed her hands up and down her face. 'Look, Ewan, there was a lot to process yesterday. I needed time to get my head around it.'

'And now?'

She thought about how she'd fought for him with Greg, how she'd said he was so good with the children. 'I'm not sure. I don't like secrets. I don't want to play games.'

'Neither. Do. I. You know why I didn't tell you about Ruby. I couldn't. I was thinking of you.' He reached out and took her hand, rubbing his thumb up and down her palm, one of his usual soothing, affectionate gestures. 'I'm always thinking of you.'

Sophie broke her hand free from his grasp and collapsed into a chair. She'd barely slept last night, the events of yesterday churning over and over in her mind. Was it possible he was telling the truth? That all he'd done was to protect her? It still left the wound over Ruby's deception weeping, and her reeling at the idea of lying in bed asleep, thinking he was beside her when he was actually out with her big sister. And all on the night of Charlotte Manning's murder.

But if he was telling the truth, it wasn't his fault. None of it was.

That morning, on the way to school, Daisy had asked if he was coming over later – to finish the game on the Xbox he'd been playing with her yesterday. She'd looked at her daughter's face in the rear-view mirror, her innocent brown eyes, eyes that were oblivious to their argument. Ewan had given up a lot for her. She came as a package. She'd made that clear from day one. It was her and the kids, equally. Yet it wasn't just a proposition he'd accepted, it was one he'd embraced. He treated those children like they were his own and the little gifts he bought them, the way he reasoned with them when they argued with tenderness in his voice, the way he rolled around the floor with them in mock combat... How many other men would do the same? Daisy and Alfie were invested in Ewan. He was generous with them. Never complained. Never moaned, even when Daisy was ill and he couldn't stay over because she slept in Sophie's bed for almost a week.

The whole package. That's what she needed to consider here. Not only her needs, but the needs of her family.

'Please, Soph. Let me make it up to you.'

Greg's words filled her mind. 'He's not what you think.' Wasn't that what Ruby had said yesterday? What was it about Ewan that made them wary?

'I'm thinking about letting Greg have the kids early this weekend,' she said, surprising herself with how quickly she'd decided. 'It might do them all good.'

'Sure,' he said. 'If you think that's best.'

–

Three hours later, Sophie watched Ewan pull off the drive in her car, on his way to collect the children from school. He'd wheedled his way into her conscience, persuading her to cancel the dentist and spend the day together because they rarely got time alone. And it had worked. She needed a rest after the events on Sunday, the sleepless night that followed. He'd been gentle with her. Ran her a bath, washed her from head to toe, paying special attention to her bruises. Then they'd made love and he'd been sweet and kind, whispering beautiful sentiments about the depth of his love.

She let the folds of curtain fall against the side of the window and turned back to the room. Why couldn't he always be that tender?

Chapter 41

Ruby stepped out of the house, shook the hands of her clients and thanked them for their time.

She bade them farewell and made her way back to her car. Monday had passed in a whirlwind of telephone calls, enquiries and appointments. Not helped by Mark leaving suddenly that morning with a family emergency, and not returning until the afternoon, leaving her, Kat and Sara to cover everything.

She crossed the road and climbed into her car. All day she'd smarted over the phone call from Colin. How dare he? Did he really think she'd chat away normally, as if he was an old friend? He clearly thought Charlotte Manning's murder exonerated him in some way. But did it? And asking her and Sophie to be careful. What did he mean by that?

Ruby scratched the back of her neck irritably and pushed the call aside. It was almost 6:30 p.m., her back and her feet were throbbing, and she still needed to go to the police station and correct her account.

Had Kat spoken with Graham? They'd been out on separate appointments for the latter part of the afternoon and she hadn't called. Ruby dialled Kat's number, tapping her foot as the phone rang out.

'Hey,' Kat said. She sounded as if she'd been running.

'Hi. I'm on my way to the police station. I wondered if you'd spoken with Graham.'

'Only just now. He's been in court all day. He said they'd be unlikely to arrest you with perverting the course of justice. You haven't deliberately lied to assist an offender, as such, you've kept unimportant stuff back. The worst-case scenario is they might look at you for wasting police time. Doesn't necessarily mean they'll take any action. If they do, it would only be a fine.'

Ruby's shoulders relaxed. 'Okay, thanks.'

'He did say you were doing the right thing by speaking up. Better late than never.' She was trying to sound upbeat, but there was a distinct rasp to her voice.

'Thanks. Did you manage to speak to Sophie?'

'I texted her this morning. She hasn't responded. I'll try calling her this evening.' Kat coughed uncomfortably. 'There's something else I need to tell you.'

'What?'

'Something Graham mentioned when I was telling him the reason for you changing your account—'

'You didn't tell him about Ewan and me? Kat!'

'I had to. You know what bloody lawyers are like. Have to know all the facts before they'll give an opinion. Don't worry, he won't tell anyone, but he did say something interesting. That he wasn't surprised.'

'What? Why?'

'He's seen Ewan out with other women.'

'What do you mean?'

'Graham was in The Crown, a month ago, having a drink with a colleague after work, and Ewan was in there with a dark-haired woman, tucked away in the snug at the back. He only saw them because they were having some work done in the pub and he had to walk right around the bar to go to the toilet.'

'It could have been a work mate or a friend.'

'I said that. He said it didn't look like a friend. "Draped all over her" was the phrase he used.'

'Maybe he was comforting her.'

Kat was quiet a second. 'It's not the first time. He also saw him in Costa in Leicester city centre with a different woman a few months back.'

This was worse than Ruby could have imagined. 'Why didn't he say anything?'

'Oh, you know Graham. Doesn't like to get involved in other people's business, he has enough drama at work. He didn't even tell me, for Christ's sake, and he knows how close I am to you and Soph.'

–

'Let me get this straight,' TDC Foster said. The light bounced off his pale forehead. 'You're now saying you did meet someone else while walking home through town on the evening of Tuesday the 18th of September.'

'Yes.' Ruby curled her fingers into tight fists beneath the table. Once again, she'd asked at the front desk for Hitesh. Once again, she'd been told he was otherwise engaged, and she got Foster. Only today, Foster was in a sombre mood.

'And you didn't tell me this in your original account because…'

'I spoke to the guy I was with that night. He didn't think it was relevant.'

'Right. Despite being specifically asked.' He looked older today, closer to thirty. He shuffled the papers in front of him – her original account, written out carefully with dates and times in his spidery scrawl. 'And you and Mr Ewan Wilson were the couple in West Way,' he said.

'Yes.' Ruby fisted her hands tighter under the table, her nails digging into the flesh. She wanted to slide off the chair and hide under the table. She bet her life Ewan hadn't felt this bad when he was in the chair. He'd only given one account, delivering all the information in one shot, which meant he could give some pathetic excuse like, 'Forgive me for not coming forward sooner, I've been busy at work, I didn't see the appeal. I do apologise.' She could almost imagine him parting his lips, widening his eyes sweetly as he spoke. All the time digging a hole and pushing her further and further into the sludge at the bottom. 'I'm sorry,' she said. It was a feeble attempt at an apology, she knew that. 'Ewan's my sister's boyfriend. We were… messing about.' She squirmed again. Her neck felt warm and clammy. 'We didn't want my sister upset. I do hope I didn't waste anyone's time.'

He raised his brow. His jaw sagged. Instead of answering, he scratched the last of her answer down. 'What time did you get home?' he asked.

'Pardon?'

'What time did you arrive back at your house?' He took his time rephrasing the sentence, enunciating the syllables.

'Around 9:20. Like I said in my last account.'

'Ah, yes. The one that isn't now accurate.'

Ruby swallowed and said nothing.

'And is there anyone who can confirm the time?'

'No, I live alone.'

'Did you make any calls from your mobile?'

'No, it was late, I didn't make any calls.' She stared across at him. 'Why do I need to confirm where I was?'

'This is a murder investigation. You weren't far from the scene of the crime.' He met her gaze. 'I should tell you a discrepancy was picked up between your account and Mr Wilson's and a detective went out to your home this afternoon. He'll have left a card.'

Ruby winced. She should have come earlier. 'I was at work.'

He gathered up the papers. 'Well, if there's nothing else…'

'I am sorry, you know.'

She expected him to leave the room, terminate the discussion. Instead, he clasped his hands together and leaned them on the table. 'This is a serious crime. The last thing we need is people being untruthful. I'd have thought you, if anyone, would understand that.'

Suddenly she felt as small as the fleck of dust on his cuff.

The conversation with Kat about wasting police time pressed on her. 'Will I be in any trouble?' she asked.

The chair scraped the floor as Foster stood. 'That's not for me to decide. You'll be hearing from us.'

—

The light was starting to fade as Ruby walked out of the police station. She'd tried to ask Foster for an update on the murder inquiry before she left, but once more, he'd said there was nothing he could tell her. According to the news, they still hadn't made an arrest and the incident continued to shake her. If Charlotte Manning had been killed on any other evening, it wouldn't have bothered her so much, but she couldn't deny the timing suggested a link to her family, her mum…

The phone call from Colin didn't help. She'd considered mentioning it to Foster, but somehow it didn't feel relevant. It wasn't as if Colin had given her anything new. He'd just continued to profess his innocence. To be expected in the circumstances.

Her phone vibrated against her thigh. A text from Tom flashed up.

> Let me know when you're free this week. Need to talk.

She was about to switch it off when the sunflower flashed up on the screen: Isla.

> I'm away in London with work this week. I'll give you a call when I get back. Not sure how much I can help you though.

Ruby's breath hitched. Central London was only an hour or so away on the train from Market Deeton. Perhaps she should travel down there. Over the telephone, people could tell all sorts of lies. Face to face their body language often betrayed them. She typed out a reply.

> I'm in London tomorrow. Any chance we could meet for a coffee somewhere near St Pancras? I wouldn't keep you too long.

She was pressing send when another idea sprang to mind. Sophie hadn't responded to Kat's message, but she couldn't avoid the mums on the school run. She checked her watch. She was due to meet Lewis in The Prince at eight. She quickly tapped out a text to him – *Running late, can we meet at nine?* There was someone else she needed to see first.

Chapter 42

Farmfield Lodge was an estate of new-builds with mock-Tudor frontages, barely a couple of years old and situated behind the sports field of Welton Primary School. Ruby parked outside a detached house in the corner, with a block-paved garden and a people carrier on the driveway. A hanging basket filled with red geraniums, looking well past their best, hung beside the front door.

It was almost 7:30 p.m. and the aroma of cooked food – a pie or a stew, something hearty – crept out to meet her, reminding Ruby she'd barely eaten apart from a sandwich she'd picked up from the petrol station in between her afternoon appointments.

The door was answered by a short woman with a curly bob and a pretty face. An oversized linen shirt with the sleeves rolled up and a pair of loose jeans hung off her frame.

'Hi, Louise. You've lost weight again.'

Sophie's friend returned Ruby's smile, exposing deep dimples in both cheeks. She peered around her, almost as if she was expecting someone else. 'Is everything all right?' she said to Ruby. 'Is Sophie okay?'

Ruby surveyed Sophie's closest friend. They'd met at antenatal classes when they'd been expecting their first children and their babies, born within a month of each other, socialised at the same mums and tots' classes, the same swim classes and the same dance classes when they were older. Now attending the same school, Daisy and Chloe were firm friends. Louise was also on the PTA. She'd been out with Sophie on the night she met Ewan, and she'd been a great support to her sister, babysitting and doing the school run during the court case. If there was anyone outside the family who knew Sophie well, it was Louise.

Ruby plastered her brightest smile on her face. 'Yes. I wondered if you had time for a quick chat?'

'Oh.' Louise looked back into the house.

The herby smell of the food was stronger now, making Ruby's mouth water. 'If you're having dinner, I can come back...'

'No, no. I've just got the kids off to sleep, haven't put ours out yet. Come on in.' She pulled the door back and Ruby stepped inside. 'Kev's watching the rugby,' Louise added, indicating for her to follow her down the hallway.

Ruby slipped off her shoes and placed them beside an over-full shoe rack.

'Australia versus England,' Sophie added. 'He won't thank me for dishing up before half-time.'

Ruby laughed. As they passed the front room, she put her head around the door frame and called 'Hi!' to Kev – a thirty-something, slender civil servant with a receding widow's peak and thick-rimmed glasses. He waved back at her, unspeaking. She'd always liked Louise and Kev. They were a strong kind family and they'd been a great support to Sophie after Greg left.

The kitchen was situated at the back of the house, a large room filled with fitted cream cupboards and a long pine table in the middle, which was littered with children's comics, drawings and crayons. Louise pushed aside a couple of sheets of paper with lines of the alphabet written in broken letters. 'Chloe's been practising her handwriting,' she said, indicating for Ruby to sit.

Ruby smiled, her gaze moving to the fridge. To the splodgy kids' paintings, the uneven writing, the drawings – all over-lapping each other and secured with various bright-coloured alphabet fridge magnets. Louise's two girls were in the same school years as Sophie's children. She often saw her when she was doing the school run for her sister and Louise could always be relied upon to show her where the homework pile was and tell her if there was anything the kids needed for the next day. At the top of the artwork was a photo curled at the edges of two girls, sitting on space hoppers in the garden. Ruby pointed to it. 'Goodness, Louise, they're growing up fast.'

'They are. I don't know where the weeks and months go.' She moved a pan off the heat and placed it at the side of the cooker. 'Can I get you a tea, or a coffee?'

'No, thank you. I'm fine.' Ruby slid into a chair. Had Sophie told Louise about their argument? If she had, she was hiding it well. 'I'm sorry to interrupt your evening.'

'Don't be silly, it's good to see you. What did you want to talk about?'

'It's a bit awkward really. I wanted to ask you about Sophie. How you think she is doing after the trial and everything.' What she actually wanted to ask was whether Louise had noticed any bruises, or any unusual behaviour, or whether she knew about Sophie's drugs, but she needed to take it slow. She was fishing, still unsure what was really going on herself. The last thing she wanted to do was to put ideas into her head. 'We've had a bit of a fall out, you see. I'm not sure if she's said anything to you.'

Louise pulled down the corners of her mouth. 'No, she hasn't. But then I haven't seen much of her these last couple of weeks.'

'How do you mean?'

Louise pulled out a chair and eased into it. 'I've only seen her briefly on the school run, she's always in such a rush. I expect she's been busy with work and the children.'

Her comment sounded amiss. Whenever she was stuck for childcare after their mother died, Sophie relied on Ewan, Ruby or Louise. Louise had helped out loads during the trial and even attended the memorial service the other day, although she hadn't come back to the house. 'I thought you two were close.'

'We are. Sometimes life gets in the way. It's been ages since we caught up for coffee.'

'What about before the trial?'

'It's difficult to say. I mean, Sophie hasn't been herself for some time.' She looked up at Ruby. 'You've all been through so much, it's hardly surprising.'

Ruby recalled Lewis's comment about her taking Valium and her stomach clenched. 'How do you mean, she hasn't been herself?'

'She's… detached, I suppose.'

'She talks to you though, doesn't she?'

'We used to talk a lot. These days, it's more passing conversation about the kids, but that's fine. I know she has a lot on.' Louise hesitated a moment. 'She hasn't been returning my calls this week. I assumed it was because of the news. You know, with Charlotte's body being found. She wasn't herself the other morning at the school when we all found out.'

'What about Ewan? Do you see much of him?'

'No. I've seen him a few times, when he's picked up the kids. They're quite a private couple, aren't they?'

The description struck Ruby as strange. When Greg was around, the two families had socialised together, enjoying BBQs in the garden, dinner at each other's houses after the first children were born. Louise and Kev continued this with Sophie after Greg had left. Yet now she was with Ewan their gatherings had petered out. What was it about Ewan and other people? He seemed to have a knack of pushing them all away.

Kev appeared at the doorway. '12–7 to England at half time,' he said. 'It's edge-of-your-seat stuff.'

Louise laughed and turned back to Ruby. 'You're welcome to join us for dinner, if you like?'

Ruby stood, not wishing to intrude into their evening further. 'No, thanks. I'll leave you to it.'

Kev retreated to the front room.

'I don't blame you. It looks like we'll be eating in front of the telly anyway!'

Louise followed Ruby into the hallway and waited for her to pull on her shoes.

'Do you mind if we keep this visit to ourselves?' Ruby said. 'I'm probably worrying for nothing. Don't want Sophie to think I'm being overprotective.'

Louise encased her in a bear hug. 'Of course. It's good to see she has her big sister looking out for her. I hope you sort out your differences.'

Ruby hoped so too, but she wasn't sure Ewan was going to let that happen any time soon.

Chapter 43

Ruby squeezed her Fiesta into a space on High Street and stared out at the empty pavements, lit in puddles of light from the intermittent streetlamps. A scene not dissimilar to last Tuesday, when she'd walked home through town under the cover of darkness, oblivious to the string of events about to unfold. Her mobile pinged as she cut the engine.

Another message from Isla. *I'll meet you at St Elms Café behind King's Cross station at 3 p.m. tomorrow.*

Finally, something positive. Whatever it was, Ruby was determined to break the mystery surrounding Ewan. She messaged back, *Thank you. See you there.*

She'd have to make up some excuse for work – a fake bug or something. There was no way she was going to miss this chance.

She dialled Kat.

Kat picked up almost immediately. 'Hey, I was about to ring you. How did it go at the police station?'

Ruby recalled Foster's stern face. 'Okay, all things considered. Did you manage to get hold of Sophie?'

'I called, she didn't answer. I've left a voicemail, asking her to ring me.'

Ruby's heart sank. Sophie didn't seem to be returning any of her friends' calls. In fact, the only person Sophie was close to at present was Ewan. 'I've just been to see Louise,' she said.

'She's looking amazing these days,' Kat gushed. 'I need to go on her diet. What did she say?'

'Not much. She and Soph have only spoken in passing since the trial.' She repeated Louise's comments about Ewan.

'I told you he was weird.'

'Hmm. I'm not sure what to think. Anyway, I need you to do something for me. Ewan's sister's been in touch. She's in London tomorrow, something to do with work, and I've persuaded her to meet me.'

'That'll be an interesting conversation.'

'I think so. I need to talk to someone, Kat. I'm going out of my bloody mind here, I'm so worried for Soph.'

'I bet. Look, don't worry. I'll square it with Mark.'

'Thanks. Is he okay?' It was so unlike her boss to leave so suddenly earlier. He practically lived at Galanti's.

'He came back late this afternoon, said it was all sorted. I doubt we'll hear any more, you know how secretive he is about his personal life.'

Ruby did. Kat had told her he'd gone through a messy divorce and had a couple of young children, the only details she'd managed to glean. But he never spoke about them and she wasn't even sure if he still saw them. Once again, she was reminded of her mother's disapproving comments. What was it that made him so mysterious?

'Anyway, it seems sorted now. I'll tell him you've got a migraine tomorrow.'

'Thanks. I owe you.'

'You do! Listen, be careful, won't you, and stay safe? I hope the outcome's positive.'

They said their goodbyes and hung up. Ruby slipped her mobile into her pocket and climbed out of her car. High Street was empty. She peered into the shopfronts, her heels tapping the paving as she walked towards the pub. The wind had picked up. She pulled her jacket across her chest, hitched her bag further up her shoulder.

Ruby was almost at the pub when a click behind her made her jump. She paused and turned. The pavement was empty.

The hairs on the back of her neck upended. She looked up and down the street, unable to shake off the feeling that someone was close by. She could almost feel the heat of their gaze, watching her. She quickened her step, relief flooding her when she entered the pub.

The Prince was a classy outfit with a round bar, lined with stools, and light oak flooring. Apart from a few couples sitting in the far corner and some locals huddled around the bar, it was quiet that evening. The sweet smell of alcohol hung in the air. She recognised Michael Bublé's voice playing out softly in the background.

Lewis was sitting at the bar, nursing the end of a pint of lager while chatting to a barman. He turned as she entered, waved her over and introduced her to the man beside him. 'Steve's recently moved into the area,' he said. 'Used to do a bit of amateur dramatics.'

'Only as an extra.' Steve, the barman, was a young scrawny chap in skinny jeans and a fitted T-shirt. He rubbed the back of his head. 'More interested in the set to be honest.'

'Everything counts,' Lewis said. 'He'd be good for the group, wouldn't he, Rubes? We could do with more set help.'

Ruby nodded and ordered a lemon and lime. Lewis opted for another lager.

'Not on the hard stuff?' Lewis said to Ruby.

'I'm driving. So, what are you doing with your week off, apart from home stuff?'

'Keeping up with the cycling.' He patted his stomach. 'This lean machine doesn't keep itself.'

Ruby snorted. Lewis was tall and thick-set. He could never be described as lean.

He picked up their drinks with a promise to ring Steve about the arts group, and they moved over to a table beside the window.

'Got your text,' Lewis said. 'You are working late tonight.'

'It wasn't all work.'

He grimaced as she told him about the visit to the police station.

'You okay?' he asked when she'd finished. 'You seem tense.'

'I don't know. I've just had one of those funny moments. You know, when you feel like someone's watching you and turn around and no one's there?'

He stretched back his brows.

'I'm serious! I've felt it a few times recently.' She told him about the face at her window, the feeling someone had been in her house, the door handle sitting awry, and cringed. It all sounded so trivial when she spoke the words aloud.

Lewis's smile fell. 'And this has all happened since last Tuesday?'

She nodded. 'The night Charlotte was killed.'

'You need to speak to someone.'

'Oh, right. I have gone mad then!'

'I meant the police.'

'And tell them what? Someone fiddled with my door handle. I saw a shadow at the window. Oh, come on, Lewis. They already think I'm crazy because I gave them half an account.'

He stiffened. 'I'm not joking, Rubes.'

'It's probably me. I've been worn out this week and with all the worry over Sophie...' She rubbed the heels of her hands into her eyes, though she couldn't erase the acidic taste sitting at the back of her mouth. 'Colin called me today.'

'Colin Halliday? How?'

'I expect they have phones in prisons. I bet it was a dodgy phone though, I can't imagine the officers letting him call me. The daughter of his victim.'

Lewis stared at her, his mouth agape. 'What did he say?'

'He'd heard about Charlotte's murder. Asked how Sophie and I were. Professed his innocence, once again. Told us to be careful.'

'He's got a nerve.'

'I thought so. I cut him off.'

'Good on you.'

Ruby nodded. It was the right thing to do. Though something about the phone call bothered her. 'Why would he call now?' she said.

'He's in prison. He's probably only just heard about Charlotte. He'll be planning his appeal. Trying to get people on side.'

She shuddered and took a sip of her drink. 'I went to see Louise this evening,' she said. 'She's one of Sophie's chums, they used to be close, yet she's barely heard from Sophie since the trial.'

'Sounds a bit odd.'

'That's what I thought.' She shared the text from Isla.

Lewis sat forward. 'You sure you want to meet her? Alone?'

'Definitely. Something about Ewan isn't right. Maybe there's something in his past... I don't know. It can't make the situation any worse, can it?' She took a sip of her drink. The bubbles fizzed on her tongue.

'I'll come to London with you.'

'No, you don't need to.'

'I don't need to, I want to. And from what you're saying, the company would do you no harm at the moment.'

'I don't need a minder.' The words sounded more defiant than she felt.

'Good, 'cos I'd make a shit bodyguard. Couldn't be doing with all that pumping iron.' He laughed. 'Anyway, I've given myself this week off, remember? I don't suppose you'll be able to make my kitchen appointment tomorrow now and there's only so much cycling I can do.'

Ruby looked out of the window. A bat fluttered by. A car cruised up the street.

'So, what do you think?' Lewis pressed.

Ruby switched back to him, realising he'd continued talking, and she'd tuned out.

'About what?'

'About me coming to London with you? To keep you company.'

'I don't know... I doubt Isla will speak to me if you're there.'

'I wouldn't come to meet Isla. I'd come for the journey. A bit of moral support. Save me twiddling my thumbs in Simon's flat.'

She wanted to say she didn't need moral support and was quite capable of doing this alone, but his jaw was set. He wanted to do this; he wanted to help. It wasn't such a bad idea. He knew London a damn sight better than she did, he probably even knew the café, and having someone with her would crush some of the paranoia.

'Okay. Just promise to keep your distance when Ewan's sister arrives. I don't want anything scaring her away.'

Her attention was caught by the door flapping back on its hinges. Ruby was surprised to see Becky enter. She was dressed in tight jeans and boots, accentuating her long legs. Her hair was pinned back off her face in that severe style she liked to wear and her face made up as if she was ready for a night on the town. She smiled as she approached.

'There you are!' she said. 'Didn't think I was going to make it. I've had a crazy evening.'

Ruby gave a polite smile and passed Lewis a quizzical look.

'What are you drinking?' she said to Ruby. 'I'm desperate for wine.'

Ruby placed her hand over the top of her glass. 'I'm fine, really.' She waited for Becky to take Lewis's order and walk over to the bar before she rounded on him. 'What's she doing here?'

He scrunched his face. 'I saw her earlier. She said she was at a loose end tonight and I mentioned we were meeting. She seemed keen to join us.'

'You could have told me. We were supposed to be talking about Sophie.'

'And we have. Come on, Rubes. I didn't think you'd mind. You should give her a chance, you know. She really likes you.'

But there was too much rolling around Ruby's mind for her to make conversation with an acquaintance right now. 'Don't say anything to her about Sophie, or London tomorrow. I'm meant to be at work. The fewer people that know about this, the better.'

Chapter 44

I sit on the edge of the bed, trepidation beating a drum inside me as I listen to the phone ring out.

The room is deliciously shaded, a trickle of light seeping in from the streetlamp outside. That is to be expected. It's 2:30 a.m., after all.

It takes you a while to answer and when you do, your voice is full of sleep. And something else: confusion. My number is withheld. You've no idea who is calling.

'Who is this?' you ask.

I listen to your voice echo in the darkness.

'Is it you, Soph?'

I chuckle to myself. My breaths are thick and strong. I couldn't be further from Sophie if I tried.

'Speak to me! Just say anything. A single word.'

You're pleading now. I inhale deeply. You need me. You need me more than I need you. You just don't realise it yet.

'Please. You're scaring me.'

I disconnect. I'm not ready to reveal any more. Not yet.

Chapter 45

Platform one was icy cold. Ruby buttoned her coat up to her chin. Puffballs of white danced out of her mouth and dispersed into the air as they waited for the train and she told Lewis about her night caller.

Lewis's face hardened. 'I don't like this,' he said.

Ruby ignored him. 'I went by the school first thing this morning.'

'You should have phoned me. I'd have taken you.'

She'd left The Prince as soon as she politely could yesterday evening and Lewis had insisted on walking her back to her car. Becky trailing at his heel like a puppy. Then he'd texted her several times after she arrived home to check she was okay. He'd also driven her to the station that morning.

'It was early.'

'You need to be more careful.'

She was beginning to wish she hadn't told him about the second phone call. This new overprotective stance didn't suit him at all.

'So, was Sophie there?'

She glanced behind. A man sat on the bench reading a newspaper. A woman in a suit was checking her mobile – other passengers waiting to board the incoming train. She lowered her voice. 'Sophie dropped off the kids as normal.' It was strange, watching her sister from afar. Clandestine. She suppressed a shudder. 'She looked fine.'

'Doesn't sound like she's your night caller then. And why would she withhold her number anyway, she'd want you to know it was her.'

'I don't know. Maybe if she'd used a different phone.' All night, the suggestion of Sophie, potentially in trouble or in danger, had bounced around her head like a string of stray bullets. She'd contemplated driving over there, although the caller hadn't given her any reason to suggest they were Sophie, and her sister certainly wouldn't welcome the intrusion – especially with the distance between them. 'I felt bloody ridiculous to be honest. Stalking my own sister.'

'It can't be a coincidence,' he said. 'Two calls, two nights in a row. You don't think it's Colin, do you?'

Ruby started. 'No. Why would he?'

'He called you yesterday.'

'Yeah, and he spoke. Whatever Colin is, whatever he's done, I don't think he'd try to frighten me.' She paused. 'You don't think it's Ewan, do you? Trying to intimidate me?'

'I can't see what he's got to gain. He's already put space between you and Sophie.'

'Perhaps his sister's been in touch and told him she's meeting me.'

'Hmm. Sounds unlikely from what you've told me about her. Anyway, I doubt he'd think a passive-aggressive phone call would stop you.'

'I can't think who else it might be.' The only other person was Bridget. Her aunt had been on her way out when she'd called earlier and didn't have time to talk. But she sounded okay and gave no indication it was her.

Lewis looked troubled. 'Why don't you contact the police? They might be able to trace the owner of the phone. You could tell them about the other stuff too.'

'I'll think about it.' A couple of phone calls sounded like a minor issue, especially when they were dealing with a murder inquiry. The caller hadn't made any threats. It could even be a mistake. And as for the other stuff, it was all so superficial. A feeling, a shadow. They'd probably think she'd lost it. She was beginning to wonder herself.

A chilling wind whistled along the platform as the train pulled into Market Deeton station. It was 10:20 a.m. The morning rush was well and truly over, the carriages half empty. Memories of her last trip to London, a meeting with one of their regular corporate clients, came to mind. Travelling during rush hour for an early appointment, being squashed against the door for the hour or so's trip. At least they wouldn't have to stand today.

They boarded the train and wandered through the carriages, looking for a seat where Lewis could stretch out his long legs. They passed a man in a suit who didn't look up from his laptop. A couple of middle-aged women engrossed in their chatter. Eventually, they found a quiet table in the corner and Lewis slipped into a seat opposite her.

They were wrestling off their jackets when a sleeping toddler with pink cheeks draped across the lap of a woman diagonally opposite caught Ruby's eye. The child plucked a heartstring. Daisy was always falling asleep on buses, cars and trains at that tender age. Ruby placed her bag at her feet. Daisy and Alfie would be running around the playground on their morning break now. It had only been a few days since she'd seen them, but the absence of their quirky little faces and funny stories pained her. The world was so different to the young. So uncomplicated.

Lewis pulled a pair of earphones out of his pocket and connected them to his phone as the train pulled out of the station.

Ruby smiled to herself. He'd read her mood, could tell she wasn't up for chit chat and she couldn't be more grateful. 'What's on the playlist?' she asked.

'Green Day, The Killers. Think there's a bit of vintage INXS on there too.' He offered her an earphone. 'Happy to move over there if you want to share.'

'No, thanks.'

She watched him insert the earpieces, lean back and close his eyes. A tinny musical beat leaked out.

The sleeping child brought another memory to the fore. Of her and Sophie throwing a sheet over their mother's dining-room table, pretending they were staying in a tent on holiday in Norfolk. Gathering pots and pans from the kitchen to cook. Bringing buckets and spades down from their bedrooms and using the front-room rug as a make-believe beach. Eventually there was so much stuff beneath the table, there was barely any room for them to sit.

She smiled. It was always Norfolk. Money was tight when they were young and every year their mother and Bridget pooled resources and rented a caravan during the first two weeks of the summer holidays. 'It's important to get away and give yourself a break,' Bridget used to say.

Ruby could almost taste the salty sea air, hear the gulls gliding overhead amidst a cloudless sky, the tide withdrawing as they clambered about the beach, furiously digging channels in the sand.

Brakes squeaked as they jolted to a stop at the next station. A man in a plaid shirt slung a rucksack over his back, narrowly missing Ruby, as he alighted. She pulled her phone out of her bag. No new messages. Kat would have gone through her diary at work by now and either taken over or rescheduled her appointments. She was such a good friend; she needed to find a way to thank her. She made a mental note to arrange to take her out for dinner at the weekend.

The train pulled off again. Ruby glanced back at her phone and switched to Google, searching Market Deeton news. She was scrolling through *Deeton Mail* posts when a familiar face graced the screen. She clicked on the article. His hair was thinner and tiny lines of grey streaked the chestnut sides, but she was in no doubt it was Charlotte Manning's father. He'd given a live interview. She scrabbled about in her bag for her earphones and plugged them in.

The footage was short, less than thirty seconds. Nigel Manning's sunken cheeks were pale, as if he hadn't slept in a week. A layer of grey stubble covered his chin. He talked about his daughter's alternative lifestyle, mentioned the difficulties they'd faced after losing her mother so young. How much he loved her and had devoted the last year to finding her. A tear rolled down his cheek when he spoke of the moment he was told of her death.

'Twenty-one stab wounds,' he said. Twenty-one stab wounds. Somebody must have noticed something – perhaps a loved one had returned with blood stains or had been displaying unusual behaviour. He implored any witnesses to contact the police, for anyone with information or who might have seen anything, however insignificant, to come forward, then swiped the tear from his cheek.

The footage ended.

It was a powerful appeal: emotional and raw. As Ruby played it through again, she felt the sting of his pain, the hollow void in his life. All those years he'd painstakingly spent helping his daughter, trying to get her life back in order, now slipping through his fingers like sand.

Darkness surrounded them as they entered a tunnel. Ruby sat back, staring into space. Sophie had mentioned something about Ewan feeling down after Charlotte's murder. Why? He claimed he'd never met Charlotte…

'Penny for them?' They'd emerged from the tunnel. Lewis had plucked an earphone from his ear and was staring straight at her.

She handed over her phone and Lewis played the footage. His face turned sad as he watched it.

'Poor bugger,' he said when it finished. He handed the phone back.

'I can't help wondering if there's some connection, you know,' she said. 'Between Charlotte and my mum.'

'You heard the police. They're treating the incidents separately.'

'What if they're wrong?'

Lewis shrugged.

Ruby pushed the thoughts aside. For the next hour, she looked out of the window and forced herself to watch the world trundling by. Flashbacks of her mum and her sister rushing in and out of her mind. Them both clapping wildly at her graduation ceremony. Of them all at the hospital together for her niece's birth. Of the surprise party they'd thrown for her mother's fortieth. Her family. Where had it all gone wrong?

Eventually, open fields gave way to buildings and warehouses. A voice filled the train, announcing St Pancras as their next stop. It was almost eleven thirty. They were early, but no matter. Plenty of time to find the café and prepare herself.

Chapter 46

St Elms tea shop was a quaint affair, sandwiched between a boutique and a chemist, with lace curtains edging the front window and less than a dozen tables inside covered in pink and white gingham tablecloths. A glass counter at the back of the café showed off flamboyantly decorated three-tiered cakes.

The clock on the wall read a few minutes to three. Lewis had helped Ruby find the place and then gone off shopping and, now she was alone, her pulse was accelerating at a rate of knots. Over the last couple of days, she'd placed so much emphasis on speaking with Ewan's sister that her nerves were starting to crystallise into a hard lump in her chest.

From her table beside the window, she watched the street outside. Burlington Row was a busy street, with a constant stream of traffic and pedestrians passing. She swallowed the last dregs of coffee in her mug. The café had filled over the last half an hour. A man with dreadlocks sat at the counter, reading on his phone. A woman and two small children occupied a table in the centre. A businessman in an open-necked shirt stared at the screen of a laptop at the table beside her.

Another glance at the clock. It was now three. Ruby chewed at the side of her thumbnail. The traffic outside was at a stand-still. A taxi driver got out of his cab and moved to talk to the car behind. No sooner did he reach the driver than the line of cars in front moved. Ruby watched him run back to his cab and climb in. Horns blasted down the road. She was concentrating so hard on what was going on in the street, she almost missed the petite young woman with cropped dark hair and spectacles push open the door.

Their eyes met briefly. She was young and pretty and dressed in a navy trouser suit – not at all how Ruby had imagined Ewan's sister. But she caught Ruby's gaze and instantly approached her table.

'Hello, Ruby,' she said warily.

She's looked me up online, Ruby thought. *Recognised me from one of the many photos on Facebook or Instagram.*

Ruby stood and shook her hand. 'You must be Isla. Thank you for coming.'

They shuffled into chairs facing each other.

'Can I get you a drink?' Ruby said.

'Thank you. Flat white, no sugar.' She spoke with a thick Glaswegian accent, much stronger than Ewan's, and there was a slight hiss when she used an 's'.

Ruby nodded and moved to the counter, ordering herself another latte at the same time. When she returned to the table, the young woman was checking her phone.

Isla was olive-skinned and well-groomed. Large owl-like eyes glanced up from her phone as Ruby sat.

'You don't look like your brother,' Ruby said.

'He's only my half-brother. I'm from my mother's second marriage. There are nine years between us.'

'I hadn't realised. You share the same name.'

'He was given my late father's surname by judge's consent when Mum married Dad and they moved to Glasgow.' That explained the difference in accent.

'I see. What brings you to London?' Ruby asked, trying to keep the conversation light.

'I've been on a training course with work. They're updating their software.'

She didn't say what her work was, but her attire indicated something corporate. Yet another thing she didn't have in common with her brother.

'You said your sister is dating Ewan.'

A slim woman with blue hair tied into teddy bear ears and a nose ring arrived with their coffees. Ruby thanked her and waited until she'd retreated to the counter before she answered. 'Yes, she's been seeing him for about a year.'

'And where's this?' Isla asked.

Ruby balked. They might have been estranged, but it hadn't crossed her mind that Ewan's sister wouldn't even know where he was living. 'Market Deeton, Leicestershire.'

'Ah.' She leaned forward, taking her time to stir her coffee, but didn't expand.

'He told Sophie, my sister, he came down from Glasgow in search of work.'

'He would say that, wouldn't he?'

Ruby wasn't sure how to answer. She decided to ignore the question. 'And… well, we know so little of his background. I was wondering if you—'

'Has something happened?'

'Not exactly. It's just—'

'What?' The interruption was harsh, direct.

The words clawed at Ruby. She needed to be careful. Ewan's argument with his sister could be perfectly normal, his intentions to Sophie honourable, if a little controlling. She could have made a mistake. 'Until I contacted you, I hadn't realised you weren't speaking,' she said.

Isla snorted. 'I'm not surprised. He usually tells people he has no family. That we are all dead.'

We. The word sent a shiver down Ruby's spine. 'We' implied numbers. Ewan had never mentioned anyone other than her. 'Why would he say that?'

'It's a long story.'

'I'd like to hear it.'

Isla studied her nails. They were short and neat and unpainted. 'I don't want to talk about it.'

'Please.' Ruby grappled to find the right words. 'I'm concerned for my sister. We lost our mother suddenly last year.' She cleared her throat. Now it was she who didn't want to share the finer details. 'She's fragile.'

Another silence. A muscle flexed in Isla's jaw. 'If she's fragile, then she needs to get away from my brother.' The accent grew stronger as she became agitated.

Ruby felt the saliva in her mouth evaporate. 'What do you mean?'

'I mean he's bad news.'

The door of the café flapped open and an Asian woman entered, bringing with her a rush of cool air.

Isla watched her take a seat at the table beside them. She gazed at the untouched coffee, shifted uncomfortably in her chair and glanced back at the door. 'This is a mistake. I shouldn't have come.'

'What?' Ruby shot forward. 'No, please don't go.'

'I don't think I'm the right person to help you.'

'Tell me why you aren't in contact any more.'

Another shifty look at the door. What was she afraid of?

'Please! I don't want to lose my sister too,' Ruby pressed.

A beat passed. Isla surveyed her a second and Ruby wasn't sure if it was her pleading or the desperation in her voice, but the woman's face softened. 'You need to tell your sister. He's one of the bad guys. I'm surprised she hasn't found that out already.'

Frustration was gnawing at Ruby now. 'What do you mean?'

'He's not nice to women. I don't know where he gets it from, our parents were never like him – God rest their souls. He's got a nasty streak, that one.'

'Has he hurt someone?'

'I shouldn't be talking about this.'

'Can you at least tell me why you are estranged?'

Isla's face slackened. 'Loads of reasons. I mean, this sounds awful, but I don't think I ever liked him as such. Yeah, he's charming, but he's also got a temper and he can be cruel.'

She recalled the argument with Sophie on Sunday, the way he'd turned the tables on her. She hadn't stood a chance. The welt on Sophie's wrist came to mind. 'Has he hurt anyone?' Ruby repeated.

'Not as far as I know. Look, it's not what you think. He's dangerous and manipulative. You should really be talking to Heather.'

'Heather?'

'Ewan's wife.'

Wife? Ruby felt blindsided. He'd never said he'd been married.

'Ay, I see he's not mentioned her either. I'm not surprised. I can't believe he left those wee ones though. They're such lovely kids.'

Wee ones. This was worse than she'd thought. 'Please. You need to explain to me what you mean.'

'I don't want to get involved.'

'Just tell me, what did you mean by dangerous and manipulative?'

Isla shook her head. 'I can't do this.'

'What about Heather? Maybe she…'

Her face froze. 'The last thing she needs is him poking his nose back in. She's worked hard to rebuild her life with those children.'

Ruby was taken aback. She didn't know what to say.

'Look, Ewan has a wandering eye. He always had, ever since he was young. He builds a relationship with someone, then delights in breaking them down, peeling away the layers. Removing every friend, every family member, anyone close. He did it with Maggie, then dropped her like a stone when he met Heather. He plays mind games, cuts them away until they have nothing apart from him. Heather even gave up her job in the end. I was at uni for most of the time they were together. I didn't know Heather until afterwards, but I'm told she was a confident woman, worked at the tax office, had her own car, her own place when they got together. Worshipped the ground he walked on. When he left, she had nothing apart from the kids and the roof over their heads.'

Ruby pictured Sophie, her beautiful vulnerable sister and her heart shrank. For a moment she couldn't speak. 'When did you become estranged?' she asked.

'We've never been close. We stopped speaking after Heather. I couldn't believe he'd treat someone like that.'

An idea crept into Ruby's mind. 'Did he ever mention a Charlotte Manning, at all?' She knew it was a long shot, especially if they hadn't spoken for some time. But it had to be worth a try.

Isla's brow furrowed. 'No. Who's she?'

Ruby's mobile trilled. 'Lewis' flashed up. She stared at it, then back up at the woman opposite her. It rang again. Isla passed her an *Are you going to get that* look.

Ruby was torn. She checked out of the window, searching the street for any sign of him and ended the call. 'I'll call them back.'

'I need to go.' Isla gathered up her bag. 'Tell your sister to steer clear. Ewan's bad news. A rotten apple.'

'No, please…'

'I shouldn't have stayed this long.'

'You've barely…' Ruby wanted to say 'touched your coffee', but the words dissolved into the air as the young woman grabbed her bag and scooted out of the café.

She grabbed her own bag and made chase. Isla was weaving through the cars, crossing the road. Ruby searched for a gap in the traffic, keeping half an eye on the patch of navy suit in the distance.

'Wait!' she called out.

If Isla heard her, she didn't acknowledge.

A van pulled up outside, blocking her view. Ruby moved further along the pavement, looking both ways, desperately craning her neck for a sight of Isla's jacket, the cropped dark hair. But she'd gone. Ruby turned on her heel 360 degrees. Numerous side streets led off Burlington Row. There was no sign of Isla. It was like she'd disappeared into thin air.

Ruby's stomach dropped away. *Dangerous and manipulative.* What did she mean by that? Why wouldn't she elaborate? Ewan had been so good with Sophie's children. Reading them stories, taking them to the park. She remembered Sophie saying how happy he was he'd found her. He had so little family, he'd never really felt he belonged after his parents died. They'd even talked about the possibility of having a baby together one day, to place the seal on their little unit. Did she know he'd been married before and already had children? Was he still married? Surely she'd have mentioned it if she did.

'Hey!'

Ruby turned to find Lewis jogging down the pavement towards her.

'Why did you ring me?' Ruby said. She cursed under her breath.

'Just checking to see if you were okay.'

'I *was* fine.' She turned back to the road. It was a hopeless task. Isla could be in a cab heading for the other side of London by now. 'Your bloody phone call spooked Isla. She's taken off.'

'Oh, no. I'm sorry.' He paused. 'How did it go?'

Ruby didn't answer. She threw her head back and stared at the sky. 'Honestly, I'm not sure what to make of it all.'

Chapter 47

'She wasn't what I expected,' Lewis said. 'I know I only saw her from a distance, but she doesn't look a bit like her brother.'

Ruby adjusted position. The train home was rammed and, perched on the edge of an aisle seat to face Lewis, the ridge of the chair was digging uncomfortably into her legs. 'She's his half-sister, from their mother's second marriage,' she said.

'Where are his parents?'

She tucked her legs to the side to allow a passenger to squeeze through. 'Passed away, I think.'

'Has he no other family?'

'I don't think so, not apart from the wife and kids. I didn't really get a chance to ask.' Her mind had been a torrent of questions since she'd left the café and even after talking it through with Lewis, she was still unsure of what she'd gleaned, or what it all meant.

The train wheels squeaked as they rolled into Market Deeton station. Ruby vacated her seat and followed Lewis through a line of standing passengers to the door. Thoughts snuck in and out of her head as she strode down the tunnel and slid her ticket through the machine to exit. Ewan was isolating Sophie from friends and family, just as he had with his other girlfriends. Keeping her to himself. Isla didn't seem to think he'd been violent. Had he changed tack? Become more intense. More controlling.

Outside the station, Lewis moved off to withdraw cash from the nearby ATM. Ruby waited for him, taking in a lungful of fresh air, a welcome change from the stuffiness of the train, and was watching other passengers stream out when a man at the roadside caught her attention. She screwed up her eyes. It was Mark.

He was thirty yards or so from her, standing beside an old red telephone box and checking his watch, as if he was waiting for someone.

She ducked down behind the people shoving tickets into their pockets, raincoats slipping down their arms, briefcases swinging by their sides. The last thing she needed was to be spotted out by her boss when she was supposed to be tucked up in bed with a migraine. But she was curious. What was he doing here? Slowly she stood, trying to peek through the passing heads, blocking her view. When she finally did find a gap, the pavement was empty. She edged around the corner, sheltered behind the door and peered up and down the road.

A hand pressed her shoulder. Ruby jumped and spun round.

'That's where you're hiding.' It was Lewis. He placed a cigarette in his mouth, cupped his hand across as he lit up, then sucked. 'I wondered where you'd gone.' Smoke rushed out of his nostrils.

She swiped a hand across her forehead. 'Mark, my boss,' she hissed. 'He was here. I can't afford for him to see me.'

He followed her eyeline, checked the road. 'Are you sure?'

'Definitely.'

He took a moment to scan the area. 'Well, if he was here, he's gone, thankfully.' He took another drag.

Ruby continued to look out for Mark as Lewis led her along the road. She watched the horde of travellers weaving through the vehicles in the station car park. Desperately trying to see if he was among them, but he wasn't.

It was five-thirty when they reached Lewis's Mondeo. They pulled out of the car park to a line of traffic.

'How are you feeling now?' Lewis asked, eyes on the road.

Ruby rubbed her forehead again, then dragged her hands down the front of her face. 'I don't know. Isla was uncomfortable, wary. It was like she was scared of talking to me.'

'I don't like the sound of it.'

'Me neither. But what can I do? Sophie already thinks I'm trying to take Ewan away from her. She won't listen to me and it's not as if I have anything concrete to give her anyway.'

'Does she know about his wife and kids?'

'I don't know. She's never mentioned them. I feel like there's something else going on here. Something deeper. Isla called him dangerous. There has to be a reason for her to say that.'

'What are you thinking?'

'I'm not sure.' She hesitated. 'Look, I know this is way out there...' She cleared her throat. 'Kat's husband reckons he's seen Ewan out with other women, more than once.'

'So, he's having affairs?'

'Maybe.'

Lewis raised a brow. 'Could have been friends,' he said. 'I've got loads of women as friends – you, Becky.'

'Graham said it was quite obvious they were more than friends. And it was recent, while he's been with Sophie. Plus, Ewan started dating Sophie two months before Mum was killed. Bit of a coincidence, don't you think?'

The nose of a car pushed out from a side street. Lewis waved them out into the traffic. 'I'm not sure where this is all going.'

'What if Mum saw Ewan with another woman and confronted him? Or maybe she threatened to tell Sophie?'

'You're not suggesting Ewan killed your mum? That's insane.'

When the idea first crept into her head on the train, Ruby had discarded it as incredulous too. But the more she percolated it, the more credible it seemed. He turned up two months before her mother died, and used Sophie's fragility afterwards to burrow deeper, cement his position. 'I'm saying the scenario is feasible, isn't it? It would give him a motive.'

'But Colin Halliday—'

'Ewan could have planted the evidence,' she interrupted. 'Made it look like Colin, then persuaded Charlotte to leave town.'

'The police found evidence of a fight at the shop. Colin's DNA was everywhere.'

'He didn't deny the fight. He said it wasn't him who killed her.' Something about Colin's voice yesterday... It sounded so innocent. Genuine. It was just the same in court. He'd stood in the dock in his fresh suits, pressed shirts. And he'd looked so small. As if it was a world so far adrift from his own. Ruby had ignored it at the time, ignored him. But now, the voice of doubt was growing louder and louder, it was deafening.

'I think you're stretching this a bit far. I mean, where was Ewan on the night of your mum's murder?'

'At home, I think. He gave a statement to the police, we all did. He wouldn't have been considered a suspect, not with all the evidence against Colin. And he had no motive at the time, or so we all thought. But this would give him a motive to kill Charlotte. And there's got to be some reason why he didn't want anyone to know he was out the night she was killed. He didn't even want to go to the police confidentially.'

'I don't know, Rubes. It's such a leap.'

They'd arrived at Ruby's house now. Lewis switched off the engine.

'It would tie everything up nicely though, wouldn't it?'

Lewis frowned. 'Except he has been to the police now. And he wouldn't be the only person who knew your mother and was out the night Charlotte was murdered.'

Ruby sighed. He was right. She'd been so consumed with Ewan, so convinced he had to be involved, she'd barely considered other possibilities. If the cases were linked, it was someone who knew her mother, someone close. She was convinced of it now. Someone her mother had upset.

She pictured the memorial service the other day. Tom sitting on the end of the row near the back. Becky behind him, sitting beside Lewis. Becky, who'd been her mother's work neighbour, the woman who found her body. Greg opposite, sitting alone. The father of Sophie's children, who Aileen had refused to speak to since he'd come back into their lives. Any one of them could have set Colin up. And then there was Mark, her boss. He hadn't even attended the memorial service, despite knowing how important it was to Ruby. The man who didn't get along with her mother, who was also out on the night Charlotte was murdered and, like Tom, was uneasy about it. What was he doing outside the station today?

But no one seemed to have a motive as strong as Ewan's.

Ruby shivered. It was getting cold in the car now the engine was off. 'Sophie said Ewan was upset after Charlotte's murder,' she said. 'Down. If he was involved, it might explain his mood.'

'I don't know. I'm more concerned with Sophie. If Ewan's sister thinks she could be in trouble, I think we should focus on her and leave the rest to the police.'

'I can't. I can't leave it, Lewis.' She twisted in her seat to face him. 'The key is to find the link between Ewan and Charlotte.'

Lewis's cheeks billowed as he exhaled a long breath. 'Okay. What about that liaison officer? Hitesh. He's been supportive. You could speak with him off the record, see if he can help. I'm sure he'd be interested to hear what Isla said.'

Ruby chewed the side of her mouth. It was a reasonable suggestion. But, following her recent dealings with the police, would Hitesh even listen?

Chapter 48

Sophie was upstairs, helping Alfie into his pyjama top when she heard the noise. A piercing scream, ringing through the house like an aeroplane on a nosedive. She rushed downstairs, closely followed by Alfie and Daisy.

In the hallway, all was quiet. She paused a split second, the children behind her, trying to place the source of the sound. The sitting-room door was open, the television switched off. The kitchen door sat ajar. She could hear Ewan in there mumbling to himself.

Sophie pushed open the door.

Ewan jolted as she entered. 'You made me jump.'

He was beside the cooker staring at Pru, who was on the opposite work surface, glowering back at him.

'What's going on?' Sophie asked. She looked from one to another. Pru cast her a cursory glance and turned back to Ewan.

'Stupid cat. I tripped over her, filling the kettle.' He licked at a line of blood, trickling from a scratch on his hand. 'When I bent down to check on her, she ripped into me.'

'I'm sure she didn't mean it. You know she's easily spooked.'

'Crazy more like. She came after me like something possessed.'

'I told you to keep your hands away from her.' She looked at the cut on his hand. 'You'd better put some ointment on that.' She pointed at the cupboard above Pru and turned to gather up the children. She really needed to get them into bed.

A sharp hiss filled the room.

Sophie started. Pru had always been a feisty girl, unwelcoming of uninvited attention. She'd lost count of the number of people she'd ragged and scratched. But she'd never seen her react like that.

'Pru,' she said softly. 'He didn't mean it.' The cat relaxed as Sophie moved beside her.

'Honestly, Soph, I don't know why you keep her.' Ewan's tone was chipped. He licked the cut again. 'I mean what if she did this to one of the kids?'

'This is her home.'

'She's clearly not happy. We really should think about finding her another place.'

'No!' It was Daisy. She dashed past her mother and stood beside the cat defiantly.

'She's never touched the children,' Sophie said. She was tempted to add it was because they'd learned to give her a wide berth but decided against it. He was already upset. No point in making the situation worse.

Ewan's forehead creased. 'I didn't mean rehome her outside the family. Of course not. Just maybe she'd be happier at Ruby's, where it's quieter.'

Sophie surveyed Pru's soft fur, the tattered edges of her ears from all the fights over the years, the pale hairs filtering into her tigery face. Remembering how her mother had found her in the shop doorway one morning, sheltering from the rain. Skinny and tired. She'd kept her there a while, put out word in the local community and waited for someone to claim her. When nobody did, she brought her home. Sophie and Ruby were teenagers then. They'd been plaguing their mother for a pet for years, and welcomed the cat with open arms. Though Pru wasn't quite the fur-baby they'd hoped for. From the moment she arrived, she was gutsy and fiery, only sitting on Aileen's knee, only letting their mother stroke her, and that was when it suited. But Aileen loved her. If Pru scratched or bit her, she'd look at the cat with sad eyes and say,

'It's not her fault, we don't know what's she's been through, bless her.'

'She stays here,' Sophie said firmly. 'Come on, kids. Let's get you up to bed.'

Chapter 49

Later that evening, Hitesh Lalvani rested his elbow on the arm of Ruby's sofa, blew out a long breath and looked down at his notes. He'd sounded intrigued when she'd called him earlier, saying she needed to speak to him urgently, and arrived within the hour. Though now, as she passed over the details of her meeting with Isla and her deliberations about Ewan, his interest was clearly waning.

'As I understand it, Mr Wilson's already been to the station and given an account of his presence in Market Deeton on the night of the murder,' Hitesh said.

'Only when he had to.'

'And you've given two conflicting accounts.'

'Yes, but he said I had to give the first one, to—'

'To keep your liaison with Mr Wilson from your sister,' he interrupted. 'Yes, you told me. How is your relationship with Sophie now?'

The sofa cushion shifted as Lewis crossed his ankles beside her. He'd stayed with her for moral support. Although, looking at the dubious expression on Hitesh's face, she was beginning to think she'd need more than moral support now if she was to convince the detective. 'We're not speaking. But she's got it all wrong.'

'She said it was you who instigated the kiss. Yes, you've made the misunderstanding quite clear.'

'It isn't a misunderstanding. He deliberately changed the facts to suit himself.'

'Why would he do that?'

'Because he wants me out of the way. He wants Sophie all to himself.'

The pen wobbled irritably between Hitesh's fingers. She was losing him. What happened to the relationship they'd built together, the mutual understanding? He'd spent time with her family, got to know them. She had assumed this mutual understanding gave them a platform of trust and he'd take her considerations seriously. But she was wrong. He was looking coldly at the facts, just like the others. And she'd lied. She'd lied herself into a corner and, when exposed, she looked like was trying to frame her sister's boyfriend.

'Did Ewan give his fingerprints and his DNA when he gave his account?' Lewis interjected.

She could see where he was going here. If they'd taken samples, they could match them against the murder scene.

'It's unlikely,' Hitesh replied. 'He was a witness. Prints and samples are only routinely taken when someone's arrested. From what you've told me, there was no reason for him to be asked.'

'There's something else,' Ruby said, desperately holding onto the final thread of his attention.

He lifted a brow as she told him about Sophie's bruises and her pathetic explanation.

'I take it Sophie hasn't complained to the police?' he asked.

'No.'

'Has she said anything about Ewan being abusive, either to you or her friends?'

'Not as far as I'm aware. It doesn't mean it isn't true. Some victims of domestic abuse protect their partners, don't they? Keep it secret because they're scared.'

He studied her a moment. 'I can alert the domestic violence team if you're concerned and ask someone to contact Sophie to ensure she is safe.'

'What about Ewan's tendency to wander, the other woman?' She was clutching at straws now.

He looked down at his notes again. 'I assume you're referring to the women your friend's boyfriend saw him with?'

'Yes.' When he put it like that, it sounded so weak, so tenuous.

'Affairs aren't a crime.'

'His sister said he was dangerous.'

'The sister he's estranged from.' Hitesh stared at her a moment. 'People say things when they argue. Our job is to establish the truth. At this stage, we've no evidence to link Ewan to a crime.' He closed his notebook, made to stand.

'Wait! If Ewan has a history of violence, you'd know, wouldn't you?' Ruby said. 'You must keep a record of offences.'

'They'll be on the police computer, yes.' He slipped his notebook into his pocket. He was at the door now. His face softened as he turned to her. 'I'm sorry to hear about your family argument. It's been a difficult time for all of you. Try to get some rest. You can be assured if I find anything to link Ewan to a crime, he will be investigated.'

'Colin called me,' she said, her voice barely a whisper.

Hitesh angled his head. 'Colin Halliday?'

Ruby nodded. She'd finally got his attention. She passed on the details of the call.

Hitesh took out his notebook and made a note. 'Why didn't you raise this earlier?'

'I didn't think it was relevant.'

'But you do now?'

Ruby closed her eyes a second. 'I don't know. I just think all the evidence should be reviewed. For both cases.'

Lewis rounded on Ruby. 'I think you should tell him everything.'

Ruby squirmed. But it was too late now, Hitesh was looking at her questioningly. She told him about the night phone calls, the face at the window, cringing as she talked about the door handle left upright, the feeling someone had been in the house. Because that's all it was, a feeling.

Hitesh's brow furrowed. He sat back down, turned a page in his notebook, made a note of dates and times.

'Will you be able to trace the details of the caller?' Lewis asked.

'We'll certainly try,' Hitesh said. He turned to Ruby. 'In the meantime, you need to think about some general safeguarding.'

'What do you mean?'

'This could be something, or nothing. But I wouldn't be doing my job properly if I didn't look into it, and ask you to check the house is locked at all times, and keep your phone with you. Is there someone who could stay with you for a while?'

'I don't know.' She hadn't expected him to take it all so seriously. 'Do you think it's Ewan, trying to intimidate me?'

'I'd prefer not to speculate. It might have nothing to do with Mr Wilson.' He placed his notebook away. 'Try not to worry. If anything else happens, then either call 999 if it's an emergency, or give me a ring. You've got my number.'

Lewis stood. 'I'll see you out, Detective.'

Ruby was aware of them wandering into the hallway. The door being pulled to. Them talking in low voices. Perhaps Lewis was pleading with him, adding his own weight to the argument. But she wasn't listening. What did all this mean? When Colin phoned, he'd implied she was in danger. He'd cautioned her to be careful. Was he right?

The front door juddered to a close. Lewis appeared at the door frame.

'He doesn't believe me about Ewan,' she said. 'He thinks I'm trying to get back at him for causing the argument with my sister.'

'Leave it now,' Lewis said. 'You've told them everything. Let them investigate.' He glanced at the sofa. 'Why don't I stay over tonight?'

'I couldn't ask you to do that.' Though she couldn't deny Hitesh's response to Colin's phone call, the feeling she was being watched, had rattled her.

'You're not asking, I'm offering. And your sofa looks a lot more comfortable than the lumpy mattress in Simon's spare room.'

Chapter 50

I watch your progress from afar and I wonder if there is still more to do.

Sometimes you don't know what's good for you. I need to point you in the right direction, make you see sense. But you need to be receptive and let me in.

Are you ready for my next move? Are you ready for the truth?

Excitement flutters inside me at the prospect. It's been a long time coming, a long time in the making, but I need to be cautious. The timing has to be perfect. When you are thinking straight, when you are stable. When you are ready to listen.

Because my next move will change everything.

Chapter 51

The following morning, Sophie was placing sandwiches in the kids' lunch boxes when Daisy ran into the kitchen.

'Mum, my coat's too small.'

'What?' It was a half-hearted reply. She was concentrating on the boxes, fastening one then the other, cursing herself for not making the lunches last night. It was almost 8:20 a.m. They should have left for the school run by now. 'Alfie!' she called. 'Have you got your shoes on?'

'My coat,' Daisy wailed. 'It's getting too tight. Look!' A rip sounded.

Sophie spun around, faster than she intended. Her hand caught a beaker of juice on the table left over from breakfast. It tumbled to the floor. Pru, who was curled up in her bed in the corner, jumped back and scowled at the splashes reaching across the tiles.

'Oh, for Christ's sake,' Sophie said. The beaker was on its side. Juice spilling off the table and pooling beneath. 'It'll have to do for today,' she said to Daisy. 'Go and check your brother is ready to go.'

She grabbed a cloth from beside the sink and started mopping up the mess. The children would definitely be late for school now. She was placing the beaker in the sink, cloth still in hand when her mobile rang. It was Ewan.

'Ewan, can I call you back? Only—'

'Sophie, this is important,' he interrupted. 'I'm at the police station. I need you to listen carefully.'

The cloth slipped out of her hand. She gripped the receiver with both hands. 'What's happened? Are you okay?'

'I'm fine. Don't worry, it's just a misunderstanding.'

'Ewan!'

'Listen, I don't have long. I need you to get me a solicitor. I'll give you a name and their practice. They need to come to the station now. I've been arrested.'

–

Ruby was running out of the door to work when her mobile rang. She gritted her teeth, fumbled with her key in the lock and waited until she was away from the house before she answered. Lewis was still sleeping in the front room; she didn't want to disturb him.

She stopped in her tracks when she saw who was calling. 'Sophie?'

A sob winged down the line.

'Sophie, is that you?'

'Yes.' The word was muffled. Another sob.

'Sophie, what is it?'

'I n-need you to come over.'

'What's happened?'

'It's E-Ewan.'

Ruby froze. 'Are you safe?' Had Ewan hurt her, or the children? *Oh, God. Please. Don't let anything happen to her.* 'Sophie?'

A car passed by on the road. Ruby pressed her free hand to her other ear to block out the sound of the engine.

'Ewan's been arrested.' Another strangled sob.

Ruby's mouth instantly dried. So, Hitesh *had* listened to her and looked into Ewan's background. Isla didn't think he'd been violent with his last two girlfriends. Perhaps there were other occasions. Hitesh must have discovered enough to spur him on to delve further. What else had he found? Something to link him to Charlotte? The whole notion, the whole scenario she'd spent the last twenty-four hours mulling over in her head was finally unfolding before her eyes. And it didn't feel good.

'Arrested for what?' she said, battling to get the words out.

'Something to do with drugs.'

Ruby jolted. Drugs?

'C-can you come over? Now?'

Confusion and frustration hammered at her. 'Of course. I'll be right there.'

The line went dead. Ruby placed her laptop and bag into the back of her car and slid into the driver's seat, gripping the steering wheel, desperately trying to order her thoughts. Had the police received other information on Ewan? Or had there been an incident? None of this made any sense.

She was reminded of the dealer in the alley. Was Ewan working with him? And the talk of Sophie's Valium habit. Could Ewan's arrest be connected to her sister? It would muddy the waters rather.

She was glad Sophie was reaching out to her. Maybe she was starting to see through Ewan. She hoped so. Still, Ruby felt an uncomfortable twist inside. It was doubtful Sophie would feel the same if she knew about her conversation with Hitesh last night.

Though, she didn't have time to think about any of these things now. Mark wouldn't welcome her taking another day off, but, whatever happened, she needed to be by Sophie's side and try to sort out this mess. She grabbed her phone and typed out a quick text to Kat.

> Something going on in the family. Can you tell Mark I'm still sick today? Sorry to have to ask, but it's important. Don't worry, will fill you in later x

As Ruby joined the line of traffic heading into town, her mind moved to her sister. She'd sounded desperate on the phone. Her stomach curdled as she pressed her right foot on the accelerator. She needed to get to Sophie before anything else happened.

Chapter 52

Ruby wandered through Sophie's back door to an eerie silence. No television blasting out, no children's voices or footsteps pitter-pattering the polished flooring. A quick glance at the kitchen clock – 8:50 a.m.

'Hello!' Her voice echoed around the walls. In the front room, Pru was curled up on the sofa in a sun puddle. She raised her head and viewed Ruby through slit eyes. Had Sophie left for the school run and forgotten to lock the back door?

Ruby moved out to the hallway. The sound of a toilet flushing was followed by thuds of footfalls.

Sophie appeared on the stairs. Her hair was tied back, her face drawn. Red rims decorated her eyes. If she was relieved to see Ruby, it didn't show.

'Where are the children?' Ruby asked.

'I called Louise, asked her to take them to school.'

One blessing. At least they weren't here, soaking up everything unfolding. They'd seen enough drama in their little lives already. 'What exactly happened?'

'I'm not really sure. He phoned as I was about to take the kids to school. Told me the police had been to his flat this morning and arrested him for drugs. Possession with intent to supply, I think he said, but it's a misunderstanding. He wanted me to contact Stephen Walkton and ask him to go down there and sort it all out.'

Stephen Walkton was a well-known criminal solicitor based in Leicester, a fifty-something eloquent man with a shrewd eye and a sensitive manner with clients. Over the years, he'd developed a magnetic attraction towards high-profile cases, or those which didn't quite fit the mould. But he was an unusual choice here. Unless Ewan was expecting the police to question him about something more sinister…

'Why Stephen?'

'Ewan's followed his cases in the news. Thinks he's impressive. The police offered to get him a solicitor, but he doesn't trust them.'

'What did he say when he called?'

'He couldn't talk for long. There was a search at his flat.' Sophie bit her lip. 'Drugs were found. Him and his flatmate were both arrested.'

'What sort of drugs?'

'Cocaine, I think. It's nothing to do with him.'

Cocaine. Not Valium. Although she imagined most dealers would have access to a range of narcotics.

Sophie wiped her nose and sniffed. 'It is going to be okay, isn't it?' She looked up at Ruby, green eyes pleading.

Suddenly they were children again, ten and eight, sitting on the floor in Bridget's spare room after their mother had been rushed to hospital with suspected appendicitis. Ruby consoling her sister, rubbing her back, telling her everything was going to be okay, when actually she had no idea herself what the outcome would be.

'It'll work out, I'm sure.' She pulled Sophie into an embrace, resting her head on her shoulder.

How was it going to work out? If Ewan was released, her sister would still be at risk. If he was kept in custody, Sophie would be broken and there would be no placating her.

The scent of Sophie's pear shampoo filled her nose as her sister pulled back. 'What am I going to do? I can't bear to lose him.'

Ruby winced. She wanted to say, 'You're not going to lose him,' though it sounded disingenuous in the circumstances. 'You said yourself, it's a misunderstanding.' This was so wrong, so sneaky. She should be honest with her sister. Tell her about Ewan's sordid past. But where to start? At least him tucked away in a police cell bought her time.

'You know what the police are like when they get their claws into somebody. And they've got this big purge on drugs at the moment. I saw it on the news.'

'What exactly have the police said?'

'Nothing. They wouldn't speak to me when I called. Perhaps I should go down there.'

'I don't think you'll get any more answers at the station. What did Stephen say?'

'He was in a conference or something, I couldn't speak with him. His secretary said she'd send someone down urgently.' She lifted her head, met Ruby's gaze. 'He will go himself, won't he? Ewan was quite specific.'

Ruby wasn't convinced, but she plastered her kindest smile on her face. 'I'm sure he'll do his best. Why don't I ring the solicitors again and find out what's happening?'

It took Ruby an age to get through to Walkton and Sons, only to be told Stephen was tied up on another case and a junior solicitor called Henry Martin had been sent. She asked them to get a message to Henry to call Sophie with an update as soon as possible.

'I bet he's straight out of law school,' Sophie said when Ruby ended the call. 'Ewan would have been better off with the duty solicitor.'

They wandered into the kitchen. The last time they'd been in there together was Sunday when they were arguing over Ewan. It seemed an age ago now.

'I'm glad you called,' Ruby said, flicking the switch on the kettle. 'I've been feeling awful about the weekend.'

'I don't want to talk about it.' A muscle flexed in Sophie's cheek.

'Okay.' But it was like an elephant in the room, huge and suffocating. Especially as the incident was all about Ewan, the person they were talking about now. 'How have you been?'

'Fine. We've all been fine, until this morning.'

Ruby busied herself with making tea, heaping sugar into Sophie's, in an effort to calm her. She hated seeing her like this.

Birds tweeted on the apple tree outside as she moved the mugs over to the table.

They sipped their drinks, the warm tea, gently soothing.

'I should call Hitesh,' Sophie said, placing her mug down and looking up suddenly, as if she'd had a light-bulb moment.

The last thing Ruby needed was a visit from Hitesh right now. She fought to remain calm and took another sip of her drink, but it was like swallowing a mouthful of sand. 'Why Hitesh?' she croaked. 'He's a liaison officer. I don't see how he could help.'

'He's police, isn't he? I bet he'll have some idea of what's happening. Or he'll be able to find out.' Sophie surveyed her sister, and frowned. 'What? Can you think of anything better...'

'No, of course. If you think it's the right thing to do.'

Ruby's throat constricted as Sophie pulled out her phone. She listened to the dial tone ring out, one, two, three, four... Would Hitesh mention his conversation with Ruby last night? Should she tell Sophie first? Or would he ask about her well-being? He might even say there had been a report of bruising, or that a member of her family has raised concerns about her safety. Her heart was in her mouth. If he said any of those things, Sophie would instantly know she'd gone behind her back.

The voicemail kicked in. Her shoulders relaxed. She listened to her sister leave a message, asking him to see what he could find out, pleading with him to call her back.

'Why don't we go and sit in the front room?' Ruby said when she called off. 'You look like you need some rest.' She needed to calm Sophie down and find a way to tell her sister what she'd been up to before she found out from elsewhere. Although she had no idea how to even start broaching the subject, especially at a time like this.

Chapter 53

Sophie placed the receiver down. 'They're interviewing him again this afternoon. Henry said they can keep him in for thirty-six hours before seeking a magistrate's authorisation for an extension. He could be there overnight.' A tear trickled down Sophie's cheek. She wiped it away with the back of her hand.

Ruby stretched her arm around her sister's shoulder. It was almost 1 p.m. and despite crying herself into an exhausted slumber in Ruby's arms, and sleeping for almost three hours, dark shadows still lingered beneath Sophie's eyes. It was awful to see her so distressed. Nothing Ruby could tell her, nothing she could say, would alleviate the pain. And when she'd finally woken and resolved to phone the solicitors again, yet more bad news was piled onto an already brimming pile.

The meeting with Isla had been plaguing her all day. Manipulative, she'd said of Ewan. Dangerous. Why wouldn't she go into detail? Perhaps it was because she had no direct evidence. If Ewan hurt his partners and persuaded them not to make a complaint, there would be nothing on police record.

She looked across at her sister now, her snow-white skin, green teardrop eyes, the vibrant ginger curls tucked behind her ears. Bridget was right, she did share their mother's worrisome streak. She could be stubborn, hard-nosed when she wanted to be, but beneath that brittle shell, she was soft and malleable, like putty. Which left her open to manipulation.

Sophie collected the used mugs from earlier and carried them through to the kitchen.

Ruby's phone buzzed. She watched her sister go, then checked the message. It was Lewis.

> Free for a coffee? I could meet you at Croft's.

She'd left him a note earlier, saying she'd gone to work and to let himself out when he was ready. He wouldn't know she was with Sophie.

She quickly typed back. *Can't today, sorry. At Sophie's atm. Will message you later.*

He replied within seconds. *Everything okay?*

Yes, don't worry. Will fill you in later. She fired off the text and placed her phone down.

It was time to be honest with her sister. To tell her about her meeting with Isla, pass along her concerns. It was only right she had all the information. And they were finally alone. This might be her only chance.

She moved into the hall. All was quiet. Had Sophie gone upstairs? She was just thinking about following her when she heard a crackle. It was coming from the kitchen. She pushed open the door.

Sophie was standing beside the table, her handbag open in front of her. Unwrapping a piece of foil. As soon as she spotted Ruby, Sophie pushed the foil into the open bag.

'What's that?' Ruby asked.

'Nothing.' Sophie made to slide the bag off the table. As she did so, the foil slipped out and three tiny blue tablets tumbled to the floor.

Sophie bent down to grab the pills, but Ruby was too quick for her. She fought off her sister as she gathered the tablets into the palm of her hand.

'It's not what you think,' Sophie said.

Ruby bristled. 'How long?'

'What?'

'How long have you been taking these?'

Sophie's nostrils flared. 'I don't have to explain myself to you.'

'No, you don't. What about the police then? You could tell them where you got these.'

'How do you know they're not legitimate?'

'Oh, come on, Sophie. There's no blister pack. I wasn't born yesterday.'

'It's none of their business, and it's certainly none of yours.'

'It's exactly my business. You're my sister. You care for my niece and nephew.'

'I'm a good mother!' she snapped.

'I'm not saying you're not. But if you need help you should go to your doctor.'

'If I need help?' She snorted. 'There you go again.'

'Well, you clearly do, otherwise why would you be taking Valium.'

'How do you know they're Valium?'

Ruby sidestepped the question. It was true, there was nothing on the pills to indicate what they were. They could be anything. Something stronger even… 'Is Ewan getting these for you?'

'It has to be about Ewan, doesn't it?'

'Well, excuse me. He's the one that's been arrested for drugs.'

Sophie's face fell. She dropped into a seat at the table. 'I just… I need them right now, okay? Since we lost Mum, I've needed a little help to keep going. It was my decision to take them. No one's forcing it on me. I checked my weight and organised the dosage online and I'm being careful.'

Ruby's heart wrenched. *Since we lost Mum…* She'd been on them a while then. Was there anything else she was taking? She was about to ask when Sophie pushed her hair out of her face, the cuff of her top sliding back to expose the welt on her wrist. It had faded in the last few days to a dusky pink. She noticed Ruby looking at it and pulled her sleeve down.

'Ewan was rough with me too, you know,' Ruby said quietly.

'What, when you kissed him?' Sophie's face contorted. 'Of course he was rough, he was trying to get you off him!'

'That's not true.' This wasn't how she wanted the conversation to unfold. But the cat was out of the bag now. Out of the bag and scrambling all over the room. 'It was Ewan who came onto me.'

'I don't believe I'm hearing this. How could you? And now, of all times, when he's locked in a police cell. When I need your support. I should never have called you.'

'If he's hurting you—'

'It's not what you think.'

'It's nothing to be ashamed of. We can get help.'

Sophie huffed. 'You've got it all wrong, as usual.'

'Then, what? Come on, Soph, tell me. I'm dying to hear it.' She leant back, folded her arms across her chest.

'Do I need to spell it out for you?'

Ruby stayed silent. She could feel Sophie's eyes boring holes into her. Hard, angry eyes.

'Look, we like to play about in the bedroom sometimes. There's no crime in that.'

Was she seriously trying to explain those marks through sex games? 'You shouldn't be ending up with bruises.'

'Oh, come on, Rubes. Don't go all prudish on me. You can't tell me you've never experimented.'

Ruby was taken aback. She *was* serious. Yes, she'd experimented. Moving into her first house with Tom was liberating. They wanted to make the most of the space, having room after room to themselves. She remembered asking Tom to tie her wrists to the bed knobs and place a blindfold over her eyes, but she'd found it hard to relax when she couldn't move and they both ended up giggling. 'Not to the extent that someone's in pain. No.'

Sophie sucked her teeth, as if she didn't believe her.

'He's done it before,' Ruby said, unable to stop herself.

'What?'

'Hurt people.' She wasn't technically telling an untruth, although the words did wedge themselves uncomfortably in her throat.

'What are you talking about?'

She was going out on a limb here, she had no firm evidence. But the need to convince Sophie, at least to get her to stop and think, was overriding any sense of normality. 'He hurt his wife.'

Sophie froze. 'What did you say?'

She doesn't know. 'Ewan left a wife and kids in Glasgow when he moved here.'

'You're lying!'

'I'm not, Soph. I spoke with his sister.'

'You did what?'

'I was worried about you. Worried about what was happening here. Between us.'

Sophie looked horrified. 'When did you speak with her?'

'Yesterday. We met in London.'

'I don't believe I'm hearing this.' She was shaking her head now, her eyes wide. 'You met with Ewan's sister behind my back?'

'There's a lot you don't know.'

'Get out!'

'Please, Soph. You need to stop seeing him. He manipulates people...'

'Ewan was right. You are jealous.'

Ruby swallowed. She didn't want to leave like this. 'I could never be jealous of you, Soph. You're my baby sister.' She reached out, but Sophie rose, and batted her away.

'Get out!' The shrill sound of her voice pierced the air. She herded her sister out of the door.

For the second time in less than a week Ruby found herself stumbling up her sister's driveway, a knot the size of a football in her chest. She pulled her phone out of her pocket and messaged Lewis. *On my way home. Meet you there?* She had to find a way to make Sophie listen to her. And soon.

Chapter 54

Ruby was so relieved to find Lewis standing on her doorstep when she arrived home, she flung her arms around him, enveloping him in a tight hug. The argument with her sister coupled with the itching sense of someone watching her, of another presence in her home over the past few days, was really starting to get to her and the sight of his welcoming face couldn't have been more comforting.

'Hey,' he said, pulling back. 'I came as soon as I got your text. What's happened?'

'Ewan was arrested this morning, possession with intent to supply cocaine. Sophie's in pieces.'

'Oh.' His jaw dropped.

She let them both into the house. 'I spent most of the day with her,' Ruby said, shrugging off her jacket. 'Really thought I was starting to get through.' She told him about catching Sophie with the tablets in the kitchen, the argument.

'I'm sorry,' he said. 'But she did need to know about Isla.'

'Not like this. An argument with her sister when she's already in a bad place. And now she's on her own. I'm frightened for her.'

Lewis checked his watch. 'It's almost time for the school run. She won't do anything silly. Not now. She adores those kids.'

Ruby wasn't so sure. 'I'm going to ring Kat. Get her to pop in, make sure she's okay. I'm sure she can make up some excuse.'

She grabbed her phone. Kat was with a client, but Ruby managed to give her a quick overview of the situation and Kat agreed to call by when she had finished her appointment, saying she was in the area and pretending not to know about Ewan's arrest. Ruby heaved a sigh of relief. It was good to think someone was checking on her.

Lewis emerged from the kitchen with two coffees. 'Thought you needed this,' he said, handing one over.

'Thanks.' They wandered into the front room and sat on the sofa. Ruby cupped the mug in her hands, relishing the warmth of the fluid trickling through her insides, inducing a moment of calm. She placed the mug down and inadvertently placed her hand in her fleece pocket. Two... no, three tiny pips slipped through her fingers. Sophie's tablets. She must have shoved them in there on the way out. 'Ewan must have been under the police radar for a while,' she said. 'Either that or they had some other evidence.'

'Possibly. I take it you had no night caller yesterday?' Lewis asked, changing the subject.

She shook her head. 'Nothing to do with Ewan's arrest though, the police only called on him this morning. And I haven't heard anything from Hitesh.'

'Ah, well. At least he's in custody. He can't hurt her while he's there.'

She told him Sophie's explanation for the bruises.

'Wow,' he said, raising a brow.

'Even if she is telling the truth and it's all consensual, Isla's comments yesterday are still worrying. I mean, he did lie about what happened with me. And he has been seeing other women— Oh, God, I didn't have a chance to tell her that.'

'A hundred grams of cocaine is pretty substantial. You're probably talking £5,000 in terms of street value,' Lewis said. 'If the police charge, they might consider him a flight risk and keep him in custody.'

'I hope so.' She was just taking another sip of coffee when his last sentence jarred her. 'How did you know how much they found?'

'Pardon?'

'A hundred grams, you said.'

'You told me.'

'I didn't. I mentioned cocaine and said he was arrested for possession with intent to supply.' She rounded on him. 'What's going on, Lewis? I checked the news reports at Sophie's. They only featured the arrest. They haven't even given out names, let alone specific details.'

He closed his eyes a second. 'Look, hear me out on this one.' She didn't like the sound of this.

'The other day at the park when you told me about Sophie… I know Valium isn't illegal, but she's been obtaining it illegally. I was worried. I asked around.'

'To whom?'

'Associates. People who occasionally use or are involved with drugs.'

'Lewis!'

'There are loads of people who dabble in my line of work, it's not difficult. More often cocaine and amphet than stuff like Valium or diazepam as most people call it now. Dealers have access to all sorts. I didn't mention any names. I didn't need to. I was told there was activity at Ewan's address.'

'Why didn't you say anything?'

'Because this goes on all the time, Rubes. It's nothing new. And I wasn't completely sure. Last night, you were so worried about Sophie, I–I mentioned it to Hitesh on the way out.'

'It was you that alerted the police.'

'I dare say they had other intelligence. It was probably the push they needed.'

'I can't believe you did that.'

His face was pained, affronted. 'I just mentioned I'd heard coke was being stored at Ewan's address and there was some activity there.'

'How could you?'

'I thought this was what you wanted. What we all wanted. Ewan's out of the way, at least for a while. Sophie's safe.'

'For how long?'

'That depends on what they've got. It might encourage Sophie to view things differently—'

'It won't! She's still taking the tablets. Chances are, it's probably him or one of his cronies supplying her. So, having him arrested for drugs isn't going to help the situation one bit.'

His face fell, contrite. 'I'm sorry, Rubes. I thought I was helping.'

She placed her head in her hands. 'I think you'd better go.' She'd called him because she hadn't wanted to come into the house alone, but now that she was here, that she knew it was safe, she was beginning to wonder at herself. This was her home.

'That's not fair.'

'Fair? Fair would have been to ask me or check with me first before you involve yourself in my family's business. Do you even realise what you've done? If she finds out this whole arrest came from me or someone close to me, she'll never speak to me again.'

'You're overreacting.'

'Believe me. Overreacting doesn't come close.' She stood.

'You're not serious?'

'I am. I want you to go. I need time to think. Alone.'

Chapter 55

Sophie placed the last of the cutlery in the dishwasher and snapped the door shut. The kids were bickering in the front room. Shrill, high-pitched voices digging at one another. They'd been hyper since Louise dropped them home from school, constantly asking where Ewan was because it was Wednesday and he usually came for dinner on a Wednesday. She'd had to make up some excuse about him working extra hours and get rid of Louise quickly – she didn't want anyone else to know about the arrest until they knew what they were dealing with. She could only imagine the fuss Greg would make at a man close to his kids involved with drugs. That was the last thing she needed. She'd baked cakes with the children to take their minds off things, yet they still wouldn't settle.

There had been no word from Ewan or the police since the call at lunchtime. No update. No news. And now it was almost 6:30 p.m. Were they still interviewing him?

She opened the door to the cupboard under the stairs, reached for her handbag and dug her hand inside, moving aside her purse, a packet of tissues, searching for the wrap of foil, when she suddenly remembered. And her heart sank. Her pills weren't there. Ruby had taken them.

She closed her eyes, shoved the bag away, was cursing her sister afresh when she heard a key in the front door.

Ewan.

Before she could reach him, Daisy and Alfie ran out into the hall and flung themselves on him. 'You came! See, Mum, he said he would!' her daughter exclaimed.

Sophie did her best to pull a smile. 'It seems you were right.'

Ewan took his time hugging the children, his blue work overalls crackling as he twirled them around. It was a while before he looked across at Sophie and she spotted the face behind the smile, the dark shadows under his eyes, the pasty white skin.

'I'm sure he's had a busy day,' Sophie said, peeling her children off him. 'Let's get him a drink and something to eat.'

'Can you read my bedtime story tonight?' Alfie asked.

Ewan ruffled his hair. 'Course I can, mate.'

Sophie steered the kids back into the front room and moved into the kitchen. She needed to speak with Ewan alone. All afternoon the idea of him in a marriage with children had tumbled around her insides, making her nauseous. A marriage he'd left, kids he'd deserted. Was it true?

'Why didn't you call when they let you out?' she said, closing the kitchen door behind him. 'I've been worried.'

'My phone's dead. I came straight here.' He pulled her into a tight embrace, stroked her hair. 'I'm sorry I worried you.'

'What exactly happened?' she said, releasing herself as soon as she was able and flicking the switch on the kettle.

'Oh, don't let's go into it now.'

'No, I want to. I need to know.'

He stared up at the ceiling, paused a moment. 'Okay. The police called at 6 a.m. I was still in bed. Ged let them in. Apparently, someone had tipped them off about a drugs den. Hardly what we were, they'd have seen that as soon as they crossed the threshold, but it didn't stop them riffling through drawers and emptying every cupboard.'

A sour taste popped at the back of Sophie's throat. 'It must have been awful.'

'It was. Ged and I were ordered to get dressed and sit in the kitchen.' His face turned stern. 'They found a bag of cocaine in the toilet cistern – Ged's private stash. The officer looked triumphant when he walked in with it, holding it up in one of those clear plastic bags as if it was a winning lottery ticket. We both said we had no idea how it got there, so we were taken to the police station, questioned for hours on end, then released under investigation.' He pulled a face. 'Worst thing about it all was the food. It was like pulp.'

'Why didn't Ged own up if it belonged to him?'

'Because he's already got a record. Even if they manage to stick a charge on him, he'll plead not guilty, say the stash was planted. There are always people coming and going at the flat.'

'What about you?'

'I'll do the same, if needs be.'

'That's not fair, Ewan, you'll get a record.'

'He's been good to me, Soph. I pay him mates' rates for the room I have there. And he gets me your V for next to nothing.'

Sophie flinched at the mention of her pills. Did that make her an accessory?

'I don't think anything will come of it,' Ewan said. 'Ged's pretty sure he can find a way out.'

The kettle switched itself off. Sophie toyed with whether to make drinks, but the next question was searing like a flame through her chest. 'There's something else I need to talk to you about. It's important.' She leaned against the kitchen side, the overwhelming desire to see his reaction dulling any consideration for the fatigue gripping them both. 'Ruby was here today.'

'Why?'

'She came over to help. But that isn't what I need to tell you. She went to London yesterday and met with your sister, Isla.'

Ewan stiffened. 'Why would she do that?'

She ignored his question. 'You didn't tell me you had a wife and kids.'

He closed his eyes, swiped his hand down the front of his face. 'It isn't what you think, Soph.'

'What? Are you telling me you aren't married then?'

He hung his head. 'It was short, a bad decision, and it's really not important.'

'How can you say that? You've got kids!'

'They're not mine. Look, Soph, if you just give me a chance to explain…'

'She said you manipulate people.'

'What?'

The door burst open and Daisy ran into the kitchen. 'I need eggs for school tomorrow. We're making fairy cakes.'

'What?' Sophie tore her gaze away from Ewan.

'Eggs – I need to take two to school tomorrow.'

Sophie cursed under her breath. 'Why didn't you tell me?'

'I'm telling you now.'

She rubbed the pads of her fingers into her eyes. She desperately wanted to probe Ewan further, but there was no way she was going to do it in front of her children. 'I'll have to go to the shop. We're out.'

'I'll go,' Ewan said.

'No. You put the children to bed. I need some air. We'll continue this conversation when I get back.' She pulled her jacket off the back of the chair, grabbed her phone and purse and marched out of the door.

Chapter 56

Ruby lay back and immersed her head beneath the surface of the bathwater, relishing the soothing heat travelling to every limb, every sensory receptor.

She'd been tough on Lewis. He was only trying to help, trying to get Ewan out of the way and safeguard Sophie, trying to be a good friend to them both. He shouldn't have meddled, not without speaking to her first, but she couldn't deny his intentions were well placed.

She dragged her head out of the water. She was dangling on the edge of a precipice, holding on by her fingernails. She needed to find a way to reason with Sophie, to make her see sense, and she needed to convince the police to dig deeper into Ewan's actions.

She climbed out of the bath, dried herself off and reached for her phone. A missed call from Lewis. He was checking up on her and she was grateful for his concern, but she didn't have the energy to deal with him. She'd call him back tomorrow, apologise with an invitation out for a beer.

Her phone rang. It was Kat.

'Hey. Did you manage to get hold of Sophie?'

'I called by, but the house was quiet. I did get a reply to yesterday's text to say she was a bit busy this week, and could we leave it until after the weekend.'

'Okay.' Ruby wasn't sure whether that was positive or not.

'What happened today? I was worried about you.'

Kat listened quietly as Ruby told her the full story about Ewan's arrest and her conversations with Sophie.

'Goodness! How long's he been into drugs?' she asked.

'I don't know if he is.'

Kat gasped when she told her about catching Sophie with Valium tablets bought off the street. 'Is he still in custody?'

'I think so. I haven't heard from Sophie since she sent me packing. I only hope they keep him in, Kat. For all our sakes.'

'Oh, I asked Graham about whether he'd seen anything in The Crown. He hasn't. He didn't even know they were pushing drugs there.'

That seemed strange, especially with Lewis claiming it to be common knowledge. Common knowledge amongst whom?

'How was work?' Ruby asked, keen to change the subject.

'Okay, the usual. Don't worry about Mark, he's still swallowing the migraine story.' Her tone lowered slightly. 'Though he is acting a bit strange.'

'What do you mean?'

'He took a two-hour lunch break today, despite you being off, and there was nothing in the diary. Bloody cheek! It was manic too.'

'That's not like him.'

'I know. When I asked him what he was up to, he said he had things to sort out. I hope he's not thinking of selling the business or something.' She groaned.

But Ruby's job was the last of her worries right now. All she could think about was that Mark had been one of the people out on Tuesday evening when Charlotte was killed. And he was behaving oddly. 'I saw him at the station yesterday,' she said.

'What time?'

'About five-ish. He looked like he was waiting for someone.'

'He told me he had an appointment on the Oakwell Estate, on the other side of town. Oh, I don't like the sound of this.'

Ruby didn't either, but for different reasons. 'I'm sure he isn't thinking of selling,' she said hastily. 'He wouldn't know what to do with himself without Galanti's.'

Kat rattled on about work and Ruby's clients she'd spoken with. Ruby zoned out, her thoughts returning to Charlotte's father, Nigel Manning, and his pitiful interview online. Charlotte's murder had to be linked to her mother's death. Every instinct in her body screamed it. Perhaps it was time to visit Charlotte's father. 'Listen, do you think you can cover for me one more day?' she asked.

'I guess so, why?'

'I need to try to sort out this stuff with Sophie.' The lie caught like barbs in her throat. Kat was a good friend. But she needed to formulate the idea in her mind before she could be sure.

'Okay. Keep me updated. And stay safe.'

Ruby swiped to end the call, switched to Google and typed in Nigel Manning. Numerous searches came up relating to Charlotte's disappearance, her murder. She worked her way through them until she found an old article mentioning their family home on Cunningham Road in Market Deeton. Cunningham Road was a few streets away from her mother's shop. She'd driven along it a couple of times, using it as a cut-through when High Street was busy.

She switched to images and various photographs graced the screen from the numerous posts and articles about him over the last year. About halfway down, there was a photo of him outside the front of a terraced house. The edge of a blue factory door cut in beside. A water droplet dripped down from her hair and landed on the phone screen. There was a shoe factory on the corner of Cunningham Road with a blue folding door. She needed to find the factory door, locate the house beside it. Maybe then, she'd get some answers.

Chapter 57

Sophie took her time walking back from the shop, scraping her heels against the paving. Leaves skittered around her ankles. The wind had picked up and after a day of being tucked up inside, sitting beside the phone, she relished the fresh air flushing out her lungs.

She was still seething at Ewan's words about his marriage – short, unimportant. What did he mean? He said the kids weren't his. When it came to it, neither were hers.

Ruby's face as she'd shared the details earlier slid into her mind. She'd looked concerned, scared. Was she scared for Sophie, or frightened at how it would affect *their* relationship? And then there were Ruby's comments about her bruises…

An evening lying on the hearth rug in front of the fire, a month or so after she'd met Ewan, sprang to mind. Wine, chatter and sex. She could still see the candle flame dancing in Ewan's eyes as she raised the subject of previous relationships. He was reluctant to join in, said the past should be left in the past. But when she told him about Greg and then talked about Dean, an old flame from school, he'd shared about a woman called Heather he'd lived with for a while in Glasgow. A relationship that morphed into a friendship, he'd said. Yet not once had he mentioned he had been married.

Her hand absently went to her throat. She stroked the bruise, flinching slightly at the tenderness beneath the skin. She hadn't enjoyed the scarf incident on Saturday; it reminded her of her poor mother. She'd told Ewan not to touch her neck again, it was out of bounds.

The conversation with Ruby, her hints at abuse pulsed through her. She wasn't being abused. She was a willing participant. Wasn't she? It certainly all started willingly. She recalled their early days when the sex was edgy, exciting, sensual. Ewan was considerate and caring, setting up safe words to ensure they stopped if either of them was uncomfortable.

Problem was, recently he hadn't always listened to the safe words.

Sophie rounded the corner, slowed her step to a dawdle, eyes unfocused as she cast her mind back. It was shortly after her mother died when he'd said he wanted them to find new ways of stimulating each other, to take them away from the worries of the day. The changes were small at first. A sharp pinch of a buttock one evening, fingernails running down her back, pressing just a little too hard into the flesh, another. Then, as time moved on, he started to tie her wrists, cover her eyes, and the pain became more intense. By day, he was the perfect boyfriend, the perfect stepfather to her children. By night, in the front room of her suburban home, he transported her to places she'd never before experienced.

She'd been wary to begin with, worried for the children. She wasn't worried they'd wake. They slept deeply and Ewan had installed baby monitors to ensure they'd hear them if they stirred. She was more concerned about the perils surrounding the world they were entering. She was a single parent, a mother and father to Alfie and Daisy for most of the week. But Ewan assured her it was all about trust. There were rules. As long as they stuck to them, it wasn't dangerous. During those moments they shared together, he took her away from everything. She was no longer Aileen McBride's grieving daughter, she was a sensual independent woman, strong and unbridled.

Since the trial, the pain had become stronger, more intense. Now she was in a whirlwind, a swirling vortex of pleasure and pain and she didn't know how to stop. A part of her didn't want to. It was intense, and… she loved him, didn't she? He was brilliant with the kids, good company, helpful around the house. She'd never loved anyone so deeply. But they were entering into more risky territory and the notion that he'd been through this with someone else, that what they were doing wasn't exclusive, changed everything.

She recalled the burning slap of his hand across her skin yesterday evening. Biting on a cushion to mute her cries. Afterwards, he'd massaged her with oil, taking great care on her sore areas, and he'd told her how special she was, how special they were. Because they did things other couples only fantasised about.

But today, as she limped along, her back crying out with pain and the question mark of a drugs charge and another family hanging over them, she was beginning to wonder. Is that what Ruby meant when she said he'd hurt someone else? Had they gone too far? She'd always believed he would stop if she really needed him to. He wouldn't push her beyond her boundaries. Now she wasn't so sure.

She walked alongside Brockleton Park. The melodic sound of the wind swishing through the trees pervaded the air, but Sophie wasn't listening. All she could think of was, how did she get to this point with Ewan? She needed to slow everything down, find a fresh foothold. At least until she really knew what was going on with the wife and kids in Glasgow.

She was almost at the children's playground when she heard a rustle and turned. A figure darted out from the bushes. Sophie froze. Dressed in black, only the whites of their eyes visible through the tight mask covering their head. She jumped back, gasped. And in that split second, they moved behind her. Fast, nimble. She opened her mouth to scream, but before any sound emitted, a hand stretched across it, wrenching her head back. The box of eggs slipped out of her hand, crashing to the floor. She struggled, pain ripping the side of her scalp as her hair was pulled under the grip.

Her phone dropped out of her pocket. Her purse followed.

The blow to the side of her head came from nowhere. She blinked away the fuzziness. Tossed, turned, struggled. A hand shot around her chest, pinning her arms by her side, the other at her mouth. And she was being dragged. Dragged towards the bushes at the side of the playground, heels scraping the concrete path. Arms fighting against the steely grip. Leaves bunching beneath her, catching the edge of her clothes. She tried to lift a foot to kick out, but gravity was defying her.

A knee hit her lumbar spine. She felt her legs wobble. The bushes starting to encase her. Sickening fear, paralysing her.

The headlights of a car, a blinding light, hurtling towards her. A weight tossed her to the ground. Excruciating pain tore through her shoulder as it connected with the concrete. A screech of brakes. The car mounted the pavement. She could only stare, mute, mouth wide open as it headed towards her. The bonnet halting inches away. Footsteps running. Running towards her, or away? She couldn't be sure. Everything was a blur.

'Are you okay?'

Sophie shrank back. She was on her side on the pavement, the concrete scratchy and hard beneath her, an elderly couple peering down.

The grey-haired man moved away. The woman slipped off a jacket and draped it over her, the wool soft and gentle on her skin. 'It's okay, you're safe,' she said. The car headlights glinted on the gold buttons of her dress as she knelt beside Sophie.

Sophie shivered.

'Try to breathe,' the woman said. 'My name's Sarah.' She wove her bony fingers through Sophie's. 'Are you hurt?'

Sophie stared back at her. She wanted to say no, but her mouth wouldn't work.

'There's an ambulance on its way,' the man said, re-joining them, concern etched into his forehead. 'Police too.'

'This is my husband,' Sarah said to Sophie. 'We saw you were in trouble, pulled over to help.' She turned to her husband. 'Turn those headlights off, will you?'

Slowly Sophie's vision started to clear. She could see Sarah's coiffed hair, the bangles jingling on her wrist. 'Ewan,' she squawked out.

'What did you say?' Sarah leant in closer. Sirens rang out in the distance now.

'Please! You need to get Ewan.'

Chapter 58

'Follow my finger,' the doctor said, covering her right eye.

Sophie blinked at the beam of light shining into her face and did as she was told, fighting to keep her left eye open. The evening had passed like a series of badly disjointed dreams, punctuated by flashing lights. The blue lights of the police car, the glare of the ambulance, the beam of the headlight driving towards her...

The figure dressed in black, grabbing her. Dragging her into the park...

'Okay, that all looks fine,' the doctor said, flicking off his torch. 'You've taken a blow to the head, you're battered and bruised and you're in shock, which means you need to rest. I'd like to examine your shoulder—'

'It's fine,' Sophie said, backing away. 'Just a bit of bruising.' She wasn't about to let him see the marks Ewan had made on her back.

The doctor paused. 'Well, if you're sure?'

She nodded.

'Okay. If you rest, you should be all right in a couple of days. I'd like to keep you in overnight though.'

'I can't, I have children.' She pictured Daisy and Alfie sleeping in their beds, blissfully unaware of the danger their mother had faced.

'I'm sure Christine will stay over with them,' Ewan said, tightening his grip on her hand.

As soon as he'd heard, Ewan had arranged for their neighbour to sit with the children and raced to the hospital. But apart from their weekends with Greg, she'd never left them all night and she couldn't bear the thought of them waking in the morning without her. 'I can't, Ewan. I can't leave them.'

'It's your choice,' the doctor said. 'You really ought to have someone with you. I don't recommend you drive either.'

'I'll take care of it,' Ewan said. He flopped to her side as the doctor left the room. 'Oh, Soph. I don't know what I would do if anything happened to you.'

She looked across at him, unable to answer, her mind a whirr. Who had attacked her? Why?

Strong arms reached around her, hugging her gently. Ewan rested his head on the top of hers. She wasn't sure how long they stayed there. She could feel the warmth of his skin, his breaths gently lifting wisps of her hair. Unspeaking. And all she could think about was – she'd been attacked. And the man consoling her, the same man she shared a bed with, who played with her children, who'd been her boyfriend for the last year, had a wife and kids. She was beginning to wonder if she really knew him at all.

The door opened and a man and woman entered, both in suits – him tall and slim with receding hair, her short and curvy. In different circumstances, they might have looked comical.

The woman pushed a bushy long fringe out of her eyes and introduced them both as detectives, flashing their cards. Sophie didn't catch their names, barely able to listen, her mind else-where. 'The couple that stopped,' she said. She wanted to see them, thank them. She couldn't even remember their names.

'They're fine,' the woman said. 'They're at the station, giving a statement.'

Goodness knows what would have happened if they hadn't arrived when they did. Sophie reached forward and pulled back the blanket covering her legs. She needed to get home.

'Why don't you rest for a while,' the female detective said, moving to her bedside. 'You've had quite a shock. We could do with asking you some questions, if you feel up to it?'

'I don't think this is a good time,' Ewan said.

The detective ignored him. 'I'm sure you'll agree, the sooner we catch whoever did this to you, the better,' she said to Sophie. 'Now, can you describe to me exactly what happened?'

Her colleague pulled a notebook out of his pocket and clicked the end of a pen.

Sophie struggled to cast her mind back to the scene. Her memory hazy, almost opaque, like an old movie. Everything happened so quickly. It was difficult to process. 'I spoke to the officer at the roadside. Gave him a description.'

The woman angled her head. 'Sometimes people remember things better afterwards.'

Sophie sighed and desperately tried to talk through the event again. Walking down Templeton Road on her way home from the shops. The park to her side. But as soon as she got to the part where the attacker emerged from the bushes, a thick fog descended.

'Tight or loose clothing?'

Sophie stared into space, thinking hard. 'Tight, I think. Like sportswear. They wore some kind of mask.' She'd seen those masks somewhere before. She tugged on her memory. Yes, on a skiing holiday in France with the school. They all wore them out one night, made fun of each other trying to guess who was who. Little did she know how frightening they would be in the wrong hands. She relayed this to the officer.

'What about an accent?' It was the male officer. The lights bounced off his shiny forehead.

'They didn't speak.'

'Not at all.'

'No.'

'Were you carrying anything?' Back to the female officer.

Sophie blinked. The criss-cross questions were making her dizzy.

She remembered her phone and her purse slipping out of her pocket, falling to the ground. A jingle of coins rolling out onto the pavement. Yet they'd ignored them, tugging at her jacket. They weren't interested in robbing her, they wanted to hurt her. 'Only my purse and my phone. Oh, and some eggs for Daisy. They didn't take anything.' She looked across at Ewan. 'We'll need to get Daisy some more eggs for school.'

'I'll sort it out,' he said. 'Don't worry.'

She looked back at the detectives. 'Who would do this?'

'Miss McBride, do you know of anyone who might want to hurt you?' The female officer again. 'Or someone you might have upset recently?' Her tone was gentle, kind.

Sophie met her gaze. They knew who she was. They had her name. Did they also know her boyfriend had been in custody today? The room started to wobble at the edges.

Ewan stepped forward. 'I think that's enough for today. I'm taking her home. You can speak with her again in the morning.'

The officers exchanged a glance, but didn't respond, instead thanking Sophie for her time and saying they'd be in touch. The woman handed her a card and asked her to call if anything came to mind, then followed her colleague out of the room.

Sophie felt the warmth of Ewan's embrace again. Him kissing her crown. 'I shouldn't have let you go out alone,' he said. 'From now on, I'm not letting you out of my sight.'

Chapter 59

Sophie sat at the breakfast bar, took another sip of tea and flinched at the sweet taste. Muffled voices filtered through from the hallway – Ewan guiding Christine out, sidestepping her questions with a promise to update her in the morning. The journey back from the hospital had taken an age and when they arrived home, Christine had fussed over them like a new mother, insisting on making tea to calm their nerves.

The front door clicked to a close. Sophie bowed her head, relishing the peace. She was aware of an unspeaking Ewan placing the throw they kept on the back of the sofa around her shoulders and sitting on the stool beside her, but she didn't look up. Gazing into space, numb, as memories from the evening crashed in and out of her thoughts. It was like living inside a dream, where events were broken, haphazard, and surrounded by a thick fog.

Time ticked past. Her nerves slowly settling like dust motes on a surface.

The cat flap snapped open and Pru climbed through. She steered around them, glowering at Ewan, before she made off into the hallway.

'Why me?' Sophie said quietly. 'Why attack me?'

'It was probably random,' Ewan said. 'Wrong place, wrong time.'

She could still feel the thick fingers pulling at her jacket, pinching at her skin. An involuntary shudder spiralled through her shoulders.

'Thank God that couple came along when they did,' Ewan added.

She turned to face him, the throw slipping off her shoulder. 'I need to thank them.'

'Of course. And we will. Don't dwell on it now. You need to rest. Doctor's orders.' He pulled the throw up, tucked the corner of it into the crook of her arm. 'You're safe. We can deal with everything else in the morning.'

He was right, of course. It had been a rollercoaster ride of an evening. Visceral. So much going on, so much to digest, all unfolding at a hundred miles an hour. But now she was home, sitting at her familiar breakfast bar, in the kitchen they'd both stood in earlier, the other matters of the day started crawling into her head. And as much as she tried, she couldn't ignore them.

'Why didn't you tell me you were married?' she asked.

'Because it's not what you think.'

'I can't believe I had to find out from my sister.'

'I would have told you myself in time.'

'Would you?'

'Of course. It just wasn't important.' He placed down his mug, hooked her gaze. 'You and me. We don't have secrets.'

But he did have a secret. A stonking big secret. One that he'd kept closely guarded for a year. 'Then tell me. Explain.'

'Not now. You've been through a terrible ordeal. You're not thinking straight.'

'I'm fine.' She mustered all her strength, tossed him a hard stare. She was worn out, drained, though the notion of going to bed, sleeping side by side, with a cloud the size of a lake hovering over them was unthinkable. 'I need to know.'

He opened his mouth to resist, but the resolve in her face silenced him. A brief hesitation. 'Okay, if you insist. Hear me out and remember this: there's only ever been you. No one has ever touched me as deeply or as tenderly as you.'

He lifted her hand, clasped it between his two, his eyes saddening.

'It was a couple of years ago. The printing firm I worked for closed down. I ended up working in a bar in Glasgow centre to pay the bills. Heather came into the bar one evening. She was the new girl in town, she'd moved with her work and she knew no one. The city can be a lonely place without friends. So much going on, no one to share it with. I felt sorry for her, showed her around, introduced her to a few people. We went out, had a bit of a fling, one of those...' He shrugged, scrunched his face. 'Whirlwind romances, I suppose. She met me after work when I was on an early shift, we'd get dinner, go for drinks. It was easy, fun. Then one evening she got a call, had to rush off. It was her babysitter.' He stretched his eyelids back. 'I didn't even know she had kids. All the discussions we'd had about life, work, our dreams for the future, yet she hadn't mentioned her children. I guess that should have rung alarm bells in itself. She said she didn't tell me because she thought it would scare me.'

'Isn't that what you did? Keep them from me. Concealed them.'

'It isn't the same, Soph. Honestly. You have to believe me. I felt awful when I met Heather's children. Connor was eight, a gorgeous lad, obsessed with golf. Jack a year younger, quieter and really sweet. I began to realise how difficult it was for her, to arrange childcare to meet me. So, I started to go there after work. We'd have dinner together. I'd play on the Xbox with the kids if they were still up.' He lifted his gaze to meet hers. 'You know what I'm like about family. Me and Isla, we were raised in a loveless household. No affection. No games. I suppose I was enjoying the company.'

'And you decided to get married.'

'No. Not at all actually. I was quite happy with how things were. We weren't even properly living together, although I spent most of my free time at her house. It all changed on my birthday weekend, about three months after we first met. Heather arranged for all of us to go away. A surprise.' He screwed up his eyes. 'I remember us heading south, stopping off at a pizza restaurant. Being plied with drinks for my birthday, them all whispering and giggling as if they had a secret.

'I was surprised when we arrived at Gretna Green. Gobsmacked when we checked into a hotel and she gave me a suit to change into. She'd planned the whole thing. I'm not sure if it was the alcohol or whether I was carried along with the excitement from the boys, but it all seemed such a thrill. Impulsively pulling in witnesses off the street, saying vows, drinking champagne afterwards. I moved in with her when we got back.'

He dipped his head, averting his gaze. 'A fortnight after the wedding, the boys' father turned up at the door. She'd told me, and the boys, he'd left them before they moved from Aberdeen. Said he used to knock her about. Was convincing too, she was terrified when he was back.'

'Didn't you call the police?'

'She wouldn't have the police involved. She'd been too frightened to report anything. I didn't know what to do. My priority was to keep her and the boys safe. Ray his name was, her ex-partner. Twenty years older than her. I met with him, organised a payment plan, a custody arrangement with the children. She didn't want him to see them, but the kids were keen. He'd never been violent with them and she said he only harmed her when they weren't around. I made sure I was there when they were collected and dropped off.'

'Weren't the kids frightened if he'd attacked their mother?'

'That was the thing. She said she'd kept it from them; he'd hit her in places they couldn't see. When they left him, she told them it was his decision. I don't know. It was hard to know what to believe. He seemed a good guy. How was I supposed to know? The kids adored him.

'He travelled down from Aberdeen, had the boys every other weekend. Heather didn't like it, but the kids were happy. And then things changed. She became clingy. Constantly calling me at work, wanting to know where I was. I just assumed she was scared, you know, coming out of an abusive relationship. It got progressively worse. If I was home late, or my phone was out of battery, she hit the roof. Became aggressive. Punched, screamed, threw things. Accused me of having affairs.'

'Why didn't you call the police?'

'I don't know. I should have. But she was a waif of a woman, half the size of me, you know? It was… odd. Anyway, I put up with it for a while. Tried to persuade her to get help. She became withdrawn, gave up her job. It was a comment from Connor that really made a difference. He mentioned her hitting his dad. I thought he was talking about a row they'd had and then he said it happened often. He said she didn't mean to, she got carried away. It was then that I realised it wasn't her being abused – she was the one abusing.

'I tried to confront her; she wouldn't talk about it. Said Connor was mistaken, his dad was trying to poison me against her. She refused to get help and as the weeks and months passed, I was facing a breakdown. I spoke to her about a break, to get my head together, and she said if I left, even for a short time, she'd stop me seeing the children. I knew she wasn't lying. She'd done it before with their real father, she'd do it again.' He looked up at Sophie. 'You know how much I adore Daisy and Alfie. Heather's boys might not have been mine, but they were good kids. The wrench when I did finally leave…' His voice splintered. 'I can't tell you.'

Sophie watched him shrink before her. Her strong capable Ewan. Her stomach clenched. But there was still one question she needed to ask.

'Did you do those things, the things that we do, with her?'

Tears filled his eyes. 'No, Soph! She was batshit crazy. Sick. What we do together is lovemaking. It's sensual, deep. Things were never like that with her, not even in the early days.'

Sophie stared at him. She wanted to believe him, though a tiny voice inside wept with doubt.

'It wasn't me being manipulative,' he said. 'It was her. She twists things, tells lies to make people believe her. She's done it before. And she's doing it again, this time with Isla.'

Chapter 60

Cunningham Road comprised two rows of terraced houses facing each other across a narrow strip, all with front doorsteps leading directly onto the pavement. Ruby walked along until she reached the last house on the right, beside the shoe factory with the blue folding door, and checked the photo on her phone. The wooden front door had discoloured to cream, the paint cracked and blistered around the letterbox. But there was no doubt it was the same door Nigel Manning was standing beside in the news piece.

She stood on the terracotta tiled step and knocked. Would Hitesh be there? He took his role as family liaison seriously, had spent a lot of time at their house after their mother died, sharing updates on the investigation, guiding them through the process of traumatic loss. It was almost 10 a.m. This was about the time he used to arrive. Oh, goodness, she hoped he wasn't there. She was pretty sure he wouldn't welcome her presence, and she'd struggle to talk frankly with Charlotte's father and get the answers she needed under his beady eye.

Nigel Manning answered the door within seconds. He seemed smaller than in the television appeal, barely five foot five. The blue jumper and jeans he wore hung off his lean frame. 'Yes?'

'Mr Manning—'

'Are you press?'

'No, I'm—'

He reached up, rubbed the back of his neck, pushing away straggles of thinning hair. 'Because if you are, you can bugger off. I'm not interested.' He made to close the door.

Ruby placed out her hand, wincing at the force with which the wood connected with her palm. 'No, Mr Manning, I'm Ruby McBride,' she said. 'My mother was killed last year.'

Comprehension spread like a stain across his face. 'You're Aileen McBride's daughter?'

'Her eldest. I wanted to come and offer our condolences. We were so sorry to hear about your daughter.'

His face slackened. 'Thank you.' He looked shocked, embarrassed, as if he didn't know what to say next. 'Do you want to come in?'

'If I'm not interrupting anything.'

He stood aside for her to enter, then glanced furtively up and down the road before closing the door. 'Sorry about that. I'm sick of bloody journalists, calling, knocking. There were hordes of them out there last week, blocking the road. It was ridiculous.'

Ruby knew that feeling only too well. They'd had to close the curtains at her mum's and sit in the rooms at the back of the house in the early days after their mother was killed. 'They can be so intrusive,' she said, quietly.

He nodded and motioned for her to follow him along a narrow hallway and into a room which was surprisingly light. The voice of a TV presenter blared on about yesterday's horse racing on the television in the corner. Used coffee mugs and beer bottles lined a brown chair opposite. A matching sofa against the back wall faced patio doors that looked out onto a lawned garden.

At least he was alone.

He gathered up some of the mugs. 'Sorry, I wasn't expecting company.'

Ruby swallowed, desperately trying to block out the damp smell clogging the air. And something else faintly in the

271

background... What was it? Sweet and musty... cannabis. No wonder he wasn't expecting company.

'Please don't worry,' she said, moving aside a newspaper to sit on the sofa.

She'd read somewhere that they didn't have any other family. There was only him and Charlotte and the room displayed all the markers of a grieving father, struggling to hold it together. It was pitiful.

'Can I get you a drink?'

'No, I'm good, thank you.'

He lowered himself into the armchair, placed the mugs down and grabbed the remote control. The presenter's voice sank to a whisper.

'How are you doing?' she asked, cringing at the hopelessness of the question. His daughter had been murdered and her killer was still on the loose. How was he supposed to be doing?

He shrugged. 'Truth is, I've no idea. I'm waiting by the phone. It's like purgatory.'

Ruby remembered those early hours and days only too well. Jumping at every ring of the doorbell, every message on her phone. After Aileen was killed, three full days passed before Colin was arrested, five until he was charged. She couldn't eat, couldn't sleep, every second a living hell. But for Nigel, it was worse. Charlotte had been dead over a week now. She couldn't begin to imagine how difficult it must be to continuously live under that cloud. 'I take it there's still no news?'

'Nothing. The police ring or call by daily. They say they're doing their best.' He sniffed, stared into space. 'Strange really, 'cos I know it isn't going to bring her back. I'd just feel easier if they got the bastard.'

She could relate to that. When they recovered from the initial shock, they'd all felt a mild sense of relief when Colin was locked away, like the calm air after a long storm.

'Did Charlotte come and see you when she came back?' Ruby asked.

Nigel was quiet a moment, his face lost in memories. 'Once. Two nights before she died. She turned up late, must have been after ten. I hardly recognised her, she was so pale and thin. Her beautiful hair lank. All she wanted was money. Wouldn't even stay to talk. She was on edge. She clearly wanted another fix of whatever it was she was taking. I made her promise to come and see me again.' His face folded, distraught.

'I'm so sorry. Did she say where she'd been or why she came back?'

'That's what the police asked me.' He placed a hand over his eyes, then gripped the bridge of his nose with his thumb and forefinger. 'I didn't ask. I was overwhelmed to see her. I thought possibly she was coming back for good, you know? That we could get her clean again. I didn't push her. I wanted to give her time. Time to rebuild things. Only, time was the one thing she didn't have.'

Ruby looked away, giving him a moment. Her gaze travelled around the room. To the thick navy drapes, hanging either side of the patio doors; the woodchipped walls, the paper curling at the corners. A sideboard beside the armchair housed a collection of framed photographs. A picture of a toddler, sitting on her dad's shoulders. A little girl on a swing, head back, laughing. A school photo of an older girl in a red cardigan, hair tied into a ponytail, two front teeth missing. The little girl with the fair complexion and the white-blonde hair bore no resemblance to the photos of the heavily made-up young woman in the press after Charlotte fled.

Nigel followed her gaze, lifted the frame on the end and stared at it a moment, forlorn.

'Do you know what's worse?' he said. 'I don't have any recent photos of her. She refused to let me take her picture when she hit her teens. I had to pinch one off her Facebook page for the police.'

He leaned across, handed over the photo in his hand. Ruby wasn't sure what to do so she took it. Charlotte must have been well into her teenage years. She was sitting on the edge of a sofa, a cola bottle clasped in her hand. The same sofa Ruby now sat on. The same clock with the roman numerals hung on the wall behind.

She shouldn't have come. It wasn't right for her to be here, probing this poor man for answers when he was wading through his puddle of grief.

'Things were so easy when she was younger,' he continued, staring into space. 'I was the most important person in her world.'

Another glance at the photo. Charlotte looked so young, so alive. 'It can't have been easy, raising her by yourself.'

'She was only twelve when the cancer took her mother and I promised that woman on her deathbed, I'd take care of our girl. Charlotte had recently started secondary school, was growing up, finding her way. Hormones flying all over the place. I won't lie, it was difficult. She desperately needed a mother figure. I did my best and not without a challenge. At fifteen, she was stopping off school, experimenting with drugs, staying out until all hours. A proper handful.' The words were strong, but his face was wistful, as if he yearned to turn the clock back. 'She could be so loving, so thoughtful at times. I remember her baking a cake for my fiftieth birthday – chocolate orange, my favourite. It sank in the middle, she was never much of a cook, and she left the kitchen in a right mess.' He gave a sad smile. 'But it was the best cake I ever tasted.'

Ruby's throat thickened. She could only imagine how difficult life must have been.

'When she reached sixteen, I knew I'd lost her,' he continued. 'She was distant, rarely at home and when she was here, she barely spoke. She was dying to leave, talked about it as if it was the big solution to all her problems – having her own space, spreading her wings.' He took the photo back from Ruby. 'When I think of what we went through afterwards. The drugs, the rehab, Colin… I didn't know about the prostitution until the trial. A call girl, they said. How could my little Charlotte become a call girl?' He sniffed. 'I should never have let her go.'

'Did she know my mother?' Ruby asked, in her most sensitive voice. She hoped that she sounded sensitive. She did feel for him, but she also desperately wanted to find the connection. For both their sakes.

'If she did, she never told me. But she was so detached by the time she went missing, I barely knew any of her friends by then.'

'Did she ever mention the name Ewan?'

He looked confused. 'No. Who's that?'

'A family friend, I wondered if she was in contact with him.'

'Not that I know of.'

'What about Mark Galanti?' she said, desperately trying to piece things together.

'From the kitchen place? No.'

She asked about Becky and even Tom, she was clutching at straws now, but he shook his head, his eyes narrowing.

'What is this?' he asked. His face scrunched in confusion.

'Sorry. I've been wondering about her connection with my mum and Colin. Looking at our links, trying to work out how it all fits together.'

'I'd be lying if I didn't say the same thing's crossed my mind, even though the police keep saying they're treating Charlotte's murder separately.'

It was comforting to hear he was thinking along the same lines. 'My sister, Sophie. She's still struggling with everything.' Ruby pulled her phone out of her pocket and worked through the photos. She was about to show him one of Sophie and the kids, when the first one she came to was a lopsided one of Ewan, Sophie and Lewis that Daisy had taken when she was playing with Ruby's phone at the memorial service. She passed it over.

'Poor thing. It's so difficult.' He leaned in further. 'Who's that with her?'

'Ewan, her boyfriend,' Ruby said, pointing at him, watching Nigel carefully.

'No, the other one.'

'Oh, Lewis. He's a friend.'

He frowned at the photo, staring at it for several seconds. 'I recognise your sister from the media coverage of your mother's trial. She looks so like your mum. Not sure about the others though. Sorry.'

Chapter 61

Ruby felt uncomfortable as she left Nigel Manning's and walked home through the back streets, as if she wasn't alone. She checked over her shoulder. A man was walking a spaniel further down the road. A jogger approaching on the other side. No one nearby. She'd left her car at home because she didn't want it spotted in town, but now she wished she'd brought it.

She quickened her step, trying to shrug off her paranoia. Nigel couldn't see a link between the families, despite, like her, believing there must be something. She needed to find the connection.

Her mind wandered as she turned the corner. She still hadn't spoken to Bridget properly since Sunday. Her aunt had been distracted when she left and too busy to talk when she'd phoned the other day. Perhaps she should call her now, check she was okay. She was just reaching for her phone when her name was called from the opposite side of the road.

Ruby jumped and turned. It was Becky. She strode across to join her.

'What are you doing at this end of town?' Becky asked.

Ruby paused for the briefest of seconds. 'I was visiting someone. Are you not working today?'

'Just running some errands,' she said, lifting her bag briefly as if it contained something important. Her face crumpled in concern. 'How are you doing? I was sorry to hear about Sophie.'

Sophie. Had Lewis told her about their argument? She was about to respond when her phone rang. It was Kat.

'Sorry, I have to get this,' she said.

Becky squeezed her arm, mumbled something about getting back to work and moved off.

'How are you?' Kat said. 'I heard about Sophie.'

'What about Sophie?' Ruby moved to the side of the pavement.

'Haven't you heard? She was attacked last night, walking home from her local shop.'

'Oh my God!' So that was what Becky was referring to. No wonder she looked concerned. Ruby had been so absorbed with Nigel Manning, about locating the right house, asking the pertinent questions, that for the first time in days she hadn't checked the news. Her pulse thumped. 'Is she okay?'

'I think so. A bit shocked, bruised and battered. Apparently, someone jumped her on Templeton Road, but they were interrupted, thankfully. I saw her neighbour, Christine. She told me Sophie was taken to hospital and she's home with Ewan now. I've tried to ring, but it goes to voicemail.'

Ewan was with her. So, he'd been released from police custody. Did this have anything to do with him?

Ruby thanked Kat, ended the call and phoned Sophie's mobile. It went straight to voicemail. What the hell was going on?

She checked her watch – almost 11:30 a.m. A low hum started in her head. She needed to get to her sister, to find out what had happened.

She turned on her heel. A car passed, then another. A woman with a buggy steered around her. A taxi approached, its yellow lamp lit. She stuck out her hand, flagged it down and climbed inside.

Ruby's stomach was churning as she arrived at Henderson Close. *Please, God. Let her be okay.*

She strode down the drive, past Ewan's Golf, his old Subaru, Sophie's Astra, about to move down the side of the house to the back door, when something stopped her. She didn't know what she was going into, who might be there, and she wasn't on speaking terms with Sophie. Without giving it another thought, she stopped at the front door and rapped hard.

The wind rippled through the bushes outside. Ruby shifted from foot to foot, cupping her hands around her eyes, squinting through the frosted glass. She turned back to the road, searching for any sign of life, and was considering trying Sophie's mobile again when the handle snapped down.

Ewan opened the door to a narrow slit. Dark circles hung beneath his eyes. There was a nick on his chin where he'd cut himself shaving.

'How is she?' Ruby asked, anxiety catching the words in her throat. 'I've only just heard.'

'She's asleep.'

'Can I come in?'

'The doctor said she needs to rest.'

'Please, Ewan? I need to see her, make sure she's okay.'

He didn't budge. 'She's shocked and bruised, but she'll be fine.' It was only then that Ruby noticed the chain fixed across the door. He had absolutely no intention of letting her in.

But she wasn't about to give in easily. 'What actually happened?'

Ewan's face softened. 'She was on her way back from the shop last night, when someone tried to grab her.'

'Who? Why?'

'We don't know yet. The police are working on it.' His body moved slightly, as if he'd shrugged. 'Could be kids, messing around.'

Ruby's chest hardened. 'Or it could be something to do with your arrest.' She couldn't help herself.

Ewan's eyes darkened. 'I think you'd better go.' He made to close the door, but Ruby shoved her boot into the gap.

'I've a right to see her. She's my sister.'

'She doesn't want you here.'

'What, like *your* sister doesn't want to see you?'

Ewan's nostrils flared. But he was unmoved. Unscathed by the words. He looked her up and down, like she was dirt on his shoe. 'You don't know anything about me.'

'I know a lot more than you think.'

The door pulled back a centimetre or so, then jammed hard into Ruby's foot.

Pain tore through her. She screamed, pulled it out. The door slammed shut.

Ruby's foot buzzed with pain, but she ignored it, the sensation overtaken by the fireball of anger bursting inside. She'd kept her temper at bay for so long, trying to protect her sister. But now wasn't the time for the softly, softly approach. She was sorry her sister had been attacked, she really was, but she needed her to be under no illusions of who she was dealing with. And there was no other way of telling her.

She thumped the door with her fists. 'Isla said you were dangerous and manipulative, a rotten apple and she was right,' she shouted. 'Your wife and kids don't want to see you either!' She raised her voice a decibel, repeated the last line. If Sophie was lying there, awake in the background, she desperately hoped she'd heard.

Chapter 62

Sophie shrank back from the bedroom curtain as Ruby walked away along the drive. Shoulders hunched, head down. Little wonder, half the street must have heard her screams and wails at the door.

A part of her was pleased she looked dejected. She deserved to be punished for trying to seduce Ewan. But there was also a concern growing. Apart from Ewan, Ruby was her only other family nearby. The only other person who unconditionally looked out for her and the kids. And the gap between them was widening by the day.

She'd been so angry with her yesterday for going behind her back and meeting with Isla. Though, as time moved on, she began to pick at the words herself. Ruby said Isla called him manipulative, a rotten apple, yet Ewan claimed the facts had been twisted.

Many times, they'd discussed a visit to Glasgow, but it was so far away and something else always came up. Alfie's birthday. Her mother's trial. She had hoped, after the memorial service, that they'd make a conscious effort to visit and get to know his family, especially if they were to share a future together.

But then, Charlotte's murder happened, Ruby made a move on Ewan, he was arrested…

A cupboard door opened and closed downstairs. Ewan had moved into the kitchen. They'd concealed the attack from the children, told them she was feeling under the weather that morning and had taken a day off work sick. It hadn't been difficult, their young minds distracted by Daddy picking them up from school, taking them to stay with him a day early for the weekend.

She thought back to Hitesh's visit earlier, following up on the police interview last night with a fresh stream of questions about her walk to the shop, the attack. Ewan sitting on the sofa, sandwiching her hands between his. Who attacked her? Was it linked to her mother's case? The incident, happening so soon after Charlotte's murder, left her terrified. And the worst of it was, she wasn't able to give Hitesh any more detail than she had given his colleagues yesterday, which was practically nothing.

Stealthy footsteps traipsed up the stairs. Sophie moved back to the bed. She was sitting on the edge beside a sleeping Pru, the duvet resting over her legs when Ewan walked in.

He placed a mug of tea beside her. 'How are you feeling?' he asked, his forehead crumpled with concern. 'I'm not sure you're ready to be up and about.'

'I'm fine.' She thanked him for the tea. He'd been a star this morning, making the children's lunches, taking them to school. Sitting with her while the police took her statement. But she couldn't rest forever, and she wasn't about to be mollycoddled.

'Drink your tea. I put in extra milk, just how you like it.'

Sophie took a sip and placed it down. 'What did Ruby want?'

'To check how you were. I said you were feeling better.'

'You could have let her in.'

'After what's she done? I don't think that would have been a good idea, do you?'

Silence hovered between them a minute. *Dangerous and manipulative.* She couldn't get those words out of her head. 'Are you sure you've told me everything? About Isla. Heather. The children.'

His eyes hardened. 'We've been through this. Heather's sick.'

'You don't talk about Isla much,' she said, manoeuvring the subject to his sister.

'There's not much to say. We don't feel the need to live in each other's pockets, we're very different. But if either of us needed the other, we'd be straight there, by their side. You'll see when you meet her.' He made to sit beside her on the bed, spotted the cat and stiffened. 'Look, you need to put this whole business out of your head, Soph. Ruby's got some twisted version of the truth. She's making you doubt your own mind.'

'Isla might not want to meet you now her head's been filled with Heather's stories.'

'I'll put her right.' He didn't seem perturbed. 'Plus, we don't know how much of this is down to Ruby.'

'What?'

'How much of this she's fabricated to suit herself.'

Sophie was flabbergasted. She couldn't imagine Ruby would go to such lengths. Though a week ago, she couldn't imagine her sister trying to seduce Ewan. It was all such a mess. But something about his comment made the hairs on the top of her arms upend. 'Let's find out, shall we?'

'What do you mean?'

'Why don't you call Isla now?'

He stared at her. 'I've tried already. Several times today. Her phone goes to voicemail. She's probably got it on silent.'

Convenient. Though Ruby did say Isla was in London. Maybe she was travelling back.

'Has Ruby always been jealous?' he asked.

Sophie smoothed a ruffle in the duvet. She wanted to say no. Instinct told her to stand up for Ruby, to fight for her sister. But she was hurt. Hurt by the way Ruby had gone behind her back and then tried to pretend everything was normal. Ruby had always sailed through life, achieving the top grades in school, the friendships with the popular kids, the cool boyfriends. Was it possible now things had fallen foul between her and Tom, for the first time she felt she was missing out on something? And if she couldn't have Ewan, she wasn't going to let Sophie have him either. She blinked, rubbed her forehead. The truth was, her head was fuzzy and she had no idea who or what to believe. 'I don't know.'

'Look, why don't I take you out tonight?' he said, caressing the back of her neck with his hand. 'You said yourself, you're feeling fine.'

Sophie pulled a face. She should quell the nerves, get back out there, show whoever had the gall to attack her that she wasn't easily scared. Though she was scared. She was very scared. At least she wouldn't be alone...

'Come on. The kids are with Greg. Let's get dressed up and go out for dinner. Somewhere special, my treat. It'll take your mind off things.'

Chapter 63

My feet pound the pavement. The soles of my running shoes connecting with the concrete, teasing it, before they swiftly draw back. Thump, thump, thump. What was I thinking of? I've always been so careful, planned so meticulously. But this time I let my guard down, acted on impulse.

I concentrate on breathing. Blood rushing through my veins. Cross the road and head down High Street. I need to put this out of my mind now, focus on the task ahead.

I pass a jogger moving in the opposite direction, the cord of his headphones running down his front. I don't need headphones to block out the drone of the traffic. The rhythm of movement: thud, thud, thud is my tune.

I turn the corner, head out of town. Relish the endorphins dripping into my system, cleansing my brain.

I now realise you weren't ready for my next move. You never will be. But it's all going to be fine. Because, you see, I have a fallback, a second choice. And it will be so much more impactive than the first.

A woman is walking two little dogs on the pavement ahead. I step out into the cycle way. A van courses around the corner, missing me by inches. 'Bastard,' I shout, scooting back onto the pavement. The wind tears at my words. I stop, wrap my arms around my head, watch it go. But it's surface anger, annoyance. The root of my real anger, an anger that burns a furnace in my soul, runs deep to the pit of my stomach.

I fall back into a jog and pick up pace. Faster and faster. Across another road and another, weaving through the constant hum of traffic, cursing it for slowing my pace. When I reach the park, evening is falling.

Twigs crackle beneath my feet. I pause, bend forward and place my hands on my knees. I'm ready to strike again. And this time I won't be thwarted.

Chapter 64

Ruby was woken by her phone, trilling beside her. She hauled herself up. Her right arm was cold and numb where it had caught beneath her. She rubbed it, checked her watch. Almost 6 p.m. She'd drifted off on the sofa after returning from Sophie's and fallen into an exhausted slumber. She must have slept for hours.

The caller was Greg. Pins and needles rippled through her arm as she pulled the phone to her ear. 'Hello.'

Greg didn't bother with preamble. 'How is Sophie? I've been trying to call. She's not picking up, or answering her messages.'

He was shooting out the words nervously, like bullets. 'What do you mean, Greg?'

'The kids told me she wasn't well. I thought maybe it was another one of her headaches. Then I had a call from an old mate in Market Deeton to say she'd been attacked. She should have told me, Ruby.'

Ruby remembered pounding Sophie's door earlier and winced, regret at losing her temper seeping into her veins. She needed to find a way to calm things down, to get through to Sophie – she still hadn't told her about the other women Ewan had been spotted with…

'Ruby?'

She switched back to her phone. Greg seemed unaware of their argument. 'She's at home, resting. She's okay.' Was she okay? She couldn't be sure. Ewan had done a good job of preventing her from seeing her sister. But the doctors had

287

discharged her. She couldn't have been seriously hurt, could she?

'She still should have told me.'

Ruby apologised on behalf of her sister and told Greg as much as she knew about the attack, which she'd picked up from scant news articles.

'What am I supposed to say to the kids? They're with me for the weekend, they clearly don't know.'

Ruby thought hard. 'Nothing at the moment. They're too young to see the news and Sophie's name wasn't specifically mentioned. If they hear a rumour or ask any questions, play it down and say she's all right. I'm sure she'll tell them what they need to know when she's feeling better.'

The doorbell chimed.

'I don't like being put in this situation, Ruby. It's not fair. We're supposed to be parenting these kids together.'

'And you are,' she said, desperately trying to placate him. Sophie wasn't doing herself any favours here. 'I'm sure Sophie will speak with you when she's up to it.'

A fist thumped the door. Someone was persistent.

'I'm going to have to go, Greg. Someone's at the door.'

She ended the call and checked her watch again. They'd normally be finishing work around now. Perhaps it was Mark, checking on her. In the hallway, she glanced at herself in the mirror. Her hair was all over her face; a sleep crease ran down the side of her cheek. Oh, well. If it was her boss, at least she looked ill.

'Hello, Ruby.' DC Hitesh Lalvani's face was stern as she opened the door. 'Can I come in?'

Ruby pushed her hair back from her face and moved aside. 'Has something happened?'

'Shall we go into the front room?'

She followed him and, as he indicated for her to sit, taking the opposing sofa himself, the back of her neck prickled. She'd been here enough times over the last year to know this wasn't a social call. 'What's going on?' she said. 'Is Sophie okay?'

'She's fine, as far as I'm aware. You've heard about her attack?'

She nodded. 'Have you arrested anyone?'

'We're still looking into it.'

'So, you don't have any idea who attacked her, or why?'

'Not yet, no. But I'll give you the same advice I did before. Keep your phone with you and make sure someone knows where you are at all times.'

She was reminded of Colin Halliday's words the other day. He'd told her to be careful. 'You think my family are in danger,' she said slowly.

'I didn't say that. It could be unrelated.'

Unrelated. There it was, that word again. A word so overused it was tired and tattered at the edges.

Her phone rang again. Bridget flashed up. Ruby bit her lip. With everything going on, she still hadn't spoken to her aunt. She made a mental note to phone her back later and rejected the call. Seconds later, a text popped up. *Are you having a good week? Call me when you are free for a catch-up.*

She cast the phone aside, aware Hitesh was watching her carefully. 'Are you sure this isn't related to what happened to Mum?' she asked.

'We've no reason to think that. But general safeguarding is never wasted.' He pushed his glasses up his nose. 'I understand you went to see Mr Manning today.'

She stayed quiet, eyeing him warily.

'And you asked him about Ewan, and whether he or Charlotte knew him, as well as other names?'

Ruby swallowed. It had all seemed rather innocent when she'd walked into Nigel Manning's front room that morning and chatted with him about her mother and his daughter. Two families united in their grief. The questions about Ewan and the others dropped into the conversation easily. If Nigel Manning was troubled, it didn't show. Though now Hitesh mentioned it, it sounded callous and conniving. 'I was trying to establish—'

'Do you know how many officers are working on this murder case?' Hitesh interrupted. 'Do you have any idea how many hours they've put in this past week? Many of them haven't seen their husbands, wives or children in days.'

'I'm sorry.'

'Mr Manning has been through hell since Charlotte disappeared. Since her body was found, it's been a twenty-four-hour job trying to keep him updated and calm, and ensure he's well supported. Then you go off on your own little investigation and put ideas into his head.'

'I didn't mean anything by it. I just thought if I could find a link, you'd look at things, well... Ewan, further.'

'We've looked at Ewan. We've checked his movements, taken samples, searched his associations. We've considered everything you've said, every little detail, and there is nothing, *nothing*, to link him to Charlotte's murder.' He took off his glasses. With his other hand, he rubbed the little indents at the top of his nose. 'I'm sorry about your argument with your sister, I really am. But you of all people should know how vulnerable someone is after losing a loved one in such tragic circumstances.'

'I was trying to help.'

He stood. 'You need to stay out of it and leave the investigation to us.'

Chapter 65

Sophie was upstairs, straightening her hair when the doorbell chimed. She glanced at her freshly ironed dress, hanging off the wardrobe. It was 7:35 p.m., the table was booked for eight and they were already running late.

'Is Miss McBride in?' A gruff tone she didn't recognise filtered up the stairs.

'We're on our way out.' Ewan's voice was tight.

It was followed by another mumbled exchange she couldn't decipher. She shrugged off her robe, slipped on the dress, grabbed the straps of her shoes and made for the stairs.

In the hallway, Ewan was face to face with a police officer in uniform, his eyes on fire.

'What's going on?' she said.

'They're just leaving.'

The officer, still standing on the doorstep, ignored Ewan. 'Miss McBride?'

She nodded.

'PC Medwell. We've got a warrant to search the property.'

'What?' It was cold with the door sitting open. She crossed her arms to hold in the little heat she had left. 'I don't understand. Why?'

'They think I'm keeping something here,' Ewan said, squaring up to the officer afresh. 'Do you think I'm mad?'

'That's enough,' Sophie said. Only now did she glimpse the line of uniforms in her driveway. Her gaze rested on an officer holding a red metal tool. Were they really thinking of forcing her door? What were they expecting to find? 'We're on our way out,' she said, shoes still hanging from her hand.

The officer's face softened. 'We want to cause as little disruption to your family as possible,' he said. 'Are your children here?'

'No, they're with their father.'

'Okay.' He pointed to the front room. 'If you could go in there, we'll get this over with as quickly as possible.'

'No way!' Ewan snarled.

Sophie pressed a hand to her forehead. 'Leave it, Ewan.'

Almost twenty-four hours had passed since her attack, the nerves still jangling, and now she was being subjected to this. Thank goodness the children weren't there.

Minutes later, they were sitting on the sofa. The sounds of footfalls seeping down the stairs. Clunks as drawers were opened and closed, wardrobes were searched. She imagined them sifting through her cupboards and personal items and cringed.

Misuse of Drugs Act, the warrant said. Did they really think Ewan was keeping drugs here?

She caught the eye of the woman in uniform, sitting on the nearby armchair. What was her name? She couldn't remember, even though she'd introduced herself twice. 'How long is this going to take?' she asked.

The officer pressed her lips together. 'It's difficult to say.'

Time ticked by. Her gaze flicking on and off the clock on the mantel. Seven forty-five. Seven fifty-five. When it reached 8 p.m., her head started to feel hot, as if she was coming down with a fever. She hadn't really wanted to get dressed up and go out, yet Ewan had been persuasive, saying it would be good for her, take her mind off things. She should be sitting down to dinner now, at a fancy restaurant, instead of sitting here all dressed up, humiliated in her own home.

A knock at the door. It was Medwell. He looked taller standing there, bearing down on them. 'Could we have the keys to the cars on the drive please?' he said, rubbing a hand over his bald head.

Sophie felt a line of sweat trickle down the back of her neck. Over the last couple of weeks, she'd faced murder, drugs, an attack. What else could life possibly throw at her? She dragged herself up and led him to the key rack in the kitchen.

She was back in the front room, considering asking if they'd finished with her bedroom so she could at least get changed, when the door knocked again.

It was Medwell. 'Do you have the keys to the Subaru?'

'Ewan has those.' She nudged him.

'This is ridiculous.' Ewan shook his head in disbelief.

'Just give them to him,' she said.

He muttered under his breath and dug his hand in his pocket. The metal chinked together as he handed them over.

The door closed and they were alone again, the three of them. It was like being under house arrest.

An hour ago, she was in the shower, the promise of a fancy meal and a long evening in front of her. Now there were officers riffling through her underwear drawer. How did they get to this point? What the hell had happened?

The door flung open. 'Mr Wilson,' Medwell said. 'Could you join me in the hallway please?'

Ewan clamped his eyes shut. 'I don't believe this.'

Sophie sat forward. 'What's going on?'

'They're trying to fit me up.'

Sophie followed him. As she stepped into the hallway, the front door opened, inviting another rush of cool air inside.

An officer in latex gloves held up a bag of white substance at Medwell. 'Another from the Subaru,' he said. 'Looks like there are several.'

Sophie's heart plummeted.

'Ewan Wilson, I'm arresting you…'

Sophie didn't hear the end of the statement amidst the ruckus that followed. She could only watch as Ewan kicked and struggled against the officers trying to hold him, a string of expletives shooting out of his mouth. He was restrained, handcuffed, led to the door.

She followed, aghast. 'How could you?' she said to him.

'This isn't what you think, Soph. It's a fit-up.'

Chapter 66

Things were getting out of hand. Ruby turned onto her side. Still exhausted, she'd taken to her bed after Hitesh left, willing sleep to rescue her from the cruel thoughts suffocating her. Only it was still early, and sleep couldn't have been further from her mind.

Could she really have been so wrong about Ewan?

His face at the door earlier, the curl of his lip, the menacing smile. If he wasn't a murderer, he knew exactly what he was doing with Sophie. She thought about her sister being ambushed on the way home from the shop yesterday. Was Sophie attacked because of Ewan's drug connections? Or was it something to do with Charlotte's murder and her mother's case?

Stay out of it… Hitesh's words made her grit her teeth. The truth was, she couldn't stay out of it. She'd needed to look further, deeper – because, as much as she tried, she couldn't shrug off the link between Charlotte's murder and her mum. It was someone close to the family, it had to be. Otherwise, none of this made sense.

A low thud made her start. Her eyes darted to the door. She'd checked and double-checked the door locks before coming up. Windows too, spurred on by Hitesh's safeguarding advice. She lay completely still. A car passed outside. Then silence. Her shoulders slackened.

A creak. It sounded like the rocking chair in Bridget's front room when they were kids. She remembered Sophie and her quarrelling over that chair many a time. It became the source of so many arguments, with Bridget eventually saying, 'Neither of you are going to sit there because I'm using it,' in her usual theatrical manner.

Bridget. She hadn't been able to bring herself to phone her back tonight. With the case flying around her head, her aunt was bound to pick up on her mood. And Bridget had sounded merrier in the text earlier. She didn't want to upset her.

Another creak, barely audible this time.

It was probably her elderly neighbour, Eric, next door. She often heard him moving about through the wall, the occasional rasp of his voice if he had company. The last place she'd lived was a flat, the top floor of an old three-storey house, and she used to lie in bed and listen to the mice scuttling about in the attic.

She relaxed into the pillow. She could bear the muffled sounds of her neighbour, or her own floorboards creaking and expanding as the house settled down for the night. At least there were no furry creatures living here.

But sleep continued to evade her and every time she closed her eyes, the case wriggled back into her mind. It was hopeless. She needed to relax, block it out. But she had no sleeping pills in the house; she'd used the last of her Kalms last Friday before her weekend off.

There was nothing for it. She pulled back the covers. She might as well get dressed, nip down to the twenty-four-hour supermarket and see what other herbal sleep remedies they stocked. Anything to give her brain a break.

She was leaning down, lacing up her Converse when the bedroom door crashed open.

Ruby spun round to face a figure dressed in black. Coming towards her, the whites of their eyes piercing through the holes in a ski mask.

She opened her mouth to scream, but they were too quick. Within a second, they were on her. One hand stretching across her mouth, the other restraining her. She fought, struggled. Scratched, tried to punch. But the hold was solid.

They were dragging her out of the room. Her heels scraping the floor. The loose Converse she hadn't yet tied slipped off her foot.

Panic struck her. Mustering every ounce of energy, she reached forward and dug an elbow into their stomach. Then lifted her foot and dropped the heel of the Converse she was still wearing down hard, right into the top of her attacker's foot. They roared like a bear. The grip loosened a split second. Enough for her to slip out. She rushed back into the bedroom, slammed the door, then dragged the bedside table across.

The door slammed against the table. And again. Every movement forcing it back further. It was only a matter of time before they were through. She grabbed her phone, fingers trembling as she swiped the screen.

The table crashed to the floor. Ruby sucked a breath. She didn't feel the blow to the side of her head. Didn't hear her phone hit the floor. Didn't notice her legs buckle and the room upturn. All she saw was the world turning black.

Chapter 67

Sophie watched the officers place their hand over Ewan's head and manoeuvre him into the car. She'd stood by him after the first arrest. Swallowed his stories about the cocaine belonging to his housemate. But this… This was a step too far. He'd brought drugs to her home. They weren't talking about her Valium here: tablets that a GP could supply. These were serious hard-core drugs. And he'd brought them to the place where her children played and slept. How could he?

The events of the last week unravelled before her. The argument with Ruby. Discovering Ewan was married and had allegedly been involved in an abusive relationship. Her attack. The arrests. It was like living inside a soap opera. Ewan had an explanation for everything, and he was convincing too. Though she was beginning to wonder how much truth there was in his words, and whether it was really all worth it. Her priority was her children, her family. This wasn't a life she wanted them exposed to.

She was thanking her lucky stars again her children weren't there this evening, to be pulled out of their beds for a police search, when she was reminded of Greg's comments about Ewan the other day. *He's not what you think*. Did he have an inkling about Ewan's involvement with drugs and prompt the raid to get him out of the way? She couldn't deny, as much as the idea galled her, he'd been right. There were drugs stored in the Subaru on her drive and Ewan was the only one with the keys – one small mercy. If the keys had been on her rack, she could have been implicated too. The idea made her recoil.

Did Greg also know about her Valium? He said he wanted to spend more time with the children. Was he looking to cast a shadow on her by showing she was buying it illegally? Surely not – she'd been so careful, kept it secret. But the suggestion left her uncomfortable and if Ruby hadn't taken those tablets off her yesterday, she'd be on her way to the police station herself now.

Ruby... Sophie moved into the front room and pulled back the curtain. The road outside was empty now. Guilt flushed through her. Ruby had tried to warn her about Ewan. She'd said he wasn't the man she thought he was, and she'd been right. What if she was right about their kiss too? What if *he* had tried to seduce her? Oh, goodness. She didn't know what to believe.

The house, with everyone gone, was screamingly quiet. She climbed the stairs, retrieved her phone from where she'd left it in the bedroom and made her way back down. In the kitchen, she pulled a bottle of red out of the wine rack, poured herself a large glass and gulped a mouthful. It slipped down easily, leaving a gentle tang on her tongue.

Another sip as she checked her phone. Two missed calls from Greg, followed by a text. *Kids are fine but need to speak with you. Call me back when you have a minute.*

Sophie placed her glass down and leant back against the kitchen side. She'd call Greg in the morning. If the kids were fine, he probably only wanted to rant about something unimportant. She'd feel compelled to tell him about the raid and she didn't have the energy to deal with that this evening.

Once again, she thought of Ruby. Of her wailing voice on Sophie's doorstep, her warning. Ruby was looking out for her sister, just as she had always done. Only this time, Sophie hadn't listened.

She glanced at her phone. She should call her. But, no... This was something she needed to do in person. It was time to go and resolve things with her sister. She just hoped she wasn't too late.

Chapter 68

Ruby blinked in the darkness. She remembered being in the bedroom, the fight. Then nothing. Where was she?

She was lying on some kind of sheet. No, a blanket, bobbly and scratchy against her skin, the floor uneven beneath. She tugged at the binds on her wrist and her ankles. Switched her head from side to side to loosen the cloth pressed over her eyes.

'Boo!'

Warm breath beside her ear made her jump. She jerked her head away.

'Ruby, Ruby, Ruby.' He was circling her now, disorientating her.

'Untie me, Lewis. We can talk.'

The laughter that filled the room was menacing. Evil.

Her limbs began to judder. What the hell was going on? 'Lewis, please? You're scaring me.'

Silence descended. He wasn't far away. She could smell him – the thick nicotine on his clothes, the sweetness of his hair gel, and another earthy odour she couldn't place. He'd made no effort to disguise himself here, introducing himself as soon as she woke, yet he'd blindfolded her.

She flinched at the displacement of air nearby. He was playing games with her.

'Why are you doing this?' she asked.

'One thing at a time.'

A whoosh of air by her face. She shrank back, her legs quaking. Why would he attack her? She couldn't work it out. Her wrists were bound tight with what felt like tape in front of her. Her ankles strapped together with something sharp. The ties cut into her flesh as she fought against them.

'You won't break out,' he said. 'You're mine to play with now.'

Sickly acid rose in her throat. She placed his voice in the darkness, turned to face it.

A cough beside her ear made her jump.

He laughed again.

'How did you get into my house?'

He tutted. 'You leave a spare set of keys in the dish in the hallway. It wasn't difficult to borrow them, get them copied. I did it ages ago.'

Ages ago. Ruby's chest tightened. She stretched her feet against the ties. One of them was still clad in her Converse, the other in a sock. She shuffled her feet back behind her, wriggled them against the ties.

'You shouldn't be so lax. And you shouldn't leave your curtains undrawn at night with the light on either: people outside can see in.'

'It was your face at the window.'

'Yup.' There was a fullness to his tone now, a definite shift. As if he was proud of himself. 'It was me who played with your door handle too. Me that followed you to Tom's the other night. And I was your secret caller in the middle of the night.' Another puff of breath beside her ear, the sweet smell of nicotine cloying her nostrils now. 'You need to pay attention.'

She tugged her head away. He'd played her. He'd played her good and proper. She'd assumed it was Ewan, warning her off, frightening her, or even Tom, when it was actually one of her best friends.

She stretched her feet again and… there was a tiny gap between her ankles. She wriggled them against each other. If she could just get her ankle through… 'I don't get it. You were in The Prince the other night when someone was following me.'

'No one was following you.'

'What?'

'You spook someone enough, you put them on edge.'

She thought of her house the other day. The odd feeling, as if someone had been in there. Convincing herself she was imagining things...

'Why?' Another tug. She flinched again as the plastic slid down a centimetre, then pinched the skin.

'Because you need me. I was trying to show you. I wanted to do this properly. But you wouldn't listen. Just when we get close, you push me aside. And you keep doing it.'

'I thought we were friends.'

'Sophie's a feisty one, isn't she?' Lewis said, ignoring her statement. 'Fights like a cat.'

Ruby's stomach pitted. 'It was you that attacked her. Oh my God, Lewis. Why?'

A stony silence. The air stilled. She tossed her head from side to side. He hadn't answered her question. Didn't seem to have moved either. What was he doing?

Suddenly, his hands were on her head. Sliding around the back, reaching for her neck. She pulled away, tried to resist. Her ankle was out of the tie now. She still had her heel to go. She lifted her bound hands, tried to fight him off, panic tearing through her.

The weight lifted. The air shifted. And everything brightened.

He'd taken the blindfold off.

She blinked several times. Bleary vision taking its time to focus. She was in the corner of a barn, lying on a blanket. Two camping lamps providing the only light. High ceilings, beams. Hay bales piled around them – the earthy smell she couldn't place. A slanted ladder halfway down the room led to a mezzanine floor, piled with more hay bales.

Lewis hovered nearby, watching the comprehension in her face with strange bulging eyes.

She dug an elbow into the blanket, levered herself into a seated position. Duct tape covered her wrists. A cable tie wound around her ankles – the plastic digging into her skin as she pushed against it. 'Where are we?'

'A long way from home.' His face was taut. Eyes as black as coal.

She pushed on the strap at her heel. The sock was bunched up, filling the gap. But she couldn't give up now. She had to keep working against it. 'Why, Lewis?' she repeated. 'Why are you doing this?'

'You rejected me. Just like your mother.'

Goosebumps prickled her scalp. 'What does this have to do with my mother?'

'It has everything to do with your mother. She fought too. Was stronger than she looked. Sophie gets it from her.'

Her heart lurched. 'I don't understand.'

'Your mother.' His tone notched up a decibel. '*Our* mother, really.'

'What do you mean?'

'Aileen gave me up for adoption.'

'What?' A torrent of breath flew out of her mouth.

'I'm your brother.'

Ruby felt as though she'd been plunged into a barrel of icy water. 'That's ridiculous!'

Beads of sweat glistened on his forehead. 'She got pregnant when she was fifteen, gave me away to an English couple.'

'No… She would have told me.'

'Would she?' He leant in close, his eyes wild.

Ruby stared back at him defiantly. For a second, she forgot all about the shackles on her wrists, her ankles. Even if death was an inevitability, she wasn't about to let him taint the memory of her mother. 'I don't believe you.'

'I don't expect you to. But it's true.' He tugged at his pocket, pulled out a pile of envelopes secured together with an elastic band. Yellowed and dog-eared at the edges. She could make out inked handwriting, the ring of a coffee stain. He waved them in front of her face. 'You see, I have proof. Your mother was a dirty cow. Six and a half months pregnant when they took her out of school and sent her to England until I was born.'

'You're making this up.'

'Am I?' He shoved the letters back into his pocket.

'I don't understand,' she repeated. Pushing again at the plastic tie, desperately trying to lever her heel through the tiny gap.

'No, you wouldn't. You see, you're all the same, you McBrides. Your mother didn't understand either, not until I explained it to her, and even then she was suspicious. Until I told her my surname – Lehane. White as a sheet she went.' Ruby recoiled. 'I bided my time, gave her a chance to get to know me. Once the cat was out of the bag, I wanted to hug her, to feel the warmth of her embrace, to be wanted. She said she needed more time. To come to terms with it. And she kept me at arm's length. Just like the woman who'd called herself my mother.'

The woman who'd called herself... Past tense. 'I thought your mother lived in London?'

He flexed his hands. For a second, she believed he was going to lash out. Then his face relaxed and he stared into space. 'Diane Lehane died just over two years ago. Peacefully in her sleep, the doctor said. She had cancer. Well, peacefully with a bit of help.'

A shiver rushed through Ruby.

'Told me exactly how I came about on her deathbed. Made me wait that long.' He sucked his teeth. 'She'd always wanted a child and couldn't have one. So, when the opportunity arose to take on someone else's, she leapt at it. Problem was, she wanted a little girl who'd sit and colour and play with dolls. She wanted to plait her hair and dress her up. Instead, she got me.' His face twisted. 'Her husband, Harry, bonded with me instantly. With her and me, there was always something missing. And after the accident, all she ever saw in me was sorrow and death.'

Ruby gulped. 'The accident?'

Lewis's eyes glazed. He gazed into space. 'I was nine. We were going to the shops, all three of us in the car. I saw a girl playing ball with a dog in a field. A Labrador it was. Black. I loved dogs, was desperate to have one. Whenever I saw them, I pointed them out to Harry. And that's all I did really. I shot forward, shrieked. Tapped his bony shoulder.' His face crumpled. 'Harry was about to pull out of a junction. I had no idea it would make him slam the brakes. Lose concentration. His foot slipped as he turned to speak to me...' He shook his head. 'I still don't know how Diane and I survived.'

He'd related the tale with such macabre preciseness it made Ruby shudder. 'I'm sorry,' she said. 'But it wasn't my mother that gave you away. It couldn't have been.'

The faraway look dropped. 'Diane kept the letters exchanged with Aileen's family in a box in the attic. There's no mistake,' he hissed. 'It all changed with your mother that last day you came into the shop,' Lewis said.

A vague memory of calling into Hattie's a week before Aileen's death tripped into her mind. Her mother was rearranging the window display. Lewis was on a ladder hanging something from the ceiling.

'She was talking about introducing me properly to you girls. "When the time is right," she said. You first, you were the easier of the two. Sophie was stand-offish. She'd take a while to come around. But as the weeks passed, I started to wonder. And then you were there, chatting, smiling. She knew we were friends. She knew I'd kept my side of the bargain and stayed quiet. Yet she wasn't prepared to keep hers.'

Ruby recalled the times he'd sat at their Sunday dinner table, the evenings she'd been out drinking with him. All the while, him knowing they shared the same blood.

'She could easily have told you that day. Dropped it into conversation, with the three of us there together. But, no. She did just what Diane had always done. Sidelined me. Poor little Lewis. Well, I wasn't about to be poor little Lewis any more.'

305

'You killed her.' The realisation was like a sharp fist in the gut.

His mouth stretched into a pernicious smile. He was enjoying himself now. 'Becky was out the afternoon she died, I was covering the shop. It was quiet. Both Aileen and I alone, with only the wall between us. I'd planned to lock up a few minutes early, access her shop through the fire escape at the back. And then I heard her and Colin in the afternoon. I sat on the stool behind the counter and listened to it all. The argument. The fight. He couldn't have made things easier for me. I waited a good hour until after he'd gone and then broke in and surprised her.'

The sheer pride in his voice clouded Ruby's vision. 'What about Charlotte?'

'Stupid cow. I spent ages looking for her. Ages following the junkies she used to hang out with. Word on the street was she ran because she was indebted to Tony G. I guess she thought she was safe to come back after he was arrested. Killing her on the night of your mum's birthday was unfortunate, but once I knew she was back, I couldn't risk the police finding her.'

He huffed, as if the conversation was becoming tedious. 'Stupidly, I still hoped there'd be a chance for us. We were making progress. Possibly, in time, Sophie would come around too. Until you threw me out of the house the other night.'

'Is that why you attacked Sophie? To get at me?'

'Oh, you're finally keeping up.' A sneer curled his lip. 'Only I picked the wrong sister.'

Chapter 69

As soon as Sophie pulled into a space opposite Ruby's she knew something was wrong. She glanced up at her sister's house. It was only just after 8:30 p.m. It was unlike her to draw the curtains so early.

Sophie grabbed her mobile, tried to call. Clicked off when the voicemail clicked in. Ruby always answered her phone, even in the middle of the night.

She was closing the door of her car when she noticed the lights to Ruby's Fiesta flick on. Sophie jumped, waved. Ruby must have left the house, seconds before she arrived. 'Hey,' she called, walking towards the Fiesta. 'Rubes!'

The car reversed. A short, jerked reaction, as if someone was in a hurry.

'Ruby!' Sophie shouted, blinking as the lights blinded her.

But the driver didn't stop. Instead, they pulled out and sped off, leaving Sophie standing in the middle of the road. Her sister must have seen her in the rear-view mirror. Must have heard her calls. They might have argued, but it wasn't like her to dash off like that. Unless she was in trouble.

Sophie called her a second time. Still in the middle of the road, phone pressed to her ear. Again, the phone rang out and went to voicemail. She looked across at her sister's desolate house, a sense of disquiet filling her. Had something happened?

Kat would know. Ruby confided in her.

Kat answered on the second ring. 'Hi, Soph! How are you?' Not the voice of anyone under strain.

Sophie said she was okay and asked if Ruby was with her.

'No. I haven't spoken to her since this morning. Everything all right?'

She didn't know. And Sophie couldn't afford to waste another moment with explanations. 'Yes, I just called round to talk to her and she's out. Don't worry.'

She rang off quickly, before Kat could ask another question, and looked again at the house. Perhaps Ruby'd had another argument with Tom. Yes. That was it. Her sister was struggling with their ailing relationship. Maybe she should call him.

Sophie bit her lip as the phone rang out. It had been a while since they'd spoken.

'Hi, Sophie.' Tom didn't disguise the surprise in his voice. 'How are you? I was shocked to hear about what happened.'

With everything that had gone on since, she'd almost forgotten about the attack. 'I'm okay, thanks. Sorry to bother you.' She paused, trying to find the right words. 'Have you spoken to Ruby this evening?'

'No. Sorry.'

Her stomach dropped to her toes. It wasn't an argument with Tom then. She explained to him how her sister had dashed off, the car revving as it sped down the street. Her phone call with Kat.

'That doesn't sound like Ruby,' he said.

'That's what I thought.'

'Do you have any idea where she was going?'

'No, we haven't spoken since the weekend.' The line crackled. 'What about Lewis?' she asked. 'I know Ruby's been spending time with him.'

'What's going on, Sophie?'

She wasn't sure how much to say. 'Ruby and I, we've not been speaking – you probably know that. I came over to sort things out and she's not here at the house. I can't reach her on her mobile either.'

Tom was quiet a moment. 'Let me try Lewis and call you back.'

308

The line cut. Sophie leant against the side of her car. She was starting to feel sick. *Please, God. Let her be okay.*

Her mobile erupted in her hand. 'No answer,' Tom said. 'I've tried Lewis and Ruby.'

'I'm worried, Tom. It's so unlike her.'

'Where are you now?'

'Outside Ruby's. The curtains are drawn. I haven't got a key.'

'I have. I'll meet you there.'

–

Sophie drummed her fingers on the steering wheel. Tom was taking an age to arrive and, back in her car, she'd bitten her nails down to the quick. There must be a simple explanation. There had to be. She was letting her mind run away with her. But she couldn't ignore the sense of foreboding growing inside.

The thrum of an engine. Headlights illuminated the street in a dazzling glow. Tom.

He was out of the car and at the house before Sophie joined him. He let them in.

Sophie called out, 'Hello!' Although she was pretty sure Ruby had driven off, she hadn't actually seen the driver. There was always a chance someone had borrowed Ruby's car. Or stolen it. Her voice echoed back at her.

They switched on the light and checked the front room. The remote control sat on the arm of the sofa, a magazine scattered to its side. In the kitchen, the sink was empty; an unopened bottle of wine stood on the side.

'Ruby!' she called out again as she climbed the stairs, Tom on her tail. The bathroom was empty. Curtains hung open in the spare room – it looked as if it hadn't been used in a while.

Ruby's bedroom door was ajar. Sophie stepped inside, and gasped. The bedclothes were pulled back, the bedside table on its side, a shoe scattered across the floor. Her gaze landed on Ruby's mobile at her feet.

'Bloody hell!' Tom said, joining her. He picked up the phone, checked the screen.

Sick rose in Sophie's throat. 'Where is she, Tom?'

He didn't answer, his jaw gaping as he scanned the room again.

She looked at the jacket clumped on the floor. Pulled back the bedclothes further. To reveal tiny spots of red. 'Oh my God.' She raised her gaze to meet Tom's. 'What's happened to her?'

'I don't know.'

'Do you think she fell getting ready? Cut herself and went to A&E?'

'And left her mobile behind. Doesn't sound like her.'

'She might be dazed.'

'I'm going to try Lewis again.' He pressed his phone to his ear. Seconds later, he shook his head. 'He isn't picking up. I don't like this. We should call the police.'

'No!'

'Come on, Sophie, she could be in trouble.'

Indecision pummelled her. Her head shouted police, but her heart screamed otherwise. She thought back to Ruby's face when she told her about Ewan giving his account at the station. Her sister hadn't exactly cast herself in a good light with law enforcement recently. 'Ruby wouldn't want the police involved. There could be another explanation.'

'For crying out loud, Sophie. It looks like she's been in a struggle.'

'Please! Give me half an hour. If we can't find her in half an hour, we'll contact the police.'

He frowned, unsure. 'Is there somewhere she could have gone?'

'Not that I can think of.' Her pulse quickened. 'Wait.' She grabbed her phone, checked the apps. 'Here.'

'What is it?'

'There's a tracker on her car.'

'What?'

'Mark's dad was an estate agent in the 90s when that poor woman' – she waved her hand in the air, snagged a memory – 'Suzy Lamplugh, vanished. They had trackers placed on all company cars afterwards as a precaution. He did the same when he set up Galanti's.'

'How come you've got the link?' he said, squishing his eyebrows together. He clearly had no idea it existed.

'There was a spare app. She put it on my phone when he gave her the company car in case it was stolen. It was before your time – three years ago now.' She opened the app. 'I never used it, always felt a bit stalker-ish. If she's taken her car, gone to hospital or something, it should show up.' She clicked a button. The wheel spun in the middle of her screen. 'Oh, Christ, I'm not even sure if it's still working.'

Chapter 70

Lewis lit a cigarette, rolling his eyes back into his head as he sucked on it.

'You won't get away with this,' Ruby said.

He took the cigarette out of his mouth, held it between his thumb and forefinger and surveyed her through a puff of smoke. 'You underestimate me. You see, I've been preparing for this for a long time. *Hope for the best, plan for the worst.* That's what Harry used to say. I have Diane's legacy. I can vanish, buy a new identity, make a new start. Once I've dealt with Sophie, of course.'

Ruby jiggled her foot again. The heel slipped a touch. She flattened it behind the other.

'What about Sophie?'

'I can't leave her out of it. It's time to show her kids what it's like to be raised by loveless adults.'

'Lewis, no...'

'Oh, come on. She's a stupid bitch with her drug-dealing boyfriend. The world won't miss her when she's gone.'

'You'll have to get past Ewan first,' she said defiantly.

'Oh, I don't think that'll be too difficult.' He checked his watch. 'In fact, if I'm not mistaken, he won't be there for much longer if he hasn't left already.'

'What have you done?'

He looked away and laughed. 'Now that would be telling.'

With all her might, Ruby tugged her foot. The skin on her heel ripped. She winced, tugged harder. Curled her toes. One last push and... she was out, leaving the sock behind. She hurled herself forward, taking him by surprise as she sidestepped him. Hay and bits of grit tore into the sole of her foot, but she ignored them.

'Bitch!' He was after her. The door was yards away, almost within her grasp, when she felt herself yanked back by the neck of her jumper. She struggled, kicked out, but he was too strong for her. A steely arm reached around her chest. And with her hands still tied, she was losing the fight. He yanked her close, put his mouth to her ear. 'You're not going anywhere.'

A rage like no other filled her. She fought like a wild dog. Kicked, elbowed, screamed. Every inch of her body resisting as he dragged her across the floor. They were almost back to the blanket now. Another blow with her foot. It was enough to knock him off balance.

'Idiot!' he snarled.

She felt her body release and thud to the floor. She was free. She didn't look back, rushed to the door. Shaking the lock. Thudding her elbow against it. Screaming for help.

A quick glance over her shoulder. He'd dropped the cigarette in their struggle, was stamping out a flame in the corner.

Then he was on her again. Pulling, tugging. Wrestling. He reached an arm around her, and she turned, stretching her neck, pulling her head back as far as she could. Then butted his head hard. A cry of pain. For a second, the barn blurred. His grip softened. She slipped out. But he'd second-guessed her and charged to the door.

She changed direction, made for the ladder up to the hay loft. Bouncing her bound hands up the rungs. Slipping, steadying herself, grateful for the slant of the ladder to keep her from falling. Waiting for a grab at her leg, a tug back down. Not daring to turn around. He'd got the door covered; there was nowhere else to go. Maybe she could get out onto the roof, or there was another exit up there. It wasn't until she reached the top that she heard the crackles, and looked back. To find he wasn't coming for her. He wasn't following her at all.

Flames tore through a hay bale, eating into the corner of the barn.

Shit, shit, shit. He hadn't put out the fire properly when he'd dropped his cigarette. A blaze was spreading across the barn. She couldn't see him.

She thrust her hands forward as far as she could reach, lifting one leg onto the landing, followed by the other. Bales were stacked high along each side, leaving only a narrow channel down the middle. But... Her chest tightened. No obvious sign of an exit.

The sound of a door slamming made her start. She peered over the side of the mezzanine landing. She could see the closed door. And hay. Lines and lines of hay. Should she go back down?

She started working at her wrists, desperately trying to twist them, to reach her fingernails to the tape. He'd secured them tight; they wouldn't budge. And getting down the ladder with bound hands wasn't going to be easy, especially with the fire blazing a trail. Her head throbbed. Her throat was bone dry. What to do?

She rushed through the bales, looking for another way out. There had to be something! She was almost at the back of the barn when she saw the edge of a door. She slid past a pile of bales. Double doors. This must be where the tractors lifted the bales onto the mezzanine for extra storage. Perhaps there was another ladder or steps the other side.

She reached for the handle and twisted, more in hope than expectation, and to her surprise it swung open. She wobbled, teetered on the edge. Steadied herself and looked down. To reveal a long drop below. No steps, nothing.

She doubled back, past the bales, rivulets of sweat running down her back. The smoke was thickening, burning her eyes. Back at the ladder, the air was hazy. The flames, long and rich, were eating through the far corner, almost as high as the mezzanine now. She lifted her jumper over her nose. She'd never make it downstairs to the door in time.

Ruby retraced her steps. Back along the landing. The heat was intense. She could barely see. A crash below made her jump. She reached the double doors. Hovered on the edge. It was dark outside, the smoke blurring her vision. And a long way to the ground.

Chapter 71

Tom's car rattled as he turned off the road and navigated the unlit track, crowded with trees either side. They were miles outside Market Deeton, surrounded by rolling countryside. 'Are you sure it's down here?' he asked.

Sophie checked her phone. 'That's what it says.'

'Are you positive the tracker's working properly? I wouldn't be surprised if Mark didn't keep up the payments. Ruby said he's been strapped for cash recently.'

Sophie's stomach lurched. She wasn't. And she couldn't for the life of her see why Ruby would come out here at this time of night.

Low clouds had drawn in, thickening the darkness. They turned a corner. The track opened up.

'What's that?' She pointed at an orange blur in the distance.

'Looks like something on fire.'

They trundled along, past an open field with wrapped straw bales dotted about. Around another corner. The barn came into view. It was richly alight, flames tearing through the far end.

Tom slowed about twenty yards away. 'The road finishes here.'

'Over there!' Sophie said. She pointed down the side of the barn. The end of a white vehicle was illuminated in their headlights. Ruby's car. Bright orange flames decimating its interior.

They jumped out, the intensity of the heat hitting them, feet pounding the ground as they ran towards it. Sophie's ankle turned on a divot. She cried out in pain, jumped, hopped a couple of times, but couldn't allow herself to stop.

Tom was circling the car when she got there. 'I think its empty.'

'Where is she?'

The heat was scorching now, as if they were in a furnace, even though the main extent of the blaze was concentrated at the other end of the barn.

Tom swiped the back of his hand across his forehead. 'Call the fire brigade,' he said, running towards the building. 'And the police. I'm going to take a look.'

Sophie followed him around the building, her feet slipping on the uneven ground, her ankle crying out in pain as she dialled 999.

'Emergency. Fire, ambulance or police?'

She dithered, wanting to say all three. Tom had disappeared from sight now. 'Fire, you need to get here soon. Someone's trapped!'

She passed on the details and location as best as she could and was searching for Tom, still on the line, when a crack made her jump. She was at the back of the building. It was followed by a series of thuds. Sophie instinctively cowered as half the ceiling tumbled into the barn. She couldn't see Tom. Flames and smoke rolled up, merging with the clouds in the gloomy sky. The far end of the barn was torched, the fire working its way along. Towards her. And with wooden walls, it didn't stand a chance.

The line on her phone cut. She stood back, placed her hands to her mouth. Shouted, 'Ruby!' Ran around the edge of the burning building, giving it a wide berth. And stopped. The barn door was fastened. Tom was rushing towards it. 'Tom, no!'

She was too late. He shouldered it, yelling as it held fast. Holding his shoulder.

'Help me find something to break down the door!' he shouted.

Sophie frantically searched the ground, working her way back towards the end of the barn. The heat was blistering.

The fire surging. If Ruby was inside, they only had a matter of minutes.

Sophie wasn't sure what made her look up at that moment. To the pair of doors hanging open on the top level. The figure silhouetted against the fire, teetering on the edge.

She screamed and pointed.

They could only watch, eyes glued as the figure lunged forward into the air.

It seemed to happen in slow motion. The movement of the air. The twirling of the body. A soft thud as it connected with the ground.

Sophie screamed again, and ran the last stretch to the end of the barn, scrabbling over a pile of loose hay outside.

'Ruby!' Sophie's heart was in her mouth. Her sister's body squirmed amidst a pile of loose hay a couple of metres thick.

Tom clambered over to her. Ruby's head hung back as he lifted her; bound hands fell limp to her side. He carried her off the hay.

'She's breathing,' he said.

Sophie viewed the duct tape on her wrists. 'What happened to her?'

'We need to get her away from the barn.'

They rushed back, the twenty yards or so to Tom's car. Ruby's eyes were open now, blinking slowly at a panting Tom.

Sophie opened the back door.

'Can you sit up?' he said to Ruby.

She didn't answer, sliding out of his arms, propping herself up against the side of the car. She cradled her ribs, bowed her head.

Sophie glanced back at the burning building, the doors on the first floor. It was a miracle she'd come out of that alive. She crouched beside her. 'Rubes. It's Sophie. You're okay now. We're here with you.'

'Is Lewis here?' Tom asked.

It was a while before Ruby looked up and when she did her face was blackened, the edges of her hair singed. She fought to catch a breath. Then became animated, pointing behind them, desperation crumpling her face.

Sophie and Tom turned. Just in time to sidestep the shovel coming for them. It plunged into the ground, missing Ruby by inches.

Lewis swung the shovel up again. His usually manicured hair was like a wild mop on his head, his pupils dilated.

Sophie shrieked, shielding her sister.

Tom hurled himself at Lewis. Pushing him back. Grabbing the handle, wrestling him to the ground. But Lewis was stronger. Within seconds, he was straddled across Tom. He twisted the wood in his hands, hurled it up. Tom rolled aside. The metal missed his head, connecting with the edge of his shoulder. But the blow dazed him, leaving him limp.

Lewis dropped the shovel and ran to Ruby. Grabbing Sophie, tossing her aside like a rag doll.

Her head thudded as it hit the ground.

Sirens filled the distance. Lewis's hands were on Ruby's neck.

Sophie made to stand, but the ground shifted.

The sirens grew louder.

She saw a flash before her eyes. Started crawling along the earth. She needed to get to Ruby. Before she could do so, Tom hauled himself up. He dashed forward. Reached for Lewis. Pulling at him. Tugging at him.

A whirlwind of lights rounded the corner. Bodies spilled out of the fire engine and flew to their side. Lewis was restrained. Someone grabbed Tom.

And Sophie could only look on as Ruby lay limp beside them.

Chapter 72

Ruby opened her eyes and blinked. A white room dazzled her. A hazy figure moved in the distance. Her chest quaked. The figure moved towards her. She fought to keep her eyes open, willing her pupils to focus. Flinched when something touched her hand.

'It's okay, Ruby.' A voice beside her. A face loomed in. 'It's me, Sophie. You're in hospital. You're safe.' She stroked her cheek. 'You're safe now.'

Ruby blinked again, her vision sharpening. She moved to sit up. A hand weighted her down. She turned to another face.

'There, now,' the nurse said. 'You need to get some rest.'

She sank back into the pillow. Her mouth felt like she'd swallowed a handful of sand. A pain split her head. She licked her lips, rubbed them together.

'Do you want a drink?' Sophie asked. She reached for a clear plastic cup on the bedside table and placed her other arm around Ruby's shoulders, pulling her forward, just enough for her lips to touch the cup.

The water was heavenly. Flowing into her mouth, flushing her senses.

'I'll pour you some more,' Sophie said, reaching for a jug on the table.

The nurse bustled out of the room.

Ruby's gaze fell to the blue bedcovers, the cannula in her wrist, the drip hovering beside the bed. She could still smell the dry smoke, the sweet earthy hay. She croaked out a cough, cleared her voice. 'How long have I been here?' Her voice was barely a whisper.

'You came in last night.' Sophie stroked her cheek again with the backs of her fingers. The gesture was warm, comforting.

A flashback. The scene outside the barn. The wolf-like eyes of Lewis. His hands on her. She placed her hands on her neck. The skin was sore, tender. 'What happened to Lewis?'

'The police got him. Don't worry, he's in custody. He went no comment, but they arrested him with attempted murder, kidnap and assault. He had letters on him…' Her voice trailed away.

Ruby closed her eyes. The letters he'd flashed in front of her face, connecting him with their mother. Why hadn't he burned them, disposed of the evidence? Though as soon as she posed the question, she knew the answer. He wanted to show them to Sophie too. Make sure she knew about them, before he made her suffer. An involuntary shudder slipped down her back. 'I had no idea,' she said.

'Of course you didn't. None of us did.' Sophie pressed a hand to the bruise on her forehead. 'I can barely believe it myself. I mean, how could we not have known we had a brother? It's strange to think of him as family.'

'He killed Mum, and Charlotte.'

'Oh my God!'

'In his warped sense of reality, he was still trying to get close to us. And when he realised he couldn't, he attacked you.' Memories of yesterday evening tumbled in and out of Ruby's mind. The barn. The fire. The fight outside. Tom. She looked up at her sister. 'How did you know where to find me?'

Sophie told her about the drive to her house, the phone call with Tom.

When she mentioned the tracker app, Ruby jolted. 'I'd forgotten all about that. I didn't even know he'd used my car; I was unconscious. He must have carried me out of the house. It's a wonder no one saw us.'

'I'm glad it still worked.' She swept a strand of hair away from Ruby's forehead. 'You've just missed Tom actually. He's popped home to get changed. He'll be relieved to see you awake.'

Blurred images of Tom outside the barn flashed before her. 'Is he okay?'

'A bit battered and bruised, but aren't we all? He's worried about you.'

Voices babbled away in the corridor beyond. Trolleys trundled past. The hospital staff were going about their business.

Every muscle, every fibre of Ruby's body relaxed back into the bed. Her head was heavy, willing sleep, her body weary. She grabbed Sophie's hand. 'I've missed you.'

Sophie swiped a tear from the well beneath her eye. 'You too.'

'I'm sorry about…' The words splintered into a husky cough.

'You've nothing to be sorry about. Kat told me about Ewan and the other women. You know, it's weird. The signs were all there – the way he refused to have his photo posted on social media, how he avoided talking about his life in Glasgow. I should have suspected something. Maybe I did, but when the kids are happy and things are good… I don't know. I pushed it to the back of my mind, I guess.' She talked Ruby through the drugs raid at her house. 'That was a step too far.' She was quiet a moment, her brain still processing. So much had happened, their lives turning upside down in the last two weeks. 'I think it was Greg who prompted the raid.'

A stream of thoughts crashed into Ruby's mind. Lewis not only knew about Ewan's connection to cocaine when his house was raided, he knew the exact amount found. He'd been specific. He knew Sophie's drugs were supplied in The Crown, and he knew the police would find something to put Ewan away, take him out of the picture last night. Information like that, on drug storage and supply, wouldn't have been easy to come by. Unless you were involved in the supply chain yourself. He'd infiltrated every part of their lives… 'It was Lewis,' she said.

Sophie widened her eyes. 'Do you really think so?'

Ruby nodded. 'I'm sure of it. He said something about getting Ewan out of the way. Does Greg know about the raid?'

'Yes, I spoke with him this morning. He was more bothered about me not telling him about my attack. Didn't flinch when I told him about the police coming over. He seemed almost relieved it put Ewan out of the picture. That's why I thought it was him. Anyway, it doesn't matter now because Ewan and I, we're over.'

'How did he take it?'

'I don't know, to be honest. He's on the remand wing at Gartree, awaiting trial. I had to send him a letter. It was either that or apply for a permit to visit the prison and I didn't fancy telling him surrounded by other prisoners.'

'What about you?' Ruby asked.

'I'm scraping through.'

Ruby lowered her voice. 'Because if you need the tablets…'

Sophie raised a flat hand. 'I've got an appointment with the GP in the morning. I'm hoping they're going to be able to give me something on prescription, just to tide me over.'

The door flapped open and Kat appeared carrying two coffees. 'You're awake! How are you feeling?'

'Probably better than I look.' Ruby gave a weak smile.

'You're not kidding. You look like you've been in the ring with Tyson Fury.'

'Kat! It's only superficial bruising,' Sophie said. 'The doc said it'll go down in a few days.'

'Well.' Ruby glanced from one to another. 'Somebody must have a mirror. I have to face it sometime.'

Kat reached into her bag, drew out a small compact, flipped it open and passed it across.

Ruby barely recognised her reflection. Her cheek was bruised and puffed out and there was a swelling the size of an egg on her forehead. She stroked her throat again and handed the mirror back to Kat. 'How's work?' she said, moving the subject on. She didn't want to talk about last night any more.

'Busy. And guess what? Mark's got a new woman.'

'He has?'

She nodded. 'I followed him out the other night, watched her meet him at his car. Apparently, she was involved in a car accident on Monday. She's fine now, but that's why he's been so elusive.' She sniffed. 'Can't say I'm surprised, to be honest. He's been after a woman for a while, hates being on his own. But he doesn't want his ex-wife finding out. Says she'll make things difficult.'

'So, you're keeping it to yourself.'

'Yeah. Well, I'm telling you, of course. At least he isn't selling up.'

Ruby rested back into the bed. *He's been looking for a woman for a while.* Was that what fractured Mark's relationship with her mother? Was he sore because she'd rejected his advances? Yesterday, she'd thought of Mark as a potential murder suspect. Today, he was having a secret relationship, and it was the tracker he'd fixed on her company car that saved her life. How things changed in twenty-four hours.

'Anyway, you need to get some rest,' Sophie said, nudging Kat. 'I'll be back in to see you this evening.'

Ruby barely heard their chairs scrape the floor. Her eyes were closed before they reached the door.

Chapter 73

Ruby looked across at Hitesh. 'Do you think they'll charge Lewis with Charlotte's murder, and my mum's?'

DC Hitesh Lalvani returned her gaze with a gentle smile. He had been sitting on the plastic chair beside her bed for the past forty minutes, listening as she talked him through yesterday evening in as much detail as she could recall. A very different Hitesh from the man who'd visited her at home twenty-four hours earlier, warning her off the investigation. No hint of his usual Kouros aftershave. He looked tired, weary, as though he hadn't slept for a week. And he kept giving her a soppy-eyed, almost paternal stare as he took down her account, carefully recording everything on his laptop.

'I'm pretty sure there's enough there to put a case together,' he said. 'Don't worry.'

'How come he was never a suspect in Mum's inquiry?'

'There were no records of the adoption. Nothing to link him. And he'd been in your mother's shop several times, so if there were fingerprints or DNA, they were to be expected.'

Ruby sighed. He'd been clever. Covered his tracks well. Pulled the wool over so many eyes. 'What happens to Colin now?'

'There's still a long way to go, with Lewis refusing to comment, but if the CPS decide to charge Lewis with your mother's murder and can show Colin wasn't involved, then his conviction will be overturned. He'll be a free man.'

The evening sun streamed through the open window. A bird was singing on the birch tree outside. A sweet, rhythmic tune.

Calming. Ruby lay back and listened while Hitesh continued to type.

'I need to ask another question,' Hitesh said, raising his head. 'Why do you think he used your car to transport you to the barn?'

'I've been thinking about that,' Ruby said. 'I guess he was being careful. Didn't want his car spotted out there.'

'How was he to get away from the barn though? Your car was burnt out.'

'Cycling,' she said.

'What?'

'He'd taken the week off work. Mentioned he'd started cycling again. He had one of those folding city bikes. Look in the back of my car, or nearby. He could have killed me, dumped my body, left my car in a deserted lane. If it wasn't for the fire...' Ruby closed her eyes. Suddenly she was back there, fighting with him, climbing the ladder. Listening to the crackles of flames as the fire took hold.

The door crashed open. It was Tom.

'Hello!' he said. He was wearing a loose white shirt over dark trousers, his hair freshly washed. The smell of his sporty shower gel wafted through the room, flushing the bad memories from her mind. A split on his lip the only clue he'd been fighting for his life the evening before.

Ruby's gaze dropped to the punnet of grapes he was carrying in one hand, the box of Milk Tray in the other. 'I'm guessing the grapes are for you,' she said. 'Since you've started running again.'

Tom laughed. 'I see you're feeling better.'

Hitesh snorted and clicked his laptop shut. 'Right, I'm off.' To Ruby's surprise, he reached forward and touched her forearm. 'Take care,' he said. 'I'll be in touch.'

They watched him leave.

'Where are your bruises?' Ruby said to Tom. 'I look like the bloody Elephant Man.'

Tom gave a short laugh. 'Well hidden. How are you feeling?'

'Been better.'

He sat in Hitesh's chair and rested the goodies on the edge of her bed. 'Do you remember much?'

'Bits. Things keep coming to mind. Did they tell you about Lewis, his background?'

He nodded. 'Sophie told me. I'm sorry, Rubes.'

'What for?'

'I should have been there for you.'

'You saved my life.'

'You know what I mean. You wouldn't have spent so much time with Lewis if I hadn't pushed you two together. He was supposed to be looking out for you. Keeping you safe.'

'He was warped, cruel. None of us knew who he was or what he was capable of.'

Tom jammed his eyes together. When he opened them, they were watery. 'If I'd been around more…'

It was agony watching him torture himself. 'Don't do this. You couldn't have known.' She reached out, rested her hand on his forearm. A simple reassuring gesture but one he immediately responded to. He placed a warm hand over hers. Then watched as he weaved his fingers in and out of her fingers, just as he used to when they were together. Sitting on the sofa watching a film. Chatting in a restaurant waiting for food to arrive. A lump climbed into her throat.

It was a moment before he lifted his gaze. 'You didn't return my text.'

Ruby didn't know what to say. The lump in her throat expanded.

'I wanted us to talk,' he said. 'Lewis was supposed to be sounding you out about the chance of us getting back together.'

She pulled back. 'I thought you were seeing someone new.'

'What?'

'When we had lunch, you told me you were out, in town, during the week.'

'It was Jake's birthday. Jake from work.'

She'd made an assumption. Put two and two together and made twenty-two. She recalled Kat's comments about her distancing herself. Tom saying she put up a barrier. They were right, she had retreated behind her own screen, shielded herself. Because she couldn't take any more pain. But in doing that she'd jumped to conclusions and almost lost one of the people most precious to her. 'I'm sorry too. I haven't exactly been easy to live with.'

'Just get better, all right.' He took her hand back. Holding it gently, as if it was a fragile piece of glass. His eyes softened. 'I'll feel so much better when you are home.'

Chapter 74

Bridget folded her hands into her lap and gazed out of the window.

'How much did you know?' Ruby asked.

Frail autumn sunlight cast a white line across the front of Bridget's jumper. 'As much as your mother told me. She was young, she made a mistake. She wanted to put it behind her.'

Ruby and Tom exchanged a glance. They were sitting on the sofa in Bridget's front room. The shrill sound of gulls screeching overhead filtered in through the open window. Four days had passed since the incident at the barn and Lewis's arrest and she needed to fill her in, update her on the events in Market Deeton as gently as possible.

'I can't believe he came to find her,' Bridget said. 'After all these years.' She listened quietly as Ruby told her about Sophie's attack and Lewis's capture. Ruby carefully keeping the details of her own abduction, the fire, the tussle at the barn, to herself. *Charlotte Manning and Aileen McBride's killer apprehended after breaking into daughter's home*, the press had reported. Thankfully the wider details weren't shared, and she saw no benefit in piling more terror onto an already toppling pile of worry for Bridget.

But she couldn't hold back on Lewis ambushing Sophie and then breaking into her house and attacking her, and her aunt's face turned ghostly pale at the danger her nieces had faced. The bruises on Ruby's face only adding to her horror.

'You must have been so frightened.'

'It's over now. He can't hurt us any more.'

'How are Sophie and the children coping?'

Ruby glanced at the empty armchair in the corner. Sophie had wanted to come, but the children were at school and, after the upset of the last few days and Ewan's arrest, they were keeping to their routine. 'Amazingly well. They're so resilient.'

She pictured their faces when she'd picked them up from school yesterday – Alfie with his stick drawing of Pru, Daisy showing off her new reading book – and her heart melted. They'd sat them down when Ruby was home and explained, in as much detail as their little ears could take, that Ewan had to go away for a while. They still had to tell them about Lewis and Colin Halliday, but there was only so much they could digest in one sitting. In time, they'd find a way. For now, routine was key and having their mother or Ruby do the school run seemed to ease the strain of Ewan's absence. A foundation on which to build. Greg had been surprisingly supportive too, pitching in. They'd manage them together. Make the best of things. Ensuring the children felt safe and cocooned in a loving family was their priority right now.

'I thought we'd all visit next weekend. Dust down the wheelchair, have a walk along the prom.'

'That would be nice.'

Quiet fell upon them.

'Why don't I make us a drink?' Tom said.

Ruby tossed him a grateful look and for the first time Bridget didn't quibble.

'Do you remember my mother's first pregnancy?' Ruby asked when he'd left the room.

'I remember it well. She didn't tell anyone until she was six months gone. Loosened her clothes, covered the bump, neat little thing that it was. Oh, that poor child! Olive went crazy when she found out. Made her stay off school. Said she'd brought shame on the family. Threatened to disown her. Your mother came to stay with me. She was only fifteen, bless her. She'd no idea about babies or children.'

'What about the father?'

Bridget's face darkened. 'That was the worst of it. She wouldn't tell our mother, she wouldn't tell anyone, but I managed to get it out of her.' Tears glittered her aunt's lashes. 'It was Patrick, your grandfather's brother. Went out on the lash one night. Raped her in a drunken state, so she said.'

'Her own uncle?'

Bridget nodded. 'Olive refused to believe her. Called her everything. Patrick denied it, but he was never the same afterwards. I think deep down Olive knew she was telling the truth. It was a difficult time. Your mother refused to have the police involved, afraid of what it would do to the family.'

She sat back in her chair, stared into space. 'I'll never forget the night your grandmother turned up and ordered your mother to pack her things. She'd found a couple through a contact at the church. "A good God-fearing couple," she said, who lived in a village north of Manchester in England. They'd agreed to look after Aileen, arrange the adoption afterwards. Your mother seemed keen. It was almost as if the decision was made for her. She spent the last months of her confinement there.'

'Alone?'

Bridget nodded. 'Your mother could be steely when she wanted to be.' A tear slid down the old woman's face. 'Those months were the hardest of my life. We didn't have mobile phones or the internet in those days. The thought of her all those miles away with strangers, and in her condition too. It was torture.'

'What happened?'

'The couple, Harry and Diane, were kind to her by all accounts. When she went into labour, they convinced her to give Diane's name and date of birth at the hospital. They told her it would make things easier when they sorted out the adoption afterwards. Aileen was a naïve fifteen-year-old in a foreign country. She had no idea how everything worked, so she did as she was told.'

'But weren't questions asked about her name, her age?'

'Apparently not. Your mother was grown up for her age. And Diane was much younger than her husband, only twenty-five, I believe. Aileen delivered in a large maternity wing, was discharged quickly. I guess the medical staff had no reason to question her. Afterwards, Olive travelled over and brought her back, leaving the baby with the Lehanes to sort out everything.'

'And that was it?'

'Not exactly. Aileen was never the same afterwards. It was like there was a hole inside of her that couldn't be filled. She couldn't stop thinking about the baby. Eventually, we agreed she'd write to the Lehanes using my address, and ask how he was doing. I thought it might put her mind at rest.' A tear trickled down her cheek. 'The letter came back. Gone away – no forwarding address.'

'I don't understand.'

'The baby was in their name. They decided to move away, to a new place where no one knew them, and keep it, I suppose.'

Ruby recalled the tiny wristband she'd found. She met her aunt's gaze. 'The hospital band in your old box of photos. It wasn't yours, was it?'

Bridget shook her head. 'Your mother begged the Lehanes to let her keep it. It was her only memory of him.'

Ruby's heart shrank. She couldn't begin to envisage what her mother had gone through as a young teenager. The pain, the anguish, the suffering. She'd battled to put it behind her and then years later it came back. 'Why didn't she accept him when he returned?' she asked.

'She'll have needed time. Time to work through how to tell you girls. Time to let it all sink in. Your mother never could make a decision in a hurry.'

The sound of crockery seeped in from the kitchen, filling the room. 'Patrick should have been charged,' Ruby said.

'You're right, he should have. But without your mother's evidence, what else was there? He contracted a brain tumour and died the following year. Poetic justice, some might say.'

Tom entered with three mugs, carrying them carefully so as not to spill the tea.

'Thanks, love,' Bridget said. 'You found everything all right?'

'Of course.' He smiled. 'You keep a very neat kitchen.'

Bridget laughed for the first time since they'd arrived, and the sound was soothing to the soul.

'I think we might take up your offer to stay over tonight,' Ruby said. She was worried about leaving her after such a shocking revelation.

Tom placed his mug down and smiled. 'Sounds like a good plan. Might even fit in an early-morning run on the beach before we head back.'

'That's settled then,' Bridget said. She sounded brighter. 'I'll make up the spare room.'

Epilogue

Two and a half months later

Two women bundled into coats, hats and scarves stopped at the crossing opposite St Peter's churchyard. A line of leaves skittered across the pathway. Winter was now in full swing, Christmas only a week away, and the skeletons of trees lining the roadside were lit with sparkling fairy lights.

Sophie linked her arm through Ruby's. 'It looks beautiful here today, doesn't it?' she said.

Ruby smiled. 'It does.'

The cars stopped. The women crossed the road and slipped through the wrought-iron gates.

Dusk was just starting to fall. A light mist curled its cool fingers around the graves as they walked up the cracked stone pathway. Past the pitted stones, lopsided and covered in lichen, the inscriptions barely readable. Past the line of mausoleums sitting proud at the side. They continued to the far corner to where the most recent burials were stowed. The earth rose into peaks in places there, pulling down protectively on their new wares below.

At the end of the third row, they stopped and stared at a newly erected grey marble headstone.

Aileen Miriam McBride, 18.9.71 – 12.11.18 Beloved mother to Ruby and Sophie, and grandmother to Daisy and Alfie. Forever in our hearts.

No 'taken too soon' or 'will be sadly missed'. This was their mother's final resting place. A happy haven. A place for her to be remembered for the wonderful woman she was.

A row of photos covered in clingfilm lined the bottom of the tombstone: Ruby and Sophie, heads pressed together, smiling. Daisy and Alfie posing on their trampoline. Bridget sitting on her patio, a clear blue sky beyond. A rare pic of Pru snoozing on the sofa. Beside them lay a splodgy picture Alfie had painted at school, covered in yet more clingfilm, and Daisy's pretty stone collection from their last holiday in Cromer.

'Hello, Mum!' Sophie said gaily, dropping to her knees. 'Look what we've brought you.'

Ruby watched her pull the wilted roses from the vase and replace them with a rainbow of carnations, and then listened to her twitter on to their mother about the renovations she was planning for the house. Sophie was looking well. Her cheeks flushed in the early-evening breeze, her eyes bright. After the separation with Ewan and the revelations about Lewis, they'd all worried about her. But as soon as Colin's conviction was overturned, Sophie became a different person. It was almost as if a huge boulder had toppled off her shoulders and she could finally breathe freely. 'The flowers aren't lasting long this time of year,' she said. 'I might ask Colin for a shrub instead.' She looked back at her sister. 'What do you think?'

Ruby's heart warmed. Since his release from prison, they met Colin Halliday regularly for coffee and they were meetings Ruby increasingly found herself looking forward to. Colin didn't talk about his time in prison. If he held a grudge about losing his home, his living and his liberty, it never showed. He'd embraced his new-found freedom with gusto and started a landscape gardening business in Leicester. He was even putting on some of the weight he'd lost. There was a time when Colin had been dear to their mother. They'd argued and seemed to be taking different paths romantically, but she was convinced they would have remained friends if her mother hadn't died. Looking at him now, his unrelenting positivity after all he'd endured, Aileen would have been proud.

'I think that's a wonderful idea,' she said.

Sophie wrapped up the dead flowers, tossed them in the nearby bin and re-joined her sister. 'Mum, Ruby has something to show you,' she said, beaming all over her face.

Ruby smiled. She didn't feel the need to come to the grave and chatter away to her mother. She was always talking to Aileen in her head. At work. At home. In the supermarket doing her weekly shop. But it meant a lot to Sophie, so she held out her left hand and angled it towards the grave. The diamond ring sparkled in the last vestiges of daylight.

'They're having a spring wedding,' Sophie said, shuddering with excitement. 'Daisy will be a flower girl and Alfie a page boy. I can't wait!'

Ruby recalled Tom's awkward proposal over dinner at Martini's Bistro the other night. He'd dropped to one knee right on top of a crushed potato on the floor. Certainly, a proposal they wouldn't forget in a hurry. 'Neither can I,' she said. Ruby placed an arm around her sister and led her out of the graveyard. 'It'll be lovely for all of us. And we'll bring the photos down to show Mum afterwards.' Although Ruby had no doubt her mother would be there, looking down on them on the day. Aileen McBride had never been one to miss a party.

A Letter From Jane

Thank you so much for reading *One Good Lie*. I do hope you enjoyed reading it as much as I enjoyed writing it! If you would like to keep up to date with all my latest releases, please visit my website at www.janeisaac.co.uk where you can sign up to my Readers' Club. Your email address will never be shared, you can unsubscribe at any time, and you will receive a FREE eBook of my short stories.

This was my first foray into psychological suspense and, after writing nine detective novels, I was keen to delve deeper into the effects of murder on victims' friends and family. I'm fascinated by the consequences of extraordinary things happening to ordinary people, particular within a domestic setting. Wrap that inside a mystery, add some sinister characters and *One Good Lie* was born!

If you have time to leave me a rating or review on Amazon, Goodreads, or wherever you purchased the novel, I'd very much appreciate it. I love hearing what you think, and your reviews help me reach new readers – which allows me to bring you more books.

Alternatively, if you would like to contact me personally, you can reach me via my website www.janeisaac.co.uk, Facebook page JaneIsaacAuthor, Twitter @JaneIsaacAuthor or Instagram @janeisaacauthor. It's always lovely to hear from readers.

Once again, thank you so much for deciding to spend time with *One Good Lie*. I'm looking forward to sharing my next book with you very soon.

Best wishes,

Jane x

Acknowledgements

I hope the people of Leicestershire will forgive me for taking liberties with their beautiful county. Market Deeton is a fictional town loosely based on the very real Market Harborough, which is a place very dear to my heart.

Books are rarely the work of one person and *One Good Lie* is certainly no exception. First, I'd like to thank my dear friend Martin Sargeant, who gave me a wonderful flavour of Cromer. I love seeing the landscape unfold in your amazing paintings.

To my agent, Caroline Montgomery at Rupert Crew, who works tirelessly on my behalf and is always at the end of the phone with a cheery note. Your support is much appreciated.

Gratitude also to Leodora Darlington and the marvellous team at Canelo. I couldn't wish for a friendlier or more dynamic publisher to work with.

Several people helped with early drafts of the novel: Debi Alper, Rebecca Bradley and Dave Sivers – heartfelt thanks to you all.

One of the nicest things about writing books is the online community. The writers who keep me sane – you know who you are! The wonderfully supportive book clubs, including Anne Cater and all at Book Connectors; Shell Baker and Llainy Swanson at Crime Book Club; Tracy Fenton, Helen Boyce and all at The Book Club (TBC); David Gilchrist at UK Crime Book Club; Susan Hunter and the guys at Crime Fiction Addict; and Wendy Clarke and the gang at The Fiction Café Book Club. Also, the reviewers and book bloggers, far too many to mention individually, who work tirelessly to spread the word about new books. I'm truly honoured to be part of such a lovely world.

So many friends have listened to my musings, reviewed cover art, proofread and generally offered a shoulder to lean on. Most notably, David and Lynne Anderson, Colin Williams, Stephanie Daniels, Ian Robinson, and Philip and Abi Bouch. And my dear friend Nicky Peacock (N. V. Peacock), a local author who fills me with coffee and cake and joviality on a regular basis.

Finally, to David and Ella. Living with a writer is never easy. You spend almost as much time with my characters as I do and I'm sure I never say thank you enough!